Lord Conrad´s Crusade

Book Seven
in the
Adventures of Conrad Stargard

A Science Fiction Novel

by

Leo Frankowski
And
Rodger Olsen

Cover Design By Chris Ciulla
Cover Art By Eugene Delacroix

With Special Thanks

To Lt. Col. Dave Grossman
For His Help, Editing, And Advice

To Mike Hubble
For His Help, Editing, And Advice

To Chris Ciulla
For His Advice And The Cover Design

To My Wife Marina
For Putting Up With Me

And
To the dozens of people who helped with editing, critique,
and encouragement.

Prolog

The Taking of Alexandria

Heavy artillery, aerial strafing, and bombardment are all very well, but there comes a time when you must go in there and clean a city out, and for that, I personally prefer to use a sword. For one thing, you don't get killed while you are reloading.

Why does the human mind insist on multi-tasking? Since fighting for my life took only half of my brain, the other half was free to distract me. I don't know why they call it "thrust, beat, and parry".

The next opponent was coming in on my left. I blocked him with my shield and hacked his arm off. That was definitely "Hacking". Poor Bastard. Why didn't he just stay home? Why couldn't they have just accepted our offer? We said that if they would free all of their slaves, we would take care of these people, send them home, and leave the inhabitants of Alexandria alive and in peace.

Faced with an overwhelmingly powerful Army, Navy, and Air Force, why was that so hard to accept? Well, yes, we had also demanded their obedience, but we had been very nice to the other places that had gone along with our program. We'd even left their leadership intact.

So, I just hacked his arm off. The next one was to my right. Small bugger. My sword knocked his aside – okay, that's "beating", but then I swung for his breastbone and damned near cut him in half. That was definitely "Hewing". When you cut something down, you are "Hewing". Okay, now a low forehand to this man's leg and a backhand to that guy's leg. That's a "backhand." So there I was, hacking and hewing and backhanding my way through an army of men I didn't know and didn't particularly want to kill, in a back alley of a city that I never really wanted to conquer.

Battle is tiring work. Half of the battles in history must have ended because the combatants were just too damned tired to swing their swords one more time. Unfortunately, my bright golden armor and polished sword seemed to attract a lot of attention. If I died on this vacation it would be because I was overdressed.

I badly needed to disengage and rest my arm. Unfortunately, my backward steps encouraged my opponents to rush harder at me and caused more work. Thankfully, red and white uniforms moved in front of me and closed the line behind these last two opponents. One went down to a throat slash. The other backed up and got a surprised look on his face when he backed into the Christian soldier who had closed the line behind him. If he had dropped his sword, he would have lived. As it was, I had to be very careful to cut him down and not take out my own man behind him. My sword is very sharp.

It was made for me by Tom, my time traveling uncle. Well, actually, he was my second cousin, but he was older than me, and I'd always called him 'uncle'. Since it was a one off, and used technology far beyond anything that we could duplicate, I was the only person who could get one.

Basically, it was a good, watered steel scimitar that had been split in half, the hard way. Then a fifty angstrom thick layer of pure diamond had been placed down the whole length of the blade, and the sandwich had been permanently bonded together. There was no way that we could make another one, here in the Thirteen

Century. Or in the Twentieth, for that matter.

Then I was able to step back a few paces. I dropped my sword to waist height and stood there panting. The battle was moving slowly away from me. If you ignored the pain, loss of blood, filth, cold, hard labor, hacking and hewing, this was not the worst vacation that I had ever taken, but I decided that next year I would go fishing.

I wished that I had some arrows left. My bow weighted less than my sword, and it doesn't attract the unwanted attention that a firearm does.

The whole thing had started one day in my castle, or palace or whatever it was.

Chapter 1 Some Papal Bull

So there I was. The Duke of Sandomierz, the Duke of Cracow, the Duke of Mazovia, the Hetman of the Christian Army, and a long way from what once was home.

'Home' used to be in Twentieth Centaury Poland for me, a decent engineer named Conrad Schwartz. Then I managed to fall asleep, drunk, in a time machine. I woke up in the Thirteenth Century, nine years before the Mongols were due to arrive and kill a third of the population of the whole country in a few weeks. By dint of some modern organization, decent technology, nine years of hard work, and a little help from my time traveling uncle, we had managed to defeat them, barely, over twenty years ago.

Now, 'home' was my headquarters and palace at Okoitz, where my two formal wives lived.

So now, I was Conrad Stargard, a Kingmaker. I was the wealthiest and most powerful man in the Western World, and I was more than slightly miffed at the letter before me.

My old friend and mentor, Father Ignacy, had long since been elected Pope, taking the name of John Paul. He had probably gained that exalted status because for many years, I'd been publishing the only magazine in Europe, and I had been distributing it across the continent. He wrote a monthly article in it. My publicity had made him what he now was.

In return, he was prevailing upon me to start a crusade to regain the Holy Lands. It seems that the Moslems had taken their City of Jerusalem back from the last bunch of Crusaders who took it from them, and the Pope wanted it back again.

I didn't want to do it, but you can't just ignore a letter from the Pope, even if he is an old friend.

There was nothing for it but to spend the afternoon writing him a long letter explaining that while I did have a very large and well trained army, the fact was that most of my men were very busy doing important things.

What I should be spending my time on was a treatise on patent law, something that Europe really needed, but what can a man do? The Pope must be answered!

We were building thousands of miles of railroads, constructing over a gross of large concrete fortresses a year, and bringing vast areas of new lands under cultivation. We were manning and expanding the mail, telegraph, and radio systems. We had steam powered river boats on most of Europe's rivers, as well as on the Amazon, the Tigris, and the Indus rivers. And we were building ocean going ships by the dozen.

They were ferrocrete ships, since we still didn't have the steel rolling capability to build them out of steel. Anyway, ferrocrete is a fine, strong material, and if it took more manpower to build with it, the material costs were much less.

The power, the wealth, and the glory of a culture is largely based on its technical expertise. What we were doing would make Christians the most powerful people in the world. Eventually, all of the other peoples in the world would fear to offend us, and wish to join us. Some day, the whole world would become Christian. This thing must be pushed forward as fast as possible.

Why fight a needless, bloody war when total victory was possible through peaceful means?

We had defeated the Mongols when they had attacked us, but a whole new generation of them was growing up in Mongolia, and we had to protect Christendom from these hooligans. It a few years, we would be in a position to counter attack, to invade Mongolia, and doing so was a military necessity.

On the other hand, the Arabs had done nothing against us except to defend themselves when Europe, mostly the French, the English, the Germans, and the Italians, had attacked them.

If the Arabs ever did anything serious to us, we were in a position to give them a very rude shock, but until such time, a war with them simply wasn't justified.

The Mongols were our natural enemies. The Arabs weren't.

There was no point in rubbing it in, so I didn't mention that one of my wives was a member of an Islamic sect, and that a colony of her co-religionists was living on my lands, in a valley near Three Walls. They were my best craftsmen, scientists, and technologists, and were responsible for setting up dozens of new industries, vastly expanding the wealth of Christendom.

I gave the rough draft to my secretary so she could have some fair copies made, hand lettered on real parchment. We were making paper by the ton, but some things still required the traditional, and very expensive, parchment. They made it out of sheep's skins.

One of my scantily dressed house girls came to invite me to dinner in my private chambers, one whole wing of the palace. Skin was back in style in Poland. It had never been really taboo, here and in Russia, the way it was farther to the west. I confess that I liked it, if the girl was pretty, but I never tried to influence fashions. I'm not abysmally stupid.

Only she wasn't scantily clad, today. Now, she was wearing a floor length dress, and everything between her neck and wrists was covered. It had to be because of the Papal messenger who was visiting us. Damn him. I mean, it was my palace, after all, and where did these idiots think that little priests came from, anyway?

I was wearing one of my usual around the castle outfits. Soft black boots, royal blue tights, and a heavily embroidered dark red tunic. I left the blue cape hanging on the wall, since it was more bother than it was worth. My old sword hung on my left hip, and my new revolver was in an ornate holster on my right.

I was becoming something of a dandy, in my old age. Not that I looked or felt all that old, especially since my Uncle Tom had given me some highly sophisticated medical treatments a while ago, but sixty-two was considered old in this century.

I really preferred to just eat in the cafeteria the way that most people did. The food there was just as good, and it saved a lot of time. But both of my wives, Francine and Celicia, had a thing about large, formal banquets, and managed to find an excuse for throwing one about four times a week. There would be a hundred and twenty people there, and they would all be ticked off if I didn't show up. I didn't seem to have much choice, but it made me feel ... imprisoned.

I found that I was becoming dissatisfied with my life, but that I really didn't know why. It was not a new feeling. The disquiet had been growing for months. More and more often I found myself reciting to myself the reasons that I was, of course, deliriously happy. I had more power than almost any other man in Christendom, two beautiful wives, more pleasurably, a abundance of other available morsels that talked less and nagged far less. Of course, I was happy.

I walked down past three very lifelike statues of beautiful, nude young women, and one that wasn't a statue at all, but one of my bodyguards. They had a habit of standing motionless, and the statues were another bit of camouflage. A few attempts had been made on my life, although I had never found out why anybody would want to do that. For the life of me, I couldn't think of anybody that I had offended that much and I had made thousands of people better off.

My Uncle Tom had decided that I needed a little protection, and had sent me one of his bio-engineered creations that had been designed to be a combination serving wench, child care worker, dancer, and God-Awfully-Deadly body guard. They looked like sweet and innocent adolescent young girls.

They weren't.

They could cut a man's throat in an instant, and not feel the least bit of guilt about it.

They reproduced by voluntary parthenogenesis, being able to crank out two litters of four every year, if you asked them to. And when the kids matured, at the age of four, they remembered everything that their mother had known, at the time of their conception. We had quite a few of them around by this time.

They had more than a few quirks, the most obvious of which was their distaste for clothing, except for the lightest and loosest of silk gowns, and then only under protest! Uncle Tom said it had to do with the fact that they did not need artificial covering to be comfortable. Thus, like normal humans who lived in the tropics, they preferred to be without the burden of clothing. I suspect that it actually had more to do with Uncle Tom's preference for skin.

And they were very pretty.

Still, I didn't like the idea of being guarded.

My dining room was large, with tapestries on the walls, an elaborate parquet floor, and a high, ornate coffered ceiling. The high table, literally a third of a yard higher than the others, had tall chairs, like bar stools, for me, my family, and my honored guests. There was room for two dozen of us on one side of the table, with men alternating with women. There were usually a few male guests who were single, or who had left their ladies home, but the cloth factories around Okoitz had plenty of attractive young women eager to take up the slack.

The other side of the narrow table was for the pretty, young house girls to serve us from.

Four more tables were set up at a right angle to the high table, like the teeth of a comb. They were the same size, and with the same seating arrangement, but at a normal table top height.

The place was packed, mostly with old and trusted friends and strikingly handsome women. The fashions that the girls had decided to wear this year were back to those approved by that old pervert, Duke Henryk the Bearded, which had the women's breasts bare, and the serving wenches wearing nothing but micro-skirts. On most of the ladies, it looked very nice, and I could hardly tell those who were fat, or old, or ugly that they shouldn't dress like the others.

But now, in deference to the visiting Cardinal, they were all wearing fashions that would be approved by the old duke's son, King Henryk, which involved a complete cover up. It ruined the scenery.

The children had their own dining hall, and had food and entertainment there more to their liking. Mostly too many sweets and clowns to amuse them. Once they became pubescent, they went through the Catholic Sacrament of Confirmation, and were treated as adults thereafter, except that most of them still went to school, or joined the army, which was much the same thing. That usually happened around the time they were fourteen or fifteen, years later than in the Twentieth Century.

I sat between my wives, as always, but lately it had started to feel constraining.

The chair next to Francine was taken by the Papal Ambassador, who was a Cardinal and the courier who had delivered the Pope's letter to me. I wasn't looking forward to talking to the guy.

He had come up from Rome using the railroad line that we had finally gotten over, or more often through, the Alps. The individual cars were each pulled by one of the Big People, and managed to average fifty miles an hour, although our hour was twice as long as the one used in the modern world.

The Big people were another gift from my uncle. They had much in common with my bodyguards, except that they looked like the finest of horses, and they couldn't speak. They could understand Polish, however. They were intelligent, they had outstanding senses, and could run all day, as fast as a modern race horse could for a quarter mile, and with an armored man on their backs.

The ambassador and his retinue had rented a whole car from us for the journey.

Why the church couldn't use our fast, inexpensive post office was beyond me. I'd even given them permission to use the mails free of charge, but no, they had to do things the hard way. The mails were faster than taking the railroads, since the mail was carried on the backs of the Big People, and lightly loaded, they averaged seventy miles in a double length hour.

Father Thomas Aquinas said grace, we all said 'Amen', and people started eating. Father Thomas was doing a good job at running our school system, but he didn't have anything like the brilliance he'd shown in my old time line. It was disappointing. Was it somehow my fault?

"So, your grace, I trust that you will accede to the Pope's request to start a New Crusade and conquer the Holy Lands for the Glory of God?" The Ambassador-courier asked loudly, so the whole room heard.

"I'm afraid not. We have too much to do here," I said quietly.

"But what could possibly be more important than taking back the very land that Christ Himself walked on?" Again, he said it loudly, playing to the crowd.

"In the first place, we can hardly 'take back' something that we never owned at any time in history. In the second, there's a little matter of a few million young Mongols growing up far to the east. The Christian Army's job is to keep them out of Christendom. The Arabs have never threatened us. To attack them would be immoral."

The courier was about to make a vehement response when Francine put her hand on his arm and spoke quietly to him. Fine, let her take up the load. She had always considered herself to be the diplomat in the family. Let her prove it. Again.

I sat back and wondered, again, if I was living in a castle or in a palace. Such nonsense thoughts had occurred more often recently. The place had tall, crenellated outer walls four yards thick, plenty of guns on those walls, and a deep moat around the whole thing, so it was certainly a defensive structure, even though the moat also served as a swimming pool in the summer time. That made it a castle. On the other hand, my real defenses, thousands of strong concrete forts, were hundreds of miles away in every direction. Our thick walls here mostly gave us a lot of thermal mass, keeping the place cool in the summer and warm in the winter.

No enemy was likely to get close enough to us to actually attack us.

The windows were all double glazed, usually with stained glass on the inside. Most of the plastered walls were covered with tapestries. The rest were hand painted, mostly with heroic battle scenes. Stands of captured arms and armor helped to brighten up the place as well. Dozens of captured battle standards hung from the ceiling.

The floors were beautifully parquet, where they weren't tiled, and then often covered with vastly expensive carpets. The furniture was all of museum quality. The place certainly looked like a palace.

A small band was playing quietly.

Four of Celicia's well trained dancers were undulating in unison in front of me. Fully clothed.

I had two beautiful wives, and all of the lovely young ladies around, the pick of the sweet young things of Poland, were eager for one-nighters with your humble servant. I had hundreds of charming servants. I had thousands of good and loyal friends. I had almost a million men in my army who would willingly go to their deaths if I commanded it.

I was certainly living the good life!

So why wasn't I happy?

As the meal finished, and the tables were moved back to allow space for dancing, people, mostly my senior military officers, felt free to come over and talk to me.

"Lord Conrad! So what's all this about a Crusade, and can I go?" Sir Miesko's son, Kolomel Wladyclaw, Commander of the Wolves said, "A good war is just what my men need! Guarding construction workers who don't need any guarding is making them all bored and stale!" The Wolves were a cavalry unit made up of the scions of the old nobility. They were the first unit to be all mounted on Anna's children, the intelligent bio-engineered species that we called 'The Big People'.

"We are not going on Crusade, Sir Wladyclaw. We have too much to do around here. But I can certainly sympathize with that business of being bored and going stale! There is a lot of it going around!" I said.

"Then let's cure it, my lord! The Wolves alone could take back the Holy Lands in a single summer! Then we could have the construction people go in and build a few dozen snowflake forts to hold it. All of Christendom would praise you and your army!"

"No. First off, there is a whole new generation of Mongols growing up who will get here sooner or later. What with all of the slave girls they captured, the word is that the average Mongol has at least four wives. At six children per wife, and half of them being boys, that means that when they return, there could be a dozen times as many of them as there were last time! Your Wolves will be needed to stop them. Then too, a Crusade would not be a just war! The Arabs have done nothing to harm us! It would not be moral to attack them without reason!"

"Nothing, my lord? They have made slaves out of thousands, maybe millions of Christians! Surely, that constitutes harm!"

"There is no way of verifying your statement, and I suspect that the real numbers are far lower than that."

"If only one Christian was enslaved by the heathens, I would say that our cause was just!"

"Well, I wouldn't, Sir Wladyclaw. Killing thousands of people, many of them our own, to revenge one crime simply isn't justified. No! We will not go on Crusade! And this conversation is ended!"

I walked away, hoping that that was the end of it, but of course it wasn't. Fully a dozen more of my senior military personnel button holed me with plans for how their particular organizations could go out alone and conquer the entire Arab world, with little or no risk or expense to anyone. Ridiculous!

The Papal Ambassador was circulating among the crowd, talking up the glories of a New Crusade. I did not love him for it.

In an hour, I was definitely getting hot under the collar.

Finally, I stood up on top of the high table and shouted, "Listen up, people! We are NOT going on Crusade! We have many other obligations and responsibilities to perform here, and they don't include attacking anybody who hasn't tried to hurt us! This discussion is over!"

"But your grace…" The Papal Ambassador said.

"And YOU will shut your mouth! You will leave tomorrow, as soon as my letter to the Pope is delivered to you. And be assured that when you get to Rome, my letter to the Pope complaining about your behavior will have gotten there days before you do, because I will send it by regular mail!"

On my way out, I left a message to my secretaries saying that my letter had to be ready by breakfast. They could take all night, if they needed to.

Francine and Celicia got to my bedroom a few minutes after I did.

The floors were a black and white checkerboard of fine marble. The walls were of red velvet interspersed with panels of fine, carved, and polished hardwood. The ceiling was again coffered, but here each square section contained the carved portrait of a good, old friend.

"That was quite a scene you made at dinner," Francine said.

"They annoyed me."

"One doesn't tell a Papal Ambassador to shut his mouth," she persisted.

"Well, this one does, and did. The guy was way out of line."

"Master, something is very wrong with you." Celicia always called me that, and insisted that she was my slave. Ridiculous, of course. "What is it that makes you so unhappy?"

"Unhappy? Yes, I suppose that I am unhappy. Somehow, I feel smothered around here. Boxed in by too much tender, loving care. Kolomel Wladyclaw said that all of his men were feeling bored and going stale. That's probably what has happened to me."

"Master, you are a warrior who has gone too long without an adventure. You need a quest."

"Well, I need a vacation, I'll go that far."

Francine said, "As you will, Conrad. Where do you want to go and when should we leave?"

"Not 'we', my loves. I need to go alone. I love you both, but don't you see? Your smothering concern for me is part of my problem. I need some time by myself. If you two need to go somewhere, why don't you take a vacation, too. You have relatives in France that you haven't seen for many years, Francine. Why don't you take a month or two off and go visit them?"

"No one in France would want to see me."

"They would if you were escorted by a company of Wolves, with three carloads of servants, and a sufficient amount of gold."

"That might be fun, but I would not want to go without you."

"Well, your choices are to either go somewhere without me, or to stay here without me. I'm going to board one of my ships and see some more of the world. Alone."

They were unhappy, but I was persistent. They left together.

I went to bed alone, knowing that I hadn't heard the last of this one.

Chapter 2 The Open Road

In the morning, I had breakfast in the cafeteria, read, signed, and sealed my letter to the Pope, and had a lance of Warriors, in full armor, deliver it to the Papal Ambassador along with the message that he was now Persona non Grata in the territories of the Christian Army, except that he could use our railroads, which he had already paid for, to return to Rome, a one way trip. The lance was instructed to speed him on his way.

Then I wrote a letter of complaint to the Pope about the way his ambassador had tried to undercut my authority. I had that one done on parchment, too, and later in the day I had it sent by regular mail. My bleary eyed secretary saw to it. Good calligraphy on parchment takes a lot of time.

"That was a good job that you just did, Nadia. Thank you for all of the extra work. But for now, take the rest of the day off, and get some sleep. Thinking about it, take the next few months off, if you want, with pay. I'll see you when I get back."

Then I called Sir Piotr Kulczynski in. He had once been my squire, and he was probably the most intelligent person in the army. I told him that I was going on vacation, and that he would be in charge until I got back.

"Very well, sir. I know pretty much what needs doing. But tell me, where are you going?"

"To start with, wherever the first ship takes me. I'll develop a plan later. Mostly, I want to see more of the world."

"Yes, sir. And when will you be returning?"

In "I'll return when I'm ready to return. I need a rest, and I'll be back when I'm feeling better. But one thing that I don't want to happen is to have all of you people out hunting for me. Understood?"

"I understand it, but I don't like it. What if you are gone for years? What if you never come back?"

"Then the world will just have to learn to get along without me."

"I'm not sure that the world can do that, sir."

"Don't be silly. I've started you guys down the right path. From this point on, you could get along quite well without me. Nobody is irreplaceable. Now, go and collect up all of our senior people who happen to be in Okoitz. I want to announce this to the group, and to leave today."

"Today, sir? Isn't that rushing things?"

"Yes, it is. But the longer I wait, the longer people will have to try and pester me out of going."

And pester me, they did. The moment I walked into the meeting room, with its great round table, and statues of Poland's ancient kings looking down on us, Sir Wladyclaw said, "I understand that you are going on vacation, your grace. Shall I call up a company of Wolves to escort you?"

"You shall not. I'm going alone."

"But, but that's improper, sir! In this world, not even the lowliest noble travels without a group of armed companions. "

"The hell I will! I'm being protected to death. I said 'alone' and I meant alone. Now, what part of that didn't you understand?"

Soon, everybody in the room was getting their penny's worth in. And most especially my wives. Who would take care of me?

I said that I had been taking care of myself for many years before I'd come here, and had done a good job of it. I was the best swordsman in the army, a good shot with my new revolver, and I was a fair cook. What else did a man need?

Problem is, that I knew I was wrong. I was acting like a petulant child, dodging my responsibilities, refusing to plan for my own safety, and running on emotion rather than brains. So I did what all men do in that situation. For fully an hour where all of them got more and more adamant, I got more and more angry. I finally compromised to the point of taking my Big Person, Silver, along. Also, I'd be taking Cynthia, one of my bodyguards. When I said that, Francine's sudden glare of jealously surprised me.

Far stronger than any man, Cynthia had incredibly fast reflexes and the training to use them. She didn't look deadly, but that was another of her advantages.

That, and Francine was right, you never knew when you might need a little sex.

"So, that's it gang. I'm going to pack, and I'll be out of here in an hour."

I packed light, one summer weight uniform and two thin civilian outfits. I packed one silk dress for Cynthia, which she didn't want, preferring like all of her kind to go nude. But once we left Poland, well, the rules out there were different.

I took my sword and my revolver, along with a box of spare ammo, the new smokeless type. Some of my old camping equipment, including my two jack knives. A shaving kit. A light weight, oiled cloak, in case of rain. It all went into my saddlebags along with some bread, sausage, and cheese.

And I took one heavy bag of gold and silver coins. The 'silver' was actually zinc, but since only my smelters could produce it, we got away with calling it a precious metal and using it for coinage. Especially since we were always willing to trade it at face value for gold.

It was enough. When I needed something else, I could buy it.

They had Silver ready when we got down to the first floor. All of the Big People were a reddish color, except for my mount, who was pure white. I'd found her after the Battle of Sandomierz. She was a true Big Person, but she understood English, modern English, and not Polish. This left no one but me to adopt her. Francine had adopted my first mount, Anna.

She was wearing one of the double saddles I'd had made up years ago. This let Cynthia sit sidesaddle in front of me.

Everyone was at the front gate to wish me goodbye. I was delayed once more, kissing my wives and children, promising to always wear my weapons, shaking hands with my friends and subordinates, and waving to all of the girls in the crowd.

But eventually, we were gone, with the open road ahead of us.

All of our railroad tracks had bridle trails running along side of them, mostly for use of the mail carriers, and also to keep civilians from cluttering up our tracks.

There was also a line of telegraph poles near the track, since this was all army property, and could be easily guarded. The wires were difficult to maintain on civilian property, since the copper was sufficiently valuable to attract thieves.

After the Mongol Invasion, this road had Mongol spears stuck into the ground, every two yards, for it's entire length. And every spear had a Mongol's head stuck on top of it. It was my way of telling the world not to mess with us.

Now, most of the spears were gone, and only a few still had a weathered skull above them. But they'd served their purpose.

Back then, the tracks had been bolted together from lengths of cast nodular iron, and the cross ties had been of untreated wood. Now, the tracks were of a rust resistant steel welded end to end with inert gas arc welders, and the cross ties were of reinforced concrete. In the long run, it was cheaper, and made for a much smoother ride.

It was a lovely spring afternoon, and Silver was running for the sheer joy of it. Cynthia was enjoying herself as well, and soon she began to sing. I'd seen her mother and her dance often enough, and they were marvelous at it. Now I learned that her voice was to be treasured as well.

I could tell that Silver loved it as well. Horses like you to sing to them, and the Big People shared the trait, not that they were horses, of course. But they looked like the finest of horses, and could impersonate them when they wanted to. Many Slavic songs were written to be sung on horseback, with the rhythm of the horse's hooves acting as the percussion section.

"You have a lovely voice! That was an old Polish folk song you were singing, wasn't it?"

"Yes, sir."

"Beautiful! But during this trip, I want you to just call me Conrad. I don't want to call any more attention to myself than necessary."

She smirked slightly, thinking perhaps that since I was well over two yards tall, was riding one of the finest of horses in the world, and was wearing a sword worth half of a kingdom, that people would have little difficulty knowing who I was.

I said, "Here's a song in English, so Silver can enjoy the words."

So we sang out the afternoon, all the way to Cracow.

Every five miles or so, we passed one of my 'snowflake' forts. These were hexagonal defensive structures made out of pre-cast concrete panels. Each had a company of men living in it, along with their families. Mostly, aside from one day a week spent in military training, they were farmers, usually with some agricultural specialty.

The number of Big People had expanded to the point where there now enough of them for almost every warrior in the army to have one. Rather than letting their numbers get out of hand, and desiring them to be strictly an army monopoly, we had asked them to slow down their breeding. They had complied, but it turned out that we had overshot our mark by a considerable margin. It would be ten years before the human population matched that of the Big People.

Many of the Big People worked in transportation and for the Post Office, where they did their jobs without needing a human rider or teamster. Yet they still preferred a one-on-one relationship with a single warrior and his family. Most often, they actually lived with the family, having very clean habits. All of our buildings were designed to permit a Big Person to move around in them without difficulty.

Much of the agricultural work was actually done by Big People. Certainly, they did all of the weeding and the hauling. Our plows didn't need a human being walking behind them, and our harvesting machinery was getting sophisticated.

Most snowflake forts had some light industry going on to take up the slack in the winter.

You could look at each fort as being a large apartment house, with a church, a school, stores, and a decent bar, a small version of my Pink Dragon Inns. They each had a co-generating power house, a library, a cafeteria, a post office, a hospital, wells, and a septic system. While a bit Spartan by modern standards, they were luxurious by those of the Thirteenth Century.

Most of the people in the Christian Army lived in snowflake forts, and were quite proud of them. They were my attempt at combining the best parts of a small city, big enough to not be stultifying, small enough so that you knew all of your neighbors, along with the best that our current technology could offer them.

The economic structure had some of the elements of Capitalism with some of the better parts of Socialism. In the army, you and your family always had a secure place to live, clothes to wear, food to eat, and such medical support as was available, along with a bit of spending money.

But every company was it's own profit center. They rented their land and buildings from the army, and then, after all expenses and salaries were paid, they split any surplus with the Christian Army, as profits. If the people of the company wanted luxuries, they had to figure out a way to be productive!

Most companies managed to do it, and some in a spectacular manner!

The snowflakes had all been cement gray when we'd first put them up, but then a company of ceramics specialists came up with a system of large, colorful decorated tiles that fitted to an external metal framework, at about the same time as a company of glass specialists had perfected a fiberglass insulation that could be placed between the tiles and the concrete.

One summer when I was a student in America, I had worked with a traveling fair, making and selling cotton candy. The same simple mechanism worked very nicely, at higher temperatures, and with different materials, to make fiberglass!

The Captains of the two companies were smart enough to get together and come up with a practical system.

The resulting system insulated the building, as well as decorating it. Most of my people were really peasants, and their tastes were peasant tastes. And those living in every fort wanted to have the beautiful tiles.

Since each fort was it's own profit center, they had to buy them on their own money, but they could afford it, most of them anyway.

Now, each of the older forts was a dazzling riot of color, with no two of them alike. The younger ones were saving their money to catch up.

The two companies that had worked out the system had each expanded over six times, each. The Captains and most of their men had earned promotions, and all of their companies were now rich.

We could have stopped at any of the snowflake forts along the way, but that would be too much like a busman's holiday. But in Cracow there was one of the finest inns in the world, and I owned it. We'd stop for the night at the Cracow Pink Dragon Inn.

As we went through the city gate, the guard snapped to attention as if he was one of my men, although he was actually hired by the city government. "Welcome, Lord Conrad! Shall I notify Wawel Castle that you have arrived?"

I halted Silver. "No, please don't do that. We only have a little time here, and then we must leave in the early morning. I would just as soon that the people on the hill didn't know that I was here at all."

"It will be as you wish, my lord."

I wish that the people who knew me better were so willing to do as I wished!

"Thank you," I said and rode on. A tip wouldn't have been appropriate. Really rich people didn't do that.

My old drinking buddy Thadeaus was the inn keeper there, as well as being the manager of the whole, huge chain, with small inns in every company in the Army, and large ones in almost every city in Christendom. And, my God, how the money rolled in!

I never drew any salary from the army, but just left it all in the Army Bank. My lavish lifestyle, my many charities, and much else, were entirely supported by the Pink Dragon Inns.

"My Lord Conrad!" Thadeaus shouted, as energetic and as fat as ever. "You haven't been by for a year! Will you be staying at the inn, tonight?"

"Yes, my friend. I'm taking a vacation, and going to the castle would be too much like work. Just take good care of Silver, with a clean stall, a nice rubdown, and all of the best that she wants to eat. Give us a room for the night. We'll eat in the common hall."

"It will be as you wish, my lord. The Ducal Chamber is available, and I will have it readied for you. I take it that you do not want your presence announced."

"You take it rightly. If the people on Wawel Hill found that I had snubbed them, they would be offended."

"Then come in, my lord, along with your lovely friend, and wash the dust of the road from your throats. Besides our usual excellent beers, we have a wide selection of wines, brandies, and whiskeys available now.

"Good. We'll do some sampling. This is Cynthia, incidentally."

It was a pleasant evening. Cynthia drank a bit, at my request, but she didn't seem to really enjoy it, and it never affected her at all. She was a totally different species, after all.

The inn's many attractive waitresses took turns dancing nude on the stage, pleasantly and enthusiastically, but not really very skillfully.

Cynthia couldn't resist the temptation to get up there and show them what dancing was all about.

Her incredibly athletic form of dancing would put an Olympic Gymnast doing floor exercises to shame. She did amazing leaps higher into the air than anyone would think possible! She did cartwheels, back flips, front flips, reverse bounces, and finished up doing three complete forward spins in the air before coming down in a splits!

The crowd went wild! They'd never seen anything like it, but they liked what they saw.

Later, up in our suite, I decided that I was ready for a bit of sex.

Cynthia was as enthusiastic and as skillful in bed as she was on the dance floor.

This was looking to be a very good vacation!

Chapter 3 (Sir Piotr's Story)   Meanwhile, Back at the Castle

Sir Piotr Kulczynski, Commander of The Mapmakers, Mathematician to the College of Inventors, Baron of Cieszyn, and Hetman (Pro Tem) of the entire Christian Army, was trying out Conrad's desk for size, in Lord Conrad's elegant office.

The walls, lined with carved bookshelves of light colored oak, and the books in their tooled leather bindings, radiated a feeling of wisdom, power, and incorruptibility. One huge wall was done all in glass, and looked out over the Polish countryside. Another looked over the magnificent courtyard, below, where the local girls were preparing decorations for the festival and dance to be held after the Easter morning mass.

The desk itself was a poor fit, since Conrad was one of the largest men in the army, and Piotr was one of the smallest. His first action was to order some furniture makers to build him a new chair, one small enough to fit him, but tall enough so he could work at the big desk.

Then, he put some books on Conrad's chair to get himself up to a height that he write from, and started making a list of the other changes he intended to make.

He and Conrad had long debated about a number of things, and they had definite differences of opinion. Basically, Conrad's feeling was that if their military technology was sufficiently better than anyone else's, it was good enough. They should work on other things, instead.

Piotr was convinced that it was necessary to continuously improve one's capabilities. In order to continue to be useful, everything had to be exercised regularly, and this was as true for organizations as it was for machines, animals, and individual human beings. A Research and Development group that did not continue to produce new things soon lost all of its best people, who became bored. They were invariably replaced by second rate people who were happy to work for nothing but their pay.

Someone else might catch up with the army, someday, and if the army did not have a creative, productive, and innovative R and D group, Christendom could be in big trouble.

At the very least, the production schedules of the new, high velocity, bolt action infantry rifles should be at least tripled, since they increased the army's fire power so much at so little cost. And they should use the new smokeless powder, even if it was more expensive than black powder. It was clearly superior!

Conrad had once discussed the navies of someplace that he has seen, with their thick armor and their huge guns, but he saw no need for such expensive things in this time and place.

Piotr felt that they were developing large, breach loading cannons for their land forces, and for coastal defenses. With a few modifications, these could be mounted on a ship!

There were three fast, big, Liner class ships being built at a time when there wasn't a strong economic justification for them. But if they could be modified into battleships . . .

And the Air Force was being deliberately held back. Conrad insisted that that they be used only for training, patrolling, and observation. But they had a new two engine, two man craft capable of staying aloft from dawn to dusk. Unlike all previous aircraft, which had been made mostly of wood and cloth, the new plane was largely made from the new magnesium alloy, which was being extracted from Mediterranean sea water. The cylinder liners and piston rings were made of cast iron, the bearings were of various alloys, and the engine cranks were bronze, but mostly, the plane was of magnesium, as was the WWII Japanese Zero.

It had a retractable, tricycle landing gear, using the new rubber pneumatic tires, and could take off and land on any field, without the need of a catapult. The pilot and the navigator-radio operator both lay prone on their stomachs, the better to observe the land below them, but this also made for a very low drag, efficient, and sleek profile.

At another installation, a tripod mounted machine gun was already in evaluation trials, in both a light and a heavy version. It used the new clean burning, smokeless powder that didn't foul the gun barrels.

Two of those machine guns could be mounted in the plane, at a cost of some of it's range, and be serviced by the radio operator. Bombs and incendiaries could also be carried by the new airplane.

And the machine guns could also be mounted on the battleships. Also, some of the new, Explorer class ships could also be heavily armed, as they were being built.

There was no reason why a heavily armed ship could not perform commercial tasks, although it might have to be subsidized, a bit, since it would require a larger crew, and the guns would cut into the cargo space.

Conrad had left him in charge, without much in the way of definite instructions. Therefore, it seemed to Piotr that he was obligated to do things as he saw best.

The worst that could happen was that he could be chastised for it. He hoped.

Conrad, after all, was an old friend.

Piotr started making up flow charts of what had to be accomplished by when, and by whom.

He must get Baron Tados Bowman, Commander of the Seagoing Forces, to agree with the changes, soonest!

And the Commander of the Air Force! Now, what was his name?

Chapter 4 Down To The Sea in Ships

After a leisurely breakfast, and taking along a picnic lunch, we again took to the road, making Sandomierz before dark. Again, we stayed at one of my Pink Dragon Inns, this one in a converted castle.

In the morning we left for Sieciechow, crossing the Vistula on a ferry powered by the river itself that I had designed myself many years ago.

The day after, we rode by the construction site of my new city of Warsaw, which was to be a combination of a university town, a tourist trap, a diplomatic center, and a trade center. But they were only putting the foundations in now, and there wasn't much to see, so we rode on.

The next three days took us through Plock, Turon, and finally to Gdansk, one of Poland's two major seaports on the Baltic Sea.

We soon discovered that one of our patrol ships, an Explorer Class vessel called The Pride of Gdansk, would be leaving in a few hours, heading east.

The army's usual practice was to divide the seas and ocean coasts up into 'patrols' that took one of our ships about two weeks to sail the circumference of. The Explorer ships were equipped with lighters, small cargo boats that didn't need much of a harbor to operate out of. The ship sailed slowly onward, while the fast, steam powered lighters scurried back and forth between the ship and a series of trading posts on the shore.

The infrastructure of most places wasn't well developed yet, and this system let us pick up and deliver cargo and passengers from nothing but a small dock, or even just a beach.

At a decent harbor, the ship could come in and transfer a lot of cargo and people easily. But we could pick up the small stuff, too.

Once there was volume enough to justify it, a second ship was added to the patrol, going around in the opposite direction. The Baltic Patrol, being our oldest, now had four ships. Every point around the southern shore could ship or receive things or people twice a week, on the average.

We had started to build a much larger and faster class of ships, the Liners, which were intended to travel between the various patrols, stopping only at improved harbors with specially built docks.

I booked us a couple of cabins, one of which was for Silver, and when they found out who I was, they wouldn't take my money. Naturally, I had stayed at my own inns for free, and we hadn't bought anything on the trip yet, so thus far we hadn't spent anything at all on my vacation.

The ship's commander, Captain Sliwa, was delighted to have us on board, and insisted that we eat at his table.

The good captain had a wife and two servants, 'servants' being a euphemism for the additional wives permitted by army regulations for our higher ranking members, but frowned on by the church. They all worked on the ship, part time because of their children, and were paid for it, as well as getting their share of the ship's profits.

The economic arrangements on shipboard were similar to those of a landed company. The ship itself was owned by the army, and rented to the crew. After all salaries and expenses were paid, the army split what was left with the people aboard, in accordance with their rank.

If they ran at a loss, they still got their pay and benefits, but they had to make up the loss before they got any profits.

A crew that perennially ran at a loss was eventually replaced.

There were about four dozen full time Warriors on the ship, about a fifth of a usual company. But Sliwa was also the commander of the other three ships in the Baltic Patrol. Also, there were always some people on leave, in school, or sick, so he commanded an average sized company.

Dinner was served in the Captain's day room, a small room with plain, painted ferrocrete walls and ceiling. A carpet and a few handicrafts had obviously been added by the Captain's wives, which gave it a bit of a homey feeling. Still, a palace, it wasn't.

At dinner with the Captain and his wives, I asked, "Are there any things of particular intrest on the Baltic?"

"Well, that of course depends on what you are interested in. Since you yourself had a major hand in her design, the operations of my ship might interest you. Then, there are four decent cities on our route. Gdansk and Szczecin Harbor were both recently built by the army, so while they are clean and well designed, they don't have a great deal of architectural interest."

"Is that a complaint?" I asked.

"Not really, my lord. In order to save our country, and the whole of Christendom besides, the army has to do things quickly, in the most efficient manner possible. We simply have not had the time and energy to build things beautifully, besides. Some day, though, I hope that it will be possible to change the emphasis, a bit."

"A good thought that, yes."

"We'll be at Tallinn in two days, and we always try to stop there for a few hours. It has a fine harbor, and it is almost as clean as an army city. That, and it's a remarkably beautiful city as well. Eight days after that, we will be in Copenhagen, and it too deserves a good looking over."

"Thank you. We'll do that. I'd been thinking in terms of getting off in Copenhagen, and linking up with the North Sea Patrol there."

"That's the place to do it, my lord."

When dinner was over, and the captain brought out flask of brandy and a small, hand made box. As soon as his wives saw it, they quickly cleared the table and departed, although Cynthia stayed with us. He poured us each a small glass of the distilled wine, a recent product made in France from inferior grapes, and opened the box.

"Are you familiar with these, my lord?"

"By God! Those look like cigars!" They looked to be made of single leaves of tobacco, rolled up tightly, and then dried.

"I'd never heard of a name for them before. They were sent to me by an old friend, the Captain of one of the explorer companies investigating the Caribbean Sea. The natives there light them afire and inhale the smoke. I rather like it, but my wives hate the smell."

"That is a common household problem where I once lived. But I haven't had a smoke in almost thirty years! I didn't even know that such a thing was available!"

"Blame it all on that 'chain of command' system of yours, where everything has to 'go through channels'. They will probably filter up to you in a year or two. I got these a month ago, with a request that I evaluate them, to see if there was any market. But you are familiar with these things?"

"Oh yes, and once I was probably addicted to something similar. But the craving never ends, and I would dearly like to try one of them."

"Then please enjoy," he said handing me one of the lighters that I'd had a hand in designing.

I inhaled, and the rough, acrid taste scorched my throat and made me cough.

"It's a little crude, but selective breeding and better curing methods will solve that. None the less, it is a lovely thing!"

We smoked and sipped the brandy in silence, for as Kipling said, conversation ruins good smoke. Eventually, we had a second cigar each, and several glasses of brandy. I saw no reason why I should restrict the use of tobacco in Europe. I mean, we already had a cure for cancer, so what harm could it do?

"I wish that I had more of these to give you, my lord, but I only have a few left."

"Don't worry about it. In a month or so I'll have a case of them sent to you, and another sent to myself."

Seventy two standard cases fit neatly into a standard army container. They were each a yard long, a half yard wide, and a half yard high. Empty, they made a convenient bench. All of our jars, cans, and bottles were similarly standardized and re-usable, with everything fitting neatly into cases. When you bought something, you also bought the container it came in, but we'd always buy the container back at the same price, if it was clean and in good shape. An efficient system.

"Thank you, my lord. On another matter, I was very pleased to meet your Big Person, Silver. Being at sea most of the time, I have had regrettably little contact with these people. But from what I have read, they have some remarkable abilities. Their eyesight and hearing are claimed to be far superior to those of us ordinary humans, and it is said that their sense of direction is remarkably good. These abilities would be very helpful when trying to navigate a ship in bad weather! What can you tell me about this?"

"Well, basically, everything that you have said is true. I suppose that we could try her out as an assistant helmsman, but there will be difficulties. Most of the Big People understand Polish, but Silver understands only English, and not the dialect that is spoken there today. In any test, I would have to translate for her."

"There might be a better way," I continued. "Cynthia here is from the same place that Silver came from. She has many of the same abilities that Silver has, and she can both understand and speak Polish. We might want to test her out as a helmsman and a navigator."

"This charming young lady is from the same place that the Big People are from? I am astounded! And where might that place be?"

"I really don't know. Perhaps the right question might be 'When was that place?', since as best as I can understand it, a very long time ago, there was a fabulously advanced culture. The people there knew so much about God's Plan that they were able to imitate some parts of it. They could actually create life! The Big People and this fine lady's people were created by them."

"And what happened to these wizards?"

"I'm not sure that anything happened to them, for they also mastered the arts of time and space, and learned to travel from one era to another. Perhaps I should not be telling you about this, but you seem to be an honorable man, and it has been building up in me for a long time."

"Such a tale would weigh on me as well, my lord. You may be assured of my discretion. But as to testing the abilities of your lady, and not those of Silver, could we start in the morning? I can see that Cynthia would be far more convenient to have on shipboard than your mount, who is overly large and couldn't climb up to the crow's nest."

I asked Cynthia if she wanted to do it, and she was agreeable. We would start after breakfast.

It was another beautiful day, but in good conditions, Cynthia could see better with her naked eyes than any of the rest of us could with a telescope. Her hearing was outstanding as well, and she seemed to have a perfect sense of direction, too. Even on the deck of a moving ship, blindfolded, and spun many times around, she could always point to true north! We were all amazed. We also tested three members of the crew in the same fashion, and none of them could begin to compare with her performance.

Soon, she was given a short course in map reading and simple navigation, and she seemed to have an eidetic memory. Once she saw a chart, and studied it for a bit, she never had to look at it again.

On the other hand, she had absolutely no ability at all in mathematics, beyond very simple arithmetic. She would never be a good navigator.

By noon, they had her steering the ship, under the watchful eye of the usual helmsman.

"Now all we have to do is hope for some foul weather, so we can see how she does there," the captain said.

"That's a strange thing for a sailor to wish for," I said.

"Isn't it though! But I'm not likely to get an opportunity like this again, and I want to make the best of it!"

But the weather stayed fine, and I got to watching the running of the ship.

The Explorer class were container ships. They hauled standard army containers which were the same size as our old war carts, and our railroad cargo cars, far smaller than the containers used on modern ships. They were six yards long, two yards wide, and a yard and a half high.

Because our ships had to be able to pick up cargo and deliver it at unscheduled destinations, they had to be able to get to any container on the ship without unloading everything above it. This was accomplished by dividing the hold into nine sections, long tunnels, each over six yards wide and over three yards high, and running two thirds of the length of the ship. Each tunnel was normally sealed, to act as a water tight floatation device.

Each container had a 'half nut' under each corner, which rode on a long screw running the length of the tunnel. Each tunnel had four of these screws, with two layers of containers, permitting each tunnel to be used for other things, like hauling cattle or even people, in an emergency, if the containers were removed.

At the aft end of the tunnels, a system of elevators and a lateral transfer system let containers be transferred from one tunnel to another, so that cargo could be shifted at will.

It was not an inexpensive or extremely efficient system, but it was a very flexible system, which also permitted the balance of the ship to be easily adjusted.

Two steam launches and several dozen towed barges (which doubled as lifeboats) were normally stored on board. The elevator, the lateral transfer system, and some davits permitted the launches and barges to be easily loaded and unloaded.

A lance of men seemed to be at work constantly, opening containers, sorting their contents to other containers that would go to particular destinations, sealing the containers back up, and sending them below to the tunnels.

We charged less for large shipments to a single destination. And we charged more for anything in a non-standard package.

A few more people were sorting mail in the same way.

The system worked well, and the fast lighters quickly picked up and delivered cargo and passengers.

The ship had five dozen small passenger cabins, which were usually underutilized. I had expected passenger travel to be greater than it was. The ship's crew and their families often used the extra rooms with the understanding that if paying passengers needed them, they had to vacate to their old, and somewhat cramped, quarters in the forecastle.

A cafeteria and a social hall were available for both the crew and passengers. They were clean and functional but not very attractive. Typical Army stuff.

The ship was painted red and white, carried a white Polish Eagle on it's red smoke stack, and I thought that it was beautiful.

The aft quarter was the business end of the ship. She used two triple expansion V-6 piston engines, each with it's own screw, which were fed by two separate tubular boilers. They usually burned coal, but in a pinch they could burn oil, wood, or anything else available. The Explorer Class ships were designed to survive, even if they were stranded off the coast of Africa!

These boilers were fed distilled water by a system of condensers and evaporators which used waste engine heat to evaporate sea water, and condense it in compartments along the bottom of the hull. This fresh water was also used by the crew. The sea salt that resulted as a byproduct turned out to be very salable, and was a source of additional revenue.

The steam used by the engines was also condensed, of course, and reused.

Besides a compass, two radios, a sonic depth gage, and a forward looking sonar rig, the bridge was equipped with one of our first radar rigs.

"Wonderful things," the captain said, "Providing that you can keep them all working. Electronic devices have a habit of going west just when you need them the most."

"Yes, well, we are working on reliability. It takes time," I said.

The ship was lightly armed, enough to repel boarders, with six steam powered pea shooters and a like number of swivel guns, but it was never intended to be a real war ship. The army had never built a war ship.

Who would such a ship fight? What we already had was superior to anything else on the sea. Our ferrocrete hulls could shrug off anything that a traditional, Thirteenth Century ship could throw at us, our upper decks were five yards higher than those of the tallest wooden ship, so boarding was nearly impossible, and being faster and not at the mercy of the wind, we could always ram them. This made everyone around very friendly and peaceful.

The weapons of our enemies were fairly primitive, at least at sea.

That night, we found that Cynthia could see almost as well in the dark as she could on a clear day, and when the helmsman deliberately took us a few degrees off course, she told him about it.

We passed one of our fishing boats the next morning. She was going after herring, judging from the look of her rig. Captain Sliwa ordered a small net put over side, on the theory that if they were catching fish here, so could he. This was not for commercial purposes, but to feed the crew. They soon pulled up a net full, enough to feed the crew and passengers for a week. The fishing was much better in the Thirteenth Century that it had been in the Twentieth.

Soon, we were eating fried herring, poached herring, stewed herring, pickled herring, and baked herring. For some variety, I asked the cook if he had ever tried deep frying. He'd never heard of it, but he did have a big bottle of cooking oil, and lots of big pots. I showed him how to bread the fish with eggs and bread crumbs, and they became an instant hit. So did the French Fries I made with them. The trick to making great fries is to soak the sliced potatoes in sugar water for a while. We didn't have anything like catsup, a Chinese invention in my old time line, but vinegar works almost as good.

I'd been responsible for introducing potatoes, and dozens of other vegetables, to the Thirteenth Century. Quite by accident, of course.

I wrote a lengthy letter to Sir Piotr telling him about the shipments of tobacco, one to me, one to Captain Sliwa, and one to our Moslem chemists, since tobacco could be refined into a very effective insecticide, and how later, this nicotine could be extracted from those parts of the plant that were not good for smoking.

A second letter was concerned with the importance of breeding superior strains of tobacco, areas of the earth where it prospered, and the importance of experimentation in developing better curing methods. I said that there was a fortune to be made with this product.

I also wrote a treatise on the subject of smoking, talking about cigars, cigarettes, and pipes. I dwelled a while on the finest of smoking pipes, the meerschaum bowled calabash pipe, how the African calabash gourd was placed over a horizontal pole while growing to give it the desired shape, and where to find meerschaum, on the south coast of the Black Sea.

I made several drawings of it as well as some of the less desirable briar pipes. I explained a bit about water pipes as well. I stressed that a good pipe was a big pipe.

I also talked about the way a cigar was used by a man to reward himself, after a good day and a fine meal. A cigarette was used by a nervous man, to calm himself. And how a pipe was used by someone who was already calm, and merely wanted to relax some more.

We got to Tallinn late one afternoon. The Captain said that he had a lot of cargo to transfer, and that we wouldn't be leaving until dawn. Although he wouldn't have time to join us, he suggested that I take a look at the city, and perhaps enjoy a night on the town.

Naturally, I took Silver and Cynthia along, with the proviso that the girl put some clothes on. She came, wearing a loose silk dress, under protest. On the ship, her nudity had scandalized some of the other passengers, but since it was an army ship, our rules applied on board. A foreign city was another matter entirely.

The town was beautiful, with dozens of fine, limestone castles and many tall, lovely churches, most of them set high on a cliff overlooking the harbor.

We found a good inn that wasn't one of my own, but was called the Red Gate Inn, the same as the inn I had stayed in the night I went from the Twentieth Century to the Thirteenth. A spooky name, but a nice place.

The decor would have been called quaint in the Twentieth Century, but here it was only ordinary. The walls and ceilings were of painted plaster, supported by heavy, squared off timbers. They were left rough, with the marks of the broad axe still on them. A low fire burned in the fireplace, slowly cooking a small pig, but providing little light. For that, you had to pay extra for a candle at your table, the usual practice in this century.

We had a fine meal, with Cynthia opting for the roast pork with bread, cabbage, and carrots, along with a light garden salad, since the waitress said that that particular meal was on an all-you-can-eat basis. I guess that the pig had been on the fire for quite a while. All of Cynthia's people were very heavy eaters, having incredibly high metabolisms. She normally ate three or four times what I did, despite the fact that I was two or three times her size. The waitress at the inn gaped at her while she ate, but she kept the food coming.

I had another inexpensive meal, a pair of lobsters. In the Twentieth Century, this would have been the most expensive meal on the menu, but in the Thirteenth, it was not highly regarded, for some reason. I went to the kitchen, and yes, they were doing it properly, with live lobsters swimming in a big tub. I picked out two of them, and they boiled them up for me.

I loved it, once I talked the cooks into serving them with melted butter, something that they had never heard of before.

Delicious!

I also enjoyed copious amounts of some of the finest dark beer that I'd ever tasted. I would definitely have to tell Thadeaus, my head innkeeper, about it. It was not usual to import beer in this century, but this stuff was outstanding, and transportation costs were going down. The army did not permit tariffs, or import - export duties. We were adamant about free trade. Any taxes had to be paid by the producers or the retailers.

Language wasn't a problem at all, despite the fact that I didn't speak a word of Estonian. Most of the people we met spoke at least some Polish, as it was fast becoming the world language. Having the only magazines, newspapers, and printing presses in the world was doing a lot for us.

It must have been midnight when I decided that it was time to return to the ship. Cynthia sat in front of me on Silver as we went down "The Street of Drunken Warriors", so named because it was so narrow that a drunk couldn't fall over sideways in it!

"Well, now. You will do very nicely!" He said in heavily accented Polish.

An armed man had stepped out in front of us, quickly followed by at least a dozen others, both ahead of us and behind. I had seen them before at the inn we'd just eaten at.

"What do you want?" I said.

"But surely that is obvious! You are a wealthy foreigner, with a large bag of gold. You have the finest horse that I've ever seen, and a very attractive young lady who will afford us with many hours of enjoyment. Just what do you think we want?"

"If you are looking for a fight, you've got one."

"As you wish. Or, you could simply dismount, leave behind your lady, your property, and your weapons, and keep your life. The choice is yours."

"So it is."

I started to reach behind Cynthia to get at my sword, but suddenly she wasn't there any more! She jumped up over my head and was going down, bouncing off Silver's rear, to take out the thugs behind us!

Silver exploded into action, kicking two of our opponents at the same time in their faces with her fore hooves while she was charging forward! She stamped, kicked, and squashed the lot of them, and finally bit the back of the neck of the fellow who had done all the talking! Shaking him the way a dog shakes a rat, she bit it clean through!

It all happened so quickly that I didn't accomplish much more than getting my sword out!

The street was so narrow that Silver had to go to the next intersection before she could turn around to return to Cynthia's aid. She had no sooner completed the turn, spitting out some bloody vertebrae out in the process, when Cynthia caught up with us.

"They're all dead, Conrad."

"No great loss. Probably a bit of civic betterment, actually. But ladies, I have a complaint! The two of you didn't let me fight even one of them! I came on this trip looking for a little adventure, and you guys are protecting me as if I was back in Okoitz!"

"It is our duty to protect you, Conrad."

"I never get to have any fun!"

"Did you want to recover the booty?"

"No time for that. Someone had to hear this ruckus, and I would not like to make the acquaintance of the city authorities. Back to the ship. And you've torn your only dress. You'll either have to repair it or I'll have to buy you another one."

We never heard about the aftermath of that affray, but I assume that the local Powers That Be were confused. They might have decided that it was a rival gang, or maybe, considering the way the gang leader's neck was bitten through, that it had been done by some marauding monster.

Well-a-day. We were healthy, and at least the girls had had a good time.

Before we left the harbor, I had the Captain order a container of that dark beer, twelve one ton, standard army barrels, and have it shipped at my expense to the Pink Dragon Inn in Cracow. A present for Thadeaus.

Within a few weeks, steins of "Lord Conrad's Choice" were selling in the seven biggest cities in Poland, at six times the price of local beers. We were sold out a week later, but more was of course ordered.

A few days later, the Captain explained that his ship only covered the southern half of the Baltic. There wasn't enough business in the northern half to justify all four ships going up there. Two of his ships could easily handle it, and anyway, there were some islands in the middle of the sea that needed tending.

Later, we passed one of our bulk cargo carriers, judging from it's lack of a passenger deck.

"It's heading to Gdansk with a load of partially refined Swedish iron, my lord.

In a few days, it will be heading north again with a load of coke, for our refinery up there. If they just brought the iron ore to Gdansk, and dead headed back north, it would have required twice as many ships ... A boring job, and I'm glad it's not mine," the Captain said.

"There doesn't seem to be much in the way of conventional shipping going on."

"No, our prices and our speed have got all the others beat hollow. The Hansianic League once did a lot of protesting, and even threatened to go to war, but they finally gave up on it when they found that they no longer had the money to equip a war fleet."

I asked, "What happened to all of their sailors?"

"Some retired, but most of them joined the army, and volunteered for shipboard duty. That's where we get our experienced men, my lord."

"Including you?"

"In a way. My father was a fisherman, and when I was a young man, I crewed for him. Now, he captains one of our trawlers, and brings in catches a hundred times as big as he did when he owned his own boat. He makes a lot more money at it, too. He was the first of our captains who made it to the Grand Banks, and was very surprised when he found a dozen Portuguese fishing boats there!"

"Fishermen never tell anybody where the fish are," I laughed.

A day away from Copenhagen, the weather turned foul. It was cloudy, rainy, and foggy, but you couldn't really call it a storm.

Cynthia performed wonderfully in the foggy, rainy night, standing naked in the cold rain, apparently quite comfortable, while the men around her were bundled up in oil skins. It was that fantastic metabolism of hers.

"That settles it, my lord. We have got to put at least one of Cynthia's sisters on each of our ships. Our losses at sea have not been small, and her eyesight, hearing and sense of direction could save a lot of lives."

"Well, right now, we are mostly using them as bodyguards for the kings and leaders of Christendom. I really don't know exactly how many of them have been distributed. But once that nitch has been filled, I don't see why your request couldn't be approved. Fill out the paperwork on it, include a report on what we've found out about her abilities, and I'll append a note suggesting that we act on your recommendation. Then you can ship it up, through channels."

"I can't ask for more than that, my lord."

"Of course, the girls would have to be willing. What do you think, Cynthia? Would your sisters want to serve on shipboard?"

"I think so, Conrad. Ships are nice."

Chapter 5 Making A Clean Break of it.

We spent a few days in Copenhagen, seeing the sights and drinking good beer. The city was truly fine. It was rich and colorful, with beautiful churches, magnificent palaces, and comfortable inns.

We found a seamstress and had three more light, simple, and loose silk gowns made for Cynthia. They looked more like Ancient Greek styles than anything else. She absolutely refused to wear any of the complicated local fashions, saying that they were horribly scratchy. She also refused to wear shoes of any kind.

But at least, she wouldn't have a gang of priests complaining to me, and who knows? Maybe she would start a new fad. We made a lot of profit, shipping silk.

Our Ambassador to Denmark looked me up. It seems that someone had spotted me, and the King of Denmark had commanded that I make a courtesy call at his palace.

"No," I told the man. "I'm on vacation, and for me, visiting royalty is too much like work. Anyway, I'm not in his chain of command. He has no right to command me."

"But, you can't possibly turn down a royal command like this!"

"I most certainly can. I command the biggest and finest army in the world, and that lets me do pretty much as I please."

"But he is a king!"

"So what? I put King Henryk on the throne of Poland, mostly because I didn't want the bother of the job myself. If I really wanted to, I could take the King of Denmark off of his throne, just by sending a message to one of my battle commanders."

"You can't possibly mean that!"

"Well, I'm not likely to do it, but I could if I wanted to. Look, just go back to this pompous ass and tell him that it was a case of mistaken identity. Okay?"

"How could I lie to His Majesty? No, it's impossible!"

"You know, you are starting to piss me off. Get out of here before I throw you out the window!"

Cynthia broke into the conversation. "Conrad, one of my sisters is a bodyguard assigned to the King of Denmark. I haven't seen her in years. Couldn't we pay her a visit?"

"Humph. Well, on that basis, sure, we'll go. We have two more days to kill here, anyway. This silly, and very relieved looking diplomat can lead us there."

We rode over to the palace, and when we got there I was still a little miffed at the thought of someone who felt that he had a perfect right to interrupt my vacation. So I rode Silver right up the steps, into the palace, and into the throne room itself, the guards being too shocked to do anything about me. Well, one brought up a halberd to block my way, so I cut the big axe head in half, and he desisted. Actually, he ran away screaming. I have a very good sword.

The throne room reminded me of something that Napoleon the First would have wanted. Rich, heavy and pompous. It was designed for only one purpose, and that was to glorify the king, to prop up his ego. I still thought that he was a pompous ass.

"Your Majesty? I'm Conrad Stargard. You wanted to talk to me about something?"

"Do you always ride your horse into throne rooms?" He said in very bad Polish. He was acting huffy, sitting on a throne that was placed on a platform six steps above everybody else.

"Silver has very clean habits. Don't worry about a thing." I didn't dismount, since that would have placed me below this ass's ass.

"And don't you believe in bowing?"

"Not as a general thing. But if you want to, feel free to do so."

"Do you know who I am?!" He was getting very red in the face.

"Well, if you are unsure about that, I'm sure that someone here could enlighten you." I turned to the crowd. "Does anyone here know who this man is? He seems to be confused."

The Polish ambassador started to answer when the man next to him elbowed him in the ribs.

"I am the King of Denmark, damn you!"

"I thought that you might be! But as to damning me, that is the prerogative of Someone with considerably more authority than you have. Please consider that from my viewpoint, you are a petty monarch of a weak little country who seems to think that he has a right to interrupt my vacation. Now, what did you want to talk to me about?"

"After these insults, absolutely nothing!"

"Fine, then I'll be going. Cynthia here is the sister of the bodyguard we sent you some years ago, and she wants to visit for a bit. Hop down, girl. I'll send Silver back for you in a few hours."

And then I rode out of the throne room, thinking that I'd just had a lot of fun, something I'd wanted to do for years. Pompous twits have always annoyed me.

Of course, King Henryk of Poland would give me hell about it eventually, but so what? He did his job and I did mine. Did people go to him and demand that he design a steamship or some such? So why should I have to worry about diplomacy?

Back at the inn, I told Silver, in English, to go back and pick up Cynthia in two hours, and went inside for another good dark beer. It wasn't as fine as that marvelous stuff from Tallinn, but it was still not to be sneezed at.

Cynthia and her sister Midge came back early, without Silver's help, looking like a pair of badly tousled, barely pubescent schoolgirls. Their clothes were in shreds, but they seemed to be unhurt.

"Well, what happened to you two?" I said.

"The king was discourteous to us," Cynthia said. "He called me a strumpet, and refused to let me visit with my sister. Midge in turn said that if her sister wasn't welcome there, then she wasn't welcome, either. The king ordered her to come back, and she said 'No'."

"Well, that was perfectly within her rights. Everyone in Poland, the army, and in any country that we have treaties with has the 'Right of Departure'. Every adult has the right to quit, and go elsewhere, except for convicted criminals, and for Warriors just before a battle, of course."

Midge took over the narrative. "Thank you, my lord. So we started to leave, and the king ordered us both arrested, chained, and thrown into the dungeon, and of course, the guards had to try and do that. We couldn't let them, since Cynthia had her duties to you. But I knew most of those guys pretty well, and we didn't want to hurt any of them really badly. Therefore, we carefully restricted it to breaking arms and legs only, and even then we were careful not to harm their knees or elbows."

"That was very courteous of you," I said, pulling on my mug of Copenhagen's Finest.

"We thought so, but the king apparently didn't. After we had disabled all of his guards and soldiers, perhaps thirty of them, the king ordered everybody in the throne room, and there must have been a hundred of them by then, to capture us or kill us. Well, what's a girl to do? We had to disable all of the rest of them as well."

"Including the Polish ambassador?"

"Yes. He'd joined in with the others."

"Humph. That guy doesn't know which side of his bread is buttered. Did you harm the king?"

"No, not really," Cynthia said.

"Not really?" I winced.

"Well, we went into the garterrobe to straighten up as best as we could, and the king rushed in there by himself! Can you imagine that? Straight into a woman's garterrobe? So Cynthia put a full chamber pot on top of his head, upside down. Then we left."

"Well, a lady should never have to endure unwelcome improprieties, but none the less, I think that this would be an auspicious time for us all to leave Copenhagen. Both of you go up to the room and put some new clothes on. Then bring all of the bags down, and I'll have Silver ready by the door.

"You're not mad at us?" Cynthia said.

"I'm a little miffed about missing out on all of the fun! But no, I think you just did what you had to do. We'll talk later. Now move!"

With Cynthia in front of me and Midge riding behind, we left town briskly, avoiding areas where there were loud sounds of soldiers moving around .

My first thought was to get to the army portion of the harbor, and see if there was an army ship leaving immediately. There wasn't. There weren't any of our ships there at all! Just bad luck. I rode on past.

"Ladies! Any suggestions?"

Cynthia said, "On the charts I saw, there was one of our small trading posts due west of Copenhagen, on the North Sea. We could get there in a few hours. From there, we should be able to get a ship, soon."

We rode west, and at dusk, directed by Cynthia, we arrived at the trading post. It was situated on a medium sized river as many of our posts were, and had the usual small dock with a man-powered derrick at the end.

It was a square, mildly defendable concrete building, with a first floor devoted to a store and a warehouse, and a second floor that contained housing for the six families living there and a few guest rooms for people awaiting transport.

A separate schoolhouse was used by the children of the soldiers and those of the surrounding villagers who wanted to come. In more barbaric areas, the school would have been built into a three story trading post, with it's own church, and with more serious defenses, but this was a civilized, Christian country.

Like all of our schools, you could send and receive mail there, buy small items, and order major ones out of the army catalog. Evenings, it was sometimes used as a social hall, and two nights a week, it served as a bar, open to the locals.

We charged the local people and travelers for these services, but the school itself was free to the students. None the less, it still paid for itself.

There was a church in the local village that the Warriors used.

The trading post was crewed by a single lance of troops, commanded by one Sir Ian MacDougal.

"We need immediate transportation out of here," I told him.

"That will be a bit difficult, my lord. A ship isn't due for at least three days. The last one left under an hour ago."

"Tell them to turn around, and come back for us."

"But, that just isn't done, my lord!"

"We're doing it now. I am Conrad Stargard, Hetman of the Christian Army, and I order you to radio that last ship and tell them that I said to come back."

"Yes, sir. Immediately, my lord!"

Two hours later, we were aboard the Northern Light, and heading for Calise.

We were soon having dinner with Knight Bannerette Igor Sorinski, captain of this ship, and his two charming wives. The army made a distinction between Captain, a military rank, and captain, the person in charge of a major ship.

The captain was fascinated by the tests run by Captain Sliwa and I on Cynthia's abilities.

"You know, my lord, the North Sea is a much more difficult environment than the Baltic. The storms are much worse here, and the Baltic has almost nothing in the way of tides. Here, they can be fierce! I wonder about these ladies' sense of timing. Could they understand when the tides were happening, or would happen? We have graphs, tables, and charts worked out, but it takes a great deal of wisdom to know exactly what will be happening where and when! And do they have a good sense of the weather?"

"We'll be aboard for a few days, captain. Perhaps these ladies would be willing to study these things for a bit, and then we can see how they do."

"And would the ladies be willing?" He asked.

They said that they would be.

I went back to my cabin and wrote a letter to King Henryk of Poland, telling him Cynthia's version of what happened in Copenhagen, complaining about his ambassador there, telling him about the king's violation of the Right of Departure. Then I politely requested his permission to invade Denmark and throw the king out. I knew that such permission would never be granted, but it put Henryk in a position of having to placate me, rather than punish me.

In the next few days, we found that in all practical shipboard matters, Cynthia and Midge could perform remarkably well. They could understand the tides with precision, once I explained the actions of the Earth, the seas, the Sun, and the Moon to them. And once an experienced old sailor spent a few days talking about the weather to them, they started to get a grip on that. Mathematics was still beyond them, but I was beginning to think that they really didn't need mathematics. They had their own way of doing things.

I decided against touring England, Scotland, and Ireland, and the western most point of captain Sorinski's patrol was at the French city of Breast. Patrol boundaries were still in a state of flux, as we worked out the most efficient way of doing things.

Midge came to me an hour before we arrived at Breast.

"My lord, I'll never be able to return to my position in Copenhagen, and Cynthia can handle the job of protecting you very well without my help. I wondered, what would you think of assigning me to help captain Sorinski? I think that I might be very useful here."

"That's an interesting thought. Understand that you are welcome to accompany Cynthia and me on my vacation, and we can find a job for you once we get back to Okoitz, but if you really want to stay on board this ship, we can probably work something out."

"Oh, my lord, I really do! All of this sailing business is fascinating, and so is captain Sorinski!"

"Oh... Well, just remember to not seriously offend either of his current wives. If you want to join his family, you will need the permission of both of them."

"Oh, I'll work very hard on that, my lord."

"Okay. You will likely have my consent, as soon as I talk this over with the good captain."

The captain was delighted to get Midge both as a crewman and as a lover. I gave them my blessings, and wrote a letter to Sir Piotr, telling him about the change of assignments.

Silver, Cynthia and I got off at Breast, and caught a ship going south within hours.

Chapter 6 (Sir Piotr's Story)

Again, Back at Okoitz

Sir Piotr had just gotten to work when he was interrupted by the an apologetic secretary. Looking up he thought I'm going to have to either get rid of all of these naked women around here, or to get them to dress properly. Maybe, I'll have to replace them with male secretaries. These girls are entirely too distracting! And you can't really invite strangers to a meeting without causing talk!

Aloud, he said, "What it is it?"

She smiled (they always smiled), looked at her feet, and said "I'm sorry to interrupt your thoughts, but we have an courier in the lobby with a message from the King."

Piotr thought, This can't be good. When the King sends a messenger instead of a letter, he always has something unpleasant on his mind.

Sure enough, it was a summons for Sir Conrad to appear NOW in front of the King, at Legnica. As acting Hetman, it would be his job to make the appearances and the excuses. Sir Conrad got away with a lot due to his long friendship with the King. Acting Hetman Piotr would have a harder time of it.

The meeting was not a meeting. It was a royal audience in the throne room. This was even worse that Piotr had expected. King Henryk sat on his throne in full regal regalia. He was even holding his scepter and wearing his formal crown. This had the look of a royal ass chewing. His countenance was determined and angry.

The usual brightly colored drapes behind him had been replaced with black velvet ones. His guards were all traditional knights, not Conrad's soldiers, and they all wore stern expressions. And none of Maud's children, his usual bodyguards seemed to be around. This did not look good at all!

King Henryk knew very well that he held his throne as a present from Conrad. Such presents do not cause great gratitude when you are reminded of them too often. He knew enough history to know that murder was the leading cause of death among royal family members and now he understood why. After all, he felt like a brother to Conrad, but brothers were not always friendly.

His voice boomed out from the throne. "Why is Conrad not here! Does he dare send a servant to answer a Royal Summons?"

Piotr lifted his head from his supplicant position and said in an apologetic voice, "But, Your Majesty, Sir Conrad is your most loyal servant. I am here in his stead only because he did not get your message and we could not deliver it too him." He paused slightly. "He is gone."

"Gone? I know he is on 'vacation'. That is one of the reasons he was summoned here. But why did you not recall him immediately?"

Piotr was caught in a voice raising dilemma. "We could not recall him, because we have no idea of where he is. He specifically forbade us to keep track of him or to have anyone accompany him. We had heard that he was intending to visit England, Scotland, and Ireland, but apparently he has not gone there. We cannot find him."

There is nothing more maddening than being angry at someone and not being able to yell at them. His Majesty's frustration was showing.

"You will find him. If you have to send messages to every soldier on the borders, and to every ship at sea, and to every inn along the roads, and you will find him! He has much to answer for! He has insulted our integrity by refusing to cooperate with the Pope's emissary. He has embarrassed me by riding his damned horse into the throne room of a brother king and mocking him. There are reports of some very strange things happening in the City of Tallinn, the very night that he spent there, with fifteen dead bodies left on the streets! I even have reports of him expressing cowardice when asked to plan attacks against the Arabs. I have the Pope threatening to excommunicate me! Every king in Europe talking about what unruly subjects I have, and I want to know why my army won't do what I tell my army to do!"

Piotr was possibly the smartest man in the Christian Army. He was one of the fastest to see an opportunity. Certainly, he never mentioned that it wasn't Henryk's army at all, but rather Conrad's.

"Your Majesty. If I might point out, Sir Conrad has given me full authority to act in his absence. We all know of the need for pious Christians to fully support the needs of the Holy Father. I can also assure you that the Army is fully in support of your desire to punish the slavers to the south of us. The Arabs cannot be allowed to continue in their pagan ways. In fact, I have some plans that I have been working on to improve our abilities to carry out you wishes. Perhaps we could meet in private and I could explain what I have in mind?"

King Henryk considered, This is more like it!

Sir Conrad was always verbally respectful but had a sly way of manipulating every conversation to get his way. Henryk never really forgot how Conrad had used his verbal games to deny him the experience of walking on fire with the rest of the soldiers. Recently his sly refusals had turned to outright refusals. This small man, Piotr, was properly respectful. Perhaps something was going right here.

"We are pleased to grant such an audience. Call those that you think are necessary for the meeting and bring them here tomorrow morning. Oh, and perhaps we should not yet disturb Sir Conrad's well deserved vacation. He has been a loyal servant for a long time and deserves his rest."

Piotr had brought the plans for the new battleships, frigates, and destroyers, along with the specifications of his new weapons to the meeting with the king. He also invited Kolomel Wladyclaw of the Wolves, Kolomel Tados of the Waterborne Forces, and Kolomel Mickolai of the Air Force with him, along with several other sympathetic members of the Army command structure.

All were anxious to begin rescuing the Holy Land.

The king was looking over the plans for the battleship conversions. "These are impressive. How many of these do you think we will need to put pressure on the Infidels?"

Piotr answered, "Two or three should do it. They have a very high speed compared to the Arab ships and can patrol wide areas. With as few as three ships, we could probably interdict ninety percent of the Arab shipping in the Mediterranean, the Red Sea, and the Indian Ocean. We already have the hulls built, so we only have the expense and delay of re-arming them and putting them to sea. In addition, we will be modifying all of the new Explorer class ships into Frigates."

A fleeting look of unhappiness crossed the royal face. King Henryk never liked the mention of 'money' or 'expense',

"How much will this cost me?"

Sir Piotr was ready with his answer. "Why, nothing, of course, your majesty! There are time honored contracts between the Christian Army and the Nation of Poland! The army has always defended Christendom at it's own expense, just as the army has always been granted Free Transit across Polish lands, and the Right of Purchase, in which any land bought by the army is owned in fee simple, and never taxed again by anyone. At the same time, we defend Poland, and the rest of Europe, and are not paid for this valuable service. And of course, any lands that might be taken by the army, and any property taken at sea would of course be ours, to offset our expenses."

King Henryk considered this. He'd planned to make a profit out of all of this. He'd hinted at this, but not actually said it.

Sir Wladyclaw interjected, "Of course, there are a lot of details to work out. We will need to equip a large invading force for the push into Jerusalem. We will need to build the new weapons that you see there in considerable quantity and there will be a significant monetary loss to the forts when the men are gone on Crusade."

One of the kings counselors spoke up heatedly, "You cannot seriously propose that we reimburse the army for money it looses when it has to go to war instead of doing other things!" His voice was very sarcastic, "It is sad that they might actually have to give up basket weaving for a while to do their real jobs, but that is the REAL business of an army."

"Well, certainly not," Sir Piotr said. "But it almost seemed to me that you were suggesting that the army should pay you for the privilege of attacking Europe's enemies!

"No, of course not," King Henryk said. "I never intended any such thing!"

As they neared resolution of the problems, tempers cooled and a feeling of comradeship – or at least shared conspiracy – pervaded the room.

Sir Wladyclaw voiced the last problem of the day. "Of course, we do have that one problem. Sir Conrad was very adamant that we should not go to war with the Arabs. He also has made it known that he does not want his aero planes to go to war and he has previously forbidden us to arm our cargo ships. His statements were as subtle as usual and therefore known to everyone in Christendom. He is gone, one hopes temporarily, but most of the army is fanatically loyal to him. How do we explain our contradiction of every order he has given?"

Sir Piotr looked earnest and a little sad. "Do not worry, good Sir Wladyclaw. Our master is in trouble. No one could possibly object to our efforts to free him from imprisonment and slavery to the Infidel."

Sir Wladyclaw looked skeptical, "Slavery and imprisonment? For all we know he is sitting in a tavern in India drinking beer by the gallon and jumping on the local dancing girls."

The king looked sympathetic, "But, Piotr has a point. How do we know? He could as easily be shoveling shit in an Arab stable while an infidel stripes his back with a whip. No one will be certain until we find him and that could take a long, long time. We will have to search all the way to Jerusalem first."

Chapter 7 Conrad's Tale

On to the Amazon?

Cynthia and I spent the next week traveling down the Atlantic coast of France and Spain. We lazed around the sun deck, stopped at a few cities, and enjoyed the wine, but nothing out of the ordinary happened, except for a storm on the fifth and sixth days.

The ship tossed, pitched, and rolled, but it never slowed down. They even managed to pick up and deliver cargo, something that surprised me. The upper deck was placed off limits to passengers, but the ship had a decent library on board, and it even had a few books that I hadn't written myself!

Cynthia, Silver, and I didn't have any problems, but some of the other passengers stayed on the railing vomiting until they emptied out. They spent the balance of the storm in their cabins, hoping for an early death, but not getting it.

The patrol ended at Lisbon, in fine weather.

This city has one of the finest natural harbors in the world, and it is in a very good location for world trade. The people there were only using one side of it, so the army cut a deal with the city fathers which got us a very long term lease on the unused half of the harbor, with plenty of land around it. The plans were to make it a center of our world trading network.

But as it stood, it was still just another concrete army city. It was clean and efficient, with good lighting, good ventilation, and good plumbing, but lacking in the architectural graces. Captain Sliwa had been right. Once this vacation was over, I'd have to see what could be done about making better looking buildings. Maybe something like the tiles they used on the snowflake forts, but in a little better taste, with more subdued colors. Say, something like Gothic.

The old part of town was more interesting, with a lot of Moorish influence in the architecture. They used a lot of intricate pierced stone and wooden screens.

On the other hand, it was a whole lot dirtier, with shit all over everything, like most Medieval cities. One day was all that I wanted to spend there, seeing the sights.

And drinking the very good wine. We took a barrel of it with us when we left, and I had twelve more barrels of wine shipped back to Okoitz. Only, after all the shit they walked through, I just hoped that the natives here washed their feet before they mashed the grapes.

I'd bought standard army barrels of wine, of course, which each held a liquid ton. They were designed to fit efficiently into our containers, a dozen to each. Sometimes, smaller packages were put into the empty spaces between the barrels. I bought some gifts for my ladies back home, like lace shawls and headpieces, and had them stuffed into the spare spaces.

From Lisbon, I'd been thinking of touring the Mediterranean Sea, or at least the northern half of it. The Crusades had made Christians unwelcome in the southern half. However, the next ship going in that direction wasn't scheduled to leave for thirteen days.

On the other hand, a new Liner class ship was going to leave for the mouth of the Amazon River in two days, and that looked interesting!

I could always check out the Med later.

I signed us up for the trip to South America, or rather to Low Brazil, as we now called it. I have never figured out just who Amerigo Vespuci was, or what great thing he had done to deserve to have two continents named after him. In this timeline, he was not so honored.

High Brazil was the civilized area high in the Andes Mountains. Maybe later, we'd take a cruise up the Amazon River.

We didn't use wooden riverboats there any more, since the local wildlife had a habit of eating them. Bugs, ants, worms and all manner of such creatures had turned our first expedition up river into a major disaster, as did the diseases that we had traded with the natives.

Both problems had been cured. We now used ferrocrete ships on the river, the same Explorer class ships we used everywhere else. The Amazon was deep enough to let them travel upstream for thousands of miles, and even their lighters were made of ferrocrete.

My Uncle Tom, the time traveler, had licked the disease problem for us. His wizards had come up with three medicines that could be made cheaply using nothing but milk, any kind of milk. You just put some of the old stuff into a sealed jar of fresh milk, and the next day you had this magic medicine.

The first of them, the butter, was used to mark all of the cells of the human body with something that identified them as being totally human. Even most cancer cells didn't qualify. It was actually cheaper to produce than normal butter, and it tasted just as good, so before long we were using it in place of butter. In trauma cases, it saved a lot of time, to have the patient already treated.

The second, the cheese, was given at least four hours later. It was a deadly poison that killed everything that hadn't been marked as being human. And I mean everything! Not only bacteria, viruses, and cancers, but your stomach flora, all of the myriad of critters living on your skin, and all of your body's other symbionts were wiped out. You had a massive case of diarrhea for half a day, and if a mosquito bit you, it died! The same thing happened if your dog licked you when the poison was acting, so you had to be careful.

We were also evaluating it for use where we needed a complete sterilization program, perhaps to kill everything in the soil before plating certain crops.

The third medication, the oil, was given the next day. It replaced all of the symbionts the second had killed, and they were a very good set of new symbionts. Infections and skin diseases became very rare. After a bath, you rubbed it all over your skin, and drank a bit of it besides. Again, this was so cheap that it was often used in place of bath oil, lamp oil, and cooking oil!

After you were cured of whatever was ailing you, there was nothing to stop you from getting the same disease again, which required the treatment again, especially with diseases like malaria. But after going through this cycle several times, your body's immune system usually had the time to take care of the disease on it's own, and you stayed healthy after that.

The second time you took the treatment wasn't nearly as bad as the first. The first time, if you had a really big, years old tumor, for example, the cheese would kill the tumor, but all of those dead cells could swamp your body's clean up system, and that could kill you even though you were now 'healthy'! A case of 'the operation was successful, but the patient died'!

We didn't lose huge numbers of people to the treatment, but we did lose some, mostly old people using it for the first time. But since they were usually already dieing of something else, well, you do what you can.

Army regulations required that all personnel take the treatment at least once a year. It was also available to anybody else who wanted it at a very minimal price. Mostly, the cost of cleaning up all of the shit. If you were really broke, and didn't mind helping out with the clean up, we could accommodate you.

The result of this treatment was that Christendom had become a very healthy place to live, even with all of the shit on the streets.

To make sure that we didn't infect any other people, quarantine lines were set up between continents, and in other places where it was thought necessary. Anyone traveling across those lines had to take the treatment.

We didn't want to spread non-human diseases, either. At the same time that the people were treated, the ship was fumigated, usually with chlorine gas flooding all compartments, while the people and animals were brought up on deck. This did a very good job on rats, insects and anything else unwanted on board. Even the occasional stowaway.

Not that there was any reason for anyone to stow away on one of our ships. There were always plenty of dirty, low skilled jobs to be done on shipboard, and army policy was to let anyone work for their passage, if they couldn't afford to pay for it.

Other quarantine measures were being evaluated, such as forbidding the transportation of any living plant or animal across quarantine lines, except to isolated, sterilized islands. There, they had to be raised for at least one generation, and the offspring could be transported to a new continent only if they appeared to be absolutely healthy. This was largely to stop the movement of insect pests.

We had once been responsible for killing many thousands of Brazilian natives, and we didn't want that to happen again!

Our ship arrived the next day on her maiden voyage from the dockyards in Szczecin Harbor. She was the first to use the special dock in Lisbon that had been built especially for use by the Liner class. Passengers came and left through the starboard side of the ship, while conveyor belts on the port side loaded and unloaded containers of cargo.

I'd gone over the plans for the new Liner class of ships, but I'd never actually seen one before. The Duke Henryk the Bearded of Poland was long and sleek and lovely. She had four times the cargo capacity of the Explorer class of ships, and three times the passenger space. And she was twice as fast as our earlier boats, capable of thirty miles an hour.

Those were long army hours, of course. The army, and just about everyone in Christendom now, used a twelve hour day, sunrise to sunrise. The world was doing it our way because we made all of the clocks.

Liner class ships also had two classes of accomodations, a Standard class, with rooms much the same as on our earlier ships, and a Noble class, which were three times larger, very nicely furnished, and six times as expensive. Time would tell whether they paid for themselves.

I took the best suite aboard, with a large living room, a nice balcony, and an extra bedroom that housed Silver. There was a stable below for ordinary horses, but Silver was a friend. The suite had it's own bathroom, although Silver couldn't fit in it, and had to use the public latrine on the Standard class deck below ours. Surely, a design flaw to be corrected on future ships.

The ship carried a single, rarely used lighter, and enough well-stocked barges to act as lifeboats for everyone aboard in the event of a disaster, but these were normally kept inboard. She didn't visit small installations, but docked only at major ports, usually the terminals of our many Patrols.

The room service was good. I used it when I didn't want to eat at the Captain Tomaz's table.

The first night out, some of the wealthier passengers enticed me into a high stakes poker game, and in a few hours, I cleaned most of them out. After all, I had introduced the game to the Thirteenth Centaury in the first place. Not that I needed the money, but winning is fun. Perhaps Cynthia's nudity distracted some of then, and surely my barrel of Lisbon wine helped. Thus far, my vacation was actually running at a profit!

Anyway, I resolved to donate the money to charity, the next chance I got.

Three days out, we hit a small problem. The Captain, Sir Tomaz, who had almost a full company subordinate to him, decided that since the weather was very fine, and since we would soon be crossing the border of a quarantine zone, we might as well all take the treatment now.

The engines were stopped, a large sea anchor, basically a big parachute, was thrown over the bow rail, and the passengers and crew were each given a pat of butter, to be eaten under the watchful eye of the ship's medical officer.

Army procedure had it that when an area was not completely explored, each ship would take a slightly different course on each trip. This permitted us to map the ocean bottom better, to chart the currents, to look out for undiscovered islands, and to locate any possible dangers to navigation. Also, our ships regularly dropped ten yard nets overboard to sample the local fisheries, usually several at different depths. You never could tell what you might find.

One of the side advantages of this was that it made each trip a 'voyage of discovery', something that the passengers seemed to like.

Occasionally, the cooks would present a fish prepared in several different ways with this announcement, "My lords and ladies! This is experimental! We've never seen a fish like this one before! It may be a tasty treat, but we don't know. Please try it, if you feel daring, and let us know what you thought of it."

Usually, they were very bad, but it contributed to the passenger's sense of adventure.

Our current course took us fairly close to the coast of Africa until we were at the equator, the latitude of the mouth of the Amazon River, and then turning due west until we got there. It was an easy bit of navigation, from a mathematical standpoint.

Latitude could always be determined by measuring the angle to the North Star at night, in the Northern Hemisphere, or the Sun at noon, although then you had to enter in a few correction factors.

Every ship had a clock that was set for "navigation time", with three o'clock being the time at high noon at our city of Three Walls. Since we had radios, we always knew the exact correct time, and with that, longitude was also easy. A single noon time sighting could give you your exact position. Well, to within a mile or so.

This was providing that you could see the Sun, of course. A few more days into the trip, we found that we couldn't. We were hit by the worst storm that I've ever encountered, on land or sea.

I was in my suite, drinking wine and playing penny ante poker with a few of the other passengers, since nobody would play for high stakes with me any more. The ship was rocking so badly that we all had to keep our money in our pouches, because it wouldn't stay still on the bolted down table!

One of my guests got so seasick that he had been monopolizing the toilet for a while, when suddenly my own stomach started to rebel violently. The toilet being unavailable, I ran out to my balcony to dump my load.

When I was finished, I looked to the side and noticed that they were dumping our cargo containers into the sea! The ship had to be in very serious trouble before the Captain would do something like that!

I was leaning over the railing to get a better look at the operation when I was hit from behind by a huge cascade of water. It had to have traveled over the top of the ship, somehow! The wave knocked me over the balcony railing, and as I fell, I saw Cynthia diving from the balcony, coming after me!

My only thought was, Oh no, not both of us!

Hitting the water, or something floating in it, knocked me unconscious.

Chapter 8 (Piotr's Story) Back at the Castle, Again

The announcement that the Christian army was going to war was greeted by happiness everywhere. The Pope was happy that the Holy Land would soon be in Christian hands. The king was happy that he would soon feel like a king again. The army was happy that they were going on a noble mission to rescue their leader from the infidels. The rest of the world was just happy because they were going away.

True, the world was a lot richer and a lot safer since the Christian army established their virtual dictatorship over Europe. People were freer and better fed than they had ever been. You went to bed at night knowing that you probably wouldn't be attacked before morning because the army was right next door.

On the other hand, it was a little like sleeping with your pet lion. He was cuddly and warm and made you feel protected. But then again, there was always that small fear that he might need a snack in the middle of the night.

And, if you weren't in the army, you might not feel so rich. Hereditary Lords were not given the respect that they once were. Everyone felt equal. Worse yet, there were a lot of dark castles where they could no longer afford candles. The estates had supported themselves with farming and small manufacturing operations. The army with it's Big People, better seeds, and expensive equipment had driven down the cost of agricultural products to the point where most of the estates could do little more than feed themselves. They were also unable to maintain most of their businesses against the mechanized competition from the army. They were reduced to small handcrafts and limited run luxury goods.

It was no better for the serfs who liked being semi-independent. True, they had been able to leave their farms, but some of them liked working alone and outdoors. With the lords going broke, the serfs were forced to join the army or starve. The army was a good life for those who liked it. Hot showers, warm clothes, good food and steady pay were hard to complain about – for those who liked to be part of an organization. For those who had been their own masters – even if pledged to a Lord, the yoke often bothered their skin.

Small businessmen were also happy to see the army occupied elsewhere. Things were good if you were tavern keeper, unless Conrad opened one of his damned Pink Dragon Inns near you, but if you were a boatman, caravan man, or building contractor you were pretty much screwed. Join the army, knuckle down, or go out of business. Not popular choices for everyone. Not everyone wanted to be in the army.

For whatever reason, everyone sincerely cheered the war.

Sir Piotr, Hetman (pro tem) of the Christian Army, was happy that his new orders were being adopted so quickly. Most of the senior staff had long been wanting to upgrade their military capabilities.

Increased production facilities for the new bolt action rifles were already being installed, and every man in the army should have one, with the new bayonet, and plenty of ammunition, within a year.

Production orders for the new artillery and machine guns had been tripled.

He was delighted to find that Sir Tados already had the designs completed to fit the new artillery to some of his ships! It was something that he had wanted to do for a long time, so he had ordered the design work done, purely as an exercise for his engineers, he said, despite Conrad's orders to the contrary. During the Battle for the Vistula, Sir Tados had once spat on Conrad's boots, when our liege lord had given an unpopular order.

Putting machine guns on the new two engine aircraft was simple, and had already been done successfully. They could only shoot forward, forcing the pilot to aim his entire aircraft, but it seemed to work well enough.

Another 'design exercise' had been going on in the flying forces, under Sir Mickolai. They had an aircraft that could land on the water! The bottom of the hull was sealed up and made waterproof, the wing was mounted very high, and the engines were even higher, to keep the props out of the water. He wanted to put a steam catapult on the bow of a fast ship to launch it. It would land on the water, and a crane would recover the plane and pilot. Like the other new aircraft, this 'sea plane' was made largely out of the new magnesium alloys.

This two man craft would give the new battleships a very good observation point, high in the air. And being able to arm the craft with machine guns and bombs delighted Sir Mickolai!

Six new Explorer class ships were being fitted out as frigates, and work had already started on modifying three of the uncompleted Liner class ships into battleships, when word came from the Captain of the Duke Henryk that the new ship had proven to be so top heavy that in a storm, he had been forced to jettison a quarter of his cargo. The entire class would need re-designing, now.

Chapter 9 Hunger, Thirst, and Death

I awoke laying on top of a cargo container, in the middle of the ocean. My head hurt, and I was thirsty. The storm was mostly over, but the waves were still choppy. Nothing else was in sight.

Cynthia was with me.

"I see that you are alive, Conrad. I was beginning to worry about you."

"I gather that you have saved my life. Thank you. How long was I unconscious?"

"Almost two days."

"Do we have any supplies of any sort?"

"No, nothing."

"And do you know what happened to the ship?"

"It was still sailing, the last time I saw it. I don't think that the Captain knew that we were gone."

"You could be right. Most of our guests were pretty drunk. It was probably a while before somebody thought to report our abrupt exit. Not that the Captain could have done much for us in that storm, anyway.

"What's in this container?" I asked, hoping for an assortment of foodstuffs.

"The bill of lading on the container says it's full of fiberglass insulation, refrigeration grade, to be delivered to the Captain of Construction, Amazon Mouth North. I suppose that's why it floated when so many of them sank."

"We'll have to check that out. Sometimes, mistakes are made. You look different. Your breasts are much larger."

"Yes. One of the uses that my kind was made for is taking care of small children. My breasts are fully functional."

"So?"

"So, we have no food or fresh water. You can not drink sea water, but I can. You can drink the milk that I can produce. Therefore, I have caused my breasts to enlarge, to keep you alive."

"So you can do this voluntarily? That's an ability that a lot of human girls would love to have! And, that's quite an offer you just made! Again, I thank you."

"Nursing isn't painful. Actually, it's very pleasant."

"Do you know where we are?"

"Yes. We are a bit north of the equator, and a few hundred miles from the coast of Africa. The wind is blowing us in the right direction, but I have no idea how long this will continue. Are you thirsty."

"Very."

She bent over me, presenting her breasts.

"Then please enjoy."

We didn't have anything like a cup, but one wasn't needed.

There was obviously a limit to how long her small body could continue to feed my big one. This was in addition to the fact that she had an extremely high metabolism, and normally ate three times as much as I did.

A Big Person could have eaten the wooden lid of the container, but Cynthia wasn't up to such a thing.

Cynthia had gone swimming a few times, hoping to catch a fish, but no luck so far.

My pistol was gone, but I still had my sword and a useless sack of gold and silver, and Cynthia had her knife. I started to cut a small hole in the container's lid, to make very sure that there was nothing useful inside. Cynthia soon took over the job, being much stronger than I was.

The container was full of fiberglass. Feeling around inside it with my sword, I found something hard! We had to cut another hole to get at whatever it was, and eventually discovered that we owned a bottle of whiskey! Stolen whiskey. I knew that because it was from my own private stock!

"Someone was probably sending a postage free gift to a friend," I said.

"At least you have something to drink."

"No, but you do. Humans don't metabolize alcohol all that well, but my impression is that your sort of body treats it just like any ordinary food."

"Yes, that's true."

"Then you should drink this, and I'll continue to drink you!"

"That does make sense, Conrad."

A further search didn't turn up any more presents in the container.

I put the gold down the hole into the container, rather than have it bouncing around on my belt.

Drinking sea water required her to urinate much more often, to dump the extra salt, I suppose. Cynthia considered nudity to be completely normal, but she was embarrassed to pee while I was watching. I obliged her and always looked in another direction. A lady has her privileges.

A few days later, Cynthia sighted a large jellyfish. She swam out to it and ate most of it on the spot, since she couldn't grab on to it to bring it back. It just ripped apart.

Just as well, since she was starting to look thin, and I was getting plenty of nourishment just getting enough to drink. The sun was fierce, and we didn't have any sort of cover. It's a pity that Cynthia's breasts couldn't make water instead of milk.

The breasts of a human woman will sacrifice her own body in order to get enough of the nutrients needed to feed her baby. I didn't know if Cynthia's people worked the same way, but I was afraid that they might.

I told her to eat the rest of the jellyfish herself, and she did.

The heat was oppressive, but I tried hard to limit my intake of milk, because it was costing Cynthia so much. The thirst was unbearable, and I only used her when I couldn't stand it any more. And while I suffered from thirst, she suffered even more from hunger.

I started to spend as much time as I could in the water, hanging on to a rope I'd made out of some of my clothes. It was cooler in the water, so I sweated less, and perhaps I absorbed a bit of the sea water through my skin. Also, this let me look down every minute or so, hoping to see a fish, or anything she could eat. But there wasn't anything.

A week later, it was becoming obvious that she couldn't go on feeding my big body with her small one. We had been able to find nothing more for her to eat. She was getting very thin and weak. She even gave up looking for fish, and most of the time she just laid there in a sort of comma.

The winds were sometimes favorable, and sometimes not. I was beginning to lose hope.

I went swimming a few more times, thinking that I might be able to kill something with my sword, but there was nothing down there for me to cut up. In all of the stories that I had read, the seas were filled with sharks, but somehow, we were now someplace where they weren't.

A few times, I cut myself on my hand, and dangled it in the water, hoping to attract some attention. Blood was supposed to attract sharks. Losing a hand to a shark would be preferable to losing Cynthia, but nothing came of it.

I finally resolved that I was going to have to stop using her. If I had to die, so be it, but I wasn't going to kill Cynthia in the process. I prayed a lot that night, trying to get my soul in order.

I slept late, and when I awoke, the container was bumping gently against the shore!

It was a deserted beach, with nothing much but sand.

Weak with thirst, and stumbling, I carried Cynthia up onto the shore. She was alive, but she wasn't capable of much movement.

I searched for something for her to eat, but it was the cleanest beach I'd ever seen. No dead fish, no seaweed. I could find no sign of crabs or clams. It was as dead as the sea before it. There weren't even any insects!

Thinking back, once I'd read of a place like this. They called it the Skeleton Coast.

A few hundred yards from the shore, there was some sparse vegetation. When I staggered up there, I found it to be a rough sort of grass. A Big Person could have eaten it, but I didn't know about Cynthia. Hacking it down with my sword, I gathered up an armful of it and headed back.

When I got there, she was so weak that I had to put some of it in her mouth, but then she started chewing it, and said, "Thank you."

I continued feeding her throughout the day, which was mostly cloudy, for a blessing. I brought her sea water with the empty whiskey bottle, and tied my money pouch back to my belt, when I was down there. The container might drift back to sea, and the gold might prove useful, now that we were on land.

Either that grass was more nutritious than it looked, or Cynthia's digestive system was more efficient than I had imagined, but she actually started to recover. When evening came, she got up, walked slowly to the ocean and took another long drink for herself.

The thirst was killing me, but I made no mention of it. But as darkness set in, she put her left breast into my mouth and said, "Your turn."

Later, working by moonlight, I gathered her yet another armful of grass, so that she could eat at night, if she wanted to.

That night, I said, "I think that we should stay here for a few days, until we are strong enough to move on. Then, we should head north along the beach. Eventually, we must find people, some sort of civilization, and then my bag of gold should be able to buy us some transportation home."

"That sounds like a good plan, Conrad."

"Another thing. I . . . I have come to admire you greatly, Cynthia. When we get home, what would you think of joining my family? What would you think of being my wife, or at least, my third wife?"

"Oh, yes! I would love that, Conrad! I would love that very much!"

We kissed, and held each other, but neither of us had the strength for real love making.

I awoke to hear men on camels approaching!

I shook Cynthia awake.

"Company's coming! Let's try to be friendly with them. Maybe, they are our ticket out of here!"

We were both still very weak, and Cynthia didn't have a tenth of her old strength, speed, and agility.

I stood and smiled with my cracked lips. I had my right hand raised in a gesture of peace. In my left, I held my bag of gold and silver.

The men, wearing voluminous blue robes, surrounded us, scowling, with their swords drawn. One of them was saying something, in a harsh language that I'd never heard before.

"They don't look very friendly, Conrad."

"Just be as calm as you can!"

Keeping my movements slow and unthreatening, I poured some of the gold into my right hand, still smiling. I gestured to the man who was doing the talking, offering it to him.

Then, one of the men behind me swung his long camel sword and cut my right hand completely off at the wrist!

Blood squirted from the end of my arm! I was aghast! How could this happen to me? Why would they do this to me? I was trying to be friendly! Yet, my hand was laying there on the sand, with gold and blood all around it.

Cynthia just had to join in to the fight, but she was still too close to total exhaustion to be able to fight well. Still, the man who had struck off my hand suddenly found her on his camel's back, behind him. Cutting his throat, with her left hand gripping his hair through his turban and her right hand jerking her knife, took less than a second!

Then she leaped to the next camel, attacking the guy on her right. Again going for the throat, she sliced every artery in it!

While she was doing that, a third Arab, or whatever these bastards were, swung a sword from behind her and cut her head completely off!

Her beautiful head went flying from her tiny body! Her people could recover from some serious wounds, but not decapitation!

I drew my sword with my left hand and tried to attack them, but I weak and clumsy. I was contemptuously kicked in the face, and landed in the dirt. I was dazed, my nose was broken, my front teeth were missing, and my face was smashed. A dozen swords were pointed at me.

It was over.

They disarmed me, keeping my sword, scabbard, and belt. They picked up all of my gold and silver, marveling at the quality and quantity of the coins, and kept it all. Their thought must have been, Why work for some of his gold when we can easily take it all for free? It must have been obvious how weak I was.

One of them tied a tourniquet to my forearm, even though it wasn't bleeding much any more. Two weeks of dehydration had thickened my blood, or perhaps my Uncle Tom had something to do with it.

Apparently, they were going to let me live. They gave me a long drink of water, too.

They took Cynthia's knife, and they stripped their own dead as well. When they stripped the bodies, I saw that their skin looked blue, too. They must have used a very cheap dye on their robes. All three bodies were just left where they laid, to eventually rot away on the surface.

Maybe, if I hadn't fed Cynthia at all, she would still be in a coma, and she couldn't have attacked these bastards. She might still be alive.

If only I had done things differently, better.

Then the gang got interested in the container, They pulled some of the fiberglass out of the holes we'd cut and examined it, arguing. They had obviously never seen anything like it.

They hauled me over, shouting and pointing at it. With gestures, I explained that they should rub it on their genitals, and that this would make them grow very long.

Most of them actually did it. This got me another beating the next morning, since the glass fibers are amazingly irritating to the skin, but it was worth it. Anything that can hurt the enemy is good.

They tied me, belly down, over one of the camels that Cynthia had emptied, and we rode on. I prayed for her, and hoped that the little girl that I loved so much had a soul, but there was nothing else that I could do. She was gone.

A mile up the coast, we found a beached, newly dead whale.

Had I just explored a bit, Cynthia would have had plenty to eat, and might have been up to strength for combat. She might still be alive. With her old strength, she could easily have killed them all, and we could have ridden north with plenty of gear and supplies.

Mea culpa, mea culpa, mea maxima culpa.

Life no longer seemed worth living.

Chapter 10   In Uncle Tom's Control Room

I hit the pause button and said, "Tom, aren't you going to do any thing for him?"

"Of course. I'm going to let him live his own life his own way, without interfering with it. He was sick to death of being smothered with affection, remember? He was tired of being overly protected, remember? He wanted to have an adventure, didn't he? Well, an adventure is someone else having a very bad time of it, long ago and far away. No sane man wants to have an adventure! Well, Conrad went out and did it his own way, and now he's getting what he asked for! He is having an adventure!"

"I still think we ought to do something. He could get killed!"

"So? There have been about a hundred billion people on this planet since time began. Every one of them dies, eventually. There isn't much we can do about that."

"I still don't like it," I said.

"You don't have to. But let a man live his own life, will you? I mean, is he trying to tell you how to live yours?"

"So what's your real reason for not doing anything?"

Tom paused for a long while, and then said, "Because it can be very dangerous for a time traveler to be around Conrad. There is something magic about that guy. It's as if he has some kind of personal control over time and space. Look at the huge split he made in the time threads in 1231, for example, by doing nothing more than saving the life of an unimportant baby girl. You know, we have tried to create such a split several times, and we have been totally unsuccessful. All of the changes that we have tried to make have just healed their way out of the continuum, always in less than a century. Conrad's split seems to go on forever!"

"So?"

"So when Conrad was fighting the Battle of Sandomierz, things got so shredded that I was killed, or one of me was! That white horse he was riding used to belong to me! And then, when I got back from that battle, there were suddenly TWO of me! A confusing situation, I assure you! We had to cut a deal, where I run things on even numbered centuries, and the other Tom runs them on odd ones! I tell you that I am very frightened about going back there, personally."

I said, "So what kind of things did you try to change?"

"Some time, when I feel like talking, ask me about the time I knocked Henry VIII of England out of the saddle."

"But you don't feel like talking now?"

Tom just looked at me and hit the start button.

Chapter 11 (Sir Piotr's Story) Once More, Back at the Castle

Conrad was missing.

Sir Piotr had had a premonition that something like this would happen.

Reports from the Captain of the ship he had been on said that he had apparently been washed over side during the storm that had nearly capsized the Duke Henryk. He had had three guests in his suite at the time, but one had been sick in the bathroom, and the other two had been so drunk that they had fallen asleep without noticing that he, or his bodyguard, Cynthia, were missing.

It was only when Conrad's mount, Silver, had started looking for him that the alarm had sounded. More time was lost, because Silver did not understand Polish, but eventually, her meaning had become obvious.

The entire ship had been searched, a process that had taken more hours, without finding them.

Finally, the Captain had turned his ship around, and went searching for the most important man in Christendom. The ship's lighter had been broken out, and six lifeboats had been equipped with radios, to aid in the search. They had cruised the African coast, and searched the seas around it for a week without finding either Conrad or Cynthia. Since they could not have had any food or water with them, after a week everyone was sure that they had to be dead.

The Captain had regretfully collected up his men and boats, turned his ship west, and continued on his journey to the Amazon river.

Sir Wladyclaw stormed into Conrad's old office, where Sir Piotr was sitting on his new chair.

"Conrad has to be alive!" Sir Wladyclaw shouted, "A man like Conrad is very hard to kill! I'm going to take a battalion of my Wolves, and go looking for him! Are you with me or against me?"

Sir Piotr said, "I'm with you, of course! But a single battalion might not be enough, not if we have to search all of Africa for him. It's a big place! Sit down. We have to plan this out very carefully, or we will end up wasting time and lives! We will need ALL of your Wolves. The Construction Corps will have to defend itself for a while. I'll give them first priority with the new rifles. We will need the Seagoing Forces to get us there, the Air Force to help in the search, and a lot of the rest of the Christian Army, besides! Now, are you with me or against me?"

"I am with you, Sir Piotr!"

"Good! We begin!"

Chapter 12 Slavery

Riding on my stomach on the back of a camel was uncomfortable, but I got enough water to drink, and all of the raw whale meat I could stomach.

Compared to my previous situation, I suppose that it was an improvement. Not that I much cared.

I survived, even though I didn't want to.

I eventually discovered that the party that had murdered Cynthia and captured me was the advanced guard of a sizeable caravan. In a few days, they were replaced by another group of blue covered men, and we waited for the caravan to catch up.

When they arrived, my stump was re-bandaged by a medic who seemed to know what he was doing, I was chained by the neck at the end of a long line of Black African slaves, and I had to walk from then on. Actually, it was preferable to riding that damned camel.

The caravan guards wore the blue outfits, too, but most of the people in the caravan itself dressed differently, and seemed to be of a slightly different racial type. They were not as absolutely brutal as the blue robed ones.

We slaves got nothing but whale meat for two weeks, but at least now it was cooked. They watered us after they watered the camels, but at least they watered us. We were valuable property, and they didn't want us needlessly damaged. Whip marks on some of the Black slaves suggested that some damage was acceptable, though.

The other slaves, mostly men, were all healthy. I suspect that this was because any who weren't had been killed before the trip began. We were not in kindly hands.

For myself, I just followed orders. I was too depressed to do anything else.

By the time the trip was over, my stump had healed over, to the amazement of the medic. Uncle Tom had done that much for me, anyway, even though he hadn't done a very good job of explaining just what he had done. I wished that he would show up and do some more nice things for me, like sending me home, but he didn't.

After two weeks of walking, we came to a fair sized city on the banks of a river. The land about it was a very dry grassland, almost a desert, but the fields around the city were irrigated and looked productive.

We spent the night in a prison, of sorts. First thing in the morning they brought us to a public bath, stripped us down, and cleaned us up. Then we were taken to a market square, where we slaves were auctioned off, naked.

Since I was at the end of the line, I was sold last. I suppose that it was because of my injuries, but I fetched less than any of the black slaves. A few trifling bits of silver. I'd paid a hundred times that much for one of Cynthia's silk dresses. It was annoying and embarrassing. It also told me that I wasn't a very valuable slave, and that if I wanted to live, I'd better be careful. They might decide that I wasn't worth the food that I was eating.

Then, they would kill me, eliminating an inefficient economic asset.

My new owner took me under guard to a pumping station that provided irrigation water for the fields. They used four big Archimedes screws for this, each with one end in the river, and the other end dumping into a tank that fed into a canal. Two men walked around inside of a big barrel to power each pump.

They took me to a pump that was barely turning, since there was but a single man inside. A door was unlocked, I was forced inside, and the door was locked behind me. A guard threatened me with a whip, and I joined my fellow slave, walking, always uphill.

I felt like a reincarnation of Sisyphus, the Greek who had offended the Gods, and was forced to push a rock uphill, always to have it roll down before his task was completed.

My fellow inmate was also missing a right hand, but you didn't need hands for our job. He was a little man, small even among these short people.

The water from the pump poured into a tank with a hole in the bottom that led to the canal. When our keeper happened by, if the water was at the proper level, he knew that we'd been working, and we were fed. Mostly, it was stale coarse bread, sometimes with some wilted, raw vegetables as well.

If the water level in the tank was low, we went hungry.

Drinking water was straight from the river. Sanitary arrangements were non-existent. You peed through the grating in the door way, you shat on the floor, and then scraped it up with your hand. If you didn't, you had to sleep in your own mess, and then walk in it the next day.

The days were very hot, but the nights were often cold, and we had nothing like blankets. Our owners simply didn't care. We huddled together for warmth, to stay alive.

Weeks went by, I don't know how long. We had to work whenever it was light out, from early dawn to darkness, and seven days a week. Yet, my depression was such that I couldn't even feel angry about it.

Chapter 13 Sir Walznik's Rescue

Shakespeare had never lived. No one had ever heard the phrase Something is rotten in Denmark, but something WAS rotten in Denmark.

Captain Kurtz was confronting his superior in that man's palatial office in Copenhagen. Fine, expensive tapestries lined the walls. Rare and priceless rugs covered the floors. Intricately carved oak furniture abounded. And an absolute twit sat behind the oversized desk.

"I do not understand these orders, my lord. We all know that Lord Conrad was lost off of the west coast of Africa. These orders tell me to interdict all Arabian shipping and demand that they turn him over to us. The one thing that we know for certain is that the Arabs don't have him."

Lord Malton was more than slightly sarcastic, his fingertips forming a bridge before him. "And how do you, in your infinite wisdom, know what the Royal Advisors do not know? They feel certain that Lord Conrad is being held by someone or he would have returned to his duties by now. Conrad is not a man to abandon his post willingly."

Captain Kurtz was feeling that total agony felt only by a reasonable man confronted by stupidity combined with power. Stupidity in another man was excusable, but proud and powerful stupidity is the most infuriating thing in the world.

"Because, Sir, Lord Conrad is the richest man in Christendom and probably the richest in the world. We all pretend that his wealth is owned by the army or the crown, but we all know that his personal wealth is beyond counting. If any Arabian leader, or any one else was holding him, they would know that he could be ransomed for more than the wealth of their entire country. They would be knocking on our door trying to sell him back."

Lord Malton help up his palm to quiet the Captain. "The crown feels that whoever is holding him has not asked for ransom because they are afraid of reprisals. We are also capable of punishing or even erasing any one who has held our leader. We feel that he is being held somewhere and no one is going to admit it. We will not know for certain, of course, until he is found."

The Captain's voice was not respectful. "If you wanted me to find him, you would let me start by searching that coastline where he fell overboard from the Henryk. Give me 20 men with rifles and enough gold and I'll have a better chance of finding him than I will running around the Mediterranean taking prizes."

Lord Malton had had enough. "Your orders, Captain, are to keep pressure on the Arabs. We have discussed the possibility of a direct search and realize that the coast is simply too big. The entire army could not search all of that sand in a hundred years. We must convince someone who knows where he is to give him up. Now, you are dismissed. You will either carry out your orders or you will be moved to a more suitable post."

Sir Tomaz, Captain of the Liner Duke Henryk the Bearded pondered his problems.

A ship's crew was as much a family as a unit of crewmates. Where once only captains brought their wives and mistresses, the Christian Army had room for everyone. Conrad had reasoned that the best men would not leave their families for the sea. In previous navies that was not important because there were three distinct classes on board. The Captain answered only to God and that on an equal basis. He occupied virtually all of the livable space on board and, like his brother gods, felt no embarrassment at being treated far differently from his mortal subjects. The officers answered to the captain. As His priesthood, they got better food, a place to actually lay down at night, and a personal locker.

Then there were the men. They were not treated badly by the standards of the time. They were usually fed the best cheap meals that the owner knew how to preserve and, on most ships, got better medical care than the land dwelling peasantry. But, they were peasants. They lived cramped lives sleeping in spare spaces.

In the Christian Army, the command structure resembled those of Conrad's time rather than those of Medieval times. It wasn't a democracy, but it felt almost like one. Within the rules of military structure, everyone felt a lot like an equal. Rank had its privileges in space and pay, but they were relatively few compared to those of other navies.

The result was a family atmosphere both figuratively and literally. No one had a wife on shore. If they were married, they rarely went to sea without their partner. Major decisions usually ended up being made by consensus, as all crew members shared both meals and income. They became a close team – or failed and went back to the land.

A company of conventional soldiers, artillerymen, had been added to the ship's company, to operate the guns and to search Arab ships for slaves. Their women were still back at their Snowflake Forts, with their children, since they were only here on a temporary basis. Women were respected more in the army than in the general society, but there was no nonsense about equality. Women worked the spinning wheel while men killed the intruders. Unless the intruders were at the gate, of course.

The Duke Henryk the Bearded of Poland had not been converted to a war ship. She was, however, huge and fast. She was capable of carrying as many field cannon as needed bolted to her decks. Her captain had no idea why he had been taken off the lucrative Brazil route to search for less profitable prizes in the Mediterranean. It seemed a waste of otherwise profitable time. His ship was invulnerable, but mostly empty and mostly without profit. He was beginning to feel the same way that Captain Kurtz had.

In Gdansk, he had boarded a company of two hundred and sixty Warriors, twelve cannons, three dozen machine guns, and sufficient supplies for six months of operations, but no Big People. The Powers That Be had decided that they would not be needed at sea. This was in addition to the six companies of men, with their Big People, and their supplies, that he would be delivering to Africa.

He had been able to convince his superiors that it would not hurt to load a few hundred containers for Lisbon and Bordeaux and drop them off on the way. Lord knows what his ship would do for cargo after that.

He wasn't too happy about the Warriors. Of course, all members of the Christian Army were on the same side and all fellow soldiers were deserving of respect, but everyone knew that the Warriors weren't, perhaps, quite as well bred as the sea going crews. Maybe it was the fact that they were traveling without their families that made them so crude. He was blissfully unaware of the Warrior's opinion of the "sissies" who sailed around in ships when there was real fighting to be done. Such mutual ignorance kept the alliance alive.

In the mean time, even for the Henryk, the extra men and Big People meant a lot work to convert cargo space into living quarters and stables. Things were civil, but a little more crowded on the ship.

Several of the cannon had been mounted more or less permanently on the deck. The Captain was not certain what good they would be. He could simply ignore, nudge, or run over any other ship at sea. The Henryk was too fast to escape from and too tough to hurt.

What really bothered him, though, was his orders. They didn't make sense. In fact, they made so little sense that he had spent several sleepless nights wondering what he should do about them.

The decision had come early that morning, the day after he had put his six companies of passengers over the side, on the north west coast of Africa.

They actually did it that way. The supplies were delivered to a deserted shore by lighter and barges, but the men, in full armor, simply rode their Big People off the deck of the ship and swam to shore! They all survived it, too!

In the cold clear sleepless night he decided to call the meeting that he now hurried too. He had rehearsed what he had to say over and over again and still worried a little about the reaction that he would get. He knew what his people would say, but the Warriors were all strangers.

The room selected for the conference was originally for use as a dining room for the noble class guests of this luxurious ocean liner. It was tastefully appointed, with magnificent furniture, excellent wall hangings, and crystal chandeliers.

When he entered the conference room, his seat was empty at the head of the table. To his left sat the first mate, navigator and three crew members. Captain Bronson of the Artillery sat at the foot of the table. His Knights Bannerette and two army engineers sat to his left. The division was obvious.

Captain Tomaz sat quickly and began briskly. Looking around the table he asked, "Has everyone filled his cup and taken a bite of breakfast? There is a good sideboard here for those who had to miss breakfast for this meeting."

Everyone nodded politely and a few murmured affirmatives.

The time for stalling was over.

"Captain Bronson and a few others know why we are here. Let me take a moment to fill in the rest of you. I opened my orders two weeks ago as we left the harbor at Gdansk. You all know in general what those orders are. We are going to join the other ships and warriors in finding Lord Conrad. Unfortunately, those orders do not make sense. We have been ordered to patrol off of the coast of the Almohades Empire. We are to interdict and capture any Arabian ships that we meet. We have specific instructions as to what to do when we capture a ship. "Now, this is very odd because Lord Conrad was lost overboard from this very ship. We were at that time a thousand miles from the Empire. We were on course for Brazil, not Constantinople."

He stood up to gesture at the map behind him.

"As you may know, when we sail for Brazil, we usually do a simple latitude run. We drop down the coast of Africa until we are about even with Brazil and then we turn West."

He tapped the map at a spot north of the equator.

"We had not yet made that turn so we were about here when we lost Sir Conrad. I say 'about' because we don't know exactly when he was lost and we were in the middle of the damnedest storm that I have ever seen. But we do know for certain that Lord Conrad is NOT in the Mediterranean."

He gave them a moment to digest what he had said. When he returned to his seat, the Captain of Artillery asked him quietly, "Have you communicated this to the Powers That Be?"

The Ship's Captain replied. "Yes, on more than one occasion. There was an extensive inquiry when we returned to port the first time and I have radioed the authorities since we received our orders. They tell me that they have reason to believe that Lord Conrad was captured by an Arab trader and is now being held in the Empire, or one of the Caliphates. Whatever the reason they have, it is, they say, too sensitive to transmit to us."

Sir Tomaz was unaware that he was fiddling his thumbs rapidly. "I, uh, maintain some skepticism about the accuracy of what we are being told. I, uh, believe that if we are to find Lord Conrad, we may have to interpret our orders somewhat more broadly than the King would find acceptable."

He became aware of his thumb fiddling and clamped his hands together on the table. "Such a decision would, of course, require the cooperation of all on board. We are here today first to assess whether we have that cooperation."

There were a lot of looks back and forth around the table. Finally Captain Bronson spoke. "I think that I can speak for the Warriors. Every morning, we pledge ourselves to God, and to the Christian Army. King Henryk has never asked for our oath. The last time I looked, Lord Conrad had not yet resigned his commission. We will, therefore, do everything in our power to honor our oath. I am certain that Sir Piotr feels the same way and has simply been unable to express his loyalty in a way that we fully understand. Now, what exactly do you have in mind?"

Taking his cue at a look from his Captain, the Ship's Navigator slid his chair back and approached the map on the wall.

"We think we were about ten dozen miles offshore when we lost Sir Conrad. About a gross miles south of here the currents begin to run westerly. The current carries you to a point just north of Brazil. That is one of the reasons that we drop south before heading out to sea. The fuel savings are considerable. However, if Sir Conrad went into the sea where we think he did, the normal currents would bring him south along the African coast. We were also in one the worst westerly winds that we ever saw here. That would have tended to drive him into shore eventually rather than out to sea. We think, therefore, that he probably came to shore on a three gross mile stretch south of the Kingdom of Senegal."

One of the banners snorted. "You're telling me that Lord Conrad went into the sea over a gross miles from shore in the middle of a gale and you want us to go look for him? Unless this huge ship of yours can also go underwater, I doubt if we can find his current residence."

"Normally, sir, I would agree with you. There are, however, a few other factors that give us hope. We were dumping cargo all during the time that he could have gone missing. The stuff was in standard waterproof containers. In fact, we recovered about a twelfth of it from the sea and the shore during our first search for

Sir Conrad. In effect, Lord Conrad fell into a sea full of small boats or life rafts. All he would have to do is to get to one of the containers to have a high probability of survival. His female bodyguard is also missing and we can assume that she went in to rescue him. Her powers are well known. In fact, the excessive use of such powers may be one of the reasons that the king is not looking harder for our lord. The odds are slightly in his favor if he got to a container. We found quite a few of them washed up on shore. If Lord Conrad got to a container, he probably got to shore."

The banner was still unconvinced. "But what if he did not get to a flotation device? What if he drowned?"

His captain shrugged, "What if the innkeeper simply discarded the Holy Grail after dinner? What if it ended up in a midden somewhere? The quest would still need to be done. Until we know that he is dead, there is no purpose in assuming it. There is a reasonable chance that he lives, so from this minute forth, he does."

Treason having been agreed upon and excuses given, the talk turned to strategy.

Captain Bronson began the meat of the discussion. "You have already done a search for survivors and found none. I assume that you plan that we should be doing something better this time."

Captain Tomaz replied, "Last time we didn't have you. As you probably know, these ships run rather light on crew. Most of the cargo handling is done with machines and the crew's pay depends upon making a profit. We found some of the cargo in various places, but we weren't able to mount a real shore search. We never got more than a dozen men ashore and they didn't have as much as a horse between them. So far as I know, no one has really searched yet. You were put aboard this vessel to encourage the Arabs to give up Lord Conrad by intimidating the crews that we captured. I plan that you should instead follow up the leads we had to pass on before. You head inland and bring him back by hook or crook."

Captain Bronson smiled, almost smirked. "I appreciate your confidence in me and my men. However, we are only two hundred and sixty men. If we go ashore, we will be on foot, since they made us leave our Big People back at the Snowflakes. We have no way to bring our artillery along. We are the best army in world with the best weapons, but we will be invading Senegal or someplace similar. We don't even have as many bullets as they have warriors. Something a little more subtle will have to be done. Perhaps we should go ashore, look around, and just ask if anyone has seen Lord Conrad."

He saw the puzzled stares around the table. "Look, if he is still alive, he is either drinking beer in some pub or he is in jail for expressing one of his not-to-subtle opinions, or he has been taken into slavery. If he is drinking, we ask him to come home. If he is in jail or a slave, we buy his way out and take him home. His captors, if he is captured, obviously don't know who he is, so a little gold should handle things easier than a little lead."

The ship's crew was obviously still skeptical. They had pictured a rousing expedition to rescue their leader from angry infidels. One of them asked, "If, as you say, they don't know who they captured or who is living among them, then how will they be able to tell you if they have seen him? If, in fact, anyone will talk to you at all."

Bronson looked at the questioner. "Well, Lord Conrad is well over two yards tall, well over a yard around the chest, blond haired, carrying a magic sword, and probably traveling with a naked magic genie. He also walks through life with the soft footsteps of an African elephant. Do you think they will remember him?"

"Ah, question withdrawn."

"I suggest that we form two parties of about four dozen men each. Both of us Captains must stay on board to cover up this treason, but no one is going to come on board and count my men. One of my platoons will form the core of each, backed up with some of your men, and some of your specialists. We will want a navigator with each group, to figure our where the hell we are, some radio operators, as well as a translator. You say that you have identified about a three gross mile stretch where cargo and Conrad should have landed. Banners Walznik and Heinrik will be dropped off at each end of the stretch, with all of the ammo and weapons that they can carry and full purses of gold. You do have supplies of gold aboard, don't you? Yes? Then they can purchase horses, pack mules, equipment, and supplies from the locals. They will head toward each other and meet in the center. At that point, we will have dropped them at least six containers of weapons, ammunition, supplies, and trade goods, with a few men to guard them. Our Banners will decide what course to take when they move inland."

The navigator piped up, "Are you certain that they will have to move inland? Perhaps Sir Conrad will be on the shore somewhere."

Sir Tomaz answered, "I somehow doubt that it will be that easy. While we talk about Lord Conrad drinking in a pub, he didn't plan to go overboard. If were on the shore, he would have signaled the ship or search parties. I hear that he wanted a vacation, but I doubt that he wanted a marooning. For one reason or another, he has moved or been taken inland. We will follow with as much subtly as possible. As we don't necessarily want the king to be informed prematurely of our interpretation of his orders, I suggest that we move as fast as possible to drop off the teams. The Henryk can then return to patrol the shores of the Empire until we rendezvous again."

There was over an hour of additional discussion over details. The Chief Navigator went over the positions of towns and villages seen on the coast line, drop off points were selected, the crew members who had gone ashore on the first search pointed out where they had found the abandoned cargo containers, and then the shore parties retired to their sections to prepare for the landings. The Henryk was fast, and she would be in position to drop the first team in less than four days.

It had taken two days to find the first village on the coast. Getting anyone to talk to them was very tricky. Everyone they met immediately ran into the jungle. When they finally caught one man by running him down and sitting on him, he just gabbled, growled, and barked until he was hoarse. The newly and temporarily promoted Captain Walznik sat on a nearby stump and waited with his head leaning on his hand until the man's struggles diminished.

Finally he called out, "Sir Toby, bring me a bottle of that good bourbon from the trade goods – and a couple of cups."

When the bottle was delivered, the Captain approached the man who had finally stopped struggling. He poured a liberal dose of the Bourbon in a cup and tried to hand it to man sitting on the ground. The result was a frightened gabble and four limbs trying desperately to move away from the cup.

Sir Toby, holding onto two of the four writhing limbs said, "I think he thinks you're trying to poison him."

Without taking his eyes from the frightened man's face, the Captain raised the cup to his own lips and took a drink. The man stopped struggling. When the Captain tried a second time to give him the cup, he still tried to pull away. The Captain took a second drink, leaned over, and breathed in the mans face. The captives eyes lit up and he reached for the cup. He drank the entire half cup twelve year old bourbon in two long swigs. He wiped his mouth with the back of his hand and said "gabble, gabble, gabble!"

When it was obvious no one understood him, he said "gooble, gooble, gooble!".

Again seeing no recognition in the eyes around him he said in passable Aramaic, "That's a pretty good drink you got there!"

Captain Walznik answered, through the Spanish scholar they'd brought with them to translate, "Glad you enjoyed it. Care for another?"

"Not right now. I have to walk back to my hut. But you are welcome to leave the bottle."

"Sorry, we can't do that. Maybe you can help us, though and we could leave you a little. We are looking for a friend of ours. He would have drifted up on shore around here a few months ago. He's a very tall white man, taller than me, with light colored hair. He had a beautiful white girl who hated to wear clothes with him. He carried a big sword longer than a mans arm with a golden handle."

The man shook his head. "Haven't heard of any strangers around these parts on sea or on foot for quite a while. I sure would have remembered a couple like that. Did get some nice new boots for the wife from the shore recently. No one stops here much anyway. If anyone does come, they stop at Armoon. Its got the only market in the area. Sells slaves, cloth, stuff from the North. They might be able to help you there. Perhaps I would have another little drink, if you don't mind."

While the nameless man sipped his second drink, the captain fished a small gold coin from his purse and handed it over. "Here's a little token of our appreciation for your help. As we get closer to our friend, our appreciation gets bigger." Before they left, they found out that Armoon was about two days walk south and that there was only one good sized village on the way.

The got to the bigger village the next day. Captain Walznik had the column stop out of site of the town while he approached the log palisade around it. He and their Spanish scholar tried several languages, calling out "Hello in there" in Polish, German, Aramaic, and Greek before they got a response to the Greek.

A voice inside called back in heavily accented Greek. "Hello out there. Go away."

The scholar called back "We have some good trade goods and a little gold. Some of our horses have died and we need replacements. We will pay you well!"

The muffled voice came back "You seem to have more weapons than horses. Go away."

The Captain said to the translator. "Well, this is going well. Tell them that we would like to buy a slave. That we will pay well for him."

The answer came back. "I am certain that you would like to have us all as slaves. We are very poor. We have no slaves, no gold, no women, no food, no horses. We cannot even get enough water to drink. Go away!"

Captain Walznik gave up. Before he left, he shouted back at the wall. "Alright, we are going away. Tell everyone that we are looking for a friend of ours. He is very tall and light colored. He may have come to the beach a few months ago. We will pay well for his safe return."

The voice came back. "We have heard of such a man. I am certain that you can find him at Armoon. It is about two days walk south of here. Better hurry before you miss him."

As they walked back to the column, the translator looked excited. "Do you really think the they have seen Lord Conrad?"

The Captain Walznik snorted. "Of course not. If fifty armed men came to your village and said they were looking for something what would you tell them? You'd say of course you know where it is. Anywhere but here! This is going to be tricky."

They did see a good sized town the next day, but decided to bypass it until they met up with the column that was working it's way north. They met the second column two days later. At that point, they had each found several empty cargo containers, but no Conrad. Some of the natives were sporting Polish cloth clothing or leather boots from Germany or wiping their butts with the remains of Polish novels, but no one had seen, or admitted to seeing Lord Conrad or Cynthia. Many people said that they had seen such a man – over that way, far away – but when pressed for details, they were always wrong.

Captain Walznik met with Hendricks and four of the knights. "Lord Conrad has been missing for several months. I think, therefore, that we can take enough time to do an organized hunt for him. Obviously, no one is going to talk straight to a column of eight dozen heavily armed men so we are going to need another approach. I'm going to take a small group into that town we passed, 'Armoon'. We've all heard that there is a market there. We are going to try to pose as representatives of a merchant caravan. I'll take enough men to bring back supplies. We'll try to buy enough horses for the rest of the men and clothes more suitable to merchants. These uniforms must be causing a lot of talk up and down the coast."

Banner Hendricks spoke up. "I assume that I will be staying here with the column. I suggest that you take Garrett and anyone else with a flair for languages with you. We'll need to learn the local lingo if we are going to travel. While you are gone, I'll try to round up a local willing to give language lessons to the Warriors. Of course, since we don't know the language, the first problem will be communicating that we don't know the language and want to learn it. We'll work that out later."

Conrad had once said that a famous linguist had claimed that any idea could be communicated if you knew the right two hundred words of a language and were willing to use a lot of words and a lot of back and forth to get your idea across. He was optimistic, but not too far off. The difference between no words and two or three hundred words was the difference between frustration and communication. Most people in the Christian Army could learn that much of anything in a few weeks.

Armoon was certainly a town rather than a village. It was surrounded by a six yard high mud brick wall. Around the top, you could see the ends of tree trunks sticking though the wall. They would hold the fighting platforms on the inside of the wall. The gate was a wide log contraption guarded by eight men in identical robes.

One of them stepped in front of the column as it approached. He spoke Aramaic. Apparently they saw at least an occasional Arab trader here.

Once the language was established, he asked their business. Walznik answered, "We are merchants. We need to buy horses and supplies for the trip inland. We also have some trade goods to sell."

The guard said, "There is a ten talent fee for entering the city. That is two small Byzantine gold coins per man or the equivalent. You will also have to leave your weapons here."

Walznik could see that many men in the town were wearing swords or daggers. He judged that the guard had never heard of a gun and was trying to steal their bayonets and swords. "I tell you what, I will give you eight of these gold coins for our passage and you will forget about our swords. We mean no offense, but my men would feel naked if they were unarmed in a strange place." All of the Warriors had their hands on their sword hilts and were staring hard at the gate guard.

The guard judged his chances of continuing to breath after a confrontation and answered, "Fair enough. While you are in our city, you may want to look for the inn of the blue pig. My cousin runs a clean place with good whores. There are stables to your left where you can leave your horses."

It was one thing to accept a fool's sword but quite another to actually fight for it.

The stable owner did not speak any common language, but gesturing and grunting got them a corral and feed for the horses. Two Warriors pitched a tent near the horses. They didn't know the moral climate around here, and they didn't want to find out by looking for stolen horses.

The Captain and the rest of the troop took rooms at an inn. It might have been clean by local standards, but by those of the Christian Army, it was filthy. The men glanced at the local whores, and passed.

The owner spoke Greek, Aramaic, Latin, and several other languages. He had a set of scales on the counter and quoted prices in ounces of gold, bronze, or silver, convertible right here. This was certainly a caravan town.

Even though this was definitely a town and not a city, there were a few other merchants in town. Merchants and tradesman in this era profited from their secrets and rarely shared information. However, a lot of drinks and gossip would often elicit the information that the other fellow thought that you already had.

The sand nomads to the north had been converted to Islam over a hundred years before. Caravans came across the desert from the Mediterranean carrying Byzantine glass, Polish manufactures, Egyptian cotton, and slaves. As a result, you could also purchase a potato or an ear of corn in most places. There was a second route overland and upriver from Egypt but it was longer and more dangerous.

Walznik desperately wished that he could disguise his men as Moslems or Jews. It would make the search much easier. The area they were in wasn't really Moslem, but they were used to Moslem traders. However, his men would fear for their immortal souls if they denied God even once. They would have to pass as Christian merchants.

Because of the trade with the Moslem areas, Aramaic was the common trade tongue although a few people would remember Greek and Latin from the older days. There was also a trade language that the Africans used among themselves. The men spent much of their time learning it. It was easier to get information in a man's native language.

By the end of the first week, they had arranged with a nearby farmer to rent a field for the column. Banner Hendricks then moved the camp closer and gave some liberty to each of the men to explore the city. It took repeated buys to purchase enough horses to mount the men without driving the prices sky high. They needed almost eight dozen additional mounts. Camels would have been cheaper, but no one knew how to ride one.

Once they had enough language to be comfortable, they started looking for information of Conrad. They went to the local slave market and asked if anyone had sold a big, blonde male slave from the north. They went to inns and taverns to ask if anyone had seen anyone of Lord Conrad's description drinking heavily and bothering the servant girls.

It them took three weeks to get a lead. One evening, Captain Walznik and Garrett were approached while at dinner. The man was wearing a Moorish headdress and was obviously not a local.

"I understand that you are looking for a friend of yours. A man who may have come in from the sea. I have also heard that you may be willing to reward the man who helps you. Is this true?"

Captain Walznik gestured to a chair. "Yes. Many men have come to us claiming to have seen our friend, but it has always turned out that it was only someone similar. We have yet to hear reliable news."

The mans voice became conspiratorial. "Would your friend have come to shore on one of those cargo boxes that we have been seeing in the market place? Perhaps with a nasty female warrior? Perhaps he was carrying a great two handed sword with the sharpest blade in Africa?"

Walznik tried hard to suppress his look of excitement. Tried, and failed. Conrad actually swung his sword with one hand, but for most men it would be a two handed blade.

"That could be our friend. Did you see the sword yourself?"

"Yes, it was a scimitar longer than my arm, and slightly curved. The pommel was in the shape of a golden eagle and had an inscription in some language that I could not read. The current owner was quite proud of it."

Current owner? That did not sound good. "May I inquire as to where you saw this man?"

The informant shuffled his feet. "Of course, you may inquire. I do want to help out a fellow traveler. However, the matter of money needs to be resolved first. I am an honest man, but this trip was not as profitable as I had hoped and I need money for the trip home. Perhaps we can help each other?"

The Captain dropped his purse on the table.

"What is your price?"

The man looked apologetic. "It will take close to 100 of those small gold coins that you have been passing around for me to get back to my home. I would not ask so much, but I am stranded here."

Walznik gestured to the purse.

"There is a little more than that in this purse. Tell us what we need to know, and you can take it with you!"

The man looked apologetic again.

"You seem to be an honest man, but I have been cheated many times on this trip. Do you swear by Allah that you will pay me that purse when I have told my story?"

"I swear by the one true God. You may call him any name you want."

The man started to reach for the purse and then decided to tell his story first.

"Several months ago, I was coming in this direction from a City called Timbuktu. I am a drover. I travel with the caravans of others. About noon we met a caravan of people who called themselves something like 'Twaregs'. They were a filthy people. They smelled as bad as a Mongol. They were an illiterate and cruel people. I think they scavenged or stole everything they could from wherever they were and took it on caravan to find a place to sell it. We stopped for a noon meal and tea with them. I think that our merchant wanted to see if he could purchase stolen goods cheaply from them or maybe he was just afraid to offend such nasty looking characters. Anyway, they had a lot of merchandise from a shipwreck here on the coast. They wanted too much money for it, so we didn't buy any.

He continued, "They also had many slaves along. Most of them were in bad shape. They tried to sell us several, but we weren't interested. We keep slaves in my country, but there are rules about how you must treat them. It was unpleasant to see how these men and women were treated. I asked the leader about one of the slaves. He was a very large man and looked very powerful. He was, however, obviously sick and he had one arm, I think his left one, bandaged. I wondered why they were hauling a one armed slave around and suggested that it might be easier to simply dump him beside the road and let him walk home.

"The leader said that they thought that they could get a few silver coins for him from someone along the road, if he lived long enough. They had found him, they said, alongside one of the merchandise boxes that they were scavenging on the shore. He was with a beautiful girl. The girl would have been worth a lot more than the man, but she had fought so hard, killing two of their men, that they had to kill her and then hurt the man. They felt bad about killing the more valuable slave and were determined to get a little money for their trouble.

"That's when I noticed him fingering the sword at his side. He told me that it had belonged to the slave. He said it was too bad the slave was too ignorant to talk like a human. He must have had money to own such a weapon and if he could talk, they might have sold him for ransom. As it was, he was almost worthless."

The story stopped while the man looked around the table. "I or anyone else here can give you directions for the road to Timbuktu. If he lives, your friend will be along there."

He looked at the purse hopefully.

Captain Walznik paused only for a moment before he reached across the table and nudged the purse closer to the man.

"Thank you, friend. You have certainly earned the purse. We must tell our men of the good news, but if you get a thirst or hunger in the future, you are welcome at our table. Perhaps we can share other tales."

Chapter 14 To Escape From A Barrel

My life as a slave in Timbuktu wasn't a pleasant one.

My cell mate wasn't a talkative man, but slowly I managed to pick up enough of the local language to communicate with him a bit.

His name was Omar, and he had once been a student at one of the many universities in the city. He was soon to graduate with what I think was the local equivalent of a law degree, but then he fell into bad company. Being hard pressed to meet his expenses, he got involved in some shady deals. When the university found out about it, he was dismissed, and his name was forever blackened.

Falling ever lower, he had been caught stealing, and lost his right hand as a judicial punishment for theft. The second time they caught him stealing, they might have killed him, but the judge was merciful. He was enslaved, and given to the city, to spend his life in unending drudgery.

I eventually found that the city that I was serving was called Timbuktu, and that the blue men who had mutilated and captured me weren't Arabs at all, but were from a people called Twaregs. Omar claimed that they were the most brutal people in the world, and I had to agree with that. They were at least on a par with the Mongols.

Not that the information did me any good.

On top of the endless drudgery, part of the annoyance was that our job was completely unnecessary. A simple undershot water wheel, turned by the river itself, could have done the work cheaply, and around the clock. Or even a wind mill. I had built many of each in Poland.

But, even if my owners, the city government, bought the idea, it could put me into much greater trouble than I was in now. Maybe they would be grateful, but maybe they would decide that if they didn't need pumping slaves any more, why feed them? They might kill us all out of hand.

A slave has very little incentive to be creative.

After a few weeks, I realized that I had not said my army oath since the I had been washed into the Atlantic Ocean. This was normally said every morning by every warrior in the Christian Army, with his right hand raised to the raising sun. I couldn't see the morning sun from my barrel, and I no longer had a right hand to raise to it, but I started to say my oath again, anyway.

"On my honor, I will do my best to do my duty to God, and to the army. I will obey the Warrior's Code, and I will keep myself physically fit, mentally awake, and morally straight.

"The Warrior's Code:

"A warrior is: Trustworthy, Loyal, and Reverent. Courteous, Kind, and Fatherly. Obedient, Cheerful, and Efficient. Brave, Clean, and Deadly."

It helped me, somehow, and I've said it every morning since.

I'd always say it in Polish, of course. I think that Omar thought that I was praying, and maybe I was.

After a month went by, I noticed something very strange. A bulge was forming at the end of my stump! It was tender and sensitive.

I thought that it might be an infection of some kind, but Omar cautioned me not to let our keepers know about it. Medical help was unavailable, and if they thought that one of the slaves was sickly, they simply killed him, threw his body into the river to feed the crocodiles, and bought another slave. Our type of slave was cheap here.

A few days later, I noticed that my front teeth were starting to grow back!

Months went by, and slowly my mind began to recover from the shocks that I had been put through. My depression and apathy eventually turned into anger, but it was an anger for which there was no release.

The door lock was strong and inaccessible. We were both completely naked, with nothing resembling a tool of any kind.

The barrel and the door were made out of the hardest wood that I'd ever seen. Something imported from the tropics, I supposed. Even chewing on it didn't accomplish much. Oh, a year's chewing might have made it through, but we were in the open, with people walking by all of the time. Any damage would soon be noticed, and punished.

The old woman who brought our food didn't have the keys, so simply grabbing her wouldn't accomplish anything, either.

Crippled as I was, I couldn't come up with a plan.

The bulge on the end of my right arm kept growing. After four months, it was as big as my other fist. There wasn't anything that I could do about it, either.

So we continued to walk, pumping water, and they continued to feed us, after a fashion. I knew that someday, something would break in my favor, and when that day happened, I'd better be ready for it. My legs were getting plenty of exercise, but my upper body wasn't. I started building my upper body strength back up, mostly using dynamic tension, since push ups and pull ups were out of the question. It's not as though I had anything better to do.

After I'd been inside that damned pump for at least six months, maybe seven, another amazing thing happened. The skin on the lump at the end of my right arm dried up, broke open, and pealed off! And inside, I had grown a whole new hand!

Omar was shocked, scared.

"Never have I ever heard of such a thing! This must be witchcraft!"

"No! I don't think so, Omar! If I could do witchcraft, I would have gotten out of this barrel long ago! I think that it is a miracle!" I said, even though I knew that this must be the result of the complete medical going over that my Uncle Tom had once given me.

One man's miracle can be just another man's technology. And how could there be anything that forbids God from using technology to attain His ends? God can do anything that He wants to do!

Frogs were able to do this same trick, growing a new limb. But frogs manage to turn out twenty to fifty new generations for every one that human beings do. This, plus their far larger number of offspring gave them a considerable evolutionary advantage. Every new baby can be looked on as being an evolutionary experiment, after all. Frogs are actually a far more advanced life form than we Homo Sapiens are.

Oh, they hadn't hit on making huge brains, and spending a third of their basal metabolism on maintaining them, but intelligence has not yet been proven to be a long term survival mechanism. In seven hundred years, we brilliant humans will be very close to destroying our entire planet!

But trying to explain that would just convince Omar that it was witchcraft, and that might cause problems.

"You think that this could be a sign from Allah?"

"Can you think of anyone else who could have done it?"

Omar said, "Indeed, no! Why would the devil help a man? It must have been Allah!"

"Then perhaps, Allah has something in mind for me to do."

"Yes, yes! Something great and important!"

"I must think on this," I said.

"Indeed! And we must pray!"

I'd never seen Omar pray before, or indeed have anything to do with any religion of any kind, but seeing a supposed miracle had quite an effect on him.

I did do some praying, but I spent more time thinking. Now that I was whole again, I didn't have to come up with a plan to sneak back home. I could damn well fight my way back!

Hours later, I said, "Omar, what is the procedure around here when someone dies?"

"Procedure? They throw his body into the river and get another slave!"

"How many men do they send to do that?"

"Two. At least the three times that my cell mate has died, they always sent two guards."

"I've told you that once, I was a famous fighting man in my own country. I think that I could take out two of them, even if they were armed and I was naked."

"You plan on some ruse, to make them think that you are dead?"

"No, actually. I was planning on making them think that you were dead. Then, when they came in here to get your body, I would jump them," I said.

"Humm... My first thought is that jumping them, merely beating them up, this would be a very dangerous thing to do. If we act violently, my large friend, we must be very violent indeed, and kill them both without mercy! Our punishment would be death whether we were kind to them or not, and if they escaped, they would sound the alarm against us! We must kill them as quickly and as silently as possible!"

"There is much wisdom in what you are saying, yes. And I certainly have no love for these slave masters. Death it is. And your second thought?"

"It is that your plan might not work, Conrad. I am a very small man, but you are a giant. The guards might just tell you to put my body outside the door. They would be afraid of you, and have their swords drawn. They would be watchful!"

I asked, "Then what do you suggest?"

"I suggest that you be the one to feign death. I have been here for many years, and they do not fear me. If you are dead, they will not fear you, either. And one so small as myself could not be expected to move one so large as you are. They will have to enter the barrel to get you. Then, we can give them a surprise!"

"That sounds like a good plan. You know, though, that if this fails, they will kill us both, don't you?

"Of course, I have already said that!" He said, "But what do we have to lose? This is not an earthly paradise that we are in, is it? There is nothing for us here but drudgery and death! Also, I think that in helping you, I will be doing the work of Allah, and thus atoning for some of my misspent life."

"Well, if we both survive this, you will be well rewarded in this life, as well as the next one. I'm a very wealthy man, you know."

"So you have told me. But we must not act too hastily! We must plan everything very carefully! Just to get out of this barrel is one thing. To get out of Timbuktu, and into your land of Europe is quite another! Let us both think, and plan further, for we will only have a single chance!"

And plan we did. We were fairly certain about our ability to trick and kill our guards, especially if we pulled it off very early on a Saturday morning, when there wouldn't be anyone working in the fields, and the streets would be nearly empty.

The big problem was in quickly getting away from Timbuktu itself. The city was surrounded by what amounted to a desert, this time of the year. A man on foot couldn't carry enough water to get across it. We had to have camels, food, clothes, and a lot of equipment.

We had no money to buy anything with, and after spending so many years in the barrel, Omar wasn't even sure of his ability to know where to go to steal any of it. I, of course, had no idea of where to get anything.

And we had to get out of town fast, because they would doubtless be after us soon with all of their forces.

And once we were out of the city, mounted on camels and with the right equipment and supplies, where would we go? The desert was trackless. You needed a guide to find the next oasis.

We talked it over for three weeks, without solving anything.

Linking up with an outgoing caravan would be nice, but that cost money which we didn't have, and cash is always a closely guarded commodity! Anyway, this wasn't the season for caravans, and one wouldn't be leaving on a Saturday morning in any event. It was the Islamic version of Sunday, and a holy day.

There had to be a way out of here, but we didn't know how to do it.

After another week, I said, "Omar, there is no way for us to sneak out of this city with any serious hope of survival, let alone of success."

"I fear that this is true, Conrad."

I paused, and then I said:

"We're just going to have to conquer it!"

Chapter 15 (Sir Piotr's Story) Back at the Castle, Again

From the diary of Sir Piotr Kulczynski:

Getting the expedition going to find and rescue Lord Conrad was far more work than anyone had imagined.

The Wolves were ready to move at short notice, but they would need the backup of at least an equal number of our new Mounted Infantry, and considerable logistical support.

Much of the problem was to decide who could go, since pretty much everybody wanted to.

But, our military system had been designed for fighting short, intense wars with the Mongols. It wasn't set up to fight long term wars on another continent!

Obviously, the Construction Corps, which was building hundreds of projects from the Ukraine to India couldn't be interrupted. This expansion of our domain was absolutely essential, and disrupting our intricate schedules might well be catastrophic.

Our ship building industry was also sacrosanct. We would likely need more shipping very badly in the near future. And the factory system was vitally needed, and could not be touched. If this attack on Africa meant a major war, and it very likely did, we would need every factory and productive facility that we had, running around the clock every day of the year!

The fishing industry was very profitable, and probably couldn't contribute much to the war effort, anyway, except to help feed our troops. Their ships were not set up to handle cargo or passengers, anyway.

But there was a lot of slack in the agricultural sector. Since the Big People had become numerous, they had taken over most of the heavy work of farming. Most of the Warriors in our Snowflake Forts were spending a majority of their time making consumer products, like clocks or violins.

Well, the world could survive for a few years without very many new violins.

We couldn't take whole companies out for long periods of time from their farming. The Big People were doing much of the heavy work, but there were many tasks that they needed human help with. Without the Warriors, their families and the land would suffer. And the Warriors themselves would each have to be mounted on a Big Person, so we would be taking members of both groups out when we invaded.

We could, however, take a third or even a half of a company out of a Snowflake, and expect it to survive, both economically and socially.

But that meant a huge amount of reorganization! Parts of companies had to be reassembled into full companies, each with a Captain, and an upper command structure had to be put together.

And, we couldn't take Warriors and Big People from every Snowflake Fort. Those new companies on our eastern frontier, pushing our way into the Baltic States, Russia and the Ukraine, had to stay fully manned. Besides needing every man to get the land ready for farming, they needed their troops to defend against the almost certain Mongol attacks which, we were sure, would be starting within a few years.

The logistics problems were equally huge. We got the shipping we needed by taking half of the ships from any patrol with more than one ship assigned to it. Shipments might take longer and cost more, but we were so superior to the old way of doing things that our customers could live with it, for a while.

We had two battleships, converted Liners, in trials, the Invincible and the Insufferable. The Intolerable wouldn't be ready for three more months. And we had six frigates, which were converted Explorers. Each Frigate had a steam catapult and two aircraft aboard, to search out enemy shipping. Each battleship carried two catapults and a dozen planes.

Each of our ships had been provided with two linguists, mostly Jewish scholars from Argon, in Spain, who spoke Arabic, and other African languages. We had to be able to talk to the captains of the ships that we intercepted.

Our land forces would need linguists, as well, and we were recruiting them.

The Liner, Duke Henryk had been on the Mediterranean Sea for months, with indifferent success. I don't think that the Captain had faith in our mission, and he lacked the aircraft to locate enemy shipping. Soon, he will be re-assigned to the commercial sector, where he had been as outstanding skipper.

I ordered the new war ships to head for the Med, as they have begun calling it, and to interrupt all of the Moslem shipping that they could find. They were to free any slaves they came across, and give them decent clothing, a little money, and free passage to wherever they wanted to go. We would confiscate any useful goods found onboard of the Moslem ships to help defray our costs, and then we would destroy the ships themselves, since wooden ships had very little value now that our ferrocrete ships commanded the seas. Our captains were ordered to release the enemy sailors not far from one of their ports. The released men would be told that we would continue this practice until such time as Lord Conrad was returned to us.

This was so that the Moslems would know who was attacking them, and why.

I have received many letters from the Pope, urging me, in Sir Conrad's absence, and probable death, to turn the energies of the Christian Army to supporting the new crusade. Finally, I have written His Holiness that we would do just that, but in our own way.

Rather than simply attacking the Holy Lands, and having the Moslems counterattack numerous times from their other domains, we would start in the west, interrupting and destroying all of their shipping, destroying their cities on the African coast, and working our way across the southern Mediterranean sea, through Egypt and into the Holy Lands. Then we would continue east, and wipe out their forces in the Middle East.

His Holiness proclaimed his blessings on our plan. Father Ignacy had been an old friend and benefactor, and it relieved me to get him off my back.

I am embarrassed to say that all of this took us five months to accomplish, during which time Conrad's wives, among many others, especially Sir Wladyclaw, became increasingly less polite.

They were making my life into a special version of Hell. Even my own wife, Krystyana, was getting rude with me.

I fear that while my technical and mathematical abilities are good, my managerial skills are obviously lacking. I found myself wishing that Conrad had left someone else in charge.

Our first probe into Africa involved Sir Wladyclaw, leading a battalion of

Wolves and a battalion of our Mounted Infantry, along with three companies of the new Artillery Corps, down the coast of West Africa, from the straights of Gibraltar, and heading south. It took all of our available shipping to get them there. They had three Explorer class ships loaded with supplies to support them, as well as one of our Frigates, the Marauder, to interrupt enemy shipping, to give Sir Wladyclaw's forces some additional firepower, and a bit of air cover, if they needed it.

It would take a month for our fleet to return and pick a similarly sized force at Gdansk, and then to take them to Tangiers, from which point the new force would head east.

After that, our forces would be traveling by land to Italy and Portugal, and travel time for the fleet would be lessened. Our two major armies could then be reinforced much more quickly.

While we had not yet explored the area, it was our understanding that the northern portion of Africa was largely a sandy desert, with very few people living there, except in Egypt, far to the east. If Conrad still lived, he had to be somewhere near the coast. This was good, because we could support our troops far more easily near the sea which we would soon control, and indeed, own.

Chapter 16 (Sir Walsnik's Rescue) Captain Walsnik's Search

It was unbelievable! Lord Conrad was alive! He was a slave, but alive. The feeling of relief among the men had been audible when they were told. The two officers were discussing the next move.

Banner Hendricks was saying, "We can be ready to move out within a week. However, we need to get word back that our Lord is, happily, alive. I don't know how we are going to do that since both or our radios are broken beyond repair! The Henryk won't be back for at least two months. We could also use some reinforcements if we are going trekking through the jungle."

Captain Walznik replied, "We can't wait for any more help. It probably wouldn't do much good anyway. We can't conquer this whole continent. Besides, now that we know Lord Conrad is a slave, we have to move as fast as possible. He is an injured slave. That means that he has to be used for brute force carrying or as a light duty house slave. He is either working as a horse or a decoration. The average life span of an injured worker is less than a year. If he is in a household, his verbal disability will kill him even sooner. The first order he gets will be answered with 'Screw You', and he will be in trouble."

Sir Hendricks thought for a moment. "We're less than four miles from the sea. I have two men in one of my lances who are good sailors. If we get them a small dhow, or other sailing ship, they should be able to sail up to Lisbon in less than a month or so. From there they can radio home. At least people will know what we are doing."

Sir Walznik thought for a minute. "The idea is a good one. If we fail, our information will not be lost and someone else can try. I hate to lose two men from our small force, but you are right, we need to send word home. Make certain that the men inform the Liner Henryk FIRST. We don't know what King Henryk will do with the information. In fact, why don't we make a short list of officers that we know can be trusted. Your men can send messages to them first. Tell them to use the radio, it is harder to stop than the mail. You and I had better finish our shopping. It may be awhile before we run into another bazaar."

In fact, it took almost a week to finish purchasing what they needed and prepare for the trek. By that time they had crude maps purchased from other travelers, horses or mules for all of the cargo, and mounts for all of the men. They had to purchase spare mounts as they became available. Speed was necessary if they were to find Lord Conrad alive.

They also bought enough Arab clothing and cloaks to look like Moslem merchants whenever needed. They packed enough grain and rice for well over a month and hoped that they would not need more. They had taken enough trade goods from the Henryk to actually function as merchants if needed.

They had finally learned the name of their informant and had invited him to a farewell dinner at the inn. Besides his company, they needed to know as exactly as possible where on the trail he had seen Lord Conrad. It would save them the time needed to search the area between Armoon and the last place Lord Conrad had been seen.

Amhad Al-Misri's name meant "Ahmad from Egypt". Captain Walznik wondered if his guest really had seen the Nile. The meal was being served in their rooms at the inn. There had been six courses of food, wine and conversation. People in this area started with desert. Rolls sweetened with honey and nuts began the meal. Vegetables, fruits, steak, and fowl were then served. This was obviously a celebration rather than the usual bowl of stew and bread. Walznik, Hendricks, and Sir Garrett sat around the table with Ahmad. Ahmad, as a Moslem, was, of course, forbidden to use alcohol but when away from home he was as faithful as most men are. He was certain that Allah would be understanding when he returned home. Besides, the bourbon was an excellent and rare treat.

Captain Walznik asked, "Are you certain that you do not want to hire on as a guide? The pay would be very good."

Ahmad belched politely and replied, "I would like to help, but I have been away from home much too long. We came down the Nile and then started across country over two years ago. It has been too long since I have slept with my wife and held my children. For a small fee and in appreciation of this marvelous meal I would, however, be happy to tell you as much as I can about the route ahead of you. For myself, I have been traveling with Ali Ben-Joseph much too long."

Sir Garrett asked, "You have a companion?"

Ahmed smiled and leaned back wearily. "Every caravaner travels with Ali Ben-Joseph. Every second man you meet claims to be Ali Ben-Joseph or his brother. Ali comes from a small caliphate east of Constantinople. It is near the area that I come from, and I am fortunate to be one the few people to have actually met the man. He was a very successful merchant in his home town. He was a personal friend of the Caliph and very respected. He had the finest family of handsome sons and one beautiful daughter who's countenance brought suitors from all of kingdoms of Allah. When she was to be married, Ali gave the finest banquet that the city had ever seen. Seven days of entertainment and feasting were provided! Wild beasts were paraded though the perfumed streets! Musicians played all over the city while people danced in the streets and houses. In his palace, Ali had hired the best dancers and entertainers and served the finest food anyone had ever seen. On the last night, Ali had eaten far too much and may even, May Allah Forgive Him, have had a little wine, such was his sorrow at seeing his daughter leave his house.

"Anyway, when he leaned over the banquet table to kiss his daughters hand one last time, he farted. It was not just an ordinary fart. It was a fart that was louder than the music and longer than a sermon. A fart that leaves color on the clothes and drops like rain in the air.

"He was mortally wounded in his soul. In his embarrassment he fled the house, mounted his horse and rode alone into the night. He took not a coin or a morsel of bread with him. For twenty years he wandered the caravan trails as a common drover. The toil aged him and bent his back. Every night he thought of his beloved family and home and suffered anew. Finally he decided that it was safe to return home. After twenty years, even his transgression would be forgotten. Anxious to see his family, he came once again to the gate of our city. In those peaceful times our older soldiers stood guard at that post. As he entered the gate, Ali stopped to chat with the old timer. 'How is the caliph? Is Muhammad Al-Rashid still in good health?'

"'Oh, you must have been away for a long time. His son Ibn Muhammad Al-Rashid has ruled for fifteen years now. He is a good man, but his father is still missed.'

"Ali looked sad. 'Are you certain that is has been fifteen years? Al-Rashid looked like such a strong and healthy man when I last saw him.'

"The guard thought for a moment and then said, 'Yes, I am certain that it has been fifteen years. I remember because that it was five years, almost to the day, after Ali Ben-Joseph farted at his daughters wedding.'

"Ali wanders the caravan trails to this day and I often see him."

When the chuckling stopped, Sir Garrett offered a toast, "To Ali Ben-Joseph. May we all meet him and never be him. To home."

When they had drunk, Ahmed leaned across the table and looked earnest. "I have noticed that all of your men carry firesticks. They may be more a problem than a help. Everyone on the caravan trail knows about them. The locals here have never seen one, but many like myself have seen firesticks that were stolen from Europe. On my last caravan, the caravan master had two in his money wagon. They are highly prized but shoot very slow. They are not good against these people if the battle goes on too long or gets too close.

"I, myself, have seen such things in battle. It is no travelers tale. I fought with the Seljuk Sultanate as a young man. I think that we would have lost the battle if it had not been for the Christians devastating half the Mongol army. You did us a great favor there."

Banner Hendricks asked "Did the Mongols actually have, uh, firesticks? I thought we had invented them."

Ahmed gestured, "Not like yours. They had things like a bamboo tube. They would set one end on fire and it would fly through the sky and then explode with loud noise. They also had iron balls the size of your head that they would set afire and throw from horseback. They would burn for awhile and then explode. The noise was scary at first, but you got used to it pretty fast. In fact, it was easier to get used to the noise than to the smell. They claim that the horse was their greatest weapon. Anyone who believes that hasn't smelled their breath."

He shuddered from the memory. "My people fight for Allah. I think that the Mongols are out looking for women. Their own probably prefer to sleep with the horses rather than the men. They are the filthiest people that I have ever met. They are even worse than the Twaregs.

"Anyway, the people that you will be traveling through allow the caravans because they are profitable. Take care, they are also envious."

The night wore down from there. Soon, the Christians left the Inn for the last time and joined the column in the early morning light.

Chapter 17   Naked Rebellion

The next Saturday morning, before the sun had even started to raise, I was laying on my back at the bottom of the barrel and Omar started howling at the top of his lungs.

Twenty minutes went by before the guards arrived.

"Shut up, you old thief!"

"But my cell mate, he is dead!"

"We heard you! When we open the door, throw him out!"

"Are you mad?! I am a very small man with only one hand. He is a giant! I could not possibly drag him, let alone get him out of the doorway. You must come in here and get him. Surely, two strong Warriors like you are not afraid of a tiny, starved, and naked old cripple like myself!"

We heard the door being unlocked.

"Step aside, you worthless old fart!"

I was still motionless on the curved floor of the barrel, with my feet toward the open door. One of the guards stepped over me and stooped to pick up my shoulders.

One of the karate blows that is sometimes taught, but never practiced, is a strike to the windpipe with one hand, using the tips of the fingers and the tip of the thumb. You hit on both sides of the trachea simultaneously, and this puts your hand deep enough in for you to grab the windpipe. Then you squeeze as hard as you can, and pull. This crushes his voice box and closes off his air supply.

Death is silent, bloodless, and fairly quick, by suffocation.

None the less, it takes a minute or two to suffocate, and this fellow had managed to pull out a knife with his right hand and was trying to use it on me, while I was fending him off with my left, waiting for him to hurry up and die!

He was on top of me, but I could see over his shoulder. The second guard had spent a fatal half second gaping at the two of us struggling on the floor. Omar used this time to steal the man's long, thin knife and drive it upward, under his jaw, through the tongue and mouth, and into his brain. Death was instantaneous and almost bloodless. He twisted the knife to free it and jerked it out before the guard had time to fall. Then he kicked the body sideways so it didn't fall on the two of us struggling on the floor, and came to my aid.

This time, he drove the knife into the back of my man's neck, between two vertebrae, and severing the spinal cord. The blow also put a small wound into the web of my right thumb, but it didn't seem polite to mention it.

All motion stopped.

"Thank you, Omar! That was some very fancy knife work!" I said as I got out from under the body and stood up.

"The result of a sadly misspent youth, I am afraid. Still, it went more smoothly than I had expected."

"Yes, well, let's get on with it."

We stripped our victims and got into the clothing that we had been so careful not to get bloodied. Fortunately, Arabian clothing is very big and bulky. Fit isn't very important. Omar was able to adjust his a bit so it didn't drag the ground much. Mine was ridiculously short on me, and there was no hope of getting the boots on, but maybe, from a distance, I could pass at a casual glance.

The head gear helped.

We collected up two decent swords and six knives. Two thick curved ones, two thin straight ones, and two that Omar said were for throwing. And we had a big set of keys!

Our next move was to take one of the guards out, naked, and lock the door behind us. We took the guard to the river, and threw him in. This was so that anyone who might be watching would think that we were the usual guards going about our normal business.

Then we went to each of the other pumps, unlocked the doors, and told the men in there that it was their choice. They could stay where they were, and live out their lives in slavery. Or, they could take their chances on their own, which would help us out since the army would also be chasing them down instead of concentrating on us alone. Or, they could join us, fight at our side, and take their chances of being killed. And maybe winning their freedom.

We said that we had a well worked out plan, and that God was certainly on our side.

They all volunteered to join us. Besides Omar, I now had three Black Africans, two Arab criminals, and a Christian seaman working for me. The Christian was a Frenchman, a Ferengi, as the Arabs called them, and he spoke no more Polish than I spoke French. But all of my new men had at least a smattering of Aramaic, so we could communicate.

We distributed the knives among the former slaves, letting them choose what they were used to.

We formed them up in a column of twos with my men trying to conceal their knives. This was not easy, since they were all naked. Omar walked on one side and I was on the other, pretending to be guards. We walked openly in the gray light to our next stop, a barracks where agricultural slaves were kept. So far, so good!

At the last possible moment, Omar traded with the Frenchman, his sword for a thin knife. He stepped into the building.

Two thuds were heard, then Omar's grinning face appeared.

"Quietly, now. There are more guards here, but I think that they are asleep," he whispered.

They were asleep, and none of them ever woke up. Omar insisted on doing it all himself, and I had no objection. At this sort of thing, he was obviously a master.

He put our troops to stripping the ten guards that he had just killed while I went to talk to the slaves in their single big room.

There looked to be about a hundred men here, and no women or children at all. Apparently, the Arabs had other uses for their female slaves, and for the children as well.

"Listen up, people! I am Conrad Stargard, Hetman of the Christian Army! I was a slave here, but now, I have re-gained my freedom! That freedom is now yours as well!

"You may stay here, if you wish, and be enslaved again.

"You may run for it, and try to make it on your own, although I do not think that your chances of success are very good.

"Or you may fight at my side! Help me to defeat the bastards who enslaved us all, and we will take this city for ourselves! We slaves built this city! We have fed it for hundreds of years with our labor! Now, we will take ownership of it! We will be the Masters of Timbuktu!

"There is no time, so you must make your choice now! Who here will follow me and obey my orders? God is on our side!"

Again, options one and two weren't taken. Slavery makes people into realists. They all knew the score.

I had all of the dead guards' uniforms filled with former slaves who looked the part, even stripping down naked myself and giving my clothes to another guy with black hair and the right look. There were enough enslaved people who at least looked like Arabs to do that, even though most of the field workers were Blacks. We found enough weapons about to give every former slave at least a knife, and all of the "guards" at least a sword, a shield, and a spear.

The land to the south and west of the city was owned by independent farmers, but that to the north was owned by the city, and worked by slaves to feed the nobles, the city workers, and the army. There were six more barracks for agricultural slaves, and we visited them all. Most of them were captured as easily as the first.

This surprised me. I'd expected that our strange actions would have been observed and that a force would have been sent out to investigate us by now. I had expected to have to fight a battle in the fields! But the Gods of Human Stupidity seemed to be smiling on us, and there was nothing for a mere human like myself to do but to give thanks to these Powers That Be, and to smile back!

There was a fight at the last barracks, where one of the guards showed a bit of intelligence. The battle didn't last long. These places were prisons, designed to keep people in, not fortresses meant to hold against an external enemy. Seven hundred mostly naked but angry men, most of us with our knives in our teeth, swarmed over the walls and made quick work of the dozen guards defending the place.

Before noon, I had more than eight hundred men, scantily armed and even more scantily dressed, most of them, walking toward the west gate of Timbuktu. The guards at the north gate might have seen and gotten curious about what had been going on. It was worth the extra time to enter somewhere else. As we walked, I explained the plan to my newly recruited troops, using my old command voice so they all could hear.

As we neared the city gate, a voice cried out.

"Halt! Who goes there?"

"Sergeant Omar with a consignment of slaves! Open up the gates!"

"Why are you here with so many slaves?"

"I have no idea! Someone came from the palace, and talked with my officer. Then Captain Abdul told me to collect up the biggest labor force that I could, and take them to the palace. I have followed my orders."

"Well, I have received no orders about this!"

"Fine. Leave the gates closed, then. Look, I did not get a chance to sleep at all last night! If you make it impossible for me to obey my officer, I will be able to go back and get some rest. I'm sure that a smart man like you can come up with some good excuses to give to the Vizier, when he asks about his labor force."

Omar turned to leave.

"Oh, the Devil! Come back here, you! Guards, open the gates!"

So we walked through the city gate, in the listless fashion of slaves, with our knives pressed tightly to our forearms, concealing them as best as we could.

There were a dozen or so guards at street level around the gate, and most of us were through the gate when one of the guards noticed something suspicious, probably a knife. This guard got a knife in the gut for his diligence, driven home by a powerful Black freedman with a huge grin on his face. He had once worked in a pump like the one I'd been in.

And naturally, the fight broke out in earnest.

The guards outside were all dead in moments. It was eight hundred of us against fifteen of them, after all.

I yelled, "Take the gate towers!" and went through a door into the northern tower that the idiots had left open and unguarded! A glance told me that Omar was leading another party up the southern gate tower. Both doors had been left open! Absolute idiots!

According to the plan, a dozen of our own fully clothed "guards" were already fanning out, to see what could be done about arousing the other slaves in the city, and rallying them to our cause. These were men who knew the city well, who spoke the language well, and who said that they knew where large concentrations of male slaves were to be found. Many of them had combat experience, and could likely take out any slave guards at need.

A straight stairway angled to one side and ended at the second floor, where there was a well, two doors, and a winding staircase.

The ground floor of the gate towers must have been built mostly solid, as a defense against battering rams, for there were no rooms coming off of the staircase near the bottom. The floor above was a guard room, and I quickly had a fight on my hands. The first two Arabs that I literally ran into were too startled to do much before I cut their throats, but the third man had time to get his sword out before I got to him, while I had nothing but a knife.

I managed to parry two of his blows, but my future wasn't looking all that secure!

Fortunately, my men were pouring in behind me, and in a fight, numbers count! We lost three ex-slaves before we killed all nine of the guards in the room, not bad considering that my men weren't trained at all. Years of pent up fury count for a lot, too.

I picked up a decent Watered Steel sword from the floor, and felt much more comfortable.

"Up! Go up!" I yelled, running up the central staircase, "And kill them all!"

The staircase twisted to the left as you went up, and had a hollow core. The stairs themselves were narrow, and two men could pass only by twisting sideways.

The next floor up contained only two soldiers that I killed quickly with my sword. I got a thrust straight into the heart on the first one, and a draw cut to the throat on the second! My new sword had the balance and the feel of my old sword, the one that had been stolen from me by the Twaregs.

The room contained the mechanism that raised the portcullis. A glance out of an arrow slit showed that while we had been going up, the portcullis had been coming down! Perhaps a quarter of our men were locked outside of the city!

I got together enough men to crank it up only after a bit of difficulty. Nobody wanted to work! My new troops weren't much on discipline, but they were eager to mix it with our enemies! They wanted to kill!

I eventually got a few men to help me with the work, but in a few moments the whole mechanism jammed. But by then we had the huge, pierced iron grating high enough for our men to crawl under it, and that would have to do. We set the latches to keep it open, then went up to join the fight.

Each floor of the tower seemed to be dedicated to some special purpose. There was an armory, a kitchen, a few barracks rooms. Some of these rooms had occupants that had to be killed. Some didn't.

The fight up the winding staircase was fierce. It had a hollow center, and twisted to the left, which gave the advantage to the man on top, assuming that both combatants were right handed. Omar might be having an easy time, being perforce a lefty, but I wasn't!

Many of our men, and many of theirs, fell bleeding down the shaft of that staircase, plugging the well at the bottom!

Inexperienced, poorly armed, and untrained, but highly motivated, my small army fought upward.

Chance had it that I was the first man to get to the top floor. While all of the other rooms we'd fought in and climbed past has been Spartan and utilitarian military places, this one was stunningly luxurious! It was obviously the commander's quarters.

One of the luxuries that I immediately noticed was a beautiful naked girl, barely pubescent, laying on the bed. I almost noticed her for too long, because the commander was also in the room, and he was attacking me!

He was a big man, well muscled, and fast. He was almost as tall as I was, and a bit wider. He'd been getting into his armor, with the chest and back pieces already on, but the arm and leg armor was still laying on the floor. I, of course, was completely naked.

He swung his sword at me, and I managed to deflect it, but I got a big surprise. I knew that sword! That was the high-tech sword that my Uncle Tom had made and had gotten to me when I first got to this century! It had a diamond edge, and could cut through anything! The Twaregs who had stolen it from me must have sold it here in Timbuktu. Oh, now the hilt and scabbard had been replaced with something beautiful made out of gold and encrusted with jewels, but that was my sword!

And now I had to fight a powerful, skillful man who was wielding it against me!

I tried a cut to his sword arm, but had it parried. His repost came down at my head, and when I blocked it, my old sword cut my new one in half! It didn't break it, you understand. It cut it, slicing through the watered steel in my hand!

I was only slightly injured when the end of my own blade bounced off my back.

The big man raised the sword again, and I knew that I was a dead man! There was just no hope left at all!

Then a spear came over my left shoulder and skewered the commander in the forehead! He dropped, obviously dead, and I quickly sat down to keep from fainting.

My God, but that was a close one!

The man who had thrown the spear was the same powerful, grinning Black man who had taken first blood in this battle. He now sported a loin cloth, a shield, and a second spear.

"You saved my life," I said. "Thank you!"

"As you saved mine by freeing me! Slavery to me was worse than death," he said while stepping on the commander's face and pulling out his spear. "But there is still much to do. My name is Juma. Among my own people, I was a prince, and a war leader. I know this city well. There is a major military barracks half way between here and the palace. We must hit them quickly, before they can get organized!"

"That would make sense. Would you want to lead the attack? I don't know my way around the city at all, and I might get lost!"

"I would be honored to do so!"

"Good! Take what men you think you might need, and wipe out that barracks!"

"To hear is to obey!"

He trotted out, shouting something in what must have been his native language. Shortly, I saw him through a window, leading perhaps five hundred Blacks down the street toward the center of the city. They wore loin cloths, and carried Arab shields and spears, besides their knives. They were silent, running fast, and maintaining good order. It seemed that some of my men were well trained, although in a different way than I was used to.

"Thus ends the life of the Great Lord Hajji," a voice behind me said.

I turned to the girl who was now sitting up on the bed.

"So, he had a name. I rarely learn the names of the people that die around me. What is yours?"

"Jasmine."

"I take it that you were a slave here?"

"It is so, my master."

"Wrong. I am not your master, and you are no longer a slave. You are now a free woman. You may go if you wish, and try to find a place of safety, or you may stay here. I couldn't honestly tell you which choice would be more dangerous."

"You must have many wounded, and I know something of bandages and salves. I would stay here, and be of what help I could."

"Excellent! You are now our medical section! Go find an empty room, and see what you can do about setting up an aid station. Get some of the men to help you. Tell them it's at Conrad's orders."

"Thank you, Conrad. I will. I notice that you are wounded."

"Not badly. It can wait, but some of my men are dying. Help them first! And get some clothes on. You are not a naked slave girl any more."

"There are clothes here," she said, dressing. "You are a Christian, aren't you?"

"Yes."

"I was a Christian, I think, although I know nothing of the religion. My father was taking me on a pilgrimage to Rome when our ship was attacked by pirates. I was only three at the time, but that's what someone told me later."

"If we live through this, you will have plenty of time to learn much more of your father's religion. But now, to work!"

There was a balcony, or fighting platform, circling the commander's apartment. I walked around it to see what was going on. I spotted Omar at the top of the southern gate tower. We waved and exchanged grins. Apparently, that tower had been secured as well.

The city wall was two stories lower than the platform that I was standing on. Below, I saw that a few of our men had had the brains to realize that the towers needed guarding at that point, and were doing it. I made a point of telling myself to find out who's idea it was, to put him in charge of expanding his force, and to tell him to keep up the good work.

At the same level, the top of the wall continued on the other side of this tower over the gate in a sort of bridge, giving communication between the gate towers. It was a sensible design, but one that would work against the city, since we now held them both.

I heard shouting and the clash of weapons, faintly in the distance. Juma was attacking. From another quarter of the city, a Moslem priest was calling the faithful to prayer, apparently oblivious to the fact that the city was under attack. Communications in a medieval city were haphazard at best.

The city about seemed calm and peaceful, but I knew that it was only the lull before the storm. Soon, all hell was about to break loose!

Chapter 18 (Sir Piotr's Story) Sir Piotr's Office

Messages were coming in constantly.

The captain of the Frigate Pirate related how he had freed some three dozen Christians from a Moslem slaver. These men had all been fishermen captured at sea. On hearing that the ship that they were imprisoned on was to be destroyed, they had begged the captain to give it to them, in lieu of the money and free transportation he had offered them. They said that their own ships had been destroyed, but that with this large ship, they could earn a decent living.

The captain had given it to them, along with enough supplies to get them started, before dumping the slavers on the coast of Africa. He felt that on this occasion, he had been right to disobey orders, but wanted my blessings on his actions.

I gave him those blessings.

The Captain of the Frigate Marauder captured a ship full of slaves that had been particularly badly treated. Although there were ample supplies of food and water on board the ship, the slaves had not been fed or given a drink for three days, even though the heat was oppressive. Many of the slaves had been wounded, and even though there was a trained medic on board, the slaves had been given no treatment at all.

The Captain's orders were that he was to drop the slavers off on the African coast, near a harbor, and he had complied with these orders. However, he had shot the slavers, first. Were his actions acceptable?

I said yes.

I sent out an all points letter, quoting these communications, and changing my orders slightly. I said that while some actions were not permitted, such as killing women, children, and the very aged, a ship's captain was expected to use his own good judgment when faced with unusual circumstances.

I received a communication from Sir Wladyclaw. He had found where Conrad came ashore on a particularly desolate shore of western Africa.

A shipping container containing nothing but fiberglass insulation was found on the shore. There were three dead bodies nearby. Two of them were of the 'Blue Men', the Twaregs, noted for their savagery. One was definitely identified as being that of Cynthia, one of Maud's children, and Conrad's bodyguard. Both the Big People present and Cynthia's own sister were adamant that it was her.

They were also positive that the dried human hand that was found nearby was Conrad's.

Our feelings at Okoitz are very mixed. We are saddened by Cynthia's loss, and Conrad's mutilation. But at the same time, we are overjoyed at the possibility that he might still be alive!

Chapter 19 (Sir Walznik's Rescue) The Search for Conrad

"Caravan trail" was a loose term. In the Ancient Roman Empire, it meant a paved road, usually wide enough for two wagons to pass. There were Inns along the road and at every mile stood a stone column where some patron paid to show the miles from Rome. Sometimes there was smaller stone sign showing the miles to the next town. If you were on the silk road, it meant a well worn path through the desert, with Imperial mile houses every few miles and forts on each horizon. In this part of Senegal, it meant the widest animal path through the jungle.

Our local guide said that things would get better as we left the jungle for the plains near the great sand desert.

We made an impressive column. Each man wore his bright red and white uniform. He also wore a beige turban wrapped around his steel helmet and a long beige cape over his shoulders. Our leather sword belts were now hidden under bright yellow silk waistbands. We succeeded in looking like the guard of a rich merchant. With every man mounted, we made good time while we were moving. Even a mule can make fourteen miles per army hour on a good road. Unfortunately, mules and horses are not mechanical and do not have headlights. We made three dozen miles the first day and considered it an accomplishment. Darkness drew the limits on our traveling day.

It took less than a month to get to the valley where Ahmed had tea with Lord Conrad's captors. We were out of the Jungle by that point and traveling through the sparsely wooded plains south of the Great Desert. From there on things would be slower. We had been avoiding every village and town by simply riding around them. Now they would have to stop at every Podunk town and look for Lord Conrad.

We established a search procedure. Every morning four troopers were designated to be village searchers. They would ride ahead looking for the villages too small to interest the entire column. They simply rode up and offered money for the slave that they were interested in. Then they spent considerable time trying to get away politely when the villagers offered every old and injured slave they had. On a few occasions when the villagers obviously had thoughts about holding onto the foolish men who rode in, the main columns appearance immediately encouraged a certain amount of courtesy.

The route was used by two types of caravans. A few Europeans were using the route to bypass the Arab lands and purchase goods from India. They usually left this main trail before it got to Egypt and moved south. Most of the caravans were Muslims searching Africa for animal furs, feathers, gold, and slaves and selling manufactured objects, glass, spices and Chinese silk. The Muslims fanned out over a large area but ended up back at the Mediterranean. There were market towns about every hundred to two hundred miles to service the caravans and exchange goods. This is where we thought we would probably find Lord Conrad.

The real problems happened in the towns.

When we got to the first town, we established a pattern that they would follow later. The column would camp in sight of the town. One of the officers and at least two of the knights would enter the town looking for Lord Conrad. We again decided that simple honesty about their goal would serve best.

At the gate they haggled about the taxes and then paid in local coin that we had acquired in Armoon. They asked the guards at the gate for directions to the slave market.

"As you can see, we are on our way to Egypt with some fine merchandise. Unfortunately, one of our friends was captured near the sea by slavers. He was a very big man. Bigger than this."

Captain Walznik raised his hand over his head. "He may have been injured on his arm when he was captured. If he has been sold here, we would like to find him. We would pay well to get him back."

The guard looked at their uniforms and tack and decided this was too good a chance to let slip. He turned to his assistant and said in a very low voice, "Run and get the slave trader. Tell him I have some very rich customers for him and remind him of my cut."

Turning to the Christians he smiled and said, "If you will wait here for a little while, we will get the man that you need to see."

The slave trader proved that fat men should not try to run in any culture. He was out of breath and sweating heavily when he approached the gate. "Gentlemen, I understand that you are looking for the finest of slaves. I am Farselee, the biggest trader in this area. Please come see my pens."

Farselee would have been a salesman in any era. You have seen this man sell used cars, water softeners, and encyclopedias. Clones of him sold silver plated idols to pilgrims in Ancient Greece and took your money that last time you bought something you didn't want.

The soldiers found themselves walking along with Farselee unable to get a word into the conversation. They ended up standing before the slave pens before they could explain that the man they were looking for would have been sold months before. Farselee insisted on displaying every male slave he had. The banner was explaining for the fourth time that the slave they wanted was over two yards tall, not one yard. This was a small town, and there were less than three dozen slaves in the pens. Only a half dozen of them were white.

They soon gave up and walked, then ran away. Lord Conrad was not in the pens.

Captain Walznik turned to the knight. "This was a mistake. We should never have looked in the pens. No slave would be there after all of these months. Go back and get your whole lance. Give each man a handful of copper coins and tell him to circulate in the marketplace, buy a little, and ask a lot of questions."

After one knight had left, the other shook his head and said to Walznik, "Sir, did you see what was in those pens? Some of those white people might be Christians. We can't leave them here!"

"Well, Sir Jan, unless you are commanding a few thousand troops that I haven't seen, we don't have much choice. We could free these slaves, but there are probably millions of slave holders between here and Lord Conrad and we didn't bring that many bullets."

"Yes, sir. But I heard you talking with Banner Hendricks about how you wanted to look like a real caravan. Right now we look more like an army than a caravan. Well, what are we missing? There's no women, no cooks, no camp followers. Now that we aint moving so fast, we could use a little help. How about we buy some of the Christians?"

The Captain looked over at the slave pens and then back at the knight. "Your suggested is noted, Sir Jan. I will discuss with the staff before we leave this place."

The next day, the two officers arrived back at the slave pens shortly after sunup. Farselee was happy to show his wares. It was like shopping for ponies or kittens. It was hard not to want them all. They began by calling out in Polish. One woman answered. She was an old woman in her 40s. Most of her teeth were gone and her hair was matted, but she seemed healthy enough. They tried German, Frankish and whatever other European languages that they knew. When they hit Latin, a man answered them.

"Thank God, Christians. Please help me, my Sons. I have been held captive by these heathens for years." He was a naked man in his 30's but his posture and expression put a priest's collar around his neck.

Captain Walznik whispered loudly to Hendricks, "Oh, my God. He's a priest. We don't want him along!"

Hendricks looked surprised. "Surely you can't leave a man of God among these heathens. It's unthinkable."

Captain Walznik groaned. "It's thinkable! A priest is the only animal louder than a jackass, more demanding than a wife, and more trouble than pestilence. He'll want to waste time on services. He'll want to stop to pray. He'll nag the men and offend every Muslim, Jew or Pagan that we meet. It's thinkable! However, you're right, we can't leave him here. I guess we can loose him along the road somewhere if he gets to be much trouble."

Hendricks was shocked into silence while Walznik bargained for the slaves. It was a long process, but he finally got them cheap.

On the way back to camp, he stopped to purchase the woman a simple cotton dress and some sandals from a stall. He thought a second time, and purchased her a cloak similar to the ones worn by the men. He felt bad about it, but he was being bothered by the sight of her old woman's breasts flopping on her chest. When she donned the dress, he was able to look at her directly.

As they walked out the gate, he asked the woman, "How's your cooking? Good. You can start out helping the mess sergeant. You'll have to ride one of the pack mules until we get you horse. You know that we don't believe in slavery any more, so you are free to leave any time you want. But if you do, nothing will stop the first African or Moslem you meet from putting you back in a slave pen, so I don't recommend that you fall behind."

He never once spoke directly to the priest. When he returned to camp, he told one of the knights, "Be sure to tell the priest that he will have to pull his weight during the trip. The more time he spends carrying water, the less energy he will have to make trouble."

Within a month, we had a full complement of camp followers. We had two dozen women and over a dozen men to do the grunt work at the camp. We had also added two wagons for the women to work in during the day. While they traveled, the women mixed bread dough and cut the meat and vegetables for the evening meal. As the advance party usually had the fires burning before the main column arrived, hot food was available by the time the animals had been unburdened and staked out.

The women also washed the clothes, did the mending, and handled the other chores that women handled at home. The men who had been slaves chopped the wood, built the fire pits, dug the latrines and did anything else that needed doing. The caravan was beginning to look like a family outing.

They also had their first trouble with the priest. When he caught a trooper and one of the women having sex in the woods, he ran around camp loudly proclaiming the evils of rape and announcing the coming wrath of God. He stormed into Captain Walznik's tent loudly demanding that the guilty man be punished. This surprised the Captain because all men of his era knew that it was the women who were the more carnal of the sexes. That is why so many of them were seduced into devil worship and witchcraft. He calmed the priest by pointing out that even Saint Thomas had written that sexual relief and prostitution were required. In fact, the saint himself had said that it was like the sewer in your castle. It might not be the most pleasant part of the building, but it was necessary. Privately, he felt that the priest was overreacting because he wasn't getting any. He also had daydreams of dropping the arrogant son of a bitch into the nearest ditch.

About that time they came to the town that began their trial.

It was almost a city rather than a town. Like Artoom, it had thick mud brick walls and a heavy gate. Unlike Artoom, the gate was closed. Sir Garrett approached the gate, "Hello in there, we are thirsty visitors and would appreciate a drink of water and maybe a little business."

From atop the gate a voice boomed out. "We are sorry to hear about your thirst, but are happy to inform you that there is a good stream less than half a days march in the direction you are going. Please think of us as you enjoy the water."

The knight called back, "We are also looking for a friend of ours. He was taken by slave traders and may be here. He is a very tall man with blond hair and blue eyes. He may have an injured arm. We are willing to pay well if you have him."

"We have no slaves here and we have no need of your gold. Thank you for visiting our humble city. Now, go away."

The officers and knights met in the command tent to consider the problem. Sir Dulka said, "I don't believe them about having no slaves. It would be the first city we've seen yet without them."

Banner Hendricks agreed. "I don't trust them. I don't want to get all the way to the Sea of India and wonder if I have missed Lord Conrad here."

Captain Walznik looked over their shoulders at the wall visible past the tent flap. "I agree, but we can't attack every town that we don't trust. Maybe there is another way. Sir Dulka, I'll need the laborers to build a large fire pit in front of the city gates. We want it clearly visible from the tower, but not in easy spear chucking range. Make it big enough to hold a side of beef. Sir Jan, take out two lances and scout around the city. See if you can find out why they are so unfriendly. Banner, who do you think our best two sharpshooters are?"

Banner Hendricks smiled, "It sounds like you have a plan."

"Yep. I think I know how we can impress them without fighting them. We'll need to move a few tents up around the fire pit to make it look homey."

It was early in the day. The stage was set shortly after noon. A fire was burning in a large stone rimmed pit built on the approach to the gate. A cow was staked out in front of the fire. The captain was going over the last minute instructions with the sharpshooters. "Pick the biggest bird you see on that wall. You just have to hit something. There are no rewards for doing it the hard way. Your cue is when I point up at the wall. No, wait. You can't take your eyes off of the target to watch me. Just fire when you hear me make the offer."

With that he picked up his rifle and walked out to stand in front of the fire pit. "Hello on the wall! We want to invite you to a meal today. We are fixing fresh meat and cakes. Does not Allah command that we offer hospitality to strangers?"

In a few minutes a voice came back from the wall. "We are not Muslims, and the Great God Whatamee does not like strangers. We are appreciative of your offer but must refuse your hospitality."

Hendricks looked up at the gate, "I am sorry to hear that. The meat will be fresh." With that, he raised his arm casually toward the cow and fired a revolver into it's head. It was probably the first powder explosion heard within a thousand miles. The cow dropped instantly. The voice on the wall was silent for a full minute. When it returned it was tremulous, "That was very impressive, but we are not eating meat during this season."

The Captain looked up at the wall. "Perhaps you would prefer fowl tonight." Another shot rang out. A large black bird on the wall fell near the feet of the voice. The voice was scared but defiant, "Shit! Uh, Uh, I do feel like a little bird tonight, but I am very hungry. Could you get me another?"

"Happy to oblige". A second shot rang out and another bird fell. The Captain hoped that they wouldn't need more convincing. Three lucky shots in a row were too much to hope for.

A head appeared over the ramparts. "Perhaps it would be inhospitable to refuse your offer. If it pleases you, I will attend at your camp shortly after sundown."

The scouting party returned shortly before nightfall. Sir Jan reported their findings to the officers. "Most of the area around here is empty. We found some abandoned farm houses. It looks like the occupants moved into town when they saw us coming. We didn't find a single person to talk too but we did find something interesting. About a mile down that road there is a graveyard. It's big. It's too big for a city that size and most of the graves are recent. Something real bad happened here, Sir."

Sir Dulka looked thoughtful. "You know, I noticed something else today. There were a lot of birds on top of that wall. We shot two, but there were a lot of others. Why weren't they spooked by the men on the parapets? Maybe there aren't any men holding those spears that are peeking over the walls."

"Ok," Captain Walznik interjected. "What are the options?"

Banner Hendricks responded, "I can only think of three. Starvation, war, and disease. There are crops in the fields, so I doubt if they are starving. The walls don't look scared or recently repaired, so war is unlikely. That leaves disease. Someone must have brought a disease here. They are either afraid of more disease, or they don't want anyone to know how weak they are. That's why the gate is shut."

Captain Walznik thought long enough to make his men uncomfortable. "Well, maybe we can try some other options."

He donned his helmet and cloak and walked out to the city wall. "Hello in there! We want to talk."

There was a delay of several minutes. "Hello down there. What do you want now? Do I have to bring my wife and most beautiful daughter with me to dinner?"

"No Sir. We do not want to cause you any more trouble. We only want our friend. If you can question your people to see if anyone saw him, we will leave you in peace."

"Please describe your friend again. I will see if anyone has news."

The delay was more than an hour. It was after dark when a door opened in the city gate and two men stepped out. The older was richly dressed in a dark red cloak, the younger was about three dozen years old and dressed in a simpler blue robe. They did not approach the Christians but spoke loudly from the gate instead.

The older man was the voice on the wall. He said, "We may have news." He turned to the younger man, "Emman, tell them what you know".

The younger man looked nervous, "Is it possible that your friend had his right arm injured instead of his left?"

Walznik answered, "It could be. Our information is from a fellow traveler."

The younger man continued. "Then he may have passed through here. A few months ago a caravan of Twaregs passed by. They are a filthy people and their merchandise is always bad. They tried to sell us some slaves. They were all in bad shape and most of them were sick. One of them was a huge male with blonde hair. His right arm was bandaged and he had the fever bad. They tried to hide his injury and sell him to us as a plow slave. We did not purchase him and they went away. The slave was alive when we last saw them."

They turned to leave. As they reached the door, the older man looked back and said, "I hope you find your friend. You are a long way from home."

Chapter 20 The Two Towers

I went back in and looked again at the big dead man on the floor. The thought occurred to me that his armor just might fit me. Armor would be a very nice thing to have in the coming fight. That, and I was sick to death of having to run around naked!

A bit of scrounging around got me a complete set of clean underwear and padded undergarments. After eight months of nudity, clothes felt amazingly good. Even the boots were a good fit. The armor itself was a bit wide and a bit short, but not by too much. A bath, a shave, and a haircut would have been wonderful, but there just wasn't time. The enemy had to be coming!

I was soon standing in front of a large and doubtlessly hideously expensive mirror, admiring myself in my fancy new outfit, complete with its ostrich plumed helmet. It was in the Turkish style, with large plates held together with chain mail. Not as good as the plate mail armor worn by the Christian Army, but vastly superior to my naked skin!

I was surprised to notice that my smashed face, missing teeth, and broken nose were completely healed and normal looking. Another gift from my Uncle Tom.

A red silk cape completed the ensemble nicely.

And having my old sword back was the fulfillment of a dream! It looked better than before, since the sheath had been replaced with a bejeweled gold thing that matched the new hand guard.

Oh, I was filthy, my beard touched my chest, and my hair came to below my shoulders, but this was still a major improvement over my condition of only that morning.

I picked up the former commander's naked body and threw it over the balcony railing, out onto the main city street. How dare he to wear MY sword, anyway?

I glanced about the fine and richly appointed quarters around me. In truth, they weren't quite up to the standards of my private rooms at Okoitz, but compared to the filthy barrel that I had been living in for much of the last year, they were the crown of luxury and beauty. This place would suit me well, if only I could keep it!

Well armed and armored, I went down to see how things were going.

They were going surprisingly well! None of my men were naked any more. Their clothing was an assortment of odds and ends, but the previous occupants had left enough spare clothes to at least cover everyone. Many of the window curtains were missing, having been re-cycled into loin cloths by the Black Africans.

Someone had gotten the kitchen running, and was serving out food. I grabbed some bread and some meat, and ate as I continued my inspection. I didn't know what kind of meat I was eating, but after living for eight months as a vegetarian, it was magnificent!

Everyone had taken his choice of weapons from the dead soldiers or from the extensive armory that we had captured. I noticed that we needed more archers, and passed the word about it. There were plenty of bows and arrows unclaimed in the armory, but everyone seemed to want to close with the Arabs, and KILL!

The girl, Jasmine, had an aid station up and running. Our wounded were being well tended. There weren't any enemy wounded. Slave revolts are like that. There is too much hatred for anyone to feel merciful.

There was even a bit of housekeeping going on, with dead bodies being pulled out of the well at the bottom of the staircase, and dead enemy soldiers being thrown out from the upper windows and into the streets or fields.

For a completely undisciplined and untrained mob, this progress was amazing!

Slaves from the city itself were starting to filter in, and more than fifty of them were here already. Most of them already had clothing, and as soon as they arrived, someone was leading them up to the armory so that they could equip themselves with whatever weapons that they thought they could handle.

One of the newcomers, a big blond man, looked up at me and shouted in Polish, "My God! Lord Conrad! Can it really be you?"

"I'm Conrad," I answered in the same language. "You have the bearing of a warrior!"

"I am one, my lord! I am Sir Stephan Stepanski, and I am a member of the Order of Radiant Warriors. I commanded a lance of Explorers mapping the West African Coast, when these Rag Heads killed two of my men without any provocation. Then after a fight, the forty of them who were left captured and enslaved the four of us who still lived."

"Were these men wearing blue robes?"

"Yes, sir. How did you know?"

"I've run into them myself. What of your Big People?"

"We had none, sir. All of this happened five years ago. There were rumors that Big People would be assigned soon to Explorer Teams, but it hadn't happened yet."

"I see. I have had similar experiences, but there is little time now for talking. I want you to form up a unit of archers, and to station a man at every window and arrow slit in this tower, with extra men on each floor to back them up. And get as many archers as you can on the fighting platform at the top. When you get that done, go over to the southern tower, and do it all over again. The people who run this city will be hitting us soon and hard, and we have to be ready!"

"Consider it done, my lord!"

I went back up to the level of the city wall, told the leader of the guard there to triple the size of his force, to include plenty of archers, and to command it in my name. Then I crossed over to the southern tower that Omar had taken and looked him up.

"Was it you who sent that Black African force out, Conrad? Suddenly, they all started shouting in a language that I didn't understand, and then they all ran away!"

"Yes. A tribal chief named Juma said that there was a barracks nearby, and he wanted to hit it before they got organized. I told him to go and do it."

"It is good, then. I had been fearing that this was a mass desertion! Do you think that we should go and support this Juma?"

"Well, I don't know exactly where he is, aside from what he said about the barracks being halfway between here and the palace. Then again, new recruits are coming in fast now, and I doubt if we could find a stronger defensive site than these two gate towers. I think that we should stay here and build our forces. The city's soldiers will have to attack us, and I think that our untrained men will be better at defense, than on the attack. At least, they won't be able to run away."

"I know the barracks that you speak of, but we shall do as you say, Conrad.

Also, I wish to know, was it you who jammed the mechanism of the portcullis?"

"Yes. Many of our men were trapped outside of the gates, and I had to let them in."

"I see. It happens that there is another mechanism in the south tower that also draws up the portcullis. These two must be used together to pull it up. I suggest that we get two groups to coordinate their efforts, raise the portcullis, and then close and bar the main gates. Our enemies might try to attack us from that direction."

"Good idea. I'll get some people on it," I said.

"Then, there is the problem of supplies. We do not know how long that we will have to stand siege here. Each tower has a good well that we are getting cleaned out, but our food supplies are limited, and we have many men to feed. We should send out foraging parties."

"You might be better at that task than I would. You know the city and I don't."

"I will organize it. You worry about our defenses," Omar said.

"Good! Let's get to it."

The little thief was good at his trade. Things stayed oddly quiet for another hour, and by that time we had a week's supply of food for over two thousand men, including bread, eggs, chickens, sheep, and six recently slaughtered camels. They had also brought in all of the charcoal that they could find for cooking it all.

When the fight started, the locals had dropped everything and had run away, usually leaving their doors open behind them. Our newly freed slaves had looted with abandon, and I'm sure that much more than food was taken. But our men had moved efficiently, and I didn't care what happened to a few trinkets.

I was just glad that Moslem homes rarely kept alcohol around, so some semblance of discipline was maintained.

And five hundred more recruits arrived.

The enemy seemed to be taking no notice of us at all! I was almost wishing that they would attack, and get it over with!

Sir Stephan had everyone who had ever pulled a bow organized into two companies of archers, one for each tower, with an officer in charge of each floor. I put him to teaching a very short course in swordsmanship, on top of the city wall.

Then, Juma came trotting back, at the head of more men than he had left with! I went down to meet him.

"You had a good fight, Juma?"

"Yes, a most glorious one, with all of the Sons of Satan killed! I lost a lot of men, but they died well, and we successfully slaughtered all of our ancient enemies that we could find!"

"Wonderful! But then how is it that you came back with more men than you left with?"

"More men, but not the same ones. The were many members of my tribe enslaved in this city! When they heard our war cries, they freed themselves and came to my aid! And even now, I have a hundred of my men searching about the city, finding more of my people."

"Great! We've been setting up our defenses and foraging for food. But come inside, rest your men, and have something to eat," I said.

"It would be better if you had food sent down to us here. My people fight best in the open field, but this street will have to suffice for now. I want to get our lines organized."

"If that's what you want," I said, shouting some orders up to the kitchen. "But at least, send your wounded up to the aid station."

"We have our own methods of healing. Do not trouble yourself. Go now. The enemy will be here in minutes, I think."

I turned to the tower and shouted, "Tell Sir Stephan that we have unwelcome guests coming!" To Juma, I said, "When the time looks right, I'll take most of the men from the towers, sally out, and hit the enemy with fresh troops. Stay as close as you can to the towers. We will be able to give you some support with our archers. The tower doors will stay guarded but open, and if you are hard pressed, retreat inside! We cannot afford to lose good men! 'The man who fights and runs away lives to fight another day!' We are here to conquer this city, not to prove how brave we are!"

"That is not the way of my people!"

"It is now! You are under my command, Juma!"

"This is so. We will obey, though it seems to be cowardly," Juma said.

"Obeying orders is not cowardly!"

He nodded, and I went into the tower to take my station on the fighting platform at the top. I was yelling orders all the way up.

I took the old commander's bow and quiver out to the fighting platform and strung the bow. It looked to be of the Mongol type, with a thin wooden center, a horn belly, and a sinew back. Commander Hajji had had good taste in weapons.

And in slave girls.

Waiting for something to happen, I got to talking to Ali Somethingoranother, who happened to be standing next to me, bow in hand.

I discovered that the agricultural slaves were not as disorganized as I had thought.

The Arabs had organized them into groups of about twenty men each, with a slave foreman in charge. Five or six of these groups were under a slave supervisor. I am sure that this explained why things had gone so smoothly after we took the gate towers.

We did have an organizational structure after all, thanks to our enemies! Right after the battle, if we lived, I was going to have to get together with these foremen and supervisors, and have a talk!

Sir Stephan had set up a system of runners to take orders to the men on the floors below. Often, this amounted to little more than shouting down the long, circular stair well, but it seemed to work.

I intended to watch the upcoming battle from the side of the tower facing the street. I put Sir Stephan on the other side of the tower, so he could watch over the top of the city wall, in case an attack happened there, and also to watch what happened on the road outside of the city.

Omar was in a similar position to mine on the southern tower of the West Gate, so we could see each other, and shout. Or at least we could gesticulate to each other, once the battle got loud.

Everything that could be done had been done, and there was nothing to do but wait and worry. There was even enough time for Juma's men to be fed and watered, down on the street.

Finally, the enemy came into sight, at the end of the long, wide, and straight street.

They had taken their time getting organized, rather than charging in piecemeal as I had hoped that they would. They came walking in toward us in a mass that was at least forty men wide and perhaps three times that deep. We were outnumbered by a considerable margin.

They were well dressed in a uniform of sorts, although officers were apparently permitted considerable latitude in their clothing and armor.

There was a hint of spit and polish about them, which might indicate crack troops, or might mean that that they were garrison troops mostly used to look pretty on parades. Time would tell which of these they were.

And while they weren't exactly marching, they were keeping in good order, which suggested some decent training. My men were essentially a bunch of untrained farmers for the most part, except for Juma's forces, and I wasn't very confident about him or them. There was something crazy and suicidal about that bunch.

On the other hand, we had the gate towers to defend us. This was a considerable advantage for us, since traditional wisdom said that it took five to ten times as many men outside of a good fortification as there were inside of it for the attackers to be victorious.

If we could bleed them hard enough for a few days, and get our own men shaken down in the process, we still might win, God willing!

Chapter 21 The Slaughter of the Slavers

Juma had most of his men near the towers, but he had also put several strong contingents in some of the buildings on either side of the street, which bothered me. I would have kept them all together, but there wasn't anything that I could do to change things now.

I passed the word that we would try a few ranging shots, but that most of the archers should hold their fire.

I seemed to have the best bow on the highest platform, so I let fly. Archery had become a sport in Poland, and I had put the word out that a gentleman wouldn't use a fire arm against a mere animal! The ancient weapons were the ones to use for hunting, as our noble ancestors had done! It had caught on, and the wildlife had stayed reasonably intact. That had meant that I had to learn how to use a bow myself, or it would have cost me a good bit of status. But I had an excellent teacher, a man named Tados who was now the commander of all of the Christian Army's Waterborne Forces.

My shot went true, into the mass of enemy troops below. I saw my man fall.

I asked Ali to try a shot. His fell short by many yards, and was well to the left. Not that accuracy was very important or even mattered in this sort of thing, as long as we didn't shoot Juma's men. It was the volume of fire that counted.

But I could hit them with my bow, and there wasn't much point in holding my fire, since we had plenty of arrows. With the soldiers in this tight of a mass, each of my arrows would take someone out, and you can't do much better than that. I emptied my quiver in short order. It wasn't more than a pinprick to the army advancing on us, but twenty dead or wounded soldiers are twenty soldiers who wouldn't be trying to kill us. I concentrated on the first few ranks, on the theory that having more men behind them stepping on them wouldn't do the wounded any good at all.

Also, it encouraged our forces. At least they were cheering a lot.

When the enemy troops stepped past Ali's arrow, I ordered the men on both fighting tops to open fire, and most of the first volley struck home. You could see the enemy lines rippling, like ripe wheat on a windy day!

When they'd come a dozen paces farther, I ordered our archers on the lower floors to join in on the fun. Enemy ranks were noticeably thinning, but they kept on coming at that walk of theirs. Juma, thank God, was holding his position, waiting for his turn to come.

I kept the archers at it. We had plenty of arrows, and I couldn't think of a better use for them than this! If we won, we could probably recover most of them. If we lost, then what difference could it make?

Finally, the enemy reached Juma's lines. The Black Africans let out a bloodthirsty roar, and the speed of death quickened. Juma's men were still considerably outnumbered, but the street and buildings stopped them from being outflanked, and only about forty of the enemy could get at them at any one time.

Those Blacks of his were very good with their shields and spears, using techniques that I'd never seen used before. Some spears were thrown, hard, fast and straight! I saw one go through three Arab soldiers! At other times, spears were used in almost the same way that an infantryman uses a bayonet. Men in their front lines often traded places with the men behind them, either to get a chance to rest, or maybe just to share the fun. Either way, it kept the front line fresh.

I got another bundle of arrows and went back to work.

I didn't see what the signal was, but from doorways on each side of the battle field, hundreds of fresh Black Africans suddenly rushed into the enemy's flanks! At first, they did tremendous damage, with each of them killing several enemy soldiers!

I called a cease fire to the archers, so that we would not be responsible for shooting any of our own troops.

Had the Blacks turned back as soon as the Arabs were aware of them, it would have been a brilliant maneuver, but they didn't! They continued to push on deep into the huge mass of enemy soldiers! They were soon surrounded, and cut down to the man!

"Those stupid, stupid suicidal idiots! Are they all mad?" I shouted to no one in particular.

"You don't know much about Juma's men, do you?" Ali said.

"That is a massive understatement!"

"Then know that they don't care if they die! They don't want their lives! They want vengeance!"

"Everybody wants to live," I said.

"That is true only for those who have something to live for. Haven't you wondered why there are so many people from his one tribe in this one city? Years ago, a collection of Arab slavers from this city organized a league of all the tribes around Juma's tribe. They all attacked at the same time, and Juma's people were wiped out, except for some of the healthy young men, who the slavers then bought at bargain prices. All of the older people, all of the children, and even most of the women were slaughtered. Juma and his people have no place to go home to. All of their elders are dead. All of their families are dead. All of their children are dead. So now, all that they want is just to kill."

"What could make the other African tribes want to kill them so badly?"

"Greed, mostly," Ali said. "Juma's people held a lot of rich land. That and they had some very bad habits, like cannibalism."

"Cannibalism! Well, I'll put a stop to that!"

"I wouldn't, Conrad. It's like a religion to them, somehow. If you tried to stop it, the least that could happen would be that we would lose their valuable services. The worst is unthinkable! We might have them for enemies! And if our supplies start running low, their strange personal habits will mean that they won't be a drain on our larder. They eat their own dead as well as their enemies, you know, although they do not deliberately slaughter their own."

"Damn! Well, the ones on the flanking attack all seem to be dead now. Archers! Resume fire!"

Both sides slugged it out for more than a long, army hour. The mutual hatred was extreme, and the fighting men on both sides knew what would happen to them if they lost!

Finally, a little before dusk, both sides started to show signs of fatigue, and we were starting to run low on arrows.

"Sir Stephan! Take over for me here! I'm going to lead a sortie of fresh troops out there and see what we can accomplish!"

Stephen said, "Please, Lord Conrad! Let me go instead! I've been taking shit from these bastards for five years now, and this is the first time that I've had a chance to get back at them!"

"Sir Stephan, I have armor, but you don't."

"I don't care, sir. Let me go!"

"Okay, I'll tell you what. Go over to the other tower and collect up everyone who isn't shooting a bow. Send a runner when you have them ready. When you hear my battle cry, rush out as fast as you can."

"Consider it done, my lord!"

"Ali!" I shouted, "Take command up here, and do whatever seems appropriate! And have someone replace Sir Stephan, watching our rear!"

"Yes, Conrad! I will do this thing!"

In a few minutes I had my men ready, everybody who could throw a spear, swing a sword, or handle a knife, barring the archers. They included the cooks, the walking wounded, and the medics! They all wanted to fight, and we needed them to do just that.

They had all been getting antsy since Juma's battle with the Arabs had started, and now they were eager to go out and join it. Most of them hadn't the slightest idea of what warfare was all about, but they would learn. Oh, yes, they would learn very soon!

Shortly, Stephan's runner said that they were ready in the other tower. I ran through the thick doorway first, and I had all of the others right behind me!

"FOR GOD AND POLAND!"

I'd naturally yelled that in Polish, a language that very few of my men spoke. But since I was shouting it, they all started shouting it too, or at least some reasonable facsimile thereof. Sir Stephan led the men of the south tower out a heartbeat later.

Battle cries are a sort of magic, I suppose, and have greater manna when no one understands them. It has much in common with why the church says much of the mass in Latin, a language which few parishioners speak.

Juma's men were more than ready for a breather, and they let our new men from both towers go through their lines to the enemy.

My size, my armor, and my incredible sword let me move forward faster into them than the others behind me. Soon, I was at the point of a wedge that we hacked forward into the still considerable mass of Arab troops.

This 'wedge attack' is normally a difficult maneuver, even for trained troops, but somehow we just managed to do it naturally!

These Arabs wore little or no armor. They were thus easy to chop up, and I think that I must have killed at least one of them with every swing of my unnaturally sharp blade. These bastards had murdered Cynthia, chopped off my right hand, and made me a slave in a stinking barrel for eight months! Killing them felt GOOD!

My impromptu army was doing surprisingly well. While untrained, they were used to long and heavy work. They had strength, fortitude, and endurance, and that paid off here. The fact that the enemy was tired helped a lot, too! I was prepared to break off and retreat if there were any signs of trouble, but so far, we seemed to be doing okay. More than okay! We were slaughtering the rag heads!

Then something very strange happened. One of the enemy officers apparently confused me with the man whose distinctive armor I was wearing.

"It is Commander Hajji! Commander Hajji has gone over to the enemy! There is treason! All is lost! Run for your lives!" he shouted at the top of his lungs.

Now, that was one hell of a thing to shout in any battle, but the effect here was astounding! Suddenly, the entire enemy army turned around and ran away!

I was bewildered, and I had no idea why they had done such a strange thing, but this was an opportunity not to be missed!

"After them! Don't let them get away!" I shouted to my men, knowing that most casualties in most battles happen after one side has lost. Once they turn their backs to you, they are dog meat, and you'd best take advantage of it before they regain their courage.

This would have been a very good time to have had some cavalry, but the enemy foot soldiers were tired while our foot soldiers were still fairly fresh, and that was enough. The slaughter went on for another quarter of an army hour.

The street was a big, ceremonial way, but the side streets leading away from it were small, narrow, and crooked, and that restricted their flight. The enemy army died in piles!

It was starting to get dark when I called my men back.

"Clean up time, people! I want every weapon you can find, theirs or ours, and especially, I want every arrow out here! Take them all back to the towers! And if any of these bastards have anything of value that you want, consider it to be my present to you!"

Christian Army rules had it that all loot must be collected and distributed fairly later on, since some men must guard while others loot, and both groups deserve a share.

I thought that these people would consider 'finders keepers' to be a more natural way of doing things. Some of them would have kept what they found anyway, causing problems later, and what the hell? I didn't need the money.

I kept an eye out for a counterattack, but none emerged.

Another thousand or so city slaves joined us during the clean up. Many had tried to come during the battle and couldn't make it, but now they were arming themselves with things that the enemy didn't need any more.

We'd asked for healthy men to join our cause, but many women and children had come as well. It hurt to send them away, but we wouldn't be doing them a favor by taking them in. This war wasn't over, not by a long shot. If we couldn't defend them, they would all be slaughtered! I told them to go back to their previous owners. We'd come and rescue them as soon as we could. It would be just a few days, I told them.

I hoped that I wasn't lying.

My red silk cape was covered with gore and ripped in a dozen places. I took it off and left it laying on the ground.

Omar had sent half of the archers down to help with the cleanup, which was helpful. There was a lot of stuff laying in the street.

Juma was doing a clean up job of his own, stripping and gutting the enemy dead. The hearts and livers were thrown back into the stomach cavity, and the dead human bodies were dragged back to his camp. The stories about cannibalism were apparently true. But in more ancient times, cannibalism was far more prevalent, even in Northern Europe, according to the church! With our ex-slave army growing, supplies could soon become a problem. And what were we supposed to do with all of these dead bodies? The streets were all paved in this city, so burying them would be difficult. This was desert country, without anything in the way of forests. We didn't have the firewood to cremate them all. And letting them rot in the open was an invitation to the plague!

I let Juma do as he wanted.

As I approached the gate towers, Juma came to me and invited me to a traditional victory feast of his people.

"Since I killed him, I will be eating the former commander myself! You are welcome to join me! He will have much manna about him!"

"His name was Hajji."

"That is good to know! I will praise him as we eat, and that will increase the manna."

"My people are Christians, Juma. We are not permitted to eat human flesh."

The Black Africans had knocked over some of the nearby buildings to get enough wooden roof beams for their cooking fires. At least fifty human bodies were starting to turn over them. And some of them were black before they started to roast.

"It is good to eat the bodies of your fallen friends," he said. "It puts their strength, their loyalty, and their courage back into the tribe!"

"I respect your thoughts and philosophy, Juma, but the customs of my people are different. I could not possibly eat human flesh. But you and yours should enjoy your feast."

"But I have honored your customs when it came to the ordering of the battle!"

"This is very true, my friend, but that was a matter of command. Consider that doing things my way has led us to victory over our enemy! Many more of them are dead than would have been the case with your tactics. Surely victory is preferable to death, provided that our enemies have all died!

"This is a matter of social custom," I continued. "I would not expect you to sing a full Catholic High Mass with me, but for now, I am very tired, and I wish to retire. I am much older than you are, after all."

"Very well, my lord. That is what your own people call you, isn't it?"

"I have many titles, but I am really not very concerned with them. Please call me Conrad, as my best friends all do."

"Then I will call you Conrad, your given name, as you call me Juma."

"This is good. I will see that your feast is not disturbed by anyone in the towers, but I urge you to keep alert sentries out all night. We have won a battle, but we have not yet won the war!"

I met Sir Stephan, coming back down from the armory.

"Get the street cleaned of at least the weapons tonight," I told him. "Keep some sentries out while the men work, and rotate them now and then so that they too get a chance at some loot. And keep everybody away from Juma's people. They might be cannibals, but they are useful cannibals."

"Will do, sir. There's a full moon tonight, and that will help with the cleanup."

"Good. It has been a very long day for me, I've been going since before dawn, and I'm not getting any younger. We'll have a meeting at midmorning with the foremen and supervisors of the agricultural slaves, and with anyone else that you think is appropriate. Maybe that Ali fellow. Discuss it with Omar."

"Yes, sir. And good night, sir."

Sir Stephan was shaping up to be a first rate executive officer. He was ready for a few major promotions, if we ever got back to Poland alive.

Chapter 22 The Fruits of Victory

I picked up more bread and much more meat in the kitchen. I ate it as I walked to the top of the tower. They'd told me that it was camel meat. That was fine by me. I'd never met a camel that I'd liked. I wouldn't eat a horse, or a dog, or a cat, you understand, but then I liked all of those critters. Camels were just fine, and they tasted good, anyway.

There had been some changes made in the old commander's quarters. Jasmine was there, and so was a huge bathtub of hot water!

She kneeled before me, her tiny breasts and puffy nipples exposed above the dress she was wearing.

"Congratulations on your victory, my lord Conrad! I have arranged for this victory gift for you, the one thing that I thought that you would most desire."

"My lady, you are spot on! Eight months without a bath is just too damn long!"

I stripped and left my weapons, armor, padding, boots, and underwear scattered on the floor. It was all too splattered with blood and gore to be put away, anyhow. I wasn't worried about being nude. We had both been naked when we had first met, anyway. I slipped into the deliciously warm water, and rejoiced. I was in Heaven!

Jasmine said, "Your back, where you were wounded. It is almost healed!"

"I do heal quickly, yes."

"I am amazed!"

"It is a useful thing for a warrior."

While I soaked, Jasmine collected up my stuff, cleaned it, and put it wherever it all belonged. Women all intuitively know where things go.

"You seem to be very efficient at that," I mentioned.

"It was one of the tasks that I did for the last commander of this tower. But I like doing it for you much better than for him. You are much nicer than he was."

"Indeed?"

"At least, you won't hang me naked on the wall for half of the night in sport!"

"He did that?" I winced. "I'm glad we killed the bastard! But shouldn't you be down in the aid station, tending to the wounded?"

"My lord, I discovered that there were three of your men who were much better doctors than I was, so I put them in charge of the aid station. Was I right to do that?"

"I suppose so, since we're a very informal bunch around here. I'll inspect the clinic in the morning, and change anything that I don't like."

"Good! Because I feel much better taking care of you!"

She had set up a small table near the tub and had it cluttered with jars of soap, shampoos, and perfumes. There were combs, brushes, scissors, razors, and some items that I couldn't immediately identify. I was apparently going to get the full treatment, and I was absolutely prepared to wallow in it!

"This was another of the things that you did for the last commander of this place?"

"Oh yes, my lord. Almost every night."

Then, Jasmine dropped her robe and got into the tub with me naked, and I saw no reason for objecting to this procedure. Forcing a slave girl to do your bidding is one thing. Accepting the willing favors of a free woman is quite another, and I planned to enjoyed myself!

I was washed, scrubbed, and shampooed. My teeth were brushed. My fingernails and toenails were cleaned, trimmed, and buffed. I looked on it, and found it to be good!

After a pleasant hour or so of this, Jasmine said, "My lord, what do you want done with your hair and your beard?"

"Well, the beard should be shaved. I've never worn a beard when I could help it. And the hair? Just take it in sort of close at the sides and longer on the top."

"You are Polish, aren't you?"

"Yes."

"I saw in a book once a drawing of a Polish Nobleman. I could do something like that, if you want."

I said, "That would be excellent!"

I had woken up this morning in a stinking barrel that was impregnated with my own shit, along with that of several other unfortunates. Much had happened, and it had been a very long day! As she worked the shaving soap into my beard, I relaxed against the wall of the tub and fell asleep.

I was gently shaken awake, I don't know how much later.

"Conrad. The water is getting cold, and I must dry you and put you to bed."

So I got out of the tub, and Jasmine scurried around me, toweling me dry and wrapping me in a nicely embroidered cotton robe. She dried herself quickly while I tried to figure out where the bedroom was.

Jasmine led me there.

I fell into the bed, which had a real mattress. 'Mattress' turns out to be an Arabic word. Jasmine got in beside me. Then, I fell asleep again.

So much for the virile Radiant Warrior!

I awoke with a lovely aroma pervading the room around me. For a few moments, I thought that I was still dreaming!

"Good God! Is that actually coffee that I smell?"

"Yes, my lord!" Jasmine called from the next room, "My last master preferred it to tea in the morning. Do you like yours sweetened?"

"Yes, please."

I followed my nose into the dining room to find the table set with fresh white bread, an assortment of butter, jams, and jellies, and a cup of lovely, honey sweetened coffee. I started in on it.

"Aren't you going to eat, too?" I asked.

"This would be permitted, my lord?"

"Of course! It has always been my custom that the people who work for me eat as well as I do. This is not so here?"

"No, my lord. Slaves do not eat as free people do. I have always wondered what coffee tasted like."

"So Hajji had you make it, but he wouldn't let you even taste it? What an asshole! I'm very glad indeed that we killed him! But sit down, pour yourself a cup of coffee, and get some breakfast into you!"

I soon noticed that Jasmine was sampling every jam and jelly on the table. Coffee wasn't the only thing that she had been forbidden.

I checked myself out in the mirror.

I was cleanly shaved, as I had asked to be, but my mustache was missing as well. I guess that I hadn't mentioned the mustache. Well, no big thing.

The haircut, though, was not quite what I'd had in mind. True, I had said that I wanted it close on the sides and longer on top, and that's what I got.

But I hadn't expected a Mohawk!

It was two fingers wide and four fingers high, and was held up straight by some sort of concoction. Apparently, Arab chroniclers had some very strange ideas about what a Polack looked like!

But so what if I looked weird. I was a stranger in a strange land, and my wives would hopefully never hear about it.

After breakfast, I said, "Well, I ought to make an inspection of the towers before we get into that organizational meeting, but there's one other thing that I want to do first."

"And what is that, my lord?"

"Sex, if you are willing."

"Oh, yes, my lord! I am not only willing but eager!"

I had been eight months without the benefits of feminine companionship, and I got to the meeting an hour late.

Dressed in a beautiful red silk robe that was heavily embroidered with gold thread, I went to the meeting of our leaders. Hajji might have been an asshole, but his taste in many things had been excellent! If I ever got back to Poland, I think that I might adopt the fashions of Timbuktu.

My new appearance raised eyebrows, and caused quite a few comments. Feelings about it were mixed, but the most prominent of them seemed to be envy, so I ignored them.

About half of those present had availed themselves of a bath, at least, and many sported clean shaven faces and haircuts. I learned that soon after I'd left it, the bathtub had been moved to the kitchen to be near the hot water, and that it had been in use all night long. They had been drawing water from the well to purify it, and figured that they might as well put the water to some good use.

Yesterday, we had managed to nearly fill the well with dead bodies, after all, and no one was very eager to drink out of it yet! We were boiling the water before anyone was allowed to drink it. Adding a little tea helped.

Omar already had the meeting going, which was fine by me. In a few hours, we had a table of organization worked out, and a head count of the number of soldiers we had fit to fight.

At present, our forces were up to three thousand, nine hundred and forty eight fighting men, and more ex-slaves were still filtering in.

I ordered an inventory made on our weapons and our food supplies, and by the end of the day we found that we could sketchily arm three times as many men as we presently had. We still had food for a week, since over half of our men were from Juma's tribe, and those guys weren't drawing from our normal supplies at all!

Many of the leaders, especially Juma, wanted to attack the palace immediately, but I talked them into waiting until dawn, and then circling around and hitting the Arabs from the east, with the early light in the enemy's eyes. And yes, we could accomplish the same thing by attacking from the west in the evening, but then we might not have enough time to get the job done!

But first, our army needed a bit of training, at least being introduced to their new captains, being told the battle plan, and then getting a lot of rest.

There was some debate as to whether the Arabs could bring in any large number of soldiers, but in truth, nobody knew what the enemy's capabilities were. We could estimate their casualties, of course, but no one knew how many soldiers they had had when this war had started. They had a slave economy, and that takes a lot of soldiers to keep the slaves from revolting, and to kill them if they do revolt. Slavery is not an economically efficient system.

Timbuktu was a city on an oasis in the middle of a desert. The nearest relief would take at least three weeks to get here. That's if some other city would come to their aid at all.

Desert peoples are not a very cooperative bunch, on the whole. Their main problem was the lack of water, and if there was a severe scarcity, the general feeling was that better I should live and you should die! In Poland and most of Northern Europe, the problem was the cold winters. There, the more people you had around you, the warmer you were! This made for some major differences in national character.

I raised a bit of a storm with my insistence that slavery would be completely abolished in Timbuktu. The idea of most of the others was that they would be freed, but that now the Arabs would be their slaves, instead of the other way around. Let those bastards do all of the work!

I persevered, though, and I knew that eventually, I would win out. We were in a position to end this abomination, and we should do it!

For now, it was simply too new of an idea for most of them.

I did find out about the strange ending of last evening's battle. It seems that some time ago, the Vizier, in the flowery praise that is common in their culture, extolling Hajji's courage, strength, and loyalty, had said that if Hajji ever proved to be disloyal, Timbuktu would vanish into the desert.

The locals took this sort of prophecy very seriously!

The fact that my back had been to the setting sun, my size, which was similar to his, and Hajji's fancy armor had all contributed to that fool's mistake. Much later, I found out that he had been executed for his stupidity.

Omar had lunch with me in my quarters. Jasmine served us roast chicken, with rice and fresh vegetables. Where she had found them, I don't know.

"Conrad," Omar said. "I see that my mistake was in running up the wrong tower! I took a similar suite of rooms at the top of the southern tower, but it had been assigned to the second in command here. The furnishings are inferior to yours, as is the wardrobe, and no one like Jasmine was there to do his bidding!"

"Warfare is largely a matter of luck, my friend. We'll take the palace tomorrow, and after that, we'll flip a coin to see who gets first choice of rooms!"

"Done! And I've no doubt that there will be others like your Jasmine available, even for an old, one handed man like myself!"

Jasmine said, "Oh, you may be assured of that, Omar. If you wish, I'll find you a few, so that you may make your choice!"

"Are you sure that it will be so easy?" Omar asked.

"Of course! If you are really going to free all of the slaves in the city, there will be a lot of girls like me who will be looking for jobs. Taking care of men is the only thing that we've been trained for!"

"Then I accept your kind offer, young lady. Please find me some young girls with lips like the reddest of berries, breasts like ripe melons, and nipples like the sweetest of raisins! Also, remember that as a true believer of Islam, I am entitled to four of them!"

"To hear is to obey!"

"The fruits of victory, indeed!" I said.

I spent the afternoon making sure that everyone knew the plan for tomorrow morning, getting to know my officers, and making the rounds of the towers. Much of a commander's job is simply walking, watching, and listening.

In normal times, the guards of the gate went to the public baths like everyone else, but they did have two bathtubs, one per tower, for emergencies, I suppose. Now, they were still in use, with three men in them at a time. If they were to die in tomorrow's attack, they would at least die clean! They seemed to be a little low on soap, scissors, and razors, so I sent word for Jasmine to lend my new toilet set to them.

Hajji's clothes, on the other hand, were entirely too big to fit any of these men, so I kept them all for myself.

Juma's men had been busy, and most of yesterday's battle field had been cleared of bodies. Many were already eaten, with the bones thrown into piles, many more were roasting over open fires, and I was told that over a thousand of them were being smoked in a big stone cellar that had been found under one of the buildings on the street! I elected to not go down and look at it!

I never measured anything, but counting the roasted sculls and doing some estimating, I got the impression that the Black Africans we had in our army must be eating over twenty pounds of human flesh per capita, per diem! That's a lot of meat! The purely vegetarian diet we'd all been on must have hurt them more than the rest of us. Or maybe 'long pork' really is that delicious!

But I didn't really want to know!

I had the other men fed supper and told them to sack out early, since we had to be up, fed, and moving out long before dawn. Desert nights were usually clear, and the moon tonight would be only one day past full, so there would be plenty of light to find our way to our attack position.

Many modern city dwellers don't realize just how bright a full moon can be, but I have often comfortably read a book well past midnight outdoors, when the moon was right.

Unlike the attack on the gate towers, there would be nothing haphazard about taking the palace. We had people with us who had actually worked there. We had reasonably accurate drawings of the gates, the approaches to them, and the private quarters of the Vizier's wing. Killing him and his staff soonest was critical to our success!

Again, I enjoyed Jasmine's cooking, and her lovemaking. And then, with the doors guarded and the sentries set, I went to sleep, after a bit.

There was a lot of noise coming from the street below. Dogs, cats, vultures, and crows were eating the offal, tripe, and intestines that Juma's men had left down there in piles, and doing it loudly.

Chapter 23   On a Staircase, Going Down

Judging by the moon, it was a little before midnight when the fight started. It sounded like it was inside the tower, so I didn't waste any time putting on armor, or indeed clothing, but just grabbed my sword and ran down the steps in a nicely embroidered Egyptian cotton sleeping robe, shouting the alarm all the way.

Four of our men had been sleeping a floor or two below me and were on the narrow, curving staircase ahead of me. They didn't last long. A large, heavily armed and armored party of Arabs was pushing up the steps from below.

"Archers to the stairwell!" I shouted as the men in front of me were chopped up.

Then it was my turn! They had armor and I didn't, but I had my old sword, and that edge didn't care much about what it was cutting. Flesh, bone, or steel, it treated them all just the same!

My first blow swung across the empty space in the middle of the stairway, cut a lesser sword than mine in half, and then continued on to take my man's head off. His swing was somewhat hampered by having the wall to his right. I suppose that he could have blamed it on the staircase, had he had any time to assign the blame.

I kicked the body down the stairs into the man behind him, and split that guy's skull while he was trying to get untangled.

The archers were arriving above me, and they started peppering the Arabs trying to climb up. I couldn't help wondering why they hadn't used archers on us when we took this tower in the first place. Maybe, they just didn't think of it.

I killed three more Arabs, while slowly descending the steps. The men following me tripped over some of them, and then they started throwing the bodies down the stair shaft, where half of them ended up in the well.

Bad design was what it was! And here we'd just gotten that damned thing cleaned out! I could see where it was convenient to be able to draw water up from any floor of the tower, with a bucket and a long rope, but why couldn't they have put a lid on the well, to keep dirt out if nothing else? And the idiot designers had never even considered of the obviously common problem of falling bodies!

I soon found that once you cut an arm or two off of an Arab, the fight usually goes right out of him, and then a neck cut is fairly easy.

Not that I was doing all of the work myself! I soon had a half dozen good men behind me, with swords and spears. They were particularly useful in getting me past the landings and doorways that led to the rooms at each level. Without someone to guard me as I passed a doorway, I would have gotten a blade in my kidney early in that fight!

All of our men were awake now, those who weren't dead, and they were pouring into every room I passed and cleaning it out!

But I was the man on the point, and for me, the enemy was down!

I was slowly working my way downward, and the archers probably got four of the Arabs for every one that I did, but the rag heads still kept coming, as though they were being pushed up from below!

How had these people gotten in here, anyhow? We'd had a strong guard on the single door below, and Juma had over two thousand of his men camped on the street.

How could they possibly have gone through the Black Africans without anybody hearing it?

Well, I'd find out eventually, once I made it to the bottom.

Damn, but my sword arm was getting sore! This was one hell of a workout!

After more time and blood than I care to think about we made it down to the second floor, where the guard room and the well were.

As my men were breaking into the guard room, the fifty or so Arabs in front of me tried to run for it, going down the steps for the tower door. They had to scramble over our slaughtered door guards to do it, but they managed to unbar the sturdy door and rush out.

Straight into Juma's forces!

Two hundred spears flew in the moonlight, and the Arabs were no more!

I stepped outside and sat down on the steps, exhausted. I was unharmed, but my sword arm ached, and my silk embroidered Egyptian cotton robe was in tatters and drenched in human blood.

I tried to find a clean spot on my robe so I could wipe my blade off, but I couldn't find one. I finally had to stand up and take the damned robe off, and then sit there naked, to get at a clean spot on the back. Aside from the diamond edge, only fifty atoms thick, my sword was high carbon steel. It needed to be kept clean, or it would rust.

After a while, Juma came over and sat down next to me.

"This business of warfare is very hard on one's wardrobe!" I said.

"So it would appear. First your pretty red silk cape, and now your bathrobe. Perhaps you should adopt my people's fashions. They are much more practical!"

"I shall consider it. How did the Arabs get past your people and into the tower?"

"They didn't," Juma said. "At least in the southern tower, they came in through a secret passage and through a hidden doorway in the side of the well. They climbed up the metal ladder set into the wall of the well, and invaded the tower. Fortunately, at the time, one of the door guards was getting a drink of water, contrary to your rules about drinking unboiled well water, and was able to alert the others before he was killed. They in turn alerted my people, who came quickly to their aid.

"You had no such luck in the northern tower," he continued. "The Arabs were able to catch your door guards unawares, slaughter them from behind, from the looks of it, and bar the door to keep us from aiding you."

"Couldn't you have crossed over to us at the level of the wall?" I asked.

"Oh, we did! But then we were above the fight, and your men were in our way!"

"Of course. I wasn't thinking. Well, we've got another mess to clean up here!"

Juma said, "I don't think so. Those bodies filling both of the wells are doing a very good job of closing off the secret doors and passages, and my people have got enough to eat for weeks. This morning, I urged attacking the palace immediately, but you rejected my advice. Had we done it my way, this attack would not have occurred. We've lost over a thousand men here, you know. They probably lost at least as many as we did, but you have always been overly concerned with such things. None the less, I must now insist that we attack the palace immediately! We are all awake now, and most of the men will not easily get to sleep again soon. They will be tired by the time your dawn attack is to occur. But we cannot delay this any more! We will all attack now, or my tribe and I will do it without you!"

"Very well. This time, you have proven to be right. Give me a few minutes to get into my armor. I will leave the wounded to hold the towers and guard this gate, so if we fail in this attack, we will have some place to fall back on."

"It is good. I will send my wounded into the towers, as well. One more thing. Since we will be attacking well before dawn, there is no point in attacking the eastern gate of the palace. We should hit the western gate, which is closer."

"Well, let's have a few archers make a demonstration at the other two gates, anyway. Lots of noise and arrows, but no real attack. They can start when they hear the main attack. It should draw off some of their forces, anyway."

"Very well, Conrad."

"And be sure that we take along all of the rope and grappling hooks we have in the armory. We're not likely to find the gates opened for us."

"Of course, we'll bring the ropes and hooks. But ask that Christian God of yours for an open gate, anyway. Now go, and put your pretty armor on!"

Women always seem to know what's going on better than men do. Jasmine had my armor out and ready. As she helped me get into it, I told her that she'd be needed in the aid station, because the regular doctors would be going with us to attack the palace. After the wounded had been taken care of, she should pack all of the clothes and anything else of value here, because we would be moving into the palace soon, with any luck.

Then I took my new bow, two quivers of arrows, my sword, and a good knife, and went down. My sword arm was still tired and sore. Let somebody else be the heroic point man next time!

I went down to the street where our men were mustering.

I was surprised to find Omar there wearing the armor of the troops who had just attacked us. With him were over two gross of men in the same uniform.

"They were polite enough to deliver this armor to us, Conrad. Wouldn't it be rude of us not to wear it on our visit to their palace?"

"Quite right, my friend. Have you thought about how we will get into the palace, or was a formal invitation included with the uniforms?"

"Since we are properly attired now, I thought that I might try simply walking up and asking them to open the gate. It worked the last time I tried it."

"That is a very good idea! Take your people to the front of the column. I'll see that Juma's people, and the rest of our raggedy band, stay out of sight," I said.

Two groups of fifty archers each were sent off at a run to create diversions at the other two gates.

Associating with the Arabs, with their base ten numbering system, was rapidly reverting me to thinking in base ten, which I had grown up using, rather than in the base twelve system that we now used in Poland.

There were again about four thousand of us as we went quietly down the street. New recruits had just about made up for all of our recent combat losses. And since we had been consistently winning, we had a surplus of weapons and armor, stolen from the dead.

Despite the nearly full moon, the streets of Timbuktu were very quiet, probably because Moslems don't go in much for night life. We didn't see anyone the whole way to the palace.

Juma had wanted to run the full distance, but I managed to convince him that we would be quieter if we simply walked. Even so, we were not exactly silent. The footsteps of four thousand quiet men are still quite loud. It is an eerie, high pitched sound, not at all what you would expect.

Juma said quietly to me, "You know, when we take the palace, we must kill them all."

"Not all of them. Many of the people there will be slaves, as you and I were. They must be spared, and freed. Many of them will join our army."

"That would be difficult! How would we tell one from the other?"

"No, it is easy," I said. "If he tries to kill you, kill him back. If he is unarmed and bows to you, throw him in jail, or whatever is available, until we can sort everything out."

"It would be easier to just kill them all. And you keep saying 'he'. The women have to die as well!"

"What for? Moslem women aren't fighters. Their men would never permit it! And the men in our army are going to want women, wives even, very soon. No, waste not, want not!" And of course, if you don't treat them too badly, most women will eventually learn to love their conquerors. They call it The Stockholm Syndrome.

"None of my tribesmen would ever take an Arab for a wife!" Juma said.

"Some of them might, given time to adjust to the idea. Once we have taken this city, you and your men will be wealthy nobles here! You could build yourselves some very good lives in Timbuktu!"

"There is no life for us! That ended when our families were killed, our tribe was butchered, and we ourselves were enslaved!"

"My people look at things differently, Juma. Once, my country of Poland was defeated, conquered, and dismembered by three of our powerful enemies. For almost two hundred years, Poland did not exist as a country! Yet my people had a song that started out, 'Poland is not yet dead, not while we still live!' And in time, Poland was reborn! Your tribe is not dead, Juma! Not while you or any one of your men still lives! Your tribe is still there, inside of you! And if you have the will and the courage, you could make it come alive again, here, in Timbuktu!"

He was silent for a long time. Then he said, "I will think on it. The palace is close. It is time to get into position."

Chapter 24   Playing The Palace

My distinctive armor had been noticed by the Arabs in an earlier battle, so I stayed back and in the shadows while Omar tried his luck with getting in the gate.

He just casually walked across the wide street surrounding the palace, with almost three hundred men at his back, and asked for the gates to be opened for him.

A voice from above the gate shouted, "Who goes there?"

"Sergeant Omar, with some re-enforcements for you!"

"We don't need any re-enforcements!"

"My captain said that you did! There's a rumor going around that the revolting slaves are planning to attack the palace soon!"

"Yes, yes! We know all about that! They'll be attacking at dawn, and hitting the Eastern Palace Gate. We've brought in twelve thousand men, and the barracks are overflowing right now. There isn't even any extra floor space in there, and men are sleeping under the bunks! Look, the attack won't happen for at least six hours. Go back to your own barracks, and come back here in five hours! We can probably find some use for you as a reserve company."

So not only did they know what our exact plans were, they outnumbered us by three to one, and they were on the inside while we were out here. This did not look auspicious!

Omar called back, "But that's a long walk! Isn't there a little room somewhere, in the gate towers, perhaps?"

"No! We've got soldiers sleeping on the stairs over here! Anyway, my orders are that these gates stay closed! Do you expect me to argue with the Vizier?"

"No, of course not, sir! We'll see you in the morning! Follow me, men!"

Only he wasn't going back the way he came. To me, it looked as though he was going to try his luck with the commander of the Southern Palace Gate.

I went back and found Juma.

"You heard?" he asked me.

"Yes, and it is not good! When we attack, we will be seriously outnumbered."

"What do you suggest?"

"We wait. Maybe Omar can come up with something. I think that he's trying to get into the Southern Palace Gate, now," I said.

"How could they have known our plans so accurately?"

"Easily enough. They could have simply have dressed a spy up to look like a slave, and had him volunteer to join our forces. We had to accept every able bodied man who wanted to join, after all. When he found out what he wanted to know, he could have slipped away, or sent a message back in any of a dozen ways. A carrier pigeon, for all I know."

Juma said, "We should have kept a double ring of guards around the towers, one to keep the enemy out and the other to keep our own forces in!"

"Well, first off, we didn't think of it. Things have been very rushed, lately. And even if we had, I'm not sure that it would have worked. We've had to forage for food, and we've been fighting battles away from the gate towers. A message could have easily been sent while either of those things was going on."

"You could have eaten our enemies, as my people do. Then you wouldn't have had to forage! And it wasn't one of my people who betrayed us!"

Ignoring the thing about eating the Arabs, I said, "No, I don't think that it was. He would have had to be someone who looked like an Arab."

We waited for what seemed like hours in this world without clocks, with no sign of Omar, nor a sound from the palace.

"Conrad, come quickly!" Juma called in a loud whisper. "Look at this!"

He pointed to a woman who was walking alongside of the palace wall. She wearing the head to toe baggy covering that all women here wore outside of their homes, but she had an exaggerated sway to her stride.

Then she stopped and tapped against the wall. Once. Four times. Then twice more. Obviously a code or signal.

Suddenly, what had looked like a solid wall became a doorway, and she was admitted to the palace!

"A prostitute, visiting a client, no doubt," Juma said. "She is the second one who has gone through that secret door! Let's you and I go knock on that wall, and see what happens!"

"It is a better plan than standing here in the dark!"

We left most of our men with Sir Stephan in charge, after talking briefly with him. If he was attacked out here, he should defend himself, but retreat, back to the city's west gate. If the palace gate opened, he should rush in. If nothing happened for another hour, he should go back to the city's west gate, and defend it without us.

I didn't want to take Juma along, since he didn't look at all like an Arab. He insisted, however, and it wasn't worth getting into a loud argument over. I did take ten other men with us, good fighters who could pass for the enemy. Juma agreed to act like a prisoner if the situation required it.

Besides my armor, I had my sword, a good knife, my bow and two quivers of arrows. I didn't know exactly what we were about to get involved with, but I planned to be ready for it.

We went across the wide street to the palace wall with Juma in the middle. Others were carrying his weapons, he had his hands held behind his back, as if bound, and his head was bowed, as if in defeat. No one seemed to notice us.

One of my men, a local who spoke Arabic without an accent, knocked the code on the secret door. It opened immediately. Someone had been stationed there, waiting. I suspected that it was a lucrative post, since anyone entering would be expected to pay a bribe for his services.

What he got from us was a cut throat, and a fast but lonely death!

Two of the men with me had been male harem slaves when they were adolescents, serving the Moslem perverts until they were thirteen and judged to be too old for the job. Then, they had been sold to the city as agricultural slaves. They knew their way around the palace, and both of them had a long standing grudge to settle.

"To the Western Palace Gate," I said, and they nodded. "We have to get it opened!"

From studying the plans, and now walking through it, I am certain that the palace was never designed, in the ordinary sense of the word. This place simply grew, over hundreds of years with hundreds of people making changes in things to suit their current whims and needs.

Nothing was simple, obvious, or straight forward. Everything was twisted, convoluted, and awkward. From the outside, the place looked simple enough, but inside, it was a maze!

Without our guides, we would have been hopelessly lost in minutes. I wondered if this was what had happened to Omar and his men.

We tried to make our way to the gate towers in a calm, unthreatening, and peaceful fashion. Twelve men cannot take on twelve thousand in either a fair fight or a sneaky one. Twice though, calm and peaceful had to give way to violent and brutal! Knives flashed and Arabs died quietly, for the most part. We hid the bodies as best as we could, quickly, and hurried on our way, without an alarm being sounded.

So far we had been lucky, losing only one of our men.

Someone said that we were almost there when we smelled smoke. Almost immediately, we heard a cry in the distance, "Fire!"

"Quickly now!" I shouted, "Let's get that gate open!"

We got outside of the building we were in and ran for the gate. A tall, military looking building was on fire to our right, with flames shooting high, and horrible screams coming from within! Soon, I realized that at least two of the gates were also ablaze. This had to be Omar's work.

Both gate towers on the Western Palace Gate were burning, but the gate between them wasn't.

Juma had our men lifting the huge bar that locked the gate when the same officer who refused to let Omar in started shouting at them.

"Get away from that gate! It was ordered closed!"

"Are you mad?" One of our men shouted back, "The palace is burning! We will all be killed if we don't get out!"

The officer looked like we was going to tell someone to stop us, so I got my bow out and shot him. He tumbled from the wall, and managed to kill one of my own men when he fell on him.

It was one of the former harem boys. Damn. Some things just don't work out.

As the gate was opened, I could see our ragtag forces coming at a run, with Sir Stephan at the head of them.

The two towers now had fire coming out of every window and arrow slit, and it occurred to me that if the ropes that held up the portcullis burned through, the heavy, iron thing would come down hard, with no way of raising it again. I got eight men to help me with the huge bar that had locked the gate, and we jammed it upright into the slot that the portcullis ran in. I hoped it would work, anyway.

"Well, Conrad. You seem to have gotten this part of the task done without me!"

The portcullis did start to come down, but it jammed against the bar that we had placed just in time! The way was still open!

I turned to see Omar's grinning face, and said, "We became worried about you! You were gone for so long, and you didn't even write to us!"

We stepped away from the gate so that we wouldn't be trampled by our own men. Juma was already leading them to the VIP wing of the palace.

"There was much work to do," Omar said. "It would have done us no good at all if our forces had been chopped to bits by an enemy three times larger than we were. It was necessary to balance the numbers of the armies involved. It took us a while to locate forty barrels of olive oil, and to see to it that they were distributed properly. The truly hard part was to carry two barrels of oil to the top of each gate tower without being noticed."

"As crowded as everything was, I can't imagine how you managed to do that!"

"We told them that the oil was needed to set signal fires, to alert the rest of the city that we were really under attack. We even got the soldiers in the towers to help us carry it up. When they went back inside to go back to sleep, we poured the oil down on the inside of the towers where the Arabs were again sleeping on the steps, and lit it afire."

"And that big building that's burning?" I asked.

"Oh, that was the main barracks. The oil was conveniently stored in the basement there. It was a simple matter of opening the barrels and leaving a stub of a candle burning in the spilled oil. We then tied all of the doors shut and let things take their course. I believe that we have burned six to eight thousand of them this night. Perhaps several thousand more."

"Death by fire," I said. "That's a rough way to go."

"I do not believe that there are any good ways to die, Conrad, but surely, it is preferable for it to happen to someone else, and not to one's own self!"

The few Arab soldiers we saw were busily trying to fight the fires, and weren't worrying about us at all.

"I suppose that we should see how things are going in the Vizier's quarters," I said.

"And I think that it would be better for us to wait a bit. Our soldiers have many years of hate to work out of their systems, and it would be best to just let them do it. Neither you nor I wish to see the things that are going on in there, just now. And if we tried to restrain them, they could easily turn on us. Let it alone, Conrad."

It seemed cowardly to simply let an atrocity take place, but I could see the wisdom of it. Unless the entire leadership of this city was destroyed, we would never be secure here. Someone would always be starting a revolt against us, every revolt would cost many thousands of lives, and one of them would probably succeed, eventually. Our plans to end slavery in Africa would then come to nothing.

Silently, I nodded my agreement.

Omar and I found our way to the roof of the palace itself, to keep an eye on things. In a half an hour, the fires had burned themselves out. The walls of the towers and buildings had been of plastered limestone blocks, but the floors and roofs had been made out of wood. The barracks building and all of the gate towers were gutted, with no hope of any survivors.

A crowd of several hundred Arab soldiers was milling around.

"Listen to me, people!" I shouted down to them. "The Vizier is dead! His family is dead! His top people are all dead! Most of your army is dead! You have fought a war, and you have lost it! If you want to be dead, too, we can arrange that! Or, if you would prefer to live, all that you have to do is go away, now. In a few days, we will be needing some experienced soldiers and policemen. If you are willing to swear allegiance to the new regime, we will soon be hiring. Perhaps, promotions will come quickly."

An officer in the crowd asked, "And who are you, to be telling us these things?"

"I am Conrad Stargard, Hetman of the Christian Army. Some of your former leaders were fools enough to try to make a slave out of me. Now, I have defeated them, and you, in just three days."

"Ha! And maybe I am Ghingus Khan!"

In one smooth motion, I drew my bow and put an arrow through the man's heart. He fell over dead.

"Does anyone else here doubt my word!" I shouted.

No one answered.

"Then go home!"

And they did!

Chapter 25 The Devil is in the Details

It was dawn before Omar and I finally entered the palace proper. Juma came over, chewing on a human forearm.

I said, "It's very strange, but I'm almost getting used to seeing things like that."

"The Vizier. He is old and stringy, but there is much manna here," he explained. "Where have you two been?"

"There was the rest of the palace complex to be attended to," Omar said. "We take it that the senior leadership of the city is no more?"

"Yes, we attended to that, first thing," Juma said.

"Have you seen Sir Stephan?" I asked.

"He took a spear in the leg when we rushed the palace here. He'll live, but he won't be walking for a while," Juma said.

"What of the palace slaves?" I asked.

"Those who claimed to be slaves are locked in the dungeon below, although I think that many of them are liars. Those women that you were so worried about are locked in the north tower, unharmed, for the most part."

"For the most part?"

"Well, most of them have been raped a few times, but that's only to be expected. I told the men not to be too rough on them. I don't think that any of the young ones were killed at all."

"The young ones," I said.

"Yes. You said that our men would be wanting those women, even for wives, so all of them young enough and the least bit attractive were spared. Even the little girls."

"You killed the older women?"

"Of course! Of what possible use is an old woman? Anyway, they were too dangerous to keep around! When you have killed an old woman's husband and all of her sons, she won't stop until either you are dead, or she is. The latter is preferable, from my point of view."

Before I could say anything, Omar said, "You are wise, Juma."

I let it go. What was done, was done, and I needed Juma and Omar.

I said, "Well, there is still work to be done. Call the Captains together, Juma. We have to set up our defenses here, and then bring our wounded out of the west city gate, along with the booty and the arsenal we won there. I think that most of the arsenals here were in the gate towers and the main barracks, and that they have been burned. We have to get the kitchens going for our men, and for our prisoners. And we have to get this place cleaned up," I said. "I expect that we can get the old palace staff to help us with much of this."

"This is all true," Omar said. "Equally important, though, we must make a proclamation to the city, stating what we have done, declaring our victory, and explaining the new rule that they will be under. We must have this read many times, in all of the market places of the city."

I said, "I would think that Omar would be the person to write that proclamation, but that the three of us together should decide exactly what should be said."

"I want no part of it," Juma said. "I was trained in the arts of war, not those of peace. I will go set up our defenses here, and send a thousand men back to the west gate for our people and our loot."

"As you wish, Juma," I said as he left. "So, Omar, shall we write a proclamation?"

"Soon. But I found this gold coin on the ground, and I consider it to be lucky. I propose to flip it in the air while you predict the fall of it. This will decide who gets first choice of apartments here, since I believe that Juma will prefer to live outside. His people do not like stone walls and heavy roofs overhead."

I called 'heads', but it came down 'tails'.

"Perhaps it is a lucky coin, for you at least," I said. "Go and chose your quarters, my friend. But please tell me where you found the second best quarters."

I found paper, a pen, and ink, and started writing up what I thought were the important points of our proclamation.

First, I stressed that while we were in a position to enslave every Arab in the city, we wouldn't be doing that. Since man was made in God's own image, slavery is an offense against God (or Allah), and was hereby forbidden. All slaves in the City of Timbuktu were immediately to be freed. From this day on, the buying, selling, and ownership of human beings was punishable by death, and the confiscation of all property.

Former slaves and former slave owners were encouraged to be sensible, however. For a three month period, freedmen and freedwomen were encouraged to work for their former masters in return for food, housing, and a small salary. Permanent arrangements that were acceptable to all parties involved were also acceptable to the city's new rulers.

The farming land that the city owned would be given in small plots to freed slaves, providing that they worked the land for two years. They could sell the surplus of what they grew as they wished. After two years of this, if they had proven that they were decent farmers, their ownership of the land would be free and clear.

Workers would be hired by the city to keep the irrigation pumps going until such time as better machinery could be built. It was planned to expand the amount of land irrigated, to increase the food supply.

Freedom of Religion was declared.

Freedom of Transit was declared.

The Right of Departure was declared.

And lastly, every adult in the city was obligated to swear an Oath of Fealty to Juma, Omar, and to myself. They might be required to repeat this oath at any time. The breaking of this oath was punishable by death. Failure to take the oath would result in expulsion from the city, with all of their real property escheating to the city, although they could take their chattel property with them.

Omar came back, and said, "The apartment that I think that you will want is at the top of that staircase, to the left. Mine is to the right. Your apartment is actually larger than mine, but I liked the balcony and the terrace on the one to the right."

I said, "It will be as you wish. Do you know if any sort of treasury was found here? We will need a supply of money, before long."

"No one said anything about a treasury, but I suppose that one must exist. I shall make some inquiries, and conduct a search if necessary."

"Good. But for now, read this and see what you think."

Omar stared at what I had written for a moment, then turned the sheet sideways and looked at it again, and finally handed it back to me. "Perhaps you should read this to me," he said.

I looked at what I had written, and realized that while it was in Arabic, I had written it in Polish phonetic script!

I laughed, "I guess that while you taught me to speak Arabic, you never taught me to write it!"

"You will recall that at the time, there was a lack of certain useful items, such as pens, ink, and paper."

"True. I'll read it to you," I chuckled.

I read through it all, while he took notes.

"This business of freeing the slaves, and not enslaving the Arabs. I take it that you are adamant about this?"

"Absolutely!" I said, "Remember that we started all of this when we both witnessed a miracle! I believe that all of this happened because God was offended by what He saw, and that He had us put an end to it! How else could we have won every battle, with the odds so heavily against us every time?"

"How, indeed? Then it will be as you say. But it will be more difficult to accomplish than you imagine."

"Nothing is difficult when you have God on your side!"

"Your faith is heartening." Omar said, "I agree with distributing the city agricultural land to the freed slaves. There are crops growing out there that must be harvested. Thanks to our revolt, there are now many fewer mouths to feed, but the freed slaves will want to eat more and better food than they got before. But what about this new machinery that you promise? Can it really pump water without slaves, or other men, working at it?"

"Certainly! In Europe, I have built many such machines, of many types. They can be powered by wind, or by water, or even by fire! They are far more efficient than slaves, since they don't revolt against their masters, they don't have to be fed, and they work all night as well as all day."

"I suppose that I must take that on faith. What exactly do you mean by 'Freedom of Religion'?"

I said, "I mean that every person's relationship with God is his own business. He can be a Christian, or a Jew, or a follower of Islam, or anything else that he wants to be. The government, by which I mean us, doesn't have the right to say anything about it, providing that he obeys the law. This is really a practical necessity, since you are Islamic, I am a Christian, and neither of us is quite sure just what Juma is! Yet we all need each other! What else can we say except that it is an individual choice?"

"I see what you are saying, but many in this city will be very offended by it! They believe that their way is the only way that is permitted by Allah. Many are willing to die for their beliefs!"

"If they are eager to do so, I am sure that Juma would be willing to accommodate them. By the way, I think that we should make him the head of our army, here."

"I agree with that last thought, Conrad. He has a sort of radiant power about him that makes men want to follow him. Do you think that there might be something to this manna thing he speaks so much of?"

"I don't know. All that I'm sure of is that I would not like to be forced to wage war against him!"

"I say amen to that!"

I said, "I also think that you would be the best man to be in charge of the civil government here. Your youthful training in the law would come in handy, I think."

"It would surely be immodest for me to say so, but I have long thought that I would make a very good City Manager. Certainly, I would love to try my hand at it! But what of you? Where do you see your own place in the governance of Timbuktu?"

"I think that for a start, I will build a number of useful machines here. Eventually, though, I will have to return to my own people. I have two wives and many children, back in Poland."

"Then it shall be as you wish it, my friend. Some day, you must again pay us a visit here in Africa!"

"Or perhaps you would want to visit with me in Poland. I can promise you a fine time there!"

He said, "Perhaps I shall. But there is work to be done, today! Now, tell me about this 'Freedom of Transit'"

I said, "It is simply that anyone may travel wherever he wishes, taking his property with him, without paying duties on it, providing that he obeys the law."

"Hmmm. No customs or gate fees?"

"That's right. Free trade enriches everyone."

"Very well," Omar said. "And this 'Right of Departure'?"

"That is a standard law in Europe that ensures that other forms of human bondage are also forbidden, including serfdom and debt bondage. Any adult may simply leave and go elsewhere, except for convicted criminals and soldiers just before a battle."

"And this last item, this 'Oath of Fealty', what exactly should it say?"

"I was going to let you write that one, Omar. Basically, I just want them to promise to be good, obedient citizens."

"Very well, I think that I can write this proclamation now, but it will be the work of some hours. I suggest that you spend some time sorting through the slaves in the dungeon, and putting as many of them as possible to work around here, cleaning up this mess. If a man has strong, rough hands, he was probably a slave. If he has well trimmed and perfumed hair, he probably wasn't. Oh, yes. And if you find a scribe who says that he can make fair copies in Arabic, please send him to me. I once had a very good hand for writing, but they cut it off."

I figured that if he could joke about it, it couldn't be troubling him too much.

I gathered up a few dozen of our soldiers, to act as a backup for me, and headed down to the dungeon. I started out by telling the six hundred odd men and boys down there that if they had been slaves or honest workingmen, they had nothing to fear. We were freeing all of the slaves in the city, and would be hiring many people to do the work that was needed. I stressed that getting their freedom also gave them the freedom to starve, if they didn't find useful work.

Then I took them aside and talked to them one at a time. Most of the men were menials of one sort or another, and if they looked the part, I asked them if they wanted their old job back, but with pay, now. We had everything from floor scrubbers to scribes to pastry chefs down there.

Most of them accepted my offer, although we hadn't worked out a pay schedule, yet.

But there were thirty five of them who just didn't look like what they claimed to be. Like one guy who said that he was a gardener, but who had beautifully manicured fingernails. I had them locked back up, resolving to see if I could get anyone to vouch for them.

It was late afternoon before I finished the job.

I looked up Sir Stephan in the palace infirmary, and found him well bandaged, but in good spirits.

"I heard that you put Juma in charge of the army, my lord."

"Yes. So many of our men were originally from his tribe, and his people are well trained, but with different weapons and tactics than we are used to. And, of course, you weren't available for the job. Then too, eventually we're going to have to figure out a way to get back to Poland. You have a lot of accumulated pay and leave time built up, and a few promotions coming!"

"I'll be up and around soon, sir, and help you plan our trip."

"Good man! But now there other things that I have to attend to."

I soon found Juma and Omar eating normal food in a small dining room off the kitchen.

Omar said, "Ah, Conrad! You must come and taste this Baklava. It is the finest that I have ever eaten!"

"So the pastry chef I sent to the kitchen really was a chef, eh?" I said.

"Oh, yes! And the others you released all seem to be doing well, including the scribe. He almost has twenty fine copies of the proclamation finished. I have already started to send out men with good voices to read them aloud in the market places!"

Juma said, "I had to make one small change in the proclamation, to insure that all of the people from my tribe came to meet me here. I want them in the army that you have given me command of."

"This sounds reasonable," I said. "But tell me what the proclamation actually said."

Omar said that he did not have a copy of it with him, but that he could recite it from memory. It was a typically Arabian flowery thing, calling on Allah every second line, telling in extreme detail about how my hand had grown back, and how our revolt was doing the work of God. Allah had been with us in every battle, and our enemies had no choice but to die before us. It said that while the people had never shown any mercy to us, we would be merciful to them, and not enslave them it turn. It eventually got around to explaining the new laws. And then there were as many literary flourishes at the end as there were in the beginning.

"Well, it wouldn't fly in Cracow," I said, "But I suppose that it's what's needed here."

Omar said, "Thank you."

Juma said, "And how went your day in the dungeons?"

"There were thirty five of those so called 'slaves' that I wasn't sure of. They are still locked up down there. Perhaps tomorrow, Omar here could look in on them. There must be someone around here who can identify them, one way or another. Free those who deserve it, and have Juma here kill the rest of them, I suppose."

"We will see to it," Omar said.

I said, "Has anybody looked into the other three city gates? We took the west gate, but the others still should have enemy soldiers in them."

"I have. They still have a few soldiers in them, but most of them were sent here to guard the palace. And those few soldiers that are left have all sworn fealty to us. It was easier to do it that way than to fight our way in and kill them," Juma said.

"Good idea," I said. "Now, what does anybody know about the city treasury? Has it been found?"

"Yes," Omar said, "And it is very extensive! I truly believe that we could go for several years without collecting any taxes at all!"

"That's a relief! Now I know that we will be able to pay all of the hundreds of people that I hired today! But don't even think about cutting taxes. We will have to pay free men to do all of the work, now, and not just give bad food to slaves! Lastly, how do I get a bath around here?"

"There is a large and beautiful public bath in the building to the west of this one, but I think that Jasmine might have something prepared for you in your new apartment," Omar said.

"Then, I won't keep her waiting! I wish you gentlemen a good evening."

Omar said, "It will be a better evening for me if Jasmine fulfills her promise to me!"

"I'll remind her of that."

Chapter 26   Omar's Conjugal Visit

I went to the top of the steps to find Jasmine leading eight beautiful, full bodied, and scantily clad young women into Omar's apartment. They reminded me of the ladies on the cover art that an American artist named Frazetta was famous for.

Jasmine said, "Omar said that he was entitled to four women, and talked about what they should look like, but he didn't tell me much else. Four of these girls were slaves before, and four were from the old nobility. It will give him some choice, although they are all of his religion," Jasmine explained.

"Should I go and tell him about what awaits him?" I asked.

"I would suggest that you don't, my lord. They will need some time to get his place tidied up, among other things. Let it be a surprize."

"I'm sure that it will be! Tell the girls to be gentle with him, won't you? He's an old man."

"They will make him young again," Jasmine said with a smile as she led me into my own apartment.

I had three nice surprises of my own waiting for me. A blond, a brunet, and a redhead. They were all very young and slender, they were naked, and they were kneeling in a line, awaiting me!

"These are Tatiana, Maria, and Colleen. Like me, they were all born Christians. I thought that you might be more comfortable among your own kind, and a man of your station deserves more than a single servant," Jasmine said.

"Uh, welcome, ladies," I said. "Thank you, Jasmine. I suppose that I'll be able to figure out a way of paying you all properly, somehow."

"But you have plenty of money, my lord."

"I do?"

"Of course!" Jasmine said, "You have Hajji's money chest, for starters. That's enough to maintain this small of a household for twenty years, at least. Plus, your share of the palace treasury must be a thousand times that."

"Why didn't you tell me about this money chest earlier?"

"Because you never asked me, my lord?"

"You know, I've heard that answer before. Show me Hajji's money chest, and then I'll be wanting dinner, followed by a bath. It's been another very long day. But first, get me out of this armor!"

The girls were all embarrassed when I insisted that they sit down and eat with me, since that wasn't the way that they had been trained. I explained that this was my household and it would be run according to my rules. Here, we all ate the same food, and we ate it together.

Arabs all sat on cushions on the floor. It gave me cramps in my legs. I resolved to get some tables and chairs made ASAP.

Despite the fact that I was now dressed in one of Hajji's elaborately decorated silk robes, I kept all of the girls naked. At their young ages, they looked better that way. There are limits to equality, after all.

I soon found out that each of them played a musical instrument or two, including Jasmine. She played a very small version of an Indian Sitar. She called it a Baby Sitar. Honest!

Music and dancing were apparently part of the training course for young women around here, along with cooking, cleaning, and properly serving their men. No time was 'wasted' on reading, writing, and arithmetic, not on a woman, anyway, since they had to be ready before they reached puberty.

Among the Arabs, the women provide the entertainment, and the men sit back and enjoy. It was a system with much to be said for it, if you were a man.

We were half way through an excelent meal when there was a knock on the door. The girls looked confused. This disturbance wasn't supposed to happen!

"Never mind," I said. "I'll get it." I took my sword with me, since things had been violent of late.

Juma was standing there.

"Do I interrupt you?"

"Not at all! Come in. We were just having some very good stewed lamb. You must sit down and join me and my new family."

The girls were suddenly covering their breasts with their hands, acting embarrassed about being naked in front of a man who wasn't their lord.

"Girls," I said, "I say again, this household will be run according to my rules. My people don't much care about nudity, and neither do Juma's. Serve him some food, and then sit down. Except for you, Jasmine. It's your turn to dance for us."

Jasmine got up and danced something smooth, slow, and sensual to the music of Maria's flute and Colleen's drum, a wide topped, narrow bottomed thing that she called an aouood, I think.

When Jasmine finished with an elaborate bow, I said, "What can I do for you, Juma? Is there something that you wanted to speak to me about, or is this just a pleasant social call?"

"Oh, there were a few details concerning the army that I was going to talk over with you, but they don't seem very important just now. It can wait until the morning. You seem to have a very comfortable existence, here."

"Happiness must be found within one's self, my brother, but friends, comfortable surroundings, and lovely women help a lot. I hope that you are beginning to think about what we talked over last night, about your tribe still being alive, inside of you."

Juma said, "I have been thinking, yes, but to live in these brick buildings, with these heavy roofs above us, it seems so unnatural to me."

"No one said that you had to live inside of the palace, if you don't want to. You could live in the courtyard, or out in the fields, if you like. You could even build a village of the sort used by your people on top of this very palace! It has a big, flat roof, you know. You could bring in the kinds of plants and animals that you are used to. I could build you wind powered pumps to water the plants and give drink to your people. Indeed, there are the thick tops of the palace walls to consider, and even the walls of the entire city. Can you imagine the difficulties that an enemy would have if he was forced to invade us right through one of your villages?"

"That is a very interesting thought! I will go up there in the morning with some of my people, and we will discuss it. There are over six thousand of us here now, you know, and more are turning up every hour."

I said, "This is excellent! We will have a fine, strong army. Have any of the women of your tribe been found?"

"No. There are plenty of Black women here, but none are from my tribe."

"Not good enough, eh? Well, here's another idea. There are many slavers in this city who are now out of business. There must be women from your tribe still living among your old enemies down south of here. We could hire some of the slavers to visit those other tribes and buy your women back. We have plenty of money in the treasury, after all. Then when they get back here with your women, we will free your ladies, and they will then be available for marriage to you and your tribesmen."

"That is an astounding idea, Conrad! Yes, yes, it might be possible! I was so afraid that we would end up watering down our sacred blood with the blood of these Arabs!"

"I'm glad that you are encouraged. Also, you know that not all of the people here are Arabs. These four ladies are Christians, for example, and were all born in Europe."

"They are indeed lovely, but you do not understand the customs of my tribe. One could have such women as servants, even as lovers, but a wife? A wife is something very special, and must be of the true blood. Especially for a nobleman like myself."

I said, "Well, for the time being, consider taking some of the local Black women on as servants, at least. Someone who at least looked like your own women might be comforting. But on the subject of the customs of your tribe, I do have something to ask of you."

"Ask, and it will be granted to you."

"Thank you. It has to do with cannibalism. You understand that this is a very offensive practice to many of the peoples of this world. I ask two things of you. The first is that while I can understand the eating of your slain enemies, as a practical matter during warfare, I beg you to not kill anyone for the sole purpose of eating them."

"But we don't do that, Conrad. There would be no manna in it."

"I am relieved to hear it. The second is that you be very discreet with these cannibal feasts of yours. Please do them out of sight of the relatives of the people that you are eating, and clean up the remains such that no one will find out what has happened. We must live among these people peacefully, after all. Consider that the money to pay your army must ultimately come from them."

"As a favor to you, it shall be as you ask."

"Thank you. Things have been quiet in the city today, and I very much want this to continue."

"It is a small thing, in return for all that you have done for me and mine."

"The meal is over, and there is another thing that I would do for you. The bathtub here has room for ten people in it. Would you like to join us in a bath? Along with a shave and a haircut, of course. Jasmine, at least, is very skilled when it comes to doing these things. We shall discover what the others can accomplish shortly."

"I accept gladly, Conrad. And I have a small gift of my own. It was taken from a captured Christian ship, but the Arabs don't use it. They call it brandy."

"Your gift is greatly appreciated, my friend. And, can you get any more of it?"

"Perhaps. At least I know where to ask about it."

"Wonderful! Jasmine, this is a liquor best drunk in small amounts out of a very large glass, so that one can enjoy the aroma. Is such a thing available?"

"Oh, yes, my lord. There is a wide variety of glassware here."

"Good. Then get three big glasses. One for me, one for Juma, and one for the rest of you to taste it, since I really don't think that you girls will like brandy."

I think that I might have been drinking out of a flower vase, but after nine months without a drink, I didn't much care. The girls all tasted the brandy, made faces, and left their glass unfinished. Juma's approach to drinking brandy resembled a Russian drinking vodka. He held the glass up, smiled, and chugged it down in one gulp. I sipped contentedly from my own glass.

"Juma, this is excellent! All I need now is a cigar, and I'd be in heaven!"

"What might a cigar be?" He asked.

"It's the rolled up leaf of a plant that grows far away from here. You light it on fire and inhale the smoke."

"Well, my people have something similar to that, except that we put the shredded leaves into a wooden pipe, and inhale the fumes from there. I bought some of it today from one of my new men, who had been a slave here in the city. Would you like to try some?"

"Yes," I said. "I definitely would."

He packed his pipe and lit it from one of the oil lamps, before passing iT to me. It wasn't tobacco. It might have been marijuana, but I had never had any experience with that sort of thing. But the evening became more colorful!

The girls were not at all adverse to smoking with us, since they were obviously familiar with whatever it was.

We were about to get into the tub when there was another knock at the door. Again, I answered it, sword in hand.

"Omar! Please come in! We have just finished eating, but there is plenty of stewed lamb left. Or perhaps, you would want to join us in a bath."

"Actually, I just dropped by to give you some gold and silver, Conrad. Juma and I received our monthly allotments earlier, as has everyone in our army, but I forgot to bring you yours. I have eaten a month's supply of pastries this afternoon, and I will not be able to eat again for some time, but a bath would be nice."

"You will be welcome, but, you know, perhaps you would be well advised to simply go home. You see, Jasmine has fulfilled her promise to you, and eight lovely girls, carefully selected to meet or exceed your exacting specifications, are awaiting your pleasure just across the hall."

"And you took this long to tell me about it?! I shall see you in the morning, Conrad! Late in the morning!"

Omar left very briskly, with my bag of gold still in his hand, and we all laughed about it.

"He was so anxious that he left with your gold undelivered!" Juma laughed.

"Omar has been living for many years in a barrel, and completely without feminine company! The gold is no big thing. Anyway, I have Hajji's gold, so I am not in want. But thinking about it, you were the one who actually killed Hajji. Maybe that gold is rightfully yours."

"Keep it, Conrad! I got his manna. You are welcome to his gold."

The bathtub was a big brass affair, with a small charcoal furnace built into the bottom to keep the water warm, and a huge lid to keep the heat in when it wasn't in use. Juma and I were soaked, scrubbed, shampooed, manicured, pedicured, shaved and barbered. He had adopted the Mohawk hairstyle that Jasmine had given me, as had a surprisingly large percentage of the men in our army. With that kind of flattery heaped on me, I didn't have much choice but to have the girls renew my own weird hairdo.

I offered him the services of one of my servants for the night, but Juma declined.

"I think that I will find my way up to the palace roof, and watch the stars from up there," he said.

When he was gone, I said, "Well, ladies, who wants to be first?"

Chapter 27   Building A New Christian Army

I enjoyed all of my ladies again in the morning, the best time for lovemaking, and then after breakfast, I lingered a while over a second lovely cup of coffee. Like Jasmine was that first morning, the new girls were fascinated with all of the new things to taste. Damn the bastards who had kept them so deprived!

I said, "The four of you are a good crew. I am satisfied with you, and will retain your services. Jasmine will be my head of household. Obey her, girls! But tell me, Jasmine, how many Christians are there in the women's quarters just now? The palace's North Tower, I mean."

"I'm not sure, my lord, but I think about forty."

"Well, some day, I will be able to go back to my home in Poland, and when I do, I intend to take with me all of the Christians who want to return. If we were to leave these women in the tower, they would eventually be dispersed among our troops here. I think that you should go to them and offer them the possibility of joining my household. That way, they would be together when the time comes to move."

"But, my lord, there isn't room in this apartment for so many people!"

"Are the other apartments around here all taken?"

"No, my lord. They are mostly empty."

"Then just commandeer the space needed, and do it in my name. Use Hajji's money to keep them well supplied with food and other things that they need. Another thing. Sir Stephen was wounded when we attacked this palace yesterday morning. He is down in the palace infirmary. Have him carried up and installed in a nice apartment near here, and set him up with a suitable number of attractive Christian servants. I think that he might heal faster in pleasant company. Also, he had two of his men, members of the Christian Army, with him. Find them, and set them up with apartments and servants, too. All of this is at my expense."

"To hear is to obey, my lord."

"Good. And help me into my armor. Things have been quiet lately, but I'm not a very trusting sort of man. I have many things to do, and I probably won't be back until evening."

The ostrich plumes on my helmet had been in a sorry state after the recent battles, but Jasmine had found replacements for them. Lovely things. If we ever get home, I'll try to bring a bale of ostrich plumes with me.

I found Juma and a few dozen of his men on the palace roof.

"We can do it, Conrad," Juma said. "With the flat roofs in the palace complex, the palace walls, and about a third of the city walls, we have room to build a proper hut for every member of my tribe, and there will be plenty of room for future expansion."

"Good. I gather that you like being high up in the air."

"Yes, of course. We are from a mountainous country."

"I didn't know that. I've been thinking that if we put a windmill on top of every gate tower in the palace and the outer walls, we will be able to supply you with water, as well as having running water in the palace and many places in the city."

"Hmm. I have seen water pour, but I have never seen it run! I've never even seen it crawl, let alone walk! I don't know what you are talking about, Conrad, but

I'll trust you. We can always carry water up in buckets, for that matter."

"Very well, I'll settle for your trust, for now, but you will like what I build for you," I said. "Have you seen Omar around yet?"

"He's been up for a while, and smiling hugely! Just now, I think that you'll find him down in the dungeon."

"Thank you. Plan your new villages carefully. Make sure that what you build is what you really want. Discuss things with your people from all levels of your society. On the outer city walls, put your people in four groups, one around each of the outer gates. And get together with Omar later about hiring those slavers who will get your women back for you."

"I've already done that. He promises to start on it in the afternoon."

I found Omar in the dungeon, interviewing the last of the prisoners in the same room that I had used yesterday.

"So, Omar. What have you learned?" I asked.

"I believe that eleven of these men are either honest workingmen, or former slaves, and I have had them released. Two very well groomed gentlemen turned out to be barbers who shaved each other. Three others were, I think, homosexuals, but I am not minded to kill a man for that, no matter what I think of his personal habits. And one fellow was a gardener who had been scheduled to be married to a girl who worked in the kitchens the very morning of our attack! Naturally, he had had himself carefully shaved, barbered, and manicured in preparation for this important event. The two will be married tomorrow morning, incidentally, if you wish to attend."

"And the other two dozen of them?"

"They were cowardly noblemen who chose to abandon their parents, their wives, and their children to our army, while trying to hide among the slaves that they had previously owned. We should kill them, but not publicly, I think. We'll just do it down here."

"I agree. Have Juma do it, if he wishes, for I am a good warrior, but a poor executioner. I need your help on another matter."

"Yes?"

"You will soon be arranging with some slavers to buy Juma some of his women back from his tribe's old enemies."

"True, I promised to do this for him, just as you and Jasmine promised to find me some suitable women."

"I trust that at least some of them suited you?"

"They ALL suited me very well! My religion permits me only four wives, but as many servants as I can afford. Now, it happens that I can afford many! Eventually, I may choose to marry some of them, but why rush things?"

"Why, indeed? Enjoy yourself. But just now, I need to make some contacts with construction companies around this city, as well as with metalworkers and carpenters, and I don't know how to do that. Can you help me with this?"

"I would be delighted to, Conrad, but I won't be able to get to it for weeks, at least! Delegations have been arriving all morning from everyone from the clergy to university presidents to the fishmonger's guild! They all have proposals to make to me. I will be busy from dawn to dusk for a very long time! Even now, I have four secretaries doing nothing but meeting with them and setting up appointments!"

"I understand, my friend. Do your job as best as you can, and I will do my work without your able help."

"Thank you, Conrad!"

"Oh. You are being careful of security, aren't you? As the civil leader of this city, you should have several hundred good fighting men around you at all times! And you might wear some decent armor under your robes, just in case. We have not settled well into this city yet, and we must be cautious."

Omar smiled, opened his robes, and displayed some very good chain mail. "And yes, I have retained those soldiers who helped me take this palace as a personal guard, almost three hundred of them. I trust that you have done something similar?"

"You know? I haven't! But I will. Soon."

So. Omar had his work set out before him, and so did Juma. I would have to solve my problems on my own. I'd done this before, and last time, it had been my ladies who had gotten things done for me!

I went back up to my apartment, to find nobody there. A walk around the upper level of the palace and a few questions taught me that Maria was getting Sir Stephan moved into his own apartment, Colleen and Tatiana were out looking for Sir Stephan's two surviving subordinates, and that Jasmine was getting forty odd Christian ladies settled into new apartments on this level.

I left word for Jasmine to come back and talk to me in our apartment, as soon as she was free.

I found Juma again, and he agreed with my plan to form all of the Christians in our army into a separate unit, under me, to act as my body guard. They would meet me in the palace courtyard at noon.

I went back to my apartment and started writing down and prioritizing all the things I had to do. First I had to contact construction companies, metalworkers and carpenters. I was hoping to find some of these skilled workers among our freed slaves.

I also needed to get the city owned farmland surveyed, and broken up into the right sized plots. How big should they be? What plants were currently growing where? I hadn't been able to see much of the fields from that barrel.

On the design side of things, I needed to design an undershot waterwheel to power one of the existing Archimedes Pumps and a windmill to fit on top of one of the burned out palace gate towers to pump water. The windmill would need a big storage tank near the top. We'd use a single windlass to raise the portcullis, instead of the current, and silly, two windlass system. I also needed to design a windmill to grind grain, using most of a gate tower as a grain silo. With Juma's men living on the adjacent walls, the towers wouldn't be needed to house soldiers.

After it was designed, I would put one of the construction companies to work with a contract for one of each of the above machines. Once we got it working properly, we'd turn put out contracts and make many of each.

And I wanted to get some proper uniforms made up for myself, Sir Stephan, and his two men. There were plenty of women around to do that. Maybe, eventually, we'd have some decent armor made up in the style of that used by the Christian Army. And maybe even some firearms!

None of this stuff was the least bit original. I'd done it all before, and I could do it again.

My reasons for doing all of this were several. For one thing, I personally enjoy building things and seeing them work. For another, I wanted to show the people of

Timbuktu that we had positive contributions to make to the city, and that machines could do much of the drudge work that once was done by slaves. Also, by spending the city treasury on useful civic projects, we would be putting money back into the local economy. This would give the people a feeling of prosperity that would be good for our cause. Ask any politician.

There would be a lot more to do before I was through, of course, but it was a start.

Jasmine got back, and I told her about the construction projects I had in mind, and how I needed to make contacts with various companies.

She said, "I'm not the one to do that for you, my lord. Until a few days ago, I was a slave girl, owned by a soldier. I've never met anyone involved with anything like that. But many of the Islamic women had wider contacts. I'll ask around this afternoon."

I guess that was the difference between the Polish peasant girls, who had been so helpful to me in the past, and an Arab's slave girl. A peasant could somehow manage to get just about anything done. Slaves led terribly restricted lives.

"Good. I'd appreciate it if you would."

We had an early lunch, and it was time to meet my Christian body guards. My first surprise was how many of them there were. Sir Wladyclaw's talk of millions of Christians enslaved by the Moslems might not have been an exaggeration after all! There seemed to be perhaps two thousand of them in this city alone, and Timbuktu was a long way from Europe. And these were all men. Surely, there were some women and children here, besides.

The courtyard was packed solid. I had to go up to a balcony to speak to them.

"Listen up, my fellow Christians!" I shouted to them in my best command voice. "I am Conrad Stargard! I am the Hetman of the Christian Army! I started this revolt in the first place! I am heartened by how many of us there are here! There is safety in numbers! Now that we have gotten our freedom, I intend to see to it that we keep it! I also intend to see to it that we all have the opportunity to get home again!"

This got me the cheer that I thought it would.

"Getting us organized is going to take a lot longer than I'd thought it would! I never thought that so many Christians had been captured by the Rag Heads! First off, are any of you members of the Christian Army? Raise your hands!"

At least forty of them raised their hands. I was astounded! We had sent very few men into Africa.

"Okay! You Warriors form a group directly below this balcony! Next, of you others, do any of you have any experience as architects, in construction, or as millwrights? We will also need skilled carpenters, draftsmen, metal workers, surveyors, and masons! Raise your hands!"

There were easily two hundred in this group.

"Okay! You people will please go over to the North-East corner of the courtyard, over there! Next, of those left, do any of you have experience in fighting on horseback, or on camelback? Raise your hands!"

There might have been two hundred and fifty in this group.

"Okay! Please congregate in the South-West corner, over there! Lastly, are there any Christian priests here? Raise your hands!"

There were five of them.

"Fathers, please meet in the center of the courtyard! The rest of you men are sorely needed, but it is going to take us time to get this organized! Please go about your business, and come back here again at noon tomorrow! Then, we will be ready to talk to you all!"

Perhaps fifteen hundred men left the courtyard, and the rest had enough room to move around. They left, but I had the feeling that we would never be truly separated again!

Once I had four distinct groups formed, I said, "Now then! I want each group to talk things over among yourselves, and if possible I would like each group to pick a temporary leader, someone who I can talk to. I'm going up to my apartment and see if I can find lots of pens, ink, and paper. I want to know who is here, what your stories are, and what your skills are."

I got up to my apartment to find Jasmine just getting back.

"Well, my lord, we got it all done. Forty six Christian ladies, five of their children, and three of your Warriors have all been assigned places on this floor, near here."

The children were all girls. Boy children had all been killed during the initial attack on the palace, since they would of necessity also be the children of the Arab rulers. I imagined that their mothers would hate us for this, but we didn't dare leave alive someone who might foment a future revolt.

"Very good Jasmine! But now you are going to have to do it all over again. I just found another forty one members of the Christian Army, and I want them up here, too."

She had a look of great dismay on her face, but all she said was, "Yes, my lord. To hear is to obey."

"And, I need all of the pens, paper and ink that you can find. Have them brought down to the courtyard. Delegate the task."

She nodded to me, and I went down stairs, again. I needed a better system of communications. Some runners, at least.

I walked over to where our future cavalry was waiting and told them that I needed some runners. Seven would be a good number. I picked the first seven who volunteered, and told the rest that I would be back again with them soon.

I went to talk to the priests. It seems that one of them was Coptic, one was a Roman Catholic, and the other three were Greek Orthodox. I found that the majority of Christians here were Orthodox, since the Mongols who had invaded Russia had discovered that it was more profitable to sell the people there than it was to kill them. The Mongol idea of perfection was to turn Russia from farm land into grazing land for their cattle and horses. The Russian people were just in their way.

None the less, the priests had decided to elect the Roman Catholic as their spokesman, since he was the oldest among them. Perhaps another reason was that the man that he would have to deal with, me, was also a Catholic.

"Fathers, your job here will need the least input from me. I want you to find a suitable building, one that isn't being used, if possible, and to convert it into a Christian Church as soon as possible. If this takes money, come to me. Get the confessionals going as quickly as possible, since too many of us have gone too long without the Sacrament of Confession. Start singing a mass in each variety of our faith, every morning, and five times every Sunday. Also, I want a school set up to teach these people about Christianity. My servant Jasmine, for example, was three years old and with her father on a pilgrimage to Rome when they were attacked by Muslim pirates. She knows nothing of her people's religion. Any questions?"

"We weren't permitted to do this, before", one of them said. "What if we have problems with the authorities?"

"Father, right now, I am the Christian authority in this city. If you have any problems, I can get a thousand soldiers to you quickly. In fact, tomorrow, I will assign several hundred Christian men to you, to protect and assist you."

"That would be most satisfactory, Lord Conrad."

"Good. For now, take these two runners with you. Have one of them find me once you find a suitable building, or if you need something from me. Keep the other around for emergencies."

The man in charge of the horsemen was an Englishman, Sir Percy, the Baron of Smallbridge.

I said, "Gentlemen. One thing that our army is sadly lacking is a wing of cavalry, and you have said that you are horsemen. Does anyone here know where we can get ahold of some horses?"

Sir Percy said, "Well, your grace, there are the palace stables. I've spent the last three years working there. They have almost two hundred good horses in that stable, perhaps fifty fast camels, and a like number of mules. We also have a full tack room, with most of the equipment that we'll need. After that, we should be able to buy anything more that we find necessary in the public markets."

"I didn't even know that there were any palace stables! Get your men sorted out and fitted up. Arrange them in the fashion of the Christian Army, with six Warriors under a knight, six knights under a knight bannerette, and as many bannerettes as you have under a captain. You are appointed temporary Captain. Understood?"

"Only temporary, your grace?"

"It will become permanent once you prove to me that you know what you are doing."

"Yes, your grace. You can count on me."

"Good. Also, I want you to find suitable housing for these men, together in one spot if possible, and near the stables."

"The stables have a third floor for that very purpose."

"Good. Make them your own. I'll be sending you some clerks from my own army, soon, to record the names, skills, and conditions of all of your men. Please cooperate with them."

"Of course, your grace."

"Your men will be needing some servants, and we captured a lot of women, taking the palace. The palace ladies were carefully selected to be very attractive. I'll have two hundred and fifty of them sent to you, later, hopefully this evening. Remember that these are free women, and not slaves. Your men will treat them decently, or they will answer to me! Sex is permissible only if the lady is willing! Is this understood?"

"They will behave in a gentlemanly fashion, or they will answer to me as well, and first!"

"Good. I've taken seven of your men to act as my runners. I want them to be issued horses and equipment, and to live with your men, but they are to be assigned to me. Take these two back for now, and send one of them to me when he knows where the stables are. I'll be wanting two runners with me at all times, each with a saddled horse in front of the palace. Carry on, Sir Percy."

About this time eight women wearing the typical Moslem tents (burnooses?), came down with their arms filled with paper, pens, and bottles of ink. I waved them over to the Christian Army group under the balcony.

"Warriors!" I said to them in Polish, "Who is the ranking man here?"

"That would be me, sir. I'm Captain Meier."

"Then you will of course be in charge of this group."

It turned out that most of my Christian Army troops were from a single ship that had gone down in a storm off the West African coast. They had been separated soon after being enslaved, and many of them hadn't known if any of the others were still alive. It was a tearful reunion for them.

I said, "There are several things that we have to get working on soonest. First, we have to get organized, here. Most of you will be spending the next day or two pretending to be company clerks. I want each of you to fill out a sheet of paper on yourself, with your name and serial number at the top. I want to know your date of enlistment, your rank, and your date of rank. I want to know your age, and about any special skills that you might have. Then, I want a short paragraph on how you happened to end up in Timbuktu. Later, we will do the same thing for every man who was here at noon. Assign each of them a serial number, starting with an "AC", for African Corps. This will all be written in Polish, so I can read it. Understood?"

Forty one men said, "Yes, sir!" in unison.

"It is lovely to hear disciplined troops again! This evening, report to the third floor of the palace. We are arranging some very nice quarters for you up there, near the ones that I've chosen for myself. You'll each be assigned an attractive Christian lady as a servant, but you can trade them around as you like, with the lady's permission. These palace servants are a very attractive bunch! Remember please that these are free women, not slaves. You will treat them with respect! Loving respect, I suppose, if they are willing, but with respect, none the less. I trust that this meets with your approval."

I got the same response as before, but this time there were smiles in it.

"Lastly, the city owned farm land will be distributed to the former slaves of this city. This must be done soon, because there are crops on the land in need of cultivating and harvesting. Some of the men in the technical group are surveyors, but I want the actual maps done by you, bilingually, in Polish and Arabic. I want to know what is growing where, and I want it divided up into plots of a size that one man can handle. Find out how big that is. In this climate, and with irrigation, I expect that the plot of land that one man can properly farm will be smaller than what we are used to in Europe. Later, we will be doing some civic improvements around here, repairing battle damage and installing some wind mills and water wheels, so those of you with technical training will have your work cut out for you. In a few days, we will start teaching most of the men who were here at noon about the fighting techniques of the Christian Army. I expect that the only way we'll get home again will be to fight our way back, and that will take training. We have some interesting times ahead of us, my brothers! You all know what to do!"

The craftsmen were waiting for me. They had decided on an older construction supervisor, a man named Jaccs Dupree, as their leader.

I had them get into lines, one for surveyors, one for masons, one for draftsmen, and so on. I promised to send them a consignment of servants, once they had found someplace where they could live together.

Then I sent them, surveyors first, to my regular troops, to get their paperwork filled out.

It was late before I could enjoy my supper, but I ate it with the intense satisfaction of a man who had laid the foundation for great things. And I even had a little energy left for my girls.

Chapter 28 Progress

The numbers turned out such that there was about one member of the Christian Army for each of the Christian ex-slave girls, plus my own four. Rather than slight Sir Stephan and some of the senior men, I had some of the best looking Arabian girls sent to them to fill out their households.

By the time that we had supplied volunteering ladies to the cavalry and the engineering company, we had just about emptied out the palace's north tower.

There were still a number of ladies who hadn't volunteered to become servants to the soldiers of the new order. I suspected that a lot of them had had their husbands and male children slaughtered during our taking of the palace, so I left them with their grief. Later, I'd ask the priests to talk with them, for what good it would do. In time, perhaps their wounds would heal. Maybe, eventually, they wouldn't hate us so much. Until then, we could afford to feed them, and their daughters.

As to the tower itself, well, we'd find something useful to do with it.

The first morning after my forty-four Christian Army troops were reunited, I had them all meet me on the roof of the palace for our Sunrise Ceremony. I even had Sir Stephan carried up there.

Our right hands raised to the raising sun, I led them in the Oath:

"On my honor, I will do my best to do my duty to God, and to the Christian Army. I will obey the Warrior's code, and I will keep myself physically fit, mentally awake, and morally straight.

"The Warrior's code:

"A Warrior is: Trustworthy, Loyal, and Reverent; Courteous, Kind, and Fatherly; Obedient, Cheerful, and Efficient; Brave, Clean, and Deadly."

There wasn't a dry eye on that roof. We were all home again.

We repeated that oath every morning in the Christian Army.

Juma's method of 'executing' the twenty-four cowardly Arabs who had tried to hide among the slaves wasn't what I had expected. It got three of his own men killed, and six more seriously wounded.

It seems that in his tribe, before a boy could be counted as a man, and have the right to have a family, he had to kill another man in combat, or at least in a fair fight. Many of his tribesmen had not yet done this, so what Juma set up was a sort of gladiatorial contest. The Arab to be executed was given his choice of weapons and put in a large room with a young and unblooded tribesman, who invariably chose the shield and two spears used by the tribe.

It wasn't absolutely fair, since if the Arab killed the Black, he was given a chance to rest up, and then he had to face another opponent. It was an execution, after all. But still, it was reasonably fair.

I watched one of the combats, and then left. It was probably better than just chopping their heads off, I suppose. Death in combat at least gives a man something else to think about than his own inevitable demise.

Omar had begged off from the beginning.

Since the victim died fighting, he had manna now, and was eligible for eating, by the victor's friends and relatives. Blacks who were killed trying to qualify for manhood were eaten as well, by their friends and relatives.

The cooking and eating took place in a locked dungeon, with no one but the Blacks, Omar, and me aware of it.

All of this cannibalism troubled me considerably, but the fact remained that I needed Juma. He had the only trained, disciplined troops in our army.

The next day, very late at night, Juma led his people back to the cellar near the west city gate where they had a thousand human bodies smoking, under guard. They transported them all down to the dungeon, for later eating.

Well, he was being discreet about it.

In a few days, we were starting to get settled in. I was still unhappy with the furniture, but I had a dining room table, big enough to seat twelve people, on order with a local furniture shop, along with six drafting tables and eighteen chairs. My Christian carpenters didn't have the equipment, or probably the skills, to do good furniture work, but they knew who did.

Mostly, my people were rough carpenters, good at building houses and other, simple buildings with simple tools. In an Arabian society, slaves weren't taught the really skilled jobs. These always went to someone's son or nephew.

Juma sent out an expedition to recover his tribe's women. It had two hundred Arab ex-slavers, six hundred pack camels, mostly carrying food and water, and a thousand of his own men as a guard. Except for the leaders, all of the Blacks sent were unblooded. This was to give them a chance to prove themselves. It also meant that they couldn't marry the best women on the way home, unless they killed somebody first! Juma's men themselves carried the gold to buy their women back, not trusting the Arabs. The Arabs would collect their pay when they got back from the three month trip.

I now had six companies of Christian infantry, each Captained by one of my Christian Army soldiers. There was a company of Roman Catholics, one of Copts, and four of Greek Orthodox soldiers. The numbers came out that way, and dividing them by religious sect reduced the chances of friction.

They were each about evenly divided between archers and pikemen, with swords, knives, and axes as secondary weapons. It takes a long time to learn how to use a sword properly, but using an axe is pretty much instinctive. They were all in training, and it might be a while before they had it down pat. They were starting to learn how to march. We had started getting uniforms made, with a triangular Arabian head covering, because of the fierce sun and blowing sand around here.

I had a company of cavalry, headed by Sir Percy, who was proving to be a valuable leader. They were all mounted now, reasonably well armed, and we had a sufficient number of spare horses, purchased in the local markets. Since none of the Christians had any experience in riding a camel, let alone fighting from the back of one, we had lent out the palace's camels to be pack animals for Juma's expedition.

And I had a company of engineers, headed up by Jaccs Dupree, a very competent older man. These people were actually under my direct command, but for administrative purposes, Sir Stephan was in charge.

Sir Stephan was also made the leader of my entire two thousand man personal body guard, even though he wouldn't be up and around for weeks. The men were mostly still in training, anyway. There were several men in my Christian Army group who outranked him, but I simply promoted him to Komander, and that was that. Captain Meier was doubtlessly a good sea captain, but he had no experience with infantry at all. There is much to be said for army discipline!

Juma complained that my surveyors wouldn't let him chop down the orchards of olive trees, date palms, figs trees, coffee trees, pomegranates, grape vines, tangerines, and other fruit trees to use as building materials for his people's huts. I explained to him just how much these trees were worth, and that many of them actually earned more money that one of his troops! I eventually managed to convince him that his men could get by for a while using Arab tents, until such time as some Arab merchants could bring authentic materials up the Niger River, on consignment.

He said that he would send some of his people south with the merchants, to make sure that they brought up the right things.

The surveying teams convinced me that we should not give these orchards, sugarcane plantations, and vineyards to unskilled ex-slaves, since they represented long term investments of considerable value, and could easily be destroyed by clumsy handling. They felt that we should keep ownership of them for ourselves, and to hire skilled workmen to maintain them.

Certainly, when it came to the coffee plantation at least, I agreed with them. I never wanted to be without coffee again!

As it turned out, many of these skilled men were already in the army. Some of our troops had been tending these same plants for many years. We cut deals with them, giving them the orchards that they were familiar with, often far larger that what we gave to the typical ex-slave, with the understanding that they owed us a bit of the profits, and that they could lose them if they were poorly tended.

We also kept the city's herds of sheep and camels. The Arabs hadn't used slaves to tend these animals, and so neither did we. We just re-hired the people who had been taking care of the animals all along.

On Sunday, I finally took a day off, telling everybody that my religion required it.

I did go to the new church, along with my ladies. I carefully coached them that they should dress well, they should expose their faces, and that they should cover their heads, with a hat or a shawl.

The church had been set up, with Omar's permission, in one of the palace's two Mosques, but it didn't have pews installed yet. Later, I offered to pay for some pews, with kneelers, but the priests got into an argument over them. It seems that in an Orthodox Church, one stood up the whole time. I guessed that eventually, we'd need to build at least three churches. That would probably be cheaper, easier, and less stressful than trying to get churchmen to agree on anything!

I spent the rest of the day mostly lazing around, eating, and enjoying my ladies' company. It had been a very long week, and I was tired.

By Monday afternoon, the drawing tables and some of the chairs had been delivered, and drafting instruments had been purchased. We set them up in the library of the bath house. My technical types went to work.

At the same time, the survey of the city's agricultural land had been completed. I was surprised to find out that the people here were growing potatoes, tomatoes, bell peppers, and corn, maize. These were plants that I had brought with me from the modern world when I first came to this centaury. There had been more communication between the Christian world and the Moslem one than I had thought!

Omar got a lottery going to distribute to the former slaves those lands which grew annual plants. He also hired about fifty retired farmers to advise the ex-slaves about the proper techniques of farming in this area.

Omar really was a very good administrator.

And I am a very good engineer. The work I was doing went surprisingly smoothly.

My next task for the surveyors was for them to go down into the wells of the west city gate, to open the secret doors, and to map out where those secret passages went to. The wells themselves had been cleaned of bodies by the palace servants, the day before.

The surveyors were five weeks doing their job!

On two occasions, they found groups of slaves chained down there. They were being kept in storage until we went away! We questioned these people, and Juma went out and settled things up with their former owners, but not in his usual way. Omar insisted on a public trial and execution, so that's what we did.

Juma did convince Omar to let him execute the miscreants in the same manner as he had used last time, but publicly, and without the traditional cannibal feast afterward. The crowds seemed to enjoy the spectacle, and it got our message across, both about obeying the law and about the expertise of Juma's Warriors. And after the executions, we confiscated all of the criminals' property, and handed it out to senior army personnel.

Several hundred newly freed slaves showed up at the palace soon afterward, and we found work for them to do. After a few weeks, a delegation of Jews came to me with a complaint. They said that there were Christian soldiers, Arab soldiers, and Juma's tribal people in our army, but we didn't have a group of Jews.

I said that they were right, and that we would welcome such an addition. We would provide equipment, pay, and training if they would provide the men. Each company was to be captained by one of my own Christian Army Warriors, however.

Soon, we had two more companies of regular infantry in training. They insisted on wearing a Star of David on their uniforms, but I had no objection to that. Also, they said that they wanted to serve under me instead of Juma. I think that many people were afraid of him.

I put them up in the palace's North Tower, since it had been largely emptied of women by now, but I let them find their own girls. Nobody had mentioned any Jewish girls in the palace.

The Jews are a remarkable people. As measured by IQ tests, they are extremely intelligent. In fact, the ultra-conservative Jews are the most intelligent people in the world! Their contributions to medicine, science, and the law have been outstanding!

Yet as a group, they have many times done the stupidest things possible! In hundreds of places, for thousands of years, they have consistently refused to assimilate and adopt to the local culture, and have managed to so anger the people around them that they have been repeatedly thrown out, robbed of all of their goods, and slaughtered.

One would think that any minority group would consider that it might be wise to at least try to assimilate a little in order to get along with the people around them, but this has apparently never occurred to the Jewish people. They believe that they are God's chosen people, and everyone else is a bit inferior to them. As individuals they are often very decent, but as a group, their behavior is completely counter productive. The mind boggles.

But in the Twentieth Century, they turned out some very good Warriors, so we took them in.

I talked with Juma about putting them under my command, and he was agreeable. Actually, I really don't think that he wanted to be responsible for anything but his own people.

Sir Stephan was hobbling around before the underground survey was completed. He brought me their finished drawings, and we were both amazed. The system of secret tunnels was huge! It had obviously been planned and built in very small sections, over hundreds of years, and had many omissions and redundancies, suggesting that the very people who had dug it hadn't know the entire plan. Many tunnels had obviously been started, and then never finished. It was an assassin's paradise! In fact, I think that assassination was the main reason why most of these tunnels had been dug in the first place. Most of the important buildings in the entire city were connected to the system, and dozens of secret entrances were in the palace itself!

I stared at the drawing for a long time before I said, "Do you know what this is?"

Sir Stephan said, "No, sir, I don't. What is it? This is a very good start on a sewer system! But for now, I want every entrance to the palace complex sealed up! And every building where our army is being housed should be treated the same way. Get our masons going at it, soonest. And there is a secret entrance from the street to the palace on the west wall, toward the south. I want that sealed up as well. I'll be damned if I want some assassin bothering me when I'm enjoying an evening with my girls! And then publish this map. Sell a copy to anyone who wants one, and recommend that they seal up the entrances to their own homes."

Omar sent out yet another proclamation on the matter.

Chapter 29 (Sir Walznik's Rescue) The Search for Conrad

Captain Walznik's men had been traveling as peaceful merchants so long that they almost forgot that they were an army patrol. It was definitely more of a search than a combat mission. They had not fired a shot in anger since landing on the first beach. There was warm food and, occasionally, the warmer companionship of a woman at night. There was enough scenery to fight boredom and servants to do the heavy work. Reality returned like a shot. It fact exactly like a shot from a bow.

Warriors Igor and Fritz were riding point when the arrow struck Igor square in the chest. He was still looking down in surprise when spears struck Fritz in the chest and leg. Fritz started to fall from his horse grasping the lance lodged in his leg. Igor simultaneously jumped from his horse and unslung his rifle. As he jumped, the arrow fell away from his chest. Seeing a movement in the underbrush, he snapped off a shot and was rewarded with a grunt of pain. He started to loosen his belt without taking his eyes off the bushes.

They would both be dead already if the Christian Army had not learned the lessons from wars that would never be fought. The stupidest idea in history was that soldiers should go into combat in cotton shirts and felt hats. Governments claimed it was because such soldiers were more maneuverable than ones burdened down with armor. The real reason was that they were cheaper.

Christian Army personnel wore steel helmets and Conrad's nickel plated steel breastplates, at the very least. In actual combat conditions, they would have been covered head to toe in plate armor, but for this mission, they decided to travel light. Unfortunately, it would stop arrows but would usually not stop crossbow bolts or lance points. Fortunately for Fritz, it would slow them down.

Igor reloaded and looked for another target. When none presented itself, he finished removing his belt and began to tourniquet Fritz's leg. He kept one hand near his rifle as he worked. A breath of air behind on his shoulder gave him enough warning to grab his rifle and turn to face the black warrior coming out of the bushes with a spear held high. Basic bayonet training did it's job. He turned, smashed the warriors shield aside with the butt of his rifle, and plunged the bayonet home just below the breastbone. Then he had to kick the body aside before it bled on Fritz's uniform.

Fritz had been watching when he wasn't busy writhing in pain. Now he moved to remove the spear from his leg. Grunting, he asked, "Now who the Hell do you think they were? What were they trying to kill us for? You been banging any of them native girls?"

Unfortunately, his bravado was running short and it was hard not to scream.

Igor knelt beside him and began pouring disinfectant on the leg wound. "How's the chest feel?"

"Bad, but not nearly as bad as the leg. I don't think I'll be able to ride."

Igor began to unbuckle Fritz's jacket. "I don't think you should try. The column will catch up to us soon enough. I'll get the bleeding stopped and we can just wait."

When both of his friend's wounds were bandaged, Igor leaned back against a tree and kept watch on the forest while his friend tried not to groan.

The column reached them about a quarter hour after the attack. They were still where they had fallen. Igor was too tired to move and his companion was being careful not to start bleeding. Neither lifted his head when they heard, "Medic to the front! Injured men!"

Medic Pulaski inspected Fritz's wounds carefully before letting him be lifted on to a stretcher. He had turned to complement Igor on his stitching when he was interrupted by Captain Walznik.

"Report Trooper. What happened here."

Igor did not rise and was not expected to do so.

"A surprise attack sir. You'll probably find that black's friend, or his blood, over there in the bushes. They were waiting on both sides of the road. We were careless and they got us by surprise. They both loosed their weapons before we knew they were there. I got luckier than Fritz."

"Alright, Warrior. Better move along and have the medic check out that scratch on your chest."

Captain Walznik slowly turned looking at the ambush spot. As he turned, he said to Hendricks, "This doesn't make sense. There's a hundred reasons for a hundred men to attack a caravan and there are plenty of reasons for one or two men to try a sneak theft. There's gold and glory enough here for most men but, I just don't see any reason for two men to attack the point guards. The only thing they can get is the clothes on their backs and the horses they're riding and there are easier ways to get horses. Well, maybe it was just an impulse to attack a traveler for his purse."

Hendricks said, "Sometimes the bad guys just don't make sense. Maybe they were just stupid. Not every enemy makes a plan and not every plan an enemy makes is good. However, I think that we should double the point guard to four men and put out some flankers. We don't want to get caught by surprise again."

They had been traveling a well marked dirt road for several days. The wooded terrain had come to seem friendly. There was plenty of water and cool protected glens to camp in. They had been on the road for two months now and had been feeling comfortable. Tonight the perimeter seemed a darker place and the nightly officers meeting was more tense than usual. As they sipped their wine, their eyes strayed to the woods around them.

Banner Hendricks was addressing the guide. "How long do you think we will be in this forest?"

The guide answered immediately, "If we continue to follow the trail the slavers took, at the rate we've been going, about two more weeks. After than we will be in a flat and dry land for 10 or 20 days march. Then we hit the desert. How long it takes will depend upon how much time you spend in the villages. There are no more real cities between here and Timbuktu."

Outside the tent, there were the sounds of an evening camp. Troopers talked, women giggled. The horses could be heard moving around on the stake line. The wood on the fires was fresh enough to crackle and pop.

Captain Walznik listened to the camp and looked worried. "As of tomorrow, we are going to change to order of march. Until we get to a clear area where we can see an enemy coming, the camp followers will follow from the center of the column. We're going to have near and far flankers on both sides and a stronger point and rear guard. That means cold camp or late dinner from now on, but it also means that we can protect our own. Gentlemen, pick your flankers and let them know tonight."

The next morning, the atmosphere was slightly more strained than usual. Everyone was concerned about the change in the order of march. It made the women nervous about their safety and the men grumpy about the prospect of a late dinner and colder camp. They had gotten sloppy about keeping the exact order of march but now the knights kept the men riding with their lances. By noon everyone felt more comfortable. They had pulled up to start the noon meal when shots rang out from the rear of the column. Four lances wheeled without needing orders and galloped toward the rear. The other lances hit the dirt and took defensive positions on both sides of the column. Forward, you could hear the sounds of the advance team returning fast to the camp. Within two minutes of hearing the shots, the column was circled with guards and the quartermaster lance had rounded up the civilians in circle in the center of the formation. All eyes looked outward.

There was silence. Nothing happened. The slowest time in the army is the time waiting for the enemy to attack. You wait forever with adrenalin pouring into your blood making time stretch, and stretch, and stretch.

Eventually more shots were fired in the rear.

A few minutes later a knight's whistle sounded from the same place. Three long whistles followed by three short ones. "All clear! Send Help!"

The medic, Banner Hendricks and two Warriors with stretchers tied to the sides of their horses galloped toward the rear. Everyone remained at the ready until the group returned. Both squads, the medic and the troopers were together. They carried four litters. Two of the faces were covered. Banner Hendricks approached Walznik while the medic started to tend wounded. "We lost the two Russian boys, Alexander and Ivan. The other two say the bastards swung out of the trees like damned apes. They were on top of them before they could draw a bead. The boys still got six of them before they went down. We killed five more of them. They were so busy fighting over the guns and trying to strip the armor off the Warriors that they didn't have time fight back. We lost two rifles, but they didn't get the Warrior's ammo pouches."

A little while later the medic reported, "Alexander got his throat cut and Ivan's neck is broken, probably by some sort of club. The other two got knife wounds and bruises, but they should pull through."

"Thanks, Doc." Walznik turned to the camp and waved his hand in the air.

"Attention. Attention everyone. We now know why they are attacking us. The locals want your rifles and your magic armor. A lot of them are willing to die for the chance to get it. Do not wander away from camp. Warriors, watch the tree tops and the bushes. These attackers came down from the trees like monkeys. Keep an eye peeled at all times."

Well, he thought, Ahmed warned us. He said don't show off the rifles and don't let them get close in. I hope we won't need that part about not facing too many of them at once.

That afternoon, the priest had his first real job. He said the service for the fallen troopers.

They did keep their eyes peeled and nothing else happened until they were out of the woods. They had come to an area of rolling hills and valleys. Vegetation was sparse and the world was turning a dusty brown. Their guide warned them to fill every canteen, jug, and water bag at every water hole because the desert would start soon. They began to relax. The were no more trees to jump from or bushes to hide behind. Wouldn't it be nice if our enemies just had the courtesy to stay stupid?

The column had kept a tighter formation since the last attack. Except for the outriders, the gross of men and women and half again more horses were in close enough to see each other from front to back. You could see the first level of Warriors riding flank a few hundred yards out and there were lances a quarter mile in front and back. Everyone else traveled together. The were going through a small rocky valley. The flankers had ridden the ridges on both sides and the forward team had passed through a few minutes before.

The wagons had at the rear had just entered the canyon when a loud trill began. It was human voices shrieking louder than the Christians had ever heard. It was a signal for boulders to begin rolling down the hills. The bastards were hidden in holes dug under the boulders! Right behind the boulders came the bandits shrieking and waving short spears and long curved swords. As the boulders passed through the column, dirt covered doors lifted from the sand and more bandits poured out. Many were armored with breastplates and all carried shields. They shrieked like banshees as they attacked.

The Christians were well rehearsed. The warriors fired carefully aimed shots and then drew swords. The lances formed up and attacked the bandits as cohesive groups. The training and organization was effective and lasted for as long as two or three minutes. Then it became a melee. Hand to hand, bayonet to spear, sword to sword. The shrieking had stopped and been replaced by grunts of effort and screams of pain. It seemed to go on forever. The Warriors dismounted after the first few minutes to be able to reach the attackers more effectively.

Captain Walznik rode back and forth down the line, shouting orders and lending a hand, or a sword, as needed. The battle began to coalesce into two lines, one of red jacketed troopers and one of brown burked attackers.

Sir Dulka formed up four lances several meters up the hill. In less than a minute, he had squad fire working. A dozen men fire while another dozen loaded. It was devastating. Within minutes, brown clad men were scrambling for the hillside and running away. When it became obvious that there was no booty, there was no reason to stay. They were not fighting for freedom, the homeland, or their country. They ran.

The officers surveyed the battlefield. It was small enough to see all of it. Warriors were bringing the wounded to a triage area where the medic and some of the more skilled troopers were working on them. Wounded and captured bandits were being herded into another area. No one was treating them. Near one of the wagons, a woman was holding a dieing Warrior's head in her lap and crying. Captain Walznik recognized her as the woman the priest had denounced for having sex with the trooper. Someone was gathering up dropped weapons and putting them in piles of trooper and bandit weapons.

Sir Bronowski was dragging a dead bandit off the trail. He grunted to the Warrior on the other end of the body, "I guess they thought we'd scatter and let them do some looting. Hold it, let some of them move the bodies. It isn't our job."

They made camp for the rest of the day. The surviving bandits were moved into a corral at one end of the canyon and pickets were set out. They finished treating all of the wounded Warriors and, in the evening, they buried their fallen comrades. The quartermaster and his women got the fires going and kept hot food available all evening. Most of them were wearing captured weapons.

It was a sad evening of shared memories and occasional songs. No one fed the prisoners.

The officers were drinking wine and looking into the fire when someone asked, "What are we going to do with the prisoners?"

One of the knights said, "We could just leave the wounded here. If they're too hurt to travel, they'll probably die anyway, and good riddance. But, Captain, what do we do with the rest?"

The Captain looked up from the fire, "I've been thinking about that. In my country, the penalty for murder is death. Unfortunately, we're an army, not executioners. I've decided to sentence them to life at hard labor."

Someone asked, "How are we gonna do that? We're thousands of miles from the nearest Polish prison."

"Well, we will use a local prison. The walking bandits go with us. We'll sell them at the next town." There were looks of disbelief. "I know that slavery is a sin and we don't believe in it. But it's the closest we can come to a fair sentence and they would have done it to us."

Around the fire, men nodded. They didn't like it, but no one had a better idea.

The next morning, for the one and only time in history, a Christian army moved out with a line of slaves roped together. The taste of it was bad, but got better as they passed the graves of the twelve brother Warriors who had been killed in the fight.

Chapter 30 Juma Finds a Bride

In two months, all four of my servants came to me and told me that they were pregnant. I was used to that sort of thing. I had hundreds of children in Poland by women that I wasn't married to. I took good care of them, and their mothers, too. When possible, I found the ladies a suitable husband. It's a wise child who really knows who his father is.

There were even a lot of children that had mothers who claimed that I was the father, but where actually, I wasn't. I acknowledged them all as my own, even if the woman in question wasn't up to my personal specifications. I wasn't about to give a baby a bad childhood over a little thing like personal vanity!

But I rather imagined that I'd raise these four kids as actually being my own. I really liked all of their mothers. My other wives, Francine and Celicia, would have to learn to live with it, somehow.

Peat moss, the fresh, green plant itself, not the brown crumbly stuff sold in modern gardening shops, is a very remarkable materiel when dried. It is very soft. It is a natural antiseptic, and is used to treat wounds. It absorbs liquids and odors, and is used as a disposable lining for a baby's diapers. And it is used by menstruating women.

One of the weird things in human physiology is that women living together tend to synchronize their menstrual cycles. Why they do this strange thing, God surely knows, but I don't! But if they are all on the moss at the same time, they are also all fertile at the same time! This meant that in seven or eight months, all four of my girls might well all give birth on the same night! This was something that I was not looking forward to.

Obviously, I needed some more women around to help out. Women trained in handling childbirth, but also someone who could keep me sexually satisfied when having sex with one of my current girls might possibly harm our child.

I asked Jasmine to expand my household. She said that she would see what she could do, but there weren't that many women still in the North Tower, and that she didn't have any contacts outside of the palace.

One of the three women she brought me was a Black girl named Mimba. There was something very familiar about her, but I couldn't quite put my finger on it. She wasn't interested in having sex with me, so of course, I didn't press her.

A few days later, Juma dropped by for dinner. When he saw Mimba, I thought he was going to faint! I mean, you wouldn't think that someone with coal black skin could turn white, but somehow, he did it!

"Juma! What's wrong?"

"Wrong?," he said after a few moments. "Nothing is wrong. Would you like to come to my wedding, Conrad? This is Mimba. She is my dead wife's little sister! She has one of the highest bloodlines of my tribe. We will be married tomorrow!"

"Congratulations. But, aren't you supposed to ask the girl first?"

"But that isn't necessary. Since her sister is dead, her family must give her to me, or return the bride price I gave them. And of course, they can't do that, since they are all dead, too. I don't think that you will ever understand our customs."

I said, "That is an understatement. None the less, I advise you to ask her to marry you. Take it from an old married man, and do it."

"Very well, as a favor to a friend. Mimba, I ask you to marry me, to be my senior wife, to cook my food, and to bear me many fine sons. In return, I will support you well, and give you honor and status in our tribe."

Mimba said, "For the honor of your family, and for the honor of mine, I will do this thing."

"There, Conrad. I have done what you asked. Now then, will you come to our wedding?"

"Will I have to eat anybody that I know?" I asked.

"At a wedding feast? Of course not! Who ever heard of such a thing? Wedding feasts are completely meatless!"

"Then I accept gladly, my brother. But please send one of your people over to guide me through the thing. I wouldn't want to do anything improper."

"Of course, my friend! Oh, and you must bring all of your ladies with you!"

And thus it was that Juma was the first man in his reconstructed tribe to have a wife. The most interesting thing about the ceremony was seeing all of my girls, and all of Omar's, wearing nothing but the traditional tribal loincloths.

Many of Juma's men had taken up with women, almost invariably Black ones, but since they didn't have the right bloodlines, they were classified as servants, not wives.

You run into racism in the damndest places.

Weeks later, Juma explained that Mimba had been embarrassed about presenting herself to him for months. She had been raped several times during her captivity, and she felt that this had sullied her, dishonoring her family and making her unsuitable for marriage to a nobleman. Juma, of course, had very different opinions.

Three months after we took this city, we had all of the city owned irrigation pumps running on undershot waterwheels, each producing twice as much water that they had under human power. It wasn't that they were turning that much faster, but that they worked all night as well as all day, the night being as long as the day at these low latitudes.

The advantages of all of these new machines were carefully explained to the people of Timbuktu in another of Omar's many public proclamations. They were told that for very little extra money, the improved pumps put out twice as much water, they didn't have to be fed, and that they would never revolt against their masters.

But now only two of them were working on the same side of the river. It happened that two of the four pumps had right handed screws and two had left handed ones. With humans providing the power, it hadn't made any difference which way the slaves walked, but with the undershot water wheels necessarily turning the way that the river flowed, only half of them worked!

Each of the pumps had been carved from a big, long, and straight tree trunk. A deep and wide helical groove had been cut into it, and then the channel had been covered with long, thin strips of wood, running the length of the tree. It wasn't at all obvious which way the screw turned, and our engineers had missed the difference between them. Nobody had thought to ask the now freed slaves who had actually turned them, even though these men had included myself, Juma, and Omar!

So, after we gave the engineers a bit of humorous chastisement, we had shifted the ones that didn't work across the river, which got them turning in the proper direction. We were now irrigating the other side of it, at first simply to provide more grass for our meat animals. Eventually, once the soil built up, we'd have farms out there.

There were nine more water pumps owned by various farmers' co-operatives in the privately owned sector, which had always been operated by the farmers on a time-sharing basis. If it was the second Tuesday of the month, it was your turn to spend the day walking around in the pump.

Well, the technology of the water wheels was available to them now, and they could do what they wanted with their own property.

A river powered ferry, of the sort that I had invented at Cracow so many years ago had been installed. Maybe someday, we'd build a bridge.

We had seven wind powered water pumps operating on the gate towers of the palace and the city gates. The outer side of the walls had merlins to defend the soldiers on the top of the walls, but the inner side didn't. These walls were remarkably level, so along the inside, we built a raised channel, coated with waterproof tar, to carry water from the wind pumps to any point on the wall. From there, someday, we might put in some aqueducts to supply the rest of the city.

For now, Juma's people just had to dip a bucket into it, and drink, bathe, or water their plants.

These pumps and troughs, too, were hyped in Omar's proclamations. It makes no sense to do things for people if you don't tell them what you are doing.

We weren't using winches to raise the portcullises, since once we had a filled water tank on the tower above each gate, it was much simpler just to hang two big buckets on ropes that went over pulleys and then were attached to the big iron things. You filled the buckets with water, they went down and the portcullis came up. You set the brake, drained the buckets into a horse trough, and when you released the brake, the portcullis went down.

Gravity works every time.

Sir Stephan thought that one up.

Each gate now had two public watering troughs, one for people and one for animals. There was some talk of carving some beautiful fountains for the city markets. We could run the pipes through the 'secret' tunnels.

We had another seven windmills, to the immediate left of each of the pumps, in use for grinding grain into flour. Again, more hype.

Jaccs Dupree and his engineers had done a number of fine jobs for us.

There was some talk between Omar and the presidents of the four main universities about setting up a system of elementary schools, to be paid for the city, that would be open to everyone, and without tuition being charged to the students. Unfortunately, there were political problems caused by the current independent schools, which were quite profitable for their owners. Also, there were economic problems due to the costs of doing all of this. The city had lost major sources of revenue when we had freed all of the slaves. The project was 'temporarily' tabled.

With all of this bright sunshine available, it seemed silly to be importing charcoal made in the forests far downstream to cook with. I came up with two types of solar cookers.

One was an oven, an insulated box with a double layer of inexpensive, poor quality glass on top. It could bake bread in about an hour and a half.

The other used a large, vaguely parabolic, polished brass reflector which concentrated sunlight on the bottom of an iron hotplate, and was used for frying, stewing, or boiling.

The girls liked them both, and sales were brisk, once we demonstrated them in the public markets. I told Omar about patent law, and assigned the rights to both devices to him. I'd used his balcony to develop both cookers, after all.

The main palace barracks had been rebuilt, but this time into a series of apartments that a man with a family could use. In the Christian Army, we didn't like to separate a man from his wife and children for long. And this time, the building was fireproof, with masonry arches supporting the stone floor above, instead of using wooden rafters and wood floors. It was actually cheaper to build that way, shipping costs of bringing wood upstream for eight hundred miles being what they were. The stone quarries were nearby, and the city was downstream of them.

All of our Christian troops had proper uniforms now, in the Christian Army's red and white, with black leather accessories and brass buttons. The Arab troops preferred traditional Arab dress, although it was now uniform, and in our colors. Juma's men stuck with their loincloths, and resisted any attempts at standardization. How they knew each other's rank was beyond me. When I asked them, they said that they could tell by a man's manna! I couldn't see any manna!

The sword makers of Timbuktu were very competent, and they had made us up some rapiers, the best secondary weapon for an infantryman, once he learns how to use one. My men carried them on their backs, high over their left shoulder in a two piece sheath that didn't get in the way. Archers carried their quivers over their right shoulders. This arrangement assumed that the warrior was right handed, of course. Lefties did it the other way.

Work was also under way to make us some decent plate armor, at least for the officers, the cavalry, and the front rank of the pikers, who each actually carried a halberd. It all had to be made individually, by hand, of course, and was expensive. But it wasn't nearly as expensive as losing a war.

Four of the Christian Army troops were trying to make gunpowder. Refining the saltpeter was the current big problem, but I was hesitant about getting Arabian alchemists in on the project. There are things which are best kept within the group.

Most importantly, the people of Timbuktu had started to accept us. I'm not saying that they loved us, or even that they were grateful, but at least their hatred wasn't as obvious as it once had been. And considering that we had 'stolen' all of their slaves, and butchered, or burned, most of their army, this was good progress.

Juma's troops had been trained from childhood, and were fanatically loyal to him. My Christian army was starting to shape up nicely. They were proud of their uniforms, and their style of marching, which seemed to impress the locals. And both groups had adopted the Mohawk haircuts, to the level of 100% of those who had any hair in the first place. This made for a strong feeling of group identification. And the Christians knew that they were training in order to fight their way home. None of them left the army.

But the Islamic troops, who had been our largest contingent at the beginning, were less satisfied with army life. Given their choice, I think that most Moslems would really rather be small scale businessmen and merchants, rather than Warriors. Oh, some of them are absolute, wild eyed fanatics, but most of them would rather just make a decent living without having to work too hard.

We had organized them in the Christian Army fashion, with our system of sixes, but many of them wanted to be discharged.

We let them go, but with the understanding that they had to train one day a week with their units, for which they received a small salary, but they could pursue civilian jobs for the rest of the week. They became our active reserve.

Many were finding wives, and were starting families. If we ever had to defend ourselves, they would be there for us. And in the mean time it saved the city money.

Those Arabs who wanted to stay in the army full time were formed up into three companies of camel cavalry. They spent much of their training time out on the desert. Their officers were mostly experienced men who had been fighting against us a few months ago, but who now had sworn loyalty to us.

The Captain of each company was one of my original Christian Army troops, who were trying hard to master the art of staying on a camel in a fight. But a Captain's job wasn't to fight efficiently. It was to direct the efforts of others. The loyalty of anyone who had survived our training program in Poland was absolute, and that was very important, too.

Originally, the Arab's sole cavalry weapon, aside from knives, was the long, heavy camel saber, so our European horse cavalry taught them the use of the lance, and about mounted archery, something that they hadn't practiced here before, for some reason that I couldn't fathom.

We also hired on a number of experienced policemen and put them to work, fighting crime.

Over the months, every single building in and around the city was searched for illicit slaves. Every former slave was questioned to see that he or she was being properly taken care of. We even set up a job placement organization to find work for those who were looking for it. Many of these people had been slaves all of their lives, and didn't know how to go about finding a job. Soon, the organization was also placing ordinary citizens, as well.

Eventually, Juma's men returned from the south. The caravan consisted of some three thousand Black women, one thousand Black Warriors, and eight hundred mostly unloaded camels, but no Arab slavers, ex- or otherwise, were with them.

"So what happened?" I asked him as we watched them entering the palace grounds.

"I don't know, but I will find out," Juma said. "I will also select four more wives for myself. My father had thirty-one wives, after all. My position requires that I have at least five of them, but more would seem greedy since we still don't have enough women."

That evening, Juma came to my apartment and explained things, over a glass of brandy.

The liquor turned out to actually be a local product, distilled from wine made illegally from our own locally grown grapes. At least, it was illegal under the old management. I'd made the production of it, and the wine itself, which was a bit weak and dry, to be legal, and taxable, but for sale only to non-Muslims. I'd also told the wine makers that adding some concentrated sugar cane juice, or honey, to their smashed grapes could improve their product. The European label on the bottle was fraudulent, and I'd had them change it. Alcohol is an Arabic word, after all.

"I was told that the caravan was attacked by a large band of Twaregs," Juma said, "The Arabs, on their fast camels, and not trusting my tribe's fighting skills, went out to fight them, but they were outnumbered, and they were all killed. When my tribesmen, who were of course on foot, got to the battle, they killed all of the now outnumbered Twaregs, with very little loss to themselves. Then they rested, and feasted, and came back to Timbuktu."

I looked at him for a while, and then I sent my six girls out of the room. This conversation wouldn't be good for them to hear!

"Girls, go to the far end of the apartment and stay there until I call you back. Don't you DARE try to overhear what we are going to talk about! It could cost you your lives!"

They left quickly. When they were gone, I said quietly, "I have never seen a battle where everybody on one side or the other was killed. There are always some survivors. This story has two complete wipeouts in it. You have told me what you were told. Now tell me what really happened!"

"I was afraid that you would say something like that. Okay. It happens that this particular group of slavers were the very same people who organized our enemies against us, just before my tribe was destroyed. These Arabs were responsible for the deaths of my father, and my mother, and my pregnant wife, and for the parents, wives, and children of everyone in my large tribe! I had never seen these particular Arabs, but many of the men that I sent on this mission recognized them! Therefore, on the return trip, my people waited until they were only two days from Timbuktu, and there was no danger of becoming lost in the desert."

Juma looked straight at me, and continued, "And then we killed them all! We feasted well, even though there is little manna in a slaver, even if they did die fighting. Two hundred more of our young men attained manhood. They also married two hundred of the best women that they had with them. Those women should have gone to older, more proven men, but that is my problem, and not yours. I say that in killing the slavers, my men acted properly. Also consider that in not returning to the city, the slavers have voided their contract. We will not have to pay them. My people have saved the city a great deal of money! What do you say?"

I looked down and shook my head.

"I don't give a damn about the money! If someone was responsible for killing my parents, and the families of everyone that I knew, yes, I would kill them! But all of this presents us with a problem. We need the support of the Arabs in this city! The true story of what actually happened must never come out on this matter. You must explain this carefully to your people! We will tell the story that was fabricated by your men, except that in the end we will have it that they merely drove the Twaregs off. That will explain why your people did not bring any Twareg camels or equipment back with them. We will hire Arabian poets to write the praises of the heroic Arabs who went to their glorious deaths to protect the people in their caravan. We will hire people to read these poems often at every marketplace in the city. Do you agree with this?"

"Of course, Conrad. We have their manna. We can let them have their 'glory'. I suppose that we will have to give their weapons and other property back to their families, but can we keep their camels?"

"No! You can't keep the damned camels! One doesn't steal from heroes!"

Like we didn't have enough problems!

I went across the hall and explained the situation to Omar. Unless we wanted to lose the services of Juma and his men, when a local mob killed them all, we had to cover this one up.

Omar agreed to contact the university presidents of his recent acquaintance, and set up a competition among the city's poets, with excellent prizes for the top five poems. The well paid judges would be chosen by the university presidents. Most of them did it personally, and kept the money for themselves.

A proclamation would go out in the morning, telling everyone about the ex-slavers heroism. It would also advertise the contest.

Omar would also see to it that the property of the deceased 'heroes' was returned to their families, and that they were paid in full for their services.

Omar and his male secretaries got to sleep very late that night, and he didn't get to enjoy his ladies at all. All secretaries in the Arabian world were male, since women here were rarely educated properly.

They just didn't know what they were missing.

Chapter 31 The Africa Corps moves North

After spending four months as one of the rulers of Timbuktu, it was time for me to leave.

My stay here had been interesting, to say the least, but these people weren't my people. I wanted to go home, and so did most of the Christians that I'd made promises to.

Besides, my wives would give me hell if they thought I'd dawdled.

The African Corps of the Christian Army, now three thousand strong, was as well trained as the Polish Army had been when we beat the Mongols, twenty years ago. We didn't have firearms, except for some crude explosives, but neither did our enemies. My people had been able to make two barrels of serpentine powder, even cruder than black powder, but you never can tell what might be useful. I resolved to bring them along with us.

The city had stayed peaceful during my stay here, and we had tried hard to be good rulers. Certainly, there had been no hint of rebellion. The Arabian people seemed to like Omar, and to fear Juma. Not a bad combination, actually. Me? Well, they all knew that I would be leaving soon, so I didn't much matter to them.

One option was to go west, following the route that I had taken when I'd come to Timbuktu, over a year ago. But the route was longer than the northerly one, and I didn't want to have to take thousands of women and children up the Skeleton Coast.

This was the right time of the year to take a large caravan north. There had been two good rain storms out on the desert to the north, and there would be enough food for the horses and camels out there.

Another factor was that my four main ladies were three months pregnant. I had apparently done them all in on a single night! If I delayed departure any more, they would soon be getting too big to travel safely.

Logistics were a problem. Counting men, women and children, I had eight thousand people coming with me. We had been collecting pack camels and mules for months, even buying them from other cities, but even so, most adults would have to walk the whole way back to Europe.

My engineering company had left Omar a good bunch of well trained Arabs to provide the city with technical services. But being Christians, they themselves would be coming with us.

Omar agreed to lend me our three companies of Arab camel cavalry, as additional security on the trip. These men would also return with the horses, the mules, and the pack camels back to the city, once we got to the Mediterranean Sea, and had arranged for some shipping to get us across it. If the prices we found at some sea port were good, they would try to bring some cargo back with them.

I was surprised when our two Jewish companies wanted to go north with us Christians. It seems that this trip was why they had wanted to join the army in the first place. Most of them had been slaves in Timbuktu, and they did not feel welcome here. I agreed to bring them, and their families, along. Especially since, at their own suggestion, they had volunteered to take care of their own costs for transportation and food. The more the merrier. And the safer.

Besides their two companies of trained men, the Jews were taking some fifteen hundred civilians with them. I felt that at least one more Jewish company should be organized out of their able bodied men, to be trained on the march, and they went along with this.

The day before we were due to leave, Juma came by.

"Conrad, the last of my five wives has announced that she is pregnant. I have thus completed, for the time being, my family obligations here. I have a good subordinate, Mishaba, one of my many half brothers, who can take care of my people in my absence, and I've been getting bored lately. There is no one here to fight, anymore. What would you think if I were to gather up, say, a thousand of my younger men, and joined you on your trip?"

"I'd say that you would be very welcome. We can use all of the fighting men we can get! But I worry about supplies on the trip. Feeding another thousand men won't be easy," I said.

"Don't worry about that. My men are all good hunters. We can easily feed ourselves and many others besides."

"If you say so. I suppose that if worse comes to worse, we can always start eating the camels."

"Trust me," Juma said.

"You know? I do! In fact, if Omar thinks that he can spare them, why don't you bring two thousand of your men along? I think that those of them who are still unproven will have plenty of chances to kill their man on this trip."

"I had been thinking that as well. It is part of my duty to them, to give them their chance. Two thousand it will be!"

Omar gifted me with a tenth of the city's treasury, much more than enough to pay the expenses of the way.

We had a surprisingly tearful departure, Omar and I. I hadn't realized how attached I had become to the man. Our months slaving together in that damned barrel, our war victories over our oppressors, and our work together in putting our new regime into working order had forged a bond between us of surprising strength. We both promised to visit each other, some day, some how.

Sir Stephan had been in charge of making all of the arrangements for the trip, and he'd done a fine job of it. We had a sufficient number of experienced Arab camel handlers to show our own men what to do, and a dozen scouts and guides to keep us on course. The caravan master, Mohamed, was a wizened old Arab with a good reputation, as were a few of the cooks, who would be teaching our ladies about cooking on the trail. The rest of my people could provide the muscle, the sweat, and the blood.

The girls had made me a copy of the Christian Army's Battle Flag, and I had a new set of shining plate armor, made in the style that we had developed over the years in Poland. Sir Stephan could have had the same thing, but he had elected to have Hajji's old armor cut down to fit him. It was pretty stuff.

I had a fine white horse that I named Whitey, who almost looked like Silver, but was, of course, only an animal, and not to be compared to a Big Person. It took me a while to get used to handling a bridle again. With a Big Person, you didn't need one, and in fact, they hated to wear them.

I also had four big camels in my personal train, one that carried a platform with a tent on top of it, big enough to hold all four of my girls, as well as their personal baggage. The last two ladies that I'd added weren't Christians, and they had said that they preferred to stay in Timbuktu. Omar had hired them, and added them to his harem.

The other three camels carried our baggage, including the Hajji's magnificent gold trimmed, Royal Blue silk tent, some three legged camp chairs that I'd had made up, and our cooking utensils, since the girls insisted on cooking for me themselves. I regretted having to leave my dining room table behind, but that's war for you.

I had a lance of men assigned to set up and take down my camp each day, which got them out of having to pull guard duty at night. I didn't want any of my pregnant girls doing any heavy work. And I had another lance of mounted runners around me at all times.

One camel had little more on his back that a lifetime supply of coffee, and a three months supply of brandy. Major food items like flour, grains, and dried meats, fish, fruits, and vegetables, were carried by the commissary caravan, although the girls had packed a lot of specialty items, just for us.

Rank has its privileges.

One of the problems that had to be settled before we even started was "Which day of the week would we rest on?" Obviously, we couldn't march for three months non-stop. But Christians like to rest on Sunday, Jews want to take off from Friday night until Saturday at sunset, and the Arabs agreed with the Jews. Juma couldn't see why we shouldn't just run the whole way, non-stop! He said that his men could do it!

I decided that we would stop on Sunday, since two thirds of us were Christians in the first place, only one sixth of us were Jewish or Arabian, and anyway, I was the boss. They went along with me, with some grumbling. Jews and Arabs pulled guard duty on Sunday, and Christians on Friday night and Saturday, but that was as far as I would go. Juma's men were soon spending a few hours a day hunting, and so were relieved from guard duty entirely.

The trail blazers of the advanced guard were relieved from guard duty as well, of course, except to guard themselves.

Fair is fair.

Our route was fairly straight forward. The first third of the trip was simply going mostly north and west along the Niger River. This would give us a dependable supply of water, firewood, and also plenty of food for the animals along the riverbank.

You have probably heard the expression, 'to eat like a horse'. Well, a war horse needs at least four dozen pounds of food a day. This means that he must feed off the land, since he can only carry a ten day supply of food on his back, even if he carries nothing else. Camels are generally bigger, and need considerably more fodder, and mules aren't light eaters, either. Keeping the animals well fed was of prime importance, since they were carrying our food, and we'd die without them.

There were many settlements along the river, where we could buy, or commandeer (that is to say, steal) additional food as needed. I also planned to relieve them of any slaves that they were keeping. Slavery was an abomination that must be stomped out! Also, I thought that we would eventually need all of the fighting men that we could get. We'd train them on the march!

Then, there was a stretch through drier land, but Mohamed, the Caravan

Master, assured us that there were water holes and the occasional oasis to provide sufficient water and fodder, especially at this time of the year.

In a few months, we would start climbing up into the Atlas Mountains. After that, there were trails that led further north. But between us and the sea, there was a little matter of getting through the Empire of Almohades. This empire was well over a thousand miles from east to west, running from Tunis in the east, to way south of Marrakech, along the Mediterranean and Atlantic seacoasts. It also included almost half of Spain. We had three hundred miles of it to get through. I was told to expect that this would be the hard part.

Well, it happened that I'd read a few history books, back when I was in the Twentieth Century, and they had said that the Almohades Empire had collapsed years ago. The Caravan Master's information had to be out of date, so I wasn't worried. Of course, I couldn't explain that to him, but what the heck.

When the day came for our departure, I'd sent an advance guard of mounted trail blazers out at daybreak, and the rest of the caravan was supposed to leave an hour later. My trained troops were ready on time, but the civilians weren't.

Inefficiency bothers the engineer in me. I fretted and fidgeted for another hour, and then gave the orders for us to move out. The trail blazers would set up our camp twenty-four miles or so ahead of us, and every minute that we were late was one more minute of sleep lost! If the rest wanted to come, they could damn well catch up with us!

I did leave the stragglers a rear guard, and Mohamed promised to hurry the twits along as best as he could. We maintained an easy pace, two dozen miles a day. It was three days before the last of the civilians caught up with us. All told, I now had twelve thousand followers with me. A fairly formidable force, and a considerable bother as well.

There were endless squabbles, that I won't trouble you with relating. Many of them were just referred to Mohamed for settlement. When I got particularly annoyed, I referred the argumentative people to Juma. Arguments had a habit of disappearing very quickly at that point, since Juma's methods were unorthodox, but decisive.

One evening, he was having dinner with us, as he often did. A few of my troops brought in two slightly battered men, who had been fighting. Each of them claimed that the other had stolen from him a bag of booty that had been won during our early conquest of Timbuktu. I didn't like the looks of one of them, to the point that I thought it might affect my judgment, so I asked Juma settle the matter. He glanced at them, and gestured them outside. He looked at the pleasant looking one and said, "You are a liar and a thief. Is that sword your favorite weapon?"

The man said it was.

"Then defend yourself with it."

Juma gestured to one of his young tribesmen, and the fight was over in a few seconds, with a spear through the heart of the man who I'd thought was innocent. The white man's body was carried away by the victor's friends.

I asked, "Juma, even if he was the guilty one, wasn't that a bit severe? I mean, killing a man for theft?"

"He was also a murder, several times over."

"How do you know that? What makes you so certain that he was the guilty one?"

"Why, it was written all over his manna, of course." He went back in to finish his meal, and I followed him.

"Juma, just what is this manna thing that you are always talking about? I can't see any manna!"

"I know, and that is very strange, for you have the strongest manna that I have ever seen. Much stronger than my father's was, even." He preferred to sit on the ground, while I sat on a camp stool.

"But that doesn't answer my question."

"Manna is something that my people and I can see, but you, and everybody else that I know of, can't. To us, it looks like a many colored glow that sort of hovers around most people, but not all of them. Some animals have it, but not many. Once, I saw a tree with manna. I don't know what it is, any more than I know what life is. It's just there, a fact of life. Manna gives you power over people and things. You, for example, were inclined to judge in favor the thief, just a while ago. This was because his manna was so strong."

"So this manna doesn't have anything to do with goodness?"

"Correct. Manna is power, nothing more or less. You can build your manna from within your own self, and also by eating that of others. It is the reason for my tribe's cannibalism, I suppose."

I said, "And no one but your people can see it. That gives you a great deal of power." It sounded a little like the 'aura' that psychics talked about in the modern world. Not that the engineer in me would let me believe in any of that stuff.

"Only we can see it, but most people can feel it, or maybe 'smell it' is a better term. People smell your manna, Conrad. That is why they so willingly follow you. And if they must battle against you, they feel your power, and become afraid."

"I'll have to think about this. But I think that from now on, I want you to handle the legal problems around here."

"No, I have enough to do. But I'll appoint a few of my people to the task, if you wish."

"Yes, please do that," I said. I've always hated having to judge people, and Juma seemed so certain of his ability to do the job properly.

Chapter 32 In Uncle Tom's Control Room

I hit the pause button.

"Tom, what's your take on this manna business?"

"Damned if I know. Superstition? Mass hallucination? Some strange psychic power? Take your pick."

"Could there actually be something to it?"

"There might be. When you've been around as long as I have, you'll have seen some damned weird things. I don't think that I could honestly say that anything is impossible."

"Huh."

"Yeah."

He hit the run button.

Chapter 33 Along The Trail

*Two dozen miles a day meant that we spent four, double length army hours a day walking, four hours setting up camp, cooking and eating, and packing things back up, and four hours sleeping, unless you were picked for guard duty. About once a week, most troops spent another annoying hour at that.

The first few days were pretty hectic and disorganized, especially since Mohamed hadn't caught up with us yet with the last of the stragglers. This forced us to figure it all out by ourselves.

By the third day, things were starting to settle down, a bit. People were slowly learning their jobs. The advanced party had selected our camp site the day before, a square more than four hundred yards to the side. They had marked out the boundaries, the gates, and the streets. We eventually got it down to a system, where the same things were set up in the same relative places every night, so people could find things.

The animals had to be unloaded and then taken down to the river for watering. This had to be done under guard, as there were some dangerous critters in that water. Just upstream, the water bags for human consumption had to be filled, loaded on some of the mules, and taken back to camp. Some people chopped wood, both for firewood and for a lightweight palisade, a fence surrounding the camp. Fire wood had to be delivered, usually by camels, to the cooking area. Our animals had to be hobbled and permitted to feed, under guard. Latrines had to be dug, food cooked, tents set up. After we ate, more food was cooked for a hot breakfast and a cold lunch.

The old Roman Legions used to build what amounted to a small city at the end of each day, complete with a dry moat and an outer wall, but I wasn't that much of a fanatic. Close, though.

And every morning, our animals had to be gathered up and watered again. Everything had to be disassembled, packed up, put on the draft animals, and the trek began again.

We usually bathed on Sunday afternoons, if we could find a clear and shallow stretch of the river. This had to be done under guard, crocodiles being what they were. Guarding the women was a highly sought after responsibility, even though many women preferred to take a sponge bath inside of their tents.

I'd had a big solar oven made up that was built on a cart that was pulled behind one of my personal camels. The idea was that we could bake bread while on the march. It turned out that it was a bad idea. Vibrations flattened the bubbles out of the dough before the bread could bake, and turned it flat and rock hard. Oh, well, it had seemed like a good idea at the time. The oven was still of use for roasting meat and making casseroles. Wild game needs a lot of roasting and stewing time, and my own party, and our guests, got a hot lunch.

Once we were away from the immediate environs of Timbuktu, the desert became a vast, green grassland. Animals in huge numbers had found there way here from someplace, and Juma's people had some very good hunting. There were wildebeests, zebras, dozens of kinds of antelopes, elephants, ostriches, rhinoceroses, and even a few giraffes. There were also lions and hyenas, which were dangerous.

There were crocodiles in the river, as well. We lost a few people to them, when we were getting water, but many more to the hippopotamuses. Those things looked fat and funny, but they are deadly! They're good eating, though. So are crocodiles, for that matter.

Without slowing down the caravan, the Black Africans were soon supplying us with over twenty thousand pounds of meat a day. They had worked out a system with the cavalry companies, where the horsemen and camel jockeys stampeded the wild animals into hidden lines of Juma's men. They were waiting near our next campsite, so they wouldn't have to haul the meat very far, but far enough away so that the scavengers who showed up in the night to eat what we threw away weren't troublesome. The Blacks generally had it all skinned out, cleaned, and cut into manageable hunks by the time the rest of us got there.

We usually had to abandon the hides, unless someone wanted to do something specific with one. Many of Juma's warriors started sporting zebra skin shields. Elephant tusks were well worth bringing along with us, though, as were rhino horns. We would have kept the ostrich plumes as well, but my Warriors always collected those up in a hurry, to wear on their helmets. Jasmine had brought a bottle of red ink along in our baggage, and this sufficed to dye the plumes used by my runners. It became their sign of authority. Everybody else had to get along with white plumes.

I was careful not to ask about exactly what I was eating. A zebra looks too much like a horse for me to be comfortable eating one. Elephant tastes pretty good, though, if you cook it long enough.

We weren't cutting into our dried rations hardly at all, except for fruit and some ground flour.

Sir Stephan had arranged for a large, wagon mounted, wood heated metal oven to be built and brought along. Many of the women helped out kneading the dough, but the oven itself was kept working all night long, every night, by bakers who slept out the day riding in the same sort of covered wagons that the sick, the children, and very pregnant women rode in. They made six thousand loaves of bread a day.

We also bought a lot of fresh vegetables from the locals as we passed through.

After a few weeks, we started salting and drying surplus meat in the sun, hanging thin strips of it over our covered wagons as we went. We were using it to replace the flour and dried fruits that we were consuming. Once we got into the mountains, the hunting might not be so good.

Juma's men killed and ate a lot of lions. It seems that according to their customs, a lion was sort of human, had a lot of manna, and killing one single handedly with a spear qualified a young man for adulthood. Primitive people live in a very complicated world, for some reason.

We came upon small settlements of farmers and herdsmen several times a day. Our message to them, from our advanced guards, traveling a day ahead of the rest of us, was always the same.

"We mean you no harm! We are just passing through, on our way homeward, to the north. We would buy food from you, especially fresh vegetables, and baked goods, at fair prices, if you are willing. We also have some trade goods for sale;

needles, knives, fish hooks, some jewelry, and some glass ware.

"However, know that we consider slavery to be an abomination! Man was made in Allah's own image, and to enslave a human being is an offense against God! If you are keeping any slaves here against their will, we will take them from you! They are welcome to join with us! Especially Christian slaves, since many of us are Christians! Hear me! We will take you home!

"Slave owners who resist us will do so at their own peril! There are eight thousand good fighting men in our huge caravan. You cannot help but to be defeated!"

Often, a few slaves just came forward, and we gave them a place in the caravan. But we also questioned every person we came across, and made sure that they were staying here willingly. Healthy male ex-slaves were armed and assigned to training companies, which we called the irregulars, because we didn't have uniforms for them.

Their armament consisted at first of a decent knife, an axe head, and a pike head. They had to carve the axe handle and pike staff themselves, from wood growing along the river. The first skill they learned was marching, of course. Many of them weren't in good shape to start with, but long hours of marching, backed up with a good diet including plenty of meat, quickly put some muscle on them!

At first we, ran into the occasional band of nomads. Some of these were Twaregs, and that inevitably meant a fight, since these people seemed to have no common sense at all! Their only thought seemed to be, 'Give us everything we want, or we will kill you!' Well, we always killed them instead. They didn't have many slaves, but we got a lot of camels and weapons from them. They rarely had a woman with them that anybody wanted, so we just left them, and other non-combatants, behind.

Those who weren't Twaregs were almost as bad, though. We tried to be reasonable, but they weren't up to it. More camels, more swords. But after a month or so, they started making a point of avoiding us whenever possible.

On the eighth day of our trek, one town did try to resist us. Lacking anything like decent city walls, they met us out in the open field.

They only had about eight hundred men. Apparently, they didn't believe what we had told them about our numbers, or their intelligence was bad. Or maybe they were just plain stupid.

Still, we had to fight them. We were traveling more slowly that word could be sent upstream. The people north of us had to learn that resisting us was a very bad idea.

I'd put Sir Percy in charge of not only his own company, but of the three companies of camel cavalry we had with us. He circled in back of the enemy forces, mostly to keep them from escaping.

Juma asked to have his own men lead the charge, and I granted his request, even though it would have been good to blood my own troops as well, on this easy of a fight. But he was, after all, my friend.

It was all over very soon. A bunch of stupid farmers do not last long against well trained troops who outnumber them by more than two to one. Eight hundred of Juma's young men attained manhood, and they held their victory feast a few miles out of town.

The rest of us took the town and looted it for what little it had. Before we went in, I talked very sternly to my men about how I would hang any man who wantonly killed a civilian, especially a woman or a child, where the punishment would also include castration, and death by fire!

Someone in the crowd called out, "How do you plan to hang a man, and give him a death by fire at the same time?"

"I'll have him hung by his heels, and have a fire built under his head! A small fire!" I shouted back. "But aside from that, you can take what you want, and do what you want. Enjoy yourselves! The victors deserve the spoils!"

A few hundred of our men brought apparently willing new wives back with them.

Chapter 34 Pigeon Polish and Rhino Rampage

In a few weeks we got used to the routine of the trek, as the people toughened up.

After two weeks, I decided that we were well enough settled into the program to start getting bored on the march, and we needed some more to do.

If I was going to take these people back to Europe, they would need to know the language, since many of them, including all four of my ladies, spoke nothing but Arabic.

Polish was fast becoming the universal European language, at least among the educated set, but Polish is a natural language, with all of the complexities of any tongue that simply grew up over the centuries. Two or three months of part time study, without any books, just wasn't long enough to teach it to them.

But the men of the Explorer's Corps had developed a highly simplified form of Polish, called 'Pigeon'.

The White Eagle was the totem of Poland, of course, and the symbol of our noble language. To name their extreme simplification of our language after a trivial bird, a scavenger, had seemed to be appropriate to them.

They had designed it so that they could quickly talk with the natives of the many lands that they visited. It consisted of only about six hundred words, mostly nouns, verbs, and adjectives, but without any articles or prepositions. Everything was absolutely regular. There was no case structure or tense structure. If you were talking about the past, you put 'was' before the verb and then talked in the present tense. For the future, you used 'will' instead. There was no sex. Everything, including your wife, was male.

It sounded very strange, but in a week or two, you could communicate with it to anyone who knew either Polish or Pigeon. With it, my people could get by, any place in Europe. Well, perhaps with a bit of gesticulation.

I had a few dozen people with us who knew Pigeon, and we all started teaching it to the others while we were on the march. After a week or so, we started encouraging people to use it throughout the day, for practice.

The girls picked it up quickly, and were soon having a lot of fun with it.

Juma liked the new language as well. I think that the simplicity of it appealed to him. And with his encouragement, his men all learned it as well.

Many of the Arabs with us were also learning pigeon, although I wasn't quite sure why. Maybe it was because there wasn't anything else to do, considering the lack of television, radio, and the movies.

We were averaging about fifty slaves freed a day, with Christians, Blacks, and Arabs showing up in about equal numbers. More than half of them were fairly healthy men, and were recruited into the army. I think that this sexual imbalance was caused because a women who has had children by a man, even if he is her owner, is less likely to leave, since this might mean abandoning her children. Or maybe, the 'Stockholm Syndrome' had a lot to do with it. And, of course, we never forced anyone to come with us.

Juma took over training the Blacks, using his traditional methods. They'd want to go back to sub-Saharan Africa, in any event.

We put the Christian and the Arab recruits into separate companies, since it was likely that the Christians would want to return to Europe, but that most of the Arabs would want to stay in Northern Africa, or return with the caravan to Timbuktu. When we finally got to the coast, the separation would be easier if they were trained separately. And as in Timbuktu, Christians were divided up according to sect. Eventually, I expected that everyone would want to go home.

There were a few Jewish slaves, and we sent those over to the Jewish companies, where they were well taken care of. They were even issued uniforms, sewn for them by the Jewish ladies. That was more than the Christians or Arabs got.

We were 'budding' off cadres from our regular troops, with six knights, and thirty-six Warriors, of fairly experienced and carefully selected men each being promoted one grade, and eventually being assigned two hundred and twelve raw recruits for training.

More promotions happened in their old company, and forty-two new recruits were added at the bottom. It was the old Christian Army system, and it worked fairly well.

Each new company was being commanded by one of my original Polish trained Christian Army Warriors. They were stunned by the speed of their promotions. But, we didn't need many surveyors or engineers anymore, although we were mapping the territory we went through. We mostly needed Warriors who could command Warriors. It was looking as though the lowest ranking member of the original ship's company would be at least a Captain before this was over.

My army was growing. We were losing a few people every day, because of wild animals, disease, the occasional skirmish, and pure stupidity, but we were adding a lot more men than we were losing.

We almost lost me one afternoon.

My girls had gotten into the habit of getting to the slaughtering grounds as early as possible, to pick out some of the best meat, normally that from one of the youngest animals killed. That day, I had accompanied them. We were a bit too early, and the cavalry was a bit late, driving the wild animals into Juma's men.

But they got there, eventually, and hundreds of big animals charged in, to be slaughtered by the Black's sharp spears, swiftly thrown with great accuracy. The whole wave of animals went down, including two female rhinos and a bull elephant.

Usually, it took a few dozen thrown spears to bring down a big bull, but this one came straight in to where Juma himself was standing. He put his spear half way into he animal's forehead, and it just crumpled, dead before it hit the ground.

"Nice shot," I said.

"I always did prefer going for the forehead," Juma answered.

He was a while getting his spear out. Finally, they had to chop it out with an axe.

The men went in for the butchering, and my girls had already picked out what they wanted, a fine young antelope. We wouldn't be eating it that night, of course. There was a brace of young warthogs roasting in the solar cooker, along with some locally purchased fresh vegetables, that my household would be eating for dinner, breakfast, and probably lunch.

Most of the hunters were working at dismembering some of the bigger animals.

Rather than wait around, Jasmine and her lovely crew took out their belt knives and started skinning and gutting the chosen antelope themselves.

I was still on horseback, since although I wanted to help out, I was wearing another one of Hajji's fancy outfits, and I didn't want to get it bloody. Anyway, the girls always acted as though they were scandalized if I tried to help out with household chores.

I heard some shouting and turned to see what it was all about.

There was a huge male rhino charging straight at us! Rhinos look fat and slow, but I assure you that when they want to move, they can! They're faster than an ordinary horse, much stronger, and a whole lot meaner. This one already had eight well thrown spears sticking into him, but they weren't slowing him down at all!

My only thought was that the two other rhinos that had been killed must have been friends of his, and that during the course of the stampede, he must have associated horsemen with the enemy.

Only, I was the only one around riding a horse!

I tried to get Whitey going in the other direction, but he panicked and froze. All that I could do was to jump out of the saddle and try not be involved with the inevitable train wreck.

I was nearly clear when the rhino caught Whitey from below, and disemboweled him while tossing him, and me, high into the air.

For some reason, things always seem to slow down for me at times like that. I remember the whole flight quite well.

I got my sword out while I was flying, and managed, more by luck than anything else, to land on my feet, not a yard from where my four frightened ladies were still crouched around the antelope.

Whitey's body fell back down on top of the rhino. I don't think that he hurt it much, but he did knock the rhino over on it's side. This gave me the moment that I needed to run over to it and pretty much take it's head off with one swipe of my sword. Most of the arteries were severed, and I'm sure that I'd done some damage to the spinal column, but somehow, the incredibly tough creature was starting to get up, again! Whitey's body slid off from his back, and I saw death in the rhino's eyes. My death!

There was nothing for it but to hit him again, and this time the head came entirely off.

All motion by the rhino stopped, which is pretty much what you'd expect, given the circumstances.

"At least this time, you didn't ruin your pretty outfit!" A voice said from behind me.

I turned to see Juma standing there, laughing.

"That was an amazing jump that you just performed, Conrad! Do you realize that you made a complete flip in the air, came down on your feet with your sword out and facing the animal, and then you killed it quite easily!"

"Not that easily," I said. "Just a moment."

I went over to Whitey, but I wasn't sure if he was dead or not. The huge gash and the torn intestines in his stomach left no doubt that if he wasn't, he soon would be. I took his head off as well. I hate to see an animal in pain.

"The rhino was a very remarkable animal. He had the heart of a true Warrior!

Did you want the body, Conrad?" Juma said.

"No. All we want is that small antelope over there. You are welcome to this big, tough character, with my blessing. Just be sure and save the horn."

"Of course. My men and I will eat this fellow tonight. I think that he might have much manna in him!"

"Enjoy your meal!"

"And your horse, Conrad. May we eat him as well? I haven't had any horse meat in a long time."

"Take it! Not that you'll find any manna in that damned coward." Whitey hadn't been a really close friend, and the whole business of a war horse freezing up in a panic had me ticked off. I was glad that I wouldn't have to take him into battle, where things can get VERY dangerous. "Just have the saddle and the bridle returned to my camp."

I told one of my runners to report the incident to Sir Percy, and to request another horse for me.

My girls eventually got over a case of the collective nervous jitters, and went back to work. I waited until they had finished with cleaning the antelope, then I cut it into four quarters with my sword for easy handling.

I walked home, limping a bit. Coming down upright had hurt my feet and ankles. I wasn't as young as I used to be.

For all of the size, strength, and speed that had been bred into them, horses are fragile animals. Maybe their fragility was because of the way they were so over bred. But for what ever reason, we lost a lot of them on the trip, and we hadn't been able to replace many of them. We were able to obtain a fair number of camels along the way, and they were mostly carrying the baggage that the pack mules used to haul, while many of our cavalry were now riding mules. They weren't happy about it, but what else could we do?

When Sir Percy came over and asked me if I would mind being assigned a mule instead of a horse, I went along with it, but only on a temporary basis. I'd never ridden a mule before.

After a few days, though, I found that I actually preferred a mule to a horse. They were smarter, for one thing. This might be the result of being sterile, and not having all those hormones around bunging up the works.

Still, I'd have given a lot to have a Big Person under me.

Walking back, I saw that the palisade was almost completed around the huge camp.

Supplies of bread, water, and firewood had been dropped off at my personal camp site. The tents were up, and the horsemen were taking care of their mounts while others were grooming our camels. Camp life had become smooth and well regulated, since people now knew what their jobs were, and did them without direction.

My household was growing, as well as was my army. I'd assigned a knight of infantry and his six Warriors to do the grunt work around my personal camp. I didn't want the girls doing any heavy work in their delicate condition. It proved more convenient for them to camp near me, although I think that the better food available at my camp had something to do with it, along with the superior entertainment.

I'd also had seven horsemen assigned to me, to act as runners. They, too, had to live nearby, so as to be immediately available for emergencies, so their tents were pitched next to mine.

I'd had six female servants in Timbuktu, but two of them, Moslems, had elected to stay there. Each of my fourteen men had originally had a servant as well, but none of them had been Christians, with a strong incentive to get home to Europe. Only two of the original fourteen had come with us.

But we were freeing slaves every day, and some of them were pretty Christian girls. I'd come across two new ones for myself, and the men of my household picked up seven more. I think that our uniforms gave us an edge over the new recruits who didn't have any to wear.

The new girls made for a very pleasant camp environment. They didn't have the training or the sophistication of Jasmine and her crew, but they were enthusiastic, and eager to learn.

They were learning how to dance, to play musical instruments, and to be absolutely obedient. The important things, in the local culture.

Chapter 35 Twisting The Tail Of One City

Six weeks into the trip, we came across a fair sized city, complete with a tall and sturdy masonry city wall. They'd heard that we were coming, and had taken the time to gather their people in from the fields and surrounding villages. At a guess, there might have been as many people inside the city as we had outside it. We were better trained, but they had the advantage of fortifications.

There was no absolute reason for us to attack them. All we really had to do was to walk around the place, and continue on our way.

The problem was that they probably had hundreds of slaves in there, maybe thousands, and I hated to just abandon those people. But assaulting that wall would probably cost us more lives than we would save from slavery.

I wished that we had Omar here. He probably would have been able to think of something.

Without him, I'd just have to wing it.

I had our camp set up in front of the city, just out of arrow range. I traded in my mule for the best looking horse available, got into one of my most impressive looking outfits, with my shiny plate mail showing around the edges, and had one of my runners ride out beside me carrying the glorious Battle Flag of the Christian Army that Jasmine and the girls had made for me, before we'd left Timbuktu.

Maybe, I could talk them into something. You never can tell.

"Hello there in the City!" I shouted in my best command voice.

"What do you want?" Someone who didn't show himself shouted back.

"For starters, I want to talk to someone in authority here."

"You're talking to him, but I don't want to talk to you!"

"What do you want, then?" I asked.

"I want you to get your damned army off of our crops, and to go away!"

"That might be arranged. But we have to talk about it."

"Go away!" The someone shouted.

"You know, talking is so much safer than having your head chopped off for no particularly good reason. Something like that can ruin your whole afternoon."

"I said, go away!"

"No, I don't think so. It's been a long, hard trip, coming north from Timbuktu. This place has a nice climate, and it has plenty of fodder for our animals. Lots of it, growing in nice neat rows! I'll bet that it could last our camels, horses and mules for a whole week, and do a lot to get their strength back up again. And those olive trees over there could be made into some very good axe handles and pike staffs. The wood we found south of here was inferior to olive wood. Yes, a nice long rest would do us all a world of good!" I said.

"All right! What will it take for you to leave here?"

"Now, you're talking! Yes, we want you to bribe us into leaving. And the bribe we want is all of your slaves. Give them to us, and we will leave peaceably."

"We heard that you had some sort of religious thing about freeing the slaves," he said.

"This is absolutely true. Allah himself told me to go out and free every slave I could find, so what can a man do? Just give us your slaves, we will free them, and then go away with them, to trouble you no further."

"We don't have any slaves. Our religion is much like yours!"

"Wonderful, my brother in God! All you have to do is to prove that to us, and we're gone!" I said.

"How is it possible to prove a negative?"

"Simple enough! Let a few of us in and let them search the city. If your city doesn't keep any slaves, we don't have any reason to be here. But if you lie to us, we will storm your walls, and put every free man in it to the sword!"

"Don't be absurd! A direct frontal attack would cost you most of your army!" He said.

"Perhaps. But when you are doing the work of Allah, you don't count the cost!"

"We'll think about it!"

"Think quickly. Our camels are hungry," I said.

We rode slowly back to where they had our camp set up, in the middle of a large vegetable garden. Our camp was growing bigger. There were about fourteen thousand of us now.

Soon, in full view of those on the city wall, our cavalry drove a fair sized herd of animals into a waiting line of Juma's men. These animals were sheep, and we ate mutton for a while.

I had my people save and stack the sheepskins, before the scavengers arrived to eat them. I was working on a plan.

Our animals ate well, that night. Horses are very fond of carrots, melons, and cabbages.

I doubled the guard, and had most of them surrounding the city, keeping out of sight in the darkness.

Soon after midnight, our guards observed a long line of people leaving the city through a small, back door. Some of them were armed, but most were not. Those who were not were chained together. Estimates ran to between two and four thousand slaves, with a tenth of that number of men guarding them. Obeying orders, my Warriors let them leave, but sent word to us and then followed them to a secluded valley some miles from the city.

They surrounded them, and then waited for reinforcements.

Juma wanted to take the slave's guards with his own people, but my own Warriors needed some battle experience, too, so I assigned six companies of regulars, my most experienced men, under Sir Stephan, to do the job. They went out in the gray dawn.

There were no archers in our force, since I didn't want the slaves hurt, and my bowmen weren't much on accuracy, yet. That is to say, the men were there, but their bows weren't. They mostly carried axes. This would be a matter settled with swords, pikes and axes. One Jewish company was included in this group. I had Sir Stephan put the Jews in the center, since I wanted to see how they'd do.

Sir Percy's cavalry was sent out to reinforce the screening guards, and to pick off any of the enemy who tried to escape.

My plan involved not letting the city fathers know that we were on to their trick.

I went along to observe the fun, but not to command, if possible. It was time to give Sir Stephan his chance.

The fight was over in a quarter of an hour. Sir Stephan had done a fine job, and

I told him so. The enemy wasn't all that incompetent, but they were terribly outnumbered. I was happy to see that all of my forces had done well, including the Jews. I told them all that, too.

We did pick up four hundred sets of decent weapons among the booty, and even a bit of good armor. I also had their uniforms brought back, but I had a feeling that we wouldn't be needing them. The boots proved useful, though.

A crew of blacksmiths arrived to cut the ex-slave's chains off, and it turned out to be an all day job.

Juma's men came along to guard the newly freed slaves throughout the day, and to 'clean up' the battlefield in their usual way. Sir Stephan insisted on burying all of our own Christian, Islamic, and Jewish casualties with full honors, over Juma's protest. Our regular forces drifted back to camp in small groups, so as to attract as little attention as possible.

I got back by mid-morning, to find that the city fathers had been trying to contact me, while still staying out of site.

"You were looking for me?" I shouted.

"Yes! Where have you been?"

"Why, I have been at my morning prayers! Surely you understand that I am a very religious man!"

"Oh. Well, we have decided to accept your offer, and permit a maximum of one hundred of your people to inspect our city to prove to you that we have no slaves here," he said.

"This is wonderful! I shall get together a proper group of leaders, and meet with you, soon. But for now, what would you say to some trade? We have the usual trade goods with us, knives and fish hooks, needles and glassware. We also have quite a collection of ivory and rhino horns! Also, our foragers came up with a very good herd of wild sheep yesterday! We now have several thousand fresh sheep skins for sale! In return, we need horses, as many as you can spare, say four hundred of them. Do you have a cloth making industry in your city? Many of my soldiers' uniforms are in poor condition, and we could use some large quantities of red and white cloth of good quality. Perhaps enough for four thousand new uniforms."

"We know about the sheep you butchered! Those were OUR sheep, damn you!"

"But surely, that is quite impossible. They were wild, without any Sheppards about. If they had been your sheep, you would have been taking proper care of them. Now, about the horses and the cloth…" I said.

"Thief! What about the inspection you promised, so your gluttonous band can get out of here?"

"As I said, we will do it soon! But today is Saturday, the Sabbath of the Jews and Moslems among us. We must not offend them by working on their Holy Day! I will go now, but think, please, about collecting up some large quantities of horses, and red and white cloth. We, for our part, will try to collect up some more of those excellent sheep skins for you!"

I went back to my camp. This was a lot of fun. We couldn't safely attack them, inside of their fortifications, and they didn't dare attack us, out in the open field, but now that we had their slaves safely out of there, I could certainly twist their tail a bit!

We spent the rest of the day doing field maneuvers with the Christian part of our army. They marched around the fields, smashing cabbages and melons, pretending to charge at each other, and practicing their archery.

The people in the city watched us, fuming. For some reason, those gardens were very important to them.

We slaughtered a few thousand more sheep at the end of the day, and after nightfall, Juma had the new ex-slaves brought into our camp. There were just over thirty-eight hundred of them.

Not a bad haul! I picked up two more pretty, well trained, Christian girls for myself, or rather, Jasmine did. She believed in keeping her only customer, me, satisfied, and in taking her duties as my head of household very seriously.

The last of the men in my household wasn't sleeping alone any more, either.

On Sunday, the people in the city were making noise again, but I ignored them until noon. Instead, I had the ivory, the rhino horns, and the sheep skins set out on display not far from the main city gate, along with what trade goods we still had with us.

After church services, and a leisurely breakfast with three cups of coffee, I again dressed well and went out to talk to our hosts once more.

The Arab and Jewish companies were out on maneuvers today, mostly doing it in the grain fields a bit to the west of the city, since we Christians had mashed up the vegetable gardens to the south the day before. I'd also sent out our Arab camel cavalry to look over the local villages, and to see what could be found. If the towns were really empty of people, they had orders to burn one of them to the ground.

I shouted at the gate tower, "You wanted to talk to me again? But why haven't your merchants been down here to examine the goods that we have for sale?

"Because we don't want what you have for sale! We want you to inspect our city for slaves and then to get out of here!" It was the same hidden voice.

"As I told you, we will do that, soon! But today is Sunday, and I am a Christian, as are more than half of my people. It would be a sin for us to work on a Holy Day!"

"If doing anything on a Holy Day is so evil, then what are all of those soldiers doing out there, ruining our barley fields?"

I said, "They are practicing military field maneuvers. Since we are fighting for the cause of Allah, training for the battle is an act of religious devotion! Surely, you can understand that! Now, have you gotten together the four hundred and fifty horses that we need, and the cloth for six thousand new uniforms?"

"Yesterday, you wanted four hundred horses and cloth for four thousand uniforms!"

"True, but a large group of new converts to our cause arrived last night, and we must provide for them, too. Surely, a righteous man like you can see that!"

He shouted, "So, now your demands have again increased!"

"But we are only offering you the opportunity to trade with us! You have not yet examined the quality of our fine products!"

"What you have down there isn't worth a quarter of what you are demanding in return!"

I said, "We can only offer what we have, as you can only donate to our noble cause what you can."

"What's that burning out there?"

"I really couldn't tell you, but if you leave whole villages unattended for any length of time, something bad is likely to happen to them."

He yelled, "Get off our land, damn you!"

"But it's not your land! The area around here is completely empty of people! But consider my offer for trade, and we'll talk again tomorrow!"

And then I went back to my camp. I was getting a kick out of this, and we really did need a rest, and a chance to practice field maneuvers.

Monday was much the same, except that we now had all of our troops out there destroying crops.

It was mid-morning before we got another call from the hidden rulers of this city.

I got suitably gussied up, and went out to talk to them once again.

"Hello! May I come down and talk with you, my Christian Lord?"

This was a different voice that the rude person that I'd yelled at before.

I said, "You certainly may, with my personal guarantee of your safety. It is pleasant indeed to speak with an educated and courteous gentleman!"

"Thank you!"

Soon, a well dressed man of middle age came through a small door in the massive city gate. He was on foot, so I got down off from my high horse.

I said, "Greetings, sir. May I have the honor of knowing your position, and your illustrious name?"

"You may indeed, my lord. It happens that I am now the new ruler of this city, and am known as Abdul Labobo Lamere."

Part of me wanted to claim to be Ivan Skavinsky-Skavar, but I decided to play this one straight. Or reasonably straight.

"Thank you, my noble sir. I am Conrad Stargard, Hetman of the Christian Army."

He said, "Indeed! I am surprised to find you in the middle of Africa, and so far from your own lands."

"It is a long and complicated tale, which would take some hours in the telling. Perhaps we could talk about it over dinner, tonight, in my camp."

"I gladly accept your invitation, my lord."

"I have many titles, but my friends simply call me Conrad," I said.

"Then you must call me only Abdul. But I am here for a purpose. As I understand it, you have said to my predecessor that if you received cloth of red and white, sufficient for six thousand uniforms, and four hundred and fifty good horses, you would be willing to leave our lands, and continue on with your duty to Allah elsewhere?"

"This is so, Abdul."

He said, "Would you swear this to Allah, and also to your Christian God?"

"There is but one God, but I will swear it to Him in both of His names, if you wish."

He said, "Then we are minded to accommodate you. We have the horses that you wish, and we will provide you with all of the necessary saddles and bridles that they need, of good quality, though not necessarily new. The cloth presents a problem. We have enough cloth of good quality to suit your needs, including plenty of white cloth, but not a sufficient quantity of the red. Could we make up the difference with other colors?"

"Yes, I would agree with that, since you are being so courteous."

"Excellent. We will add to it sufficient thread for the sewing. And, if I were to give you these gifts immediately, could you leave immediately?"

"Well, I could immediately call in all of my men, who are presently doing impolite things to your city's property, and leave in the first hour tomorrow morning," I said.

"That would be sufficient. What of your requirement that you inspect our city for slaves?"

"Abdul, you are a true gentleman. If you would swear to Allah that there are no slaves in your city, I would believe you."

"Willingly would I do that," he said.

"Then we are in agreement. Could you have the cloth and horses out here, say in the middle of the afternoon?"

"That could be arranged."

"Then do so. We will each bring, say, fifty of our best men here to hear our oaths. And we will be gone in the morning. But come to my camp when the sun is a hand's breath above the horizon, and have dinner with me and my household," I said.

I told my runner to get word out immediately to call in all of our troops, and for them to come back doing as little damage to the crops as possible.

I said, "And our payment for this. You will be taking that back with you?"

"As to that, rhino horns have a very high value far to the east, where they make dagger and sword handles out of them. I would very much appreciate them as a personal gift. We have jewelers, glass blowers, and smiths in this city, and so your trade goods have little value here. Keep them for later trading. The raw sheep skins aren't worth your trouble to haul them away, so we might as well send them to a local tannery. And the ivory? I have heard that it is highly valued in your homeland of Europe, but it has little value here. Take it back with you."

"Thank you. And please have the rhino horns as my personal gift to you."

As I rode back to my camp, I couldn't help smiling.

Abdul Labobo Lamere! What a laugh!

I was a school boy when I first read the poem about the fight between Abdul Labobo Lamere and Ivan Skavinsky-Skavar.

That was over forty years ago, and I don't remember it all any more, but it started out, "The sons of the Prophet are braver than most, and quite unaccustomed to fear, but the bravest of all was a man wide and tall, one Abdul Labobo Lamere! If you needed a man to encourage the band, or attack at the enemy's rear, you had only to shout for that big bounding lout, one Abdul Labobo Lamere!"

The Russian got similar praise, until he walked through a tavern to hear "I'll have you to know that you have trod on the toe of one Abdul Labobo Lamere!"

Somewhat later, it went on, "And historian blokes, who seldom make jokes, say that hash was first made on that spot!"

But it couldn't possibly be the same guy. Funny coincidences like that happen, like the time when two of my peasants came to me for permission to get married. I always granted such permission, but when I found out their names, I'd almost fallen off my chair. His was Nickolai Copernic, and hers was Maria Slodowska, perhaps better known by her married name, Marie Currie. The names of two famous scientists. I kept track of their kids, in case we had a family of Einsteins coming along, but they were just ordinary people.

In the afternoon, all oaths had been sworn, and promises had been carried out. The horses and cloth were taken to my camp. They were good horses, with decent tack. The cloth was of good enough quality, and since the usual Arab outfit needs twice as much material as a European one, we had plenty of red cloth for our Warrior's uniforms. And enough of other colors to satisfy our ladies as well.

I ordered that all of the city's ex-slaves be kept well out of sight for Abdul's visit.

At dinner in my camp, I told the story of my being washed off my ship, Cynthia's death, and my enslavement in Timbuktu. I told about how my hand regrew, our rebellion, and all that happened afterward. Abdul was amazed, and this was the first time that two of my girls had heard the story. They were enraptured.

Later that evening, I asked Abdul about the former ruler of the city.

"He was a great fool who had great prestige because of the wisdom of his father. But when he was willing to ruin an entire harvest over so trivial a matter as some cloth and a few horses, well, he became suddenly ill, and died in his sleep."

"Of a knife in the throat?"

"In the heart, actually. Strange, these new diseases. I wish you well, Conrad Stargard. As odd as it sounds, I owe my recent advancement to you."

Chapter 36 (Sir Walznik's Rescue) The Trip to Timbuktu

They had been traveling through the desert for two weeks. It was the brownest and driest place they had ever seen. Every building was built of brown mud bricks, every person robed in brown cotton. The dust was under their clothes and gritting under their tongues and in their teeth. The eyes of men and beast alike had to be swathed in cotton to keep the sun and sand away. They all hoped they would find the end of their quest in Timbuktu. It was only a few gritty days away.

They had stopped at the last of an endless succession of boring mud hut villages. They asked the endless question again.

"We are looking for a friend. He is tall and he has…" Banner Hendricks had asked the questions so many times that he was beginning to loose interest in finding anyone – even Lord Conrad. The weariness and boredom were becoming unbearable. Please, he thought, let this end soon. I don't mind the danger and I can face death, but if I have to have this conversation one more time…

It was a town of brown mud huts. The town had no walls, no streets, and, obviously, no tradition of bathing.

"Slaves! Do we look like we have any slaves? They all ran off. Look at my poor wife over there drawing her own water from the well. The slaves are all gone! Every slave in this country has rebelled. They stole all of the food, molested the women, beat most of the men and then ran off. My wife can't sleep at night for fear that they might come back and attack us! You look like soldiers. Maybe you can bring them back."

He resisted the urge to pat the pathetic man on the head and said, "Oh, don't worry. If we see them, we'll send them right back. How long have they been gone?"

"About a month. Some rebellious slaves came to the village talking about how all of the slaves in Timbuktu were free and the army was gone. Pretty soon, our slaves were gone too. Now there are bands of slaves roaming the countryside raping and murdering and stealing. My wife is terrified! Thank the gods, they seem to going away from us."

"Did you hear what started it?"

The mans voice got earnest, "You wouldn't believe it! They say a great blond god dropped out of the sky into Timbuktu. He is bigger than two men and swings a huge magic sword. He slaughtered hundred of soldiers and brought lightening down on the city walls. When the people defied him, he made floods run through the street and drowned them all. Now he leads the slaves east, destroying all that he sees. It is a bad time."

The banner was whistling as he sauntered back to his horse. I think that we have found Lord Conrad, Hetman of the Christian Army, and a gentle soul throughout.

As they approached Timbuktu, they saw their first evidence of Lord Conrad's presence. Beside the road, an undershot water wheel was patiently lifting water from the stream to an irrigation ditch. This was the first mechanical power they had seen on this continent. When one has slaves, the cost of water wheels and windmills is often unjustified. It seems that the tales of Lord Conrad and free slaves were true. A tired smile passed down the column as the each trooper came into sight of the wheels.

The pace picked up as confidence grew that they no longer had to search foot by dusty foot for their leader. Within an hour they were on the outskirts of the city. Irrigated fields become more numerous and they began to pass surprised farmers who stood in small clumps to watch the column go by.

The city was impressive. It was still as brown as dirt, but impressive. The walls and the large building beyond were built with plastered limestone, not the mud brick and palm trees of most of the towns they had passed. Moreover, the other towns had been tiny compared this one and had not had windmills on top of the gate towers. The soldiers watching the gate were actually paying attention to the farmers and peddlers walking through. More impressive, both they and their uniforms were clean and in good repair. And the uniforms were colored red and white!

The Captain signaled the column to halt about four dozen yards from the gate and rode forward with Banner Hendricks and two Warriors. He halted in front of the two guards that had moved into the road in front of him and saluted, "I am Captain Walznik of the Christian Army. I have come with a message for Lord Conrad Stargard, whom I have reason to believe is residing in your city."

The guard snapped back a proper Christian Army salute! "Very good, Sir. I will inform the officer of the watch. If you please, kindly wait here."

The wait was short. A short and muscular man dressed in uniform and bright shiny breastplate appeared from a guardhouse inside the gate. He saluted when he stopped in front of the Captain.

"I hear that you are part of the Christian Army. Of course we are happy to greet our allies. However, you understand that I cannot allow an armed column into the city without more authority. I suggest that you allow your men and animals to rest on that level spot near river while I confer with the officer of the day. If you wish to water your animals, please put out guards. Occasionally, there are dangerous beasts in the water. You and your retinue are, of course, welcome to share the comforts of the guard post while wait."

The Captain motioned to Hendricks, who turned his horse around to return to the column, and then dismounted to enter the gate. He tried very hard to ignore the archers who had quietly appeared above the gate. Mother had always said that it wasn't polite to stare, particularly when you were staring at arrows pointed at your chest.

This time the wait was longer. The watch officer offered them something called "coffee" and wine and then left them alone in his office. They sipped the coffee and then decided that it must have some medicinal use as no one would drink something so bitter unless they had too. The wine wasn't bad, though.

Over half an hour passed before the door of the office banged open. Two men entered. The banger was a very short but powerful looking Arab man in his 40s. He had a rich cloak tossed over his wide shoulders. His sword was gilded, but visibly nicked by use. His right hand was missing. The other man was obviously his aid.

He returned their salute in a casual manner, with his left hand. "Captain, uh, Walznik. I hear that you are a member of the Christian Army and that you are looking for our Friend Lord Conrad." He said this in Arabic, and then continued in practiced pigeon Polish, "Where come you from?"

Walznik was still absorbing "our friend" and was caught off guard by the sudden switch to Polish. "We started inland from a city on the coast named from Armoon. We have followed the caravan trail looking for Lord Conrad."

The mans face squinted fleetingly and his finger wagged at them, "No talk fast. Small words. How long to come?"

Walznik said in Aramaic, "Perhaps it would be more convenient for you to speak in this language. We come from Armoon, on the ocean. It took us five months to travel up the old road."

Their questioner smiled and continued in fluent Aramaic. "So there really is a Christian Army? I am Omar and a friend of your Lord Conrad Stargaurd. It is with his help that I assumed command of this desert paradise. Is he really a great Lord in your land?"

Walznik was surprised at the question. "Very great. Our army is the largest in Christendom and our Lord's lands are greater than any king's. If you have fought along side him, you surely know that."

Omar almost looked jolly, "Well, I knew that there were men here who claimed to be part of a vast army and that Lord Conrad claimed to be their leader. However, every man more than a hundred miles from home is a king in his own land and it is not polite to question a man who has saved your life so many times. I am almost disappointed to learn that his truth may have been as strong as his sword arm.

"Unfortunately, Lord Conrad was unable to wait for your arrival," he continued. "He left for home several weeks ago. I suggest that we let your men and animals rest. Armoon is a long way away. I'll have my aid show you where you can unburden your animals and rest your men. If you will join me for the evening meal, we can discuss your future plans." With that, Omar left the room.

After a few moments, his aid gestured for Captain Walznik to follow.

"We have several empty barracks which are normally occupied by the troops that are with Lord Conrad. We can put you up there. I'll have some people bring over supplies and re-open the cafeteria for you. Your men should have some real rest so I'll send some servants for the cooking and cleaning."

As they walked past the gates, the Captain asked, "Several barracks? How many retainers did Lord Conrad take with him."

The aid bit his lip as he thought, "I don't know exactly. Perhaps twelve thousand or so."

So much for "rescuing" Lord Conrad. He seemed to have done that without help.

The evening meal was a pleasant experience for everyone. It was like a slice of home for the troops to eat in a real cafeteria again. There were even Polish Eagles in the wall decorations. Most of the food was not what they were used to. Curried Mutton, dates, figs and spiced camel meat pies were not common in Poland. However, there were also piles of steaming corn on the cob, platters of boiled and baked potatoes, baked sweet potatoes, chunks of roasted beef and stewed tomatoes. It was heaven on Earth which was cooked by heavy sweaty cooks and served up by slender, scantily clad female servants. It was almost worth the trip.

A few gross yards away and five stories higher up, the officers were enjoying fancier service but the same food. They lay back on silken pillows and were served on silver plates by women even more comely than the cafeteria servants. The conversation had been about their trip. All during dinner, they had traded tales of the road and tales of Lord Conrad. As the last dinner dishes were cleared away, they settled back for business.

Omar opened the conversation. "I assume that, having come this far, you will want to continue on your quest to find Lord Conrad."

It was hard to tell whether Captain Walznik groaned or smiled. "Of course, we are anxious to find him. It has been a hard trip and we intend to see it through." Omar tried to sound reassuring. "Your trip is almost over. Lord Conrad left here about six weeks ago. He had between twelve and thirteen thousand soldiers and civilians in his column so I doubt that he can make more than 25 or 30 miles a day. I suspect that he is also stopping to free slaves and make an impression on the local population. If you rode like a Mongol, you'd probably catch him in a few days. Of course, that's not realistic because you have you own column to carry with you."

Walznik sat forward on his cushion. "I plan that we should leave as soon as possible. My men are tough but tired. The longer we stay here, the harder it will be to get them back up to speed. We'll purchase what supplies we can, rest for two or three days and then get on the way. I noticed that you do have a building that looks like a church. If it is, some of my men will want to celebrate the mass there before they go on."

"It is, but Conrad took all of our Christian priests with him on the journey."

"Well, I suppose that we could use the one that we brought with us."

"Then please make any use of the church that pleases you," Omar replied. "You are officially either allies or part of our army and unofficially, you are pledged to a good friend of mine. We can find the money to re-supply your larders and provide you with fresh mounts. Call it a repayment of debts to old friends."

He looked thoughtful. "In fact, I am glad you are going to join my old friend. He has a lot of trained soldiers with him, but your men could be a big help to him. My staff says that you are carrying many firearms and I assume that you are carrying some bombs and hand grenades. You are only eighty-four men, but you are worth ten times that number because of your weapons and training. Somehow, he is going to have to get past the Almohades Empire and I doubt that it will be an easy passage."

Dinner ended with more planning, lists of supplies, music, and sleepy goodbyes.

They were on the road again four days later. Their horses and mules had been replaced where necessary and they now had spare mounts. Even the women and cooks were mounted on their own horses. The supply wagons had been repaired with new bearings and metal tires. The mules were laden with dried meat and fruits as well as corn meal and flour.

This was the final leg and they were stripped for speed. At least, they did not have to ask if anyone had seen Lord Conrad. Twelve thousand people would be hard to miss.

Almost every day was the same. They had loading, saddling, and tent striking down to a half hour pattern. They ate cold corn dodgers, bread, and dried fruit while they worked. At midday, there was time for hot tea, dried meat, and bread from the night before while they unpacked and unsaddled almost every horse and mule and saddled and packed the spare animals. The night meal was the only real hot meal of the day. There as more time for human meals because the animals had to graze and be cared for. Half of the night was given to baking tomorrow's food.

Chapter 37   Into The Mountains

We left early on Tuesday morning, and headed north, before Abdul could find out what had happened to his city's slaves and the men guarding them.

For weeks, the scissors and needles were busy every night, and everyone in the caravan was eventually well clothed. The buttons were made of wood or bone, instead of brass or gold, but they were recognizably uniforms, which is important for morale.

With the new uniforms as an incentive, we found some tanners and cobblers among our people, and boots started to be made. The tanning was crude, and we didn't have any way of dying the leather, but they were better than nothing. A uniform without boots just didn't make it.

Elephant hide makes a very good sole for an infantryman's shoe, and one thickness of it made a good heel for a cavalryman's boot.

The mules were back to doing mule work, and Sir Percy had used the rest of the new horses to form up a second company of horse cavalry.

Many of our new cavalrymen were now wearing leather armor. Boiled rawhide, stretched over a reusable wooden frame, dried, trimmed, and then heavily waxed, was remarkably effective. Pound for pound, it was almost as good as steel.

The infantry were equipping themselves with armor, too, at least to the point of helmets and breast plates. The preferred helmet was halfway between a German WWII helmet, and something that might have come from Medieval Japan. It gave fairly decent protection to the sides of the head and the back of the neck. Individual companies were coming up with distinctive decorations, panache, for the tops of them. I let them have their fun, so long as the basic colors were red and white, from a distance. I wanted it always to be obvious who the good guys were.

Battles have been lost because someone confused the enemy with their own forces. And vice versa.

I don't know why we hadn't started doing this leather armor thing sooner. Maybe, because nobody thought of it.

We were well equipped by the time we started climbing up into the Atlas Mountains. It was just as well, because as the terrain became more rugged, we started finding fewer large animals with good leather on them.

Juma's spear chuckers were feeding themselves well enough, but they weren't bagging the huge surpluses they'd been getting on the plains.

This meant that less meat was coming into the camp, but we still had just as much food as when we had left Timbuktu. Flour was getting scarce, and we had cut bread production down to three thousand loaves a day. I suppose that I should have hit Abdul up for a supply of flour, or at least grain, but it didn't occur to me at the time. Perhaps I am getting old. We were buying more of it from the few farmers we were coming across.

Still, we had plenty of dried and salted meat, packed in old flour barrels.

It amounted to a two month supply, at least, without any rationing. It wasn't a three month supply because we had more than eighteen thousand people with us now. We had started out with twelve.

The reduced meat supply was somewhat alleviated by the fact that our archers were finally learning to shoot. We let them spend an hour a day hunting, and what anyone in a lance could shoot, the men in that lance could eat. Going after rabbits and birds improves a man's marksmanship considerably! And occasionally, they got something big enough to contribute to the common pot.

Mohamed said that if we weren't stopped by the Almohades Empire, we should get to the sea coast in five or six weeks. And if we really did empty the commissary camels, we could always eat the camels themselves. Try that one with a modern truck!

We were running into fewer people now, and only about ten or twenty slaves were being freed a day.

Finally, the day came for us to leave the Niger river, which was bending to the west, and take to a trail heading north again.

The trail was narrow, and with eighteen thousand people and many animals, we had a caravan that was almost nineteen miles long! We had to break it up into four groups, each traveling a day behind the one in front. The first consisted of healthy men, mostly, who broke trail, built camps, and left what supplies of wood behind that they could. They also dug a lot of wells. Juma, Mohamed, and I went with the first caravan. The last one had a strong rearguard, under Sir Meier. Other Warriors were in the middle two caravans, as were the trainees, along with the bulk of the non-combatants.

The next three groups followed in order. There weren't many people living here, so there wasn't really a security problem. Still, my basic paranoia was working overtime, thinking about everything that could go wrong.

Our cavalry kept the groups in touch with one another, and told the ones behind about the problems to be faced up ahead.

We had to carry our water with us now, since while we crossed many stream beds, they weren't always running with water. When we found water, we always drank deep, and topped off the water bags. A few times, we had to dig wells in a dry stream bed to get enough water to take care of the animals. It was horses first, then women and children, then the mules, followed by the men. Camels came last, since they could take it.

But at least these mountain streams were clean, and without crocodiles and hippos.

The rugged terrain was starting to turn into real mountains now, and we were making for a mountain pass with almost vertical walls, they told me, which had been cut by a small river. We'd have to wade in that river for two days, and spend a night sleeping on horseback.

We found the pass, but there wasn't any river at the bottom of it.

A day later, we found out why. A huge rock slide had blocked the pass and the river as well. A vigorous man could easily have climbed over the slide, but there was no way to get the caravan through, not with our pack animals, horses, and wagons filled with the children, the sick, and the severely pregnant women.

The rock slide was made up of huge boulders of hard rock, way beyond our ability to cut, break, or move. My sword could scratch this stuff, but our ordinary tools could not. Our two barrels of serpentine powder couldn't have moved a tenth of it.

The standard way of doing the job would be to cover the rocks with dirt, building a ramp over it, but the old streambed was made up of scowered stone. The nearest dirt was a day's march back, toward where we had come from. My first eyeball estimates said that even with all of our animals, men and healthy women working on it, the job would take four months to complete, even if there was any fodder for the animals, which there wasn't in here.

We didn't have the supplies to do that.

We might possibly be able to climb the sheer rock walls to the top of the plateau, but we didn't have anything like enough rope to haul up all of our baggage, animals, wagons, and people. And the top of the plateau might be impassable, anyway. Nobody knew.

Plan Z involved asking the eight thousand ladies we had with us to cut off their long hair, so that we could make rope out of it. I put that one off, for a bit. I knew that if I asked them, they would do it, but I saw a lifetime of nagging ahead for all of us if we asked it.

I sent the first caravan back to a small spring we'd passed a while ago, and told them to pitch camp. I also sent runners back to the other three caravans behind us, telling them to find a good place to wait for a while.

Along with most of my best technical people, I climbed the huge rock fall.

When we finally got to the top, we had another problem in front of us. The river had backed up against the rock fall, half filling the valley beyond, like the water behind a dam. So even if we could somehow get the caravan over this natural dam, it wouldn't do us any good at all without a fleet of boats! And if we could somehow have blown it up, we all would be promptly killed by a tidal wave of water!

I pondered the problem all night, but I could see no technically feasible way to get us over the rock slide. Climbing up the rock face was a very 'iffy' proposition. I talked it over with the men in our engineering company, but nothing workable came of it. My Old Christian Army Warriors also drew a blank.

In the morning, I called a meeting of our leaders to discuss the problem. After an hour of useless talk, the Caravan Master, Mohamed, said, "Well, there is another route…"

"There is WHAT?!" I shouted. "Why didn't you tell us about this before?"

"Because the other route has certain difficulties associated with it. We would never be permitted to use it."

"Please tell us more," I said, exasperated.

"There is a large and pleasant valley to the west of here, which is completely surrounded by high mountains, except for one place that is much like this very valley that we are in right now. The narrow valley then splits into two valleys, one going to the north and one to the south. The inhabitants of the big valley have built very strong walls across these two narrow valleys, with extremely strong gates and portcullises. They sometimes permit small caravans through, for a price, and while they are largely self sufficient, they do engage in a small amount of trade."

"But they would be afraid of letting a group as big as ours in?" I asked.

"Precisely. By now, they have probably heard of our pervious difficulties on this trip, and what has happened to some of the people that we encountered. They would not love us for what we have done," Mohamed said.

"And these people own slaves?"

"Doesn't everyone?"

Mohamed told us the name of the city, but I couldn't begin to pronounce it. From his description of it, I started calling it Shangri La, and the name caught on.

"Okay, people. Break camp. We're going to look this situation over, and anyway, this valley is not a safe place to stay in. Besides the lack of forage for our animals, there's no telling just how long that natural dam will hold. Certainly, it won't last forever. Lead us to this city you talk of, Mohamed. Runners, tell the other caravans to follow us."

We were six days getting to the gates of the city that was apparently in our way. As before, I tried talking to them.

I tried what had worked before. I got into my most impressive outfit and rode our best horse, with but a single runner beside me, carrying the Christian Battle Flag.

"Hello, the gate!" I shouted.

"Hello, yourself!"

"I am Conrad Stargard, Hetman of the Christian Army, and I request passage through your city!"

"We know who you are, and we don't want your sort here. Your request is denied. Go away!" The man said.

"Who are you, to be denying us passage?"

"I am the keeper of this gate, and I am following the orders of my betters. Go away!"

I said, "But we could pay you very well if you allowed us passage! We have a tenth of the entire treasury of the City of Timbuktu with us!"

"We are unimpressed, having gold mines of our own in the valley. Most of the gold you carry probably came from here in the first place. Go away!"

"I know that you would feel unconfident, with such a large force as we are passing through. But we could go in small groups, such that your guards would at all times outnumber us."

He said, "The matter has been considered already, and been rejected. Go away!"

"Can nothing that I say convince you of our sincerity? Does not pity make you want to help us in our need?"

"Not in the least! You are liars, murderers and thieves! Go away!"

"Well, please convey my words to your superiors. I will return at this time tomorrow to talk to you, or hopefully to them tomorrow," I said.

It seemed to me to be about as serious a rejection as a man could get!

That gate looked strong enough to stand up to any sort of battering ram we could come up with.

What we needed was a company of heavy artillery, but that was sadly unavailable.

We had a couple of barrels of serpentine powder loaded on one of the camels in my personal train. We needed to build a petard!

When I got back to the caravan, I started giving orders. The engineering company was to meet me as soon as possible. The others were to set up camp somewhere that Mohamed selected. I wanted it to be big enough to hold all of our forces, with a separate place to put all of our animals. I wanted it surrounded with a ditch three yards deep, and have an earth rampart three yards high inside of that. Then I wanted a sturdy palisade built on top of the rampart.

I wanted some wooden towers built on all four corners of our fort, and some drawbridges going over the ditch, or dry moat. I wanted wells dug inside the fort, at least thirty yards from the latrines.

I put Sir Stephan in charge of construction, went to talk to the assembled engineering company, and told them what I wanted done to get rid of that gate.

Then I went to where my personal camp had already been set up, changed back into comfortable clothes, had a glass of brandy, and watched everyone scurrying around me.

Delegation is a wonderful thing.

Chapter 38 Taking Shangri La

The fort was completed by the time the last caravan got there. Sir Stephan had added a few refinements of his own, such as lining the dry moat and ramparts with small, vertically placed logs that had been cleaned of their bark. Even though it was only at a forty-five degree angle, it was almost impossible to climb up the slippery stuff.

The wells had been lined with short lengths of interlocking logs, to make sure that they wouldn't collapse at the wrong time, they each had a roof over them, and featured a crank system to haul up the buckets of water. The latrines had proper wooden seats and were enclosed for privacy.

Collecting up all of this wood had cleared the surrounding area for almost a mile, so no one was going to sneak up on us. Plus, the chips and small pieces left over gave us a month's supply of firewood.

All told, it was a first class job considering that we'd only spent three days at it. Sir Stephan said that if we had another two days, he'd have a bath house ready.

The purpose of the fort was that if the petard failed to do it's job, the citizens of what we were calling Shangri La would be unhappy with us, and just might attack us. Since from what Mohamed had said about them, they considerably out numbered us, and I would much rather fight them from a defendable position.

The petard was ready as well. A petard is simply an explosive in a strong container that is braced against a door, and then ignited. In the Late Middle Ages, the container often looked like a church bell, but we didn't have a church bell. We had some wooden barrels, which by themselves wouldn't be strong enough. Unless the barrels held together for the first instant after ignition, the force of the explosion would go sideways, not forward. We were dealing with a fairly low grade explosive here. With a modern, high explosive, like plastique, that wouldn't have been so important.

We reinforced the barrels by first emptying them out, tightly winding them with many layers of wet rawhide, and then drying the raw leather slowly over a low fire. You get a really long strip of leather by skinning a big animal before you gut him, cutting the skin around the shoulders, and in front of the hips, and pulling a big tube of skin back over its hind legs. From there, you can cut off a long strip in a helix. How many layers did we use? Until we ran out of leather, actually. We only had six cattle available at the time. This was rule of thumb engineering we were doing here.

The leather shrinks on drying, squeezing the barrel tightly together. The back of the barrels would be up against a large tree trunk, which would be wedged into the hole left when we lifted a big paving stone, so the barrel itself didn't have to be strong there. The front of the barrels would be tight against the gate, at the level that we were sure the bar was at. The object of this exercise was to break that bar.

Our tree trunk had to fit tightly, so the distance from the paving stone to the gate had to be exactly right.

Getting the dimensions correct was done with a measuring rod, by two of our engineers the night after my first conversation with the gate keeper. They were ready to say that they were looking for my lost, silver handled dagger, but fortunately, they weren't noticed at all.

The petard was mounted on a pivot in one of our covered wagons. While one team was prying up the right paving stone, another would be pushing the wagon up to the gate, just before gray dawn.

The serpentine powder was carefully mixed, put back into the barrels, and the lids put back on.

This was necessary because with serpentine powder, the ingredients (fifteen parts of saltpeter, three of ground charcoal, and two of sulfur), are simply mixed together. During travel, the materials separate out, and with all of the charcoal at the top, it won't explode. Before we left Timbuktu, there hadn't been time to wet the mixture, press it into cakes, dry the cakes, grind them up again, and then sift the black powder.

While our men worked on the fort, most of our leaders went over our battle plan with me. Except for the less than fifty men who had served with the Old Christian Army (I couldn't help but think of it that way!), most of our people had no experience with explosives. Three quarters of them had never even heard of them. Some things had to be explained over and over again.

Finally, I just had to say, "There will be a big, loud noise, like thunder, or like lightning hitting near by! There will be a lot of dust and a terrible smell! Don't worry about it. It is supposed to be like that. If the gate falls down, or is broken open, charge the enemy, because they won't have had any idea of what is going on. They will be confused, and that will make them easy to kill."

I said, "Remember our rules of engagement. Kill anyone who is trying to kill you. Kill anyone who is armed, and not one of us. Accept the surrender of those who throw down their arms, or who say that they surrender, but keep them under close guard. Do not kill women, children, harmless old people, or anyone who says that he is a slave, unless they are trying to kill you. Able bodied men who claim to be slaves will be locked up somewhere, until we can sort them out later. Breaking these rules can get a man hung, unless I'm really mad at him, at which point things can get painful. Surely, that is easy enough!"

"Also," I continued, "There will be no looting until the entire big valley is taken. Then, you can loot to your heart's content. We'll pool all the loot, and a soldier's committee will decide on a fair division of the booty. Fancy weapons, clothing, and art works are 'finders keepers'. Gold and silver are not. We'll share that equally. Women may be taken home with you only if they are willing, but as long as you don't harm them, there's nothing wrong with a little sex. Just be gentle, huh? Make sure that this is drilled into all of your men. First you conquer, then you rape, then you pillage, AND THEN you burn! And tell them not to do much burning. There will be a lot of stuff in there that we can use. A full granary would be nice."

I'd learned long ago that stopping rape after a battle was impossible without killing half of my own men, and I had a sneaking suspicion that the women wanted it as much as my troops did. Sex is a very good thing to remove your anxieties and tensions with. The best that I could do was to try to cut down on the sexual violence.

I'd visited the gate every day, hoping to generate some sanity in the opposition, but I'd really known from the beginning that it was hopeless. They were so convinced that they were invulnerable that they wouldn't even talk with me. Mostly, I just didn't want to blame myself later about not doing everything possible to prevent major bloodshed. Because major was just what this one was going to be.

Juma came over to my blue and gold silk tent for dinner, something that he often did.

He said, "You know, I was very impressed with those mills you built in Timbuktu. Machines that did useful work, and acted almost as if they were alive! It sometimes seemed to me that they should have manna in them, but of course, they didn't. But this thing that you plan to use on the big gate has me baffled. Could there be a kind of manna that I cannot see, or feel?"

I said, "I suppose that you could look at it that way. You have said that manna is power, nothing but power. Well, there are many kinds of power in this world. The machines we built in Timbuktu worked on wind power, some of them, and the rest on water power. Those two food cookers worked on solar power. The petard works on chemical power, or at least I hope it works. Neither the device nor the powder in it have ever been tested properly, except in very small amounts. And I don't really know exactly how strong that gate is. All we can do is try it."

"We will hope that this chemical manna of yours is strong enough!"

I gave the men a day to rest up, and then we attacked.

I left our least well trained company to guard the fort, backed up by Mohamed, his camel handlers, the cooks, about a hundred women who said that they could shoot a bow, and a thousand more with axes and hatchets. And of course, everyone in the middle ages carried a knife. Our ladies had no intentions of ever becoming slaves again!

The wheels on the petard wagon were well greased, and a layer of fur had been wrapped around the wagon's steel tires to keep them quiet.

A lance of masons went first, followed by four lances of engineers, pushing and pulling the wagon. Juma's men went next. They would be our shock troops, if we got the gate open. Regular companies of infantry followed, in order of seniority, with the most experienced companies first. The cavalry went last. They probably wouldn't be needed until we were through the main defenses, and into the big valley behind them.

I was near the front, with my sword and bow, but riding a mule. I wasn't planning on leading any cavalry charges. I just needed a steady animal to lift me up high enough to see what was going on.

We got to the gate without attracting any obvious attention in the cold, gray dawn. The masons started trying to pry up the paving stone that had to be removed to get a hole to anchor the petard in. It wasn't coming. Neither were the stones on either side of it. They couldn't get any of them loose! As a backup, they had brought pickaxes and sledge hammers with them, so they started pounding on the offending rock with a great deal of energy.

This, of course was a noisy procedure, and now we were attracting attention. I saw four soldiers running out to the battlements, bows in hand.

"What are you doing down there!" One of them shouted from above.

"We're bringing you a present, to show you what kind of people we really are!" Jaccs Dupree, our Captain of the engineers, shouted. The masons kept on hammering.

"You will stop tearing up our streets, or we will shoot you!"

"Oh, come now! That wouldn't be very polite! Don't you like presents?" He said, while the masons kept at it.

I got my own bow ready and let fly at about the same time as the enemy did. But they were up there, and we were down here. Their arrows were hitting a whole lot harder than mine were, and there were more of them than there was of me. I should have thought of this possibility, and put a company of archers first, but I hadn't.

I shouted, "Archers to the front!"

It didn't do any good. The nearest archers were three gross yards back, and Juma's men were in their way, slowing them down, and stopping them from getting to where they could do some damage.

One of Juma's men let fly with a spear, and it actually got all the way up to the high battlements, but by then it was moving so slowly that it was just swatted aside, but cutting the swatter's hand, I was pleased to note.

They killed six of my men, three of the masons and three of the engineers standing with the wagon, before I got the four of them. But even while their friends around them were dying, the masons didn't stop. They just kept on smashing that stone into powder!

Each time a mason fell, an engineer ran up and took his place! Damn, but these were fine troops!

Two dozen more archers were running out to the fighting platform above us, some of them only half dressed. That was more men than I had arrows left!

It probably only took the masons a minute to pulverize that damned stone, but it seemed a lot longer at the time. The masons left quickly, leaving their tools on the street, but dragging their dead and wounded with them.

The engineers wheeled the petard forward, dropped the pivoting log into the hole, and hammered the wedges behind it tight. Everything fit!

Our ignition system had a minute's worth of slow match, to give everybody a chance to run away, then two short pieces of quick match, one to each barrel of powder. The Captain of the engineering company, Jaccs Dupree, had insisted on lighting the wick himself, but when the time came to do that, he found that an enemy arrow had managed to cut the quick match within an inch of one of the barrels. He knew that it was vital for both barrels to go off at the same time!

I later found out that he had taken an arrow just above the right collar bone, angling down into his gut, and driven in as far as the fletching, but I couldn't see that from where I was. He probably knew that he was dead, or rather dying. But that doesn't change what he did. I just hope that when my time comes, I have the courage to finish off as well as Jaccs Dupree did.

Spraying blood from his mouth, he shouted, "Run, you fools!"

Then he grabbed the oil lamp that he'd brought to light the fuse, grabbed it in his bare fist, and smashed it on top of the barrels. As it burst into flame, he smeared the burning oil with his bare hand over both wicks, and the petard detonated. The explosion threw him, the rest of the petard and its wagon, back over thirty yards. It stopped sliding barely a yard in front of Juma's men.

The gate not only flew open, with its bar broken, but was knocked completely off of its hinges, blown backward into the lowered portcullis behind it, and the cast iron portcullis itself was broken into at least a dozen pieces! Our two barrels of serpentine powder were more effective than I had expected!

The way to Shangri La was open!

Juma lost not a moment exploiting the opportunity. His original two thousand tribal warriors had more than doubled in the past two months what with the Black slaves we had been freeing. A Black hoard of some forty-five hundred men with spears and shields, and wearing nothing but loincloths, ran through the smoke and dirt to face the enemy who had dared to bar our path!

And most of the rest of the Africa Corps was right behind them!

Juma's men swarmed up both gate towers, through doors that had been left open, just like the ones on the West City Gates of Timbuktu. Of course here, maybe the defenders had some sort of an excuse. They couldn't possibly have expected our petard.

These towers had been partially built from large blocks of stone, and partially cut from the living rock. Juma's men cleaned them out, with some of the defenders flying out of the upper windows or falling, bleeding from the battlements.

It looked as though the enemy had been forming a company up when Jaccs had set the thing off. For what purpose, I couldn't imagine. Surely, they couldn't have been planning to go out and chase us away! The blast had taken that company out, although Juma's people had stuck spears into a lot of them, just for form's sake, and maybe to be able to claim a kill.

I stayed to the side and watched. There didn't seem to be much else to do. My men knew what they were doing. After the cavalry rode past, I followed.

According to the plan, my troops followed the steep walled canyon until it branched, and then turned left. We could always take the north gate towers later, easily done from the inside. The west branch of the canyon opened out into a fairly small city, which was mostly carved out of the soft, limestone cliff face. Much of the architecture looked as though it belonged in Ancient Rome. Most of the population here lived in villages scattered around the large valley.

The defenders tried to put up a fight, but they were disorganized, and locally outnumbered.

The city was ours within an hour, about the time that most of the locals were just getting up. It wouldn't be a good day for them.

Juma had slaughtered the city's leaders, mostly just because they were there, and since we'd done that last time. Here, it wasn't really needed. Oh, well. They had been stupid, and stupidity always has been a capital offense.

Chapter 39 (Sir Walznik's Rescue) Rescuing Conrad

It wasn't Mongol movement, but it came as close as any Christian Army did, riding real horses. Where Lord Conrad could make two dozen miles a day, they could make well over a seven dozen miles on a good day. Part of their new supplies were very light robes that could be worn over their uniforms without adding a lot of weight or heat. It hurt their pride to hide their identity as part of the Christian Army, but there was neither time nor purpose in fighting people mad because Lord Conrad had freed their slaves or appropriated their crops. Cites and towns were avoided unless there were no other water holes or no way to bypass them.

They had been on the road less than four weeks when they heard an explosion in the distance. Captain Walznik needlessly signaled for a stop.

His leaders had already spurred their mounts to join him. "What the Hell was that?"

The Captain shouted back "It has to be Mongols or Lord Conrad and the Mongols are a damned long ways away! Get ready for a gallop! Sir Garret, take your lance and stay with the baggage train. Tell them to follow at their best pace. The rest of us leave in five minutes!"

In less than five minutes, the officers, ten knights, and most of the men were moving out full speed. The brown cloaks were gone and they shown in full red and white uniform. One of the knights had brought a fast pack horse with a supply of hand grenades and spare ammo.

Within a mile, they began to run into Lord Conrad's baggage train. As they passed the encampments, a veritable fortress, actually, Captain Walznik called out in Pigeon, "Where battle?"

The people on the ground shouted back "That way!" and mostly pointed in the same direction.

His warriors kept moving. Eventually, they crested a hill and saw the ruined gate below them. The great gaping hole and destroyed gates showed that this had been the source of the explosion. So did the smoke and dust still hanging in the air.

The battle of the gate was over, but the gate was crowded with troops pouring through. The Captain raised his rifle over his head and fired into the air. The explosion got enough peoples attention. The road ahead cleared enough for them to pass through at a gallop. They reigned up on the far side of the wall. They were in a small village apparently set up for the gate keepers, mostly carved out of the rock walls. There were a lot of dead bodies around, but the battle had moved elsewhere. They got another three gross yards past the village before they spied a familiar red and white uniform. The Captain called out in Pigeon, "Where Conrad? Where Lord Conrad?"

He couldn't hear the answer, but a red clad arm made an overhand gesture showing 'take the left branch, ahead, ahead.' The canyon opened out into a city of sorts, with fluted columns on the buildings, and more rooms carved right into the cliffs. The Captain looked around quickly for a place that his troop could be of greatest use. They were on the floor of a rather large valley. The ground slopped up on both sides.

Turning in his saddle, he called out, "Left column, take the high ground on the left side of the valley! Don't shoot anything that isn't attacking a red and white suit!

We don't know what forces Lord Conrad has. Give supporting fire where you can! Right column follow me!"

While Banner Hendricks peeled his column off left, the Captain started his column up the hill, looking for a firing position. They met no one for a quarter mile. This battle was moving fast. Then they came in sight of a pitched battle on the valley floor. Through his field glasses, he could see a large man standing just behind the front lines, using a large recurved bow to pick off enemy soldiers. The man was in gaudy armor and large enough to be Lord Conrad.

Gesturing at a group of boulders he shouted, "Take positions here and support the troops below. The red uniforms and the Black soldiers seem to be on our side. Kill the rest."

They were dismounted by the time he finished his instructions. The soldiers took kneeling or prone positions behind the boulders and began to look for targets. Below them, one of the enemy soldiers had slipped through the line and was bearing down on the presumed Lord Conrad. Two shots sounded and the enemy dropped about six feet short of his target. Lord Conrad lowered his bow and looked up at the hill. After a moment, he waved broadly and then went back to shooting his bow.

The battle was going well anyway and the rifles accelerated the end. The enemy was in full retreat within moments. The Captain called for his men to mount up and they rode down the hillside.

When they approached Lord Conrad, the officers did a showy dismount while the horses were still moving. They were out of breath and before they could say anything, Lord Conrad looked at them and asked, "Doctor Livingston, I presume."

Captain Walznik came to attention and saluted smartly. "No sir. Captain Walznik, attached to his majesty's ship Duke Henryk and, as strange as it might sound now, in command of your rescue party."

Lord Conrad asked, "What force do you command?"

"I have seven dozen active riflemen, all mounted, all with bolt action rifles and some small explosives."

"Well, Captain, the black warriors and the guys wearing the Star Of David are on our side. Accept surrender when offered and don't kill anyone who doesn't need killing. You, sir, will use your riflemen to reinforce our flanks. We can talk later."

With that Lord Conrad turned to the battle and Walznik rode out to the flanks with his men. It was good to be home.

Chapter 40 Looting Shangri La

From there, it was a matter of freeing the slaves, some nine thousand of them, as we visited each village and told the citizens about their bad luck. We gathered up enough provisions to feed the whole lot of us for three months, enough weapons to arm the new troops, and enough pack animals to carry it all.

We even got a good start at making uniforms for all of our new troops. We got enough boots by stealing them. The ladies who had been slaves just took what they wanted in the way of clothes and jewelry from their former owners. The ladies of our caravan treated the looting as though it was the greatest of all shopping sprees, where everything was free!

We robbed from the rich, we robbed from the poor, and we kept it all for ourselves. I couldn't generate much pity for slave owners. These people did some really rotten things! I mean, they had crucifixes around with dead bodies hanging from them!

The city had a well stocked treasury, and we stole it all. I appointed five men from all ranks to be our Spoils Distribution Committee, and they decided on an equal distribution scheme, with every man in our army getting the same amount. That was fine by me. I was already wealthy, and our top men would be well paid by the Christian Army, eventually.

The lowest ranking man among us would get home rich, if he got home at all. They even voted a share to each of the new male slaves who joined the army, at a quarter of what the rest of us got. This being the Middle Ages, it never occurred to anyone on the committee to give any of the booty to the women. The feeling among many was that women were booty.

The men wanted the money shared out, now. I had misgivings about that, but I granted their request.

In a week, we were ready to pull out.

I gave a speech to the people we were leaving behind in their ransacked valley.

I told them to pick themselves some leaders with some common sense, next time.

I told them to dismantle the north gate, and build a new one at the mouth of the west tunnel, so that travelers could use the pass without bothering anybody. They should place the new gate far back from the junction, to give their merchants room to display their wares. I said that if they didn't do that, the next time I came through here, I would blow all of their gates down, and their city besides.

I told them that even though we could have enslaved and sold them all, we hadn't done that. I also said that the next time I came through here, if I found them keeping slaves again, I still wouldn't enslave them, but I would kill every single one of their adult citizens in the entire valley.

I meant it, too, all of it.

The death of Jaccs Dupree would not be in vain!

Chapter 41 North To The Sea

It took us six days to leave the city. With a fairly narrow trail, twenty-seven thousand people, and a very long baggage train, spreading it out was the only way to do it efficiently. When you are well over a day's march long, you can't all camp together at night!

A company of trail blazers went out a day before the rest of us started. Their job was to explore the trail, map it, and to lay out the campsites that the rest of us would use. They were also to tell the rest of us about anything that we should know about, like an approaching enemy army.

I put our best men in the first caravan, to break trail, to dig more wells where needed, and to build camps. The prepared camp sites could then be used by the caravans behind us. The last caravan had a strong rear guard, and the middle three held the trainees, their cadres, and most of the non-combatants.

I broke Captain Walznik's men into three groups and put them with the central caravans, to help out with training all of the newly freed slaves. I bumped over half of them up to at least Captain, to their considerable surprise, and put them in charge of companies. I made Walznik a full Komander.

Officers, knight bannerette and up, got to bring their ladies with them, but the others had to leave theirs with the three 'safe' caravans in the center. After the extended debauchery of our stay in Shangri La, the men could live with that, and the trainees loved it.

Juma, Mohamed, Sir Stephan and I went with the first caravan.

Despite the fun of looting a city, just about the only person who really hated leaving was Sir Stephan.

"It wasn't leaving the city that bothered me so much," he told me the first night. He and his four ladies had accepted my dinner invitation. I was up to twelve girls, now, six of whom were pregnant. A high percentage of the slaves in Shangri La had been Christians.

"It was abandoning the fort I'd had so much fun building," he continued. "I'd gotten a beautiful fort built in only three days, we stayed in it for only two nights, and then we had to leave it!"

I said, "True. But if that petard hadn't worked, we might have had to stay there for a very long time. Maybe for the rest of our short lives!"

"I suppose that you're right, sir."

"You really get a kick out of building things, don't you."

"Yes, sir. I guess that my feelings about making buildings is a lot like yours are, making machines."

"Well, we do a lot of building in the Christian Army. Besides a lot of new rank, you've also earned a lot of pull from the guy on top, me, so if you want to transfer over to construction, or design, you can do it. I've been thinking that we should do something about making our army cities more beautiful."

"Thank you, sir. I'll think on it."

The next night, Juma was over. We sat around, me on a stool, him on the ground. We were sampling the liquor of Shangri La. It was a brandy, in that it had been made from distilled grape wine, but then it had been stored in wooden barrels for years, and had some of the flavor of a good whiskey. I'd brought along a few barrels, rather liking it, myself.

I said, "You know, I was a little worried when the men wanted to divide up the loot we took at Shangri La. I was sure that we'd see an outbreak of theft and violence with that much money lying around, but it hasn't happened."

"Nor will it, Conrad. We have a fine bunch of good and honest people, here."

"We certainly do! But how could that be? Most of these people were slaves. Often, they were born into slavery, with poor food, poor living conditions, sexual abuse, and often no family life at all. That should have resulted in a lot of violent misfits."

"Which, of course, it did. But, months ago, you asked me, or rather some of my people, to act as judges for you. We have done this, though among my people, a judge is also a prosecutor and sometimes an executioner. We have seen to it that many of your people have corrected their ways, or have been eliminated."

I said, "Uh, you made 'preemptive strikes' on criminals?"

"One could say that. A person's moral structure is obvious when you look at his manna. If several very good readers study a person for a while, they can pick up a lot of specific information about him, and what he has done. In extreme cases, such as one man, who had deliberately killed both of his parents, his sister, and six other people besides, all on separate occasions, there was nothing for it but to take him away from camp and to kill him. Usually, though, it is sufficient to take them aside, tell them exactly about all of the crimes that they have committed, and to tell them that they are being watched. We don't have to kill them unless they sin again, and they know this."

"Remarkable. How many people have you killed in this way?

He said, "Not many. Only about one man in a hundred, and one woman in three hundred."

"That's still a lot of people."

"Perhaps two hundred, I suppose. But those criminals had killed many more innocent people than that, and likely would have killed again."

I said, "I'd feel a lot better about it if I could see their manna as you do, and not have to take it on faith."

"But you have seen proof of what we are doing in the lack of crime in this camp."

"That's true. Still, I wish that you had told me about this earlier," I said.

"To what purpose? It would only have troubled you, to no good effect."

"I suppose so. But you've got them all weeded out now?"

"Mostly." He said, "There are still a few in this last batch that you have freed that we are unsure of. Best to move slowly on them. And, of course, our techniques only work on people who have manna. Not all people do. There will always be a criminal element, but now there are many fewer of them."

"Well, thank you, I suppose."

Juma said, "You are most welcome, my friend."

We were coming out of the mountains, and getting into a rough, hilly area. It was dry here, but nothing like the endless sand dunes you see in the movies. There was some dry grass, thorn bushes, and so on. It was enough to feed the camels, but the horses and mules needed some grain as a supplement.

There were a few animals about, the biggest being antelopes, along with some birds, including ostriches, and rodents. Juma's men managed to feed themselves, somehow, but they didn't generate a surplus. The archers brought down some small game, mostly keeping in practice. The rest of us lived on dried food and bread.

We had the traveling oven with us in the first caravan, the plan being to bake at least six thousand loaves a day, and to bury most of it at our campsite in big, sturdy, oiled bags. Each of the other caravans would then be able to dig up their bags of bread as they passed through. This plan had the advantage of ensuring that my household, at least, got fresh bread! The rearguard might be getting some pretty stale stuff, but that's war for you. Maybe the bugs wouldn't get in.

Often, the trail followed a stream, and sometimes, it actually had running water in it. More often, it was a dry stream bed, but there was usually still water there. You just had to dig for it. We dug a lot of wells. These were temporary affairs, since the next time it rained, the wells would quickly be filled with silt and mud.

If we ever decided to civilize this place, we'd put in some permanent wells back away from the river bed. But by then, we'd likely be putting in railroads with cars pulled by Big People capable of traveling three hundred miles a day, or six hundred if you changed Big People twice a day, and traveled around the clock. Rest spots would be much farther apart.

When we were three weeks from Shangri La, Mohamed said that we were in the Empire of Almohades now, but things didn't look much different. We came across a few subsistence type farming and herding villages, but the people had somehow gotten word that we were coming and had headed for the hills. We left their villages unmolested. For one thing, they didn't have anything that we needed, and also, they weren't trying to give us any trouble. A few times, when it was convenient to use a village's well, I left a small gold coin in payment for the service. It seemed the right thing to do.

But we didn't see any evidence of an Empire around!

Then one morning, our point knight bannerette and his people came riding back at a gallop, shouting, "Battle Stations!"

This was something that we had often drilled, but had never done in earnest. Mohamed immediately collected up his men, the baggage train, and all of the non-combatants and turned them around. He'd take them back to the nearest hiding place he remembered, and try to keep them out of harm's way.

Sir Percy was with us with two companies of cavalry, one of horse and one of camels. He quickly had them in the vanguard, ready to be our first line of defense.

Juma's men, two thousand strong, were right behind the jockeys. After him were the remaining eight companies of regular troops, in strict order of seniority.

They were almost formed up by the time I got there on my mule.

"So what's happening?" I asked our point man.

"Sir, there is a major battle going on two miles ahead of us! To the north, they look like perhaps two battalions of our own Christian Army Troops. At least, they are all wearing Red and White uniforms, and they are all mounted on very fast horses. To the south, near us, they have at least five times that many men, and the uniforms match Mohamed's descriptions of the army of the Empire of Almohades! There were many strange and loud noises coming from that fight, of a sort that I've never heard before."

I was surprised. The Empire of Almohades really existed? Were the history books I'd read so many years before that inaccurate? Or had history changed here, as it had in Europe?

I said to our point man, "First off, relax. If Christian Army troops are only outnumbered by five to one, they aren't in any trouble. The loud noises have to be gunfire, and our friends are making it. Still, it would be polite to lend them a hand, and we'll want to link up with them anyway."

I spotted Sir Percy, and switched to my command voice.

"Sir Percy, there are hostiles ahead of us, engaging elements of the Christian Army! Take your forces forward and harass the enemy's rear. Use arrows only! Don't mix with them, since they greatly outnumber you! The rest of us will be along as soon as we can. Do you understand?"

"Yes, sir! Arrow attacks, without any contact if possible, and you'll be along directly!"

"Right! Carry on! Now, the rest of you! Advance at a quick step! We're going to war!"

A loud "Hurrah!" rippled down our lines, and we marched forward!

I sent three of my runners with three lances of our point men ahead on good horses to see what was going on to the north, and to give me a report on the lay of the land.

I sent another two runners, with spare horses, to go back south, and report to me where Mohamed had decided to hole up with our non-combatants. The second runner was to continue south to the next caravan back, and to tell them to either find a good place to hide, or at Sir Meier's discretion, to team up with Mohamed's group, and to support them. From there, other runners would eventually get the message back to our rearguard, four days back. They were to tell everyone that we had found our people, and thus, a way home!

I kept the last two runners with me, since you never can tell when you might need to send another message.

Two miles, at an army quick step, took a third of an army hour to walk, and I felt that it was best to stay with the bulk of my army until I was sure just exactly what was going down.

The army hour was twice as long as the modern hour mostly for mechanical reasons. When I was building our first clock, our tooling was primitive, and things had to be kept as simple as possible. After a week or so of playing with numbers, I discovered that if I had two pairs of double gears rotating on, but not attached to, two parallel shafts, a twelve to one gear reduction was fairly simple, with many similar parts. That was to say, a four to one reduction going from the upper shaft to the lower, and a three to one going back to the upper.

The upper shaft consisted of a central shaft and three concentric tubes, the inner of which, a solid shaft, turned the fastest, and was connected to a drum with a wavy groove cut around the outside of it. A small wheel attached to a pendulum traveled inside of this groove, controlling the speed of the drum. At the time, I couldn't remember exactly how a normal clock's escapement worked. I still can't.

At the slow end of the gear train, a weight on a chain slowly turned the slowest tube, the one that took an entire day to revolve once. This tube was attached to the hour hand. The next fastest tube was attached to the twelfthhour hand, which turned once in one of our hours. The third tube was connected to the dozsecound hand, twelve times faster yet, and the center shaft was attached to the second hand.

The clock face was divided into twelve parts, with zero being where the nine o'clock mark would be on a modern clock. This was reset daily at sunrise. Poland, being at a high latitude, had a considerable variation in the length of the day, but things started happening at sunrise, when the army went out and said their oath. With the clock placed on a south wall, the hour hand moved about as the sun did, and people learned the system quickly.

This gave us a simple clock that didn't have the silly modern AM and PM ambiguity. Our numbering system was a duodecimal one, and so it fit right in.

Admittedly, our hour was twice as long as the modern one, but so what? Modern people would never use this thing, anyway. And yes, the pendulum went forward and back, instead of side to side. You want to fight about that? And it didn't go tick-tock-tick. It went swish-swish-swish. In the modern world, it might have started a series of Polack jokes, but I didn't care.

It worked, and we sold a lot of them!

This clock was also the basis for our angular measurement system, the way we navigated, and our system of map making. On our maps, south was at the top, because that was the direction you were looking when you looked at a clock. That, and the fact that in Poland, the mountains are to the south, and the low plains are to the north. Of course, the higher ground was 'up', at the top.

Having a dependable clock made a major improvement in efficiency. Before it was introduced, people spent a lot of their time just sitting around waiting for everybody else to get there!

I could see my runners coming back from the front about the time I could hear the sounds of gunfire. It was a lot different from what I had once become used to.

The low pitched 'foof' of the old pivot guns was no more. Now, there was a high pitched sonic crack of what had to be our new high velocity bolt action rifles. Those had been in final development when I had left Poland, over a year ago. The rapid fire of the Wolves' blowback operated sub-machine guns was still there, but there were two other types of machine guns operating as well. One had the same timbre as the rifles, obviously a light machine gun. The other was lower pitched, probably a heavy machine gun. And there was the roar of what had to be artillery!

Sir Piotr had been doing a lot of unauthorized things since I had left!

Chapter 42   Silver, Midge, And the New Old Christian Army

With the good guys putting out this much fire power, I didn't think that it would be a bright idea for my small force to attack the Imperial Army in their rear. Too many of my people in the Africa Corps would be hit by friendly fire.

One of my runners brought me a sketch of the battle field. There was a low ridge running east - west about a half mile south of the fight. It was just high enough to conceal my forces while we deployed. Then, we would be in a position to advance when the enemy eventually broke and ran, and keep them contained for a more complete wipeout.

I put Juma's forces in the center, and my more conventional forces to both sides of him. The old Christian Army was less likely to shoot at anyone wearing red and white, so it would be easier to make contact between them with our uniformed troops. It looked like we could cover the front with a double line of men, one of pikers in front, and a line of archers backing them up. That should be strong enough to hold broken troops.

I gave the necessary orders, stressing the need to stay behind the ridge until I told them to advance, and then to go only far enough to put the archers on top of the ridge, and the pikers just a bit in front of them. Juma's forces, having neither archers or pikers, would do things their own, traditional way.

I went to the top of the ridge, to see what was going on. One man on a mule wasn't going to bother the enemy. The roar of gunfire was loud and continuous. I'd commandeered Sir Walznik's field glasses, and I put them to good use.

Sir Percy's cavalry was just breaking off, apparently having exhausted their supply of arrows. Using hand signals, I sent the horse cavalry to my right, and the camels to the left, so they would be in a position to seal off the ends of the trap.

Sir Percy later told me that the enemy was so involved with attacking the main force that they had largely ignored his cavalry, even though he had put 20,000 arrows into them with good effect. He had lost some twenty of his men, and twice that number of horses, to our own gunfire, however. Those heavy machine gun bullets each ripped through a lot of men before they lost momentum!

Meanwhile, I waited for the enemy to take so many casualties that they broke, or for the Christian Army to start running low on ammunition, at which point they would need our help.

Our people seemed to have plenty of ammo, though, and their rate of fire didn't slack off. And the enemy seemed to be willing to take an awful lot of punishment. They hadn't learned that the only way to defend yourself against bullets was to dig a hole in the ground and then get in to it. I was keeping that bit of information as a military secret. I hadn't even told my top people about it. And I wouldn't, until such time as somebody started shooting at us!

Sir Stephan rode up to ask me what was going on, and I explained the situation to him. Then I asked him to ride along our troops to the west, and to tell them what was happening. A runner was sent east, with the same instructions.

After waiting a bit more, using the field glasses, I saw a very fast and powerful horse leave the rear of the Christian Army formation, and circle the battle before angling toward me. She wasn't wearing a bridle, so she had to be a Big Person. And she was white, so she just had to be Silver! A huge smile broke out on my face.

There was a small naked girl riding on her back, and I knew that she had to be one of Maud's children, one of Cynthia's sisters, one of my body guards! With their astounding eyesight, they must have spotted me up here.

I got off of my mule to greet them properly. Silver skidded to a stop right in front of me. I hugged her around the neck, I spoke to her in English, and I told her how much I had missed her. She nudged my right hand, inquiring how it was that I still had one, and I told her how it had grown back. She nodded, having a considerable knowledge of my Uncle Tom. Before I'd found her, he had been her principal rider.

It was a while before I noticed that the girl on her back was Midge, Cynthia's sister! I was about to greet her as well, when she jumped down from the double saddle on Silver's back, gave me a rib crackling hug, and a huge, slobbering kiss!

In Polish, she said, "Conrad, you are alive! And whole! But, how? I mean, I was there when they found Cynthia's body, and your hand! I smelled them both, and there couldn't be any doubt but that you had lost your right hand!"

"I lost my hand, but it grew back. Uncle Tom's doing, I suppose."

"That's so wonderful! You must tell me the whole story!"

I said, "I will, but just now, there is a battle going on. I need some information. First off, who is in command on our side out there?"

"In theory, that would be Sir Vladimir, who is senior, and commands the battalion of Mounted Infantry, along with the three companies of artillery. But in fact, he generally goes along with what Sir Wladyclaw says. He commands the battalion of Wolves."

"Good. They are both old friends of mine. Next, I had a company of mapmakers and trail breakers riding a day ahead of us, but I haven't heard from them. Do you have any idea of what happened to them?"

"Oh, yes," Midge said. "We met them yesterday. They said that you would be following them, but that their orders were to go ahead and lay out your next camp site."

"So the twit followed his orders, instead of using his brain! I can't punish him for that, but he'll never get promoted again! But at least, they are not all dead, which is what I was worried about.

"Next," I continued, "I need to communicate with Sir Vladimir and Sir Wladyclaw. I want them to send me a radio out here, and men to operate it.

"Also, tell them that I have almost five thousand troops out here. Most of them are Christian slaves that we have freed and trained, but some two thousand of them are Black Africans who are fighting on our side. We are in a position to advance on the enemy, but I have been hesitating because of the army's fire power. I sent in two companies of cavalry out earlier, to harass the enemy, and they took casualties from our own guns. We are limited to arrows, pikes, and swords."

I said, "If they need us to form a blockade against the enemy, ask them to send up two white signal rockets. If they need us to engage the Imperials, send up three red rockets. Also tell them that I have twenty-two thousand more people following me in four caravans, one day apart each. Many of them are non-combatants, or only partially trained. But mostly tell them to get me a radio and a team to operate it!"

Midge said, "Yes sir. I understand that. Do you want me to recite it back to you?"

"No, I trust you and your memory. But I need you and Silver to run this message back to Sir Vladimir and to Sir Wladyclaw, since most of my people here speak only Arabic, and some Pigeon. You will be understood more easily than they would."

"We'll go, Conrad, and lead the radio people back here."

"Good girl!"

I told Silver, in English, that I wanted them to go the long way around the battle, to play it safe, and then to come back when Midge said so. My mount nodded her head, and left with Midge on her back.

"This was an amazing thing!"

I looked down and saw Juma standing below me, behind the ridge, but high enough to see the battle.

"Indeed?" I said.

"That little girl had almost as much manna as you do. And the horse was as powerful as she was!"

"Well, first off, 'that little girl' wasn't exactly human. She is an intelligent person, you understand, but she is twice as strong as you are! And faster! And better trained! And the horse wasn't a horse, either. Silver is also a person, and mentally very similar to Midge. Look at her run! Could a mere horse do that? But manna? That astounds me! Why would one of my Uncle Tom's creations have manna?"

"I have very little idea of what you are talking about, Conrad, but I would like to get to know both of them better!"

"You'll have that opportunity soon, my friend. They will be back shortly with a radio."

"Now you've used another new word on me."

"A radio is a device that lets you talk to people a long ways away."

"With one, we could talk to the people in Timbuktu?"

"Yes, if they had a radio, too."

"Then we must get one to them!"

"I, too, had had that thought. I would like to keep in touch with Omar."

"Yes, and with my own people as well. Those noises are the guns you told me of?"

"Yes. There are some new sorts that I'm not all that familiar with. The people that I left in Poland have been very creative since I left them, well over a year ago. From the sounds, they have rifles, sub-machine guns, two sizes of machine guns and at least two sizes of cannons."

As we talked, an artillery shell exploded about ten yards above a concentration of the Imperial soldiers, killing perhaps four dozen of them. Either our designers had come up with a proximity switch, or one of our gunners was very good at setting a timer. Or maybe he was just lucky.

"Would that my own people were so armed," Juma said.

"I could arrange that, if you wish. Your forces are part of the Christian Army, after all, and you should be equipped like the rest of our forces. You could have guns, and armor. In time, you could each have one of those manna filled 'horses' that you admired, as well."

"We don't wear armor, it is unmanly! And I don't think that we would like to be on horseback."

"You can always change your mind. But if want Big People, you'd have to change your uniforms. You cannot go mounted in a loincloth. The skin on your crotch would be bleeding by the end of the day. Boots are needed, too."

"I will think on it."

"Good. But first, you must take a very good look at our weapons and the Big People. Perhaps tomorrow, there will be time."

As we talked, I saw Silver and Midge reach our headquarters. They'd be coming back soon.

An airplane of a type that I had never seen before flew overhead. It had a high, stubby wing, and two radial engines rigged as pushers, set higher yet, above the wing. There was no observable landing gear. I decided that this must be a seaplane.

Then, it dipped down and flew over the battlefield. Two heavy machineguns in the fuselage opened fire, and it strafed the imperials. Piotr was at it again!

"This is one of the airplanes you told me about?" Juma asked.

"Yes."

"It has killed many of the enemy."

The plane came back twice more, while the imperials on the ground could do absolutely nothing about it but die. It seemed to be the straw that broke the Imperial Army's back. Their formations started to get raggedy.

A minute later, I saw a white signal rocket go up. A few moments after that, there was a second one.

Juma said, "Those mean something?"

"Yes. How did you know?

"It was obviously important by the change in your manna."

"Indeed. They are telling me that it's time to put our men on top of the ridge."

I shouted a few orders, and the troops walked up the low ridge and got into position, in a double line with just enough room between the men to give some freedom of action.

Juma said, "But if they are subordinate to you, why are you obeying their orders?"

"Because they have the superior force here. This is their battle, not mine. My job is to help them out where I can."

"I don't think that I will ever understand your people, Conrad."

"I've often had similar thoughts about yours, my friend."

One of my runners brought up the Christian Army Battle Flag, and unfurled it. It was time to let everyone know who we were.

Yes, the Imperial troops were definitely on the run. Gunfire slacked off and then almost stopped, with little more than short bursts of sub-machine gun fire and revolver shots as the Wolves and the Mounted Infantry went after the enemy on their big people. Swords and lances flashed.

Juma said, "I don't think that they will leave any of them for us!"

"We are just here to make sure than very few of them get away," I said as I signaled Sir Percy's cavalry to go in and join the fun.

This time, Juma was wrong. A mass of Imperial Soldiers, perhaps a thousand of them, stayed together and managed to make it all the way to our lines. The Wolves were after them, but every time they got close, a few squads of Imperial

Pikemen would form a line and ground their pikes, forcing our Big People to veer off.

Noticing the obvious differences between Juma's forces and the rest of us, their commander must have decided that the Blacks were the lesser of two evils. He soon discovered his error. They hit our center, and then they fell apart! Most of them went down with thrown spears in them, and the few who made it to our lines didn't get any farther.

The Blacks were using the same basic maneuver that they had practiced every day for the past three months, killing wild animals to put meat on our plates. They had gotten very good at it!

I saw one younger man miss his throw as an Imperial ducked under his spear. An older man in the rank behind him handed the boy his unused spare spear. The boy smiled at him, threw the spear, and this time, he killed his enemy, with a shaft straight through the Arab's heart. The old man and the young one laughed and hugged each other, and then prepared to defend the line against the Imperials.

Not one of the enemy made it through!

"I think that just about all of my men have attained manhood now," Juma said. "There will be a mighty feast, tonight!"

"Enjoy your meal, my friend. I'll see you in the morning. Ah, here comes Silver and Midge. I'll have to go and talk to some old friends. Sir Stephan, take command here. Set up camp, and send some runners back to find Mohamed! Send some others to find our Trail Breakers, and tell the twits to come back here!"

Chapter 43 Old Friends

I took off my silver spurs and threw them away. I never wanted to have to use them again. Wearing spurs while riding a Big Person was not polite.

Climbing up on Silver's back was like going up to heaven, even though I found myself reaching for the non-existent reins for a moment. Midge jumped up to the side saddle built in front of mine, and it was just like old times again, when Cynthia was alive.

"Midge, why are you here, instead of with captain Sorinski and his family, on the north sea patrol?"

"Well, first off, he's not down there any more. He was promoted to full Captain, and got command of the Marauder, one of the new Frigate class ships. He's only about four dozen miles from here, out on the Mediterranean. I visit him often. He is my husband, after all."

"That brings me to about six more questions. First off, these 'Frigates' are war ships, aren't they? What are they doing here?"

She said, "They are destroying all Moslem shipping, and freeing every slave they can find, until such time as the Arabs release you. But then, I guess that you released yourself, didn't you?"

"Yes. Just how many of these 'Frigates' are there, anyway?"

"There are only eleven of them, right now, but they are building lots more of them, as fast as they can. They're really just Explorer class ships, with a lot of big guns on board. They have some airplanes, too. Right now, there seven of them on the Mediterranean, two on the West African coast, and two more heading around Africa to disrupt trade and slavery in the Red Sea. Then, there are three big Battleships, which are based on the Liner Class. They can't work well with the Frigates, since they are so much faster, but there is a new class being built, the Destroyers, that will be as fast as the Battleships, but with the fire power of the Frigates, so that problem will soon be taken care of."

I said, "Sir Piotr has some explaining to do."

"Well, everybody thought that you were dead, except for some of your best friends. Certainly, the Pope did."

"Grumble. But if Captain Sorinski is out at sea, why are you here on dry land?"

"My lord, ever since you were reported missing, I've been feeling terribly guilty about it." She said, "I selfishly did what I wanted to do, when I should have gone on with you and Cynthia. Maybe, if I'd been there, things would have happened differently. So when I heard that Sir Wladyclaw was taking a battalion of Wolves to Africa, to search for you, I wanted to go along, to help out. As my commanding officer, my husband gave me permission to apply for a posting with the African Expeditionary Force, and I was accepted. He then applied for a sea job, supporting Sir Wladyclaw's forces, and got a promotion and a new ship. I still see him fairly often, but we're under different commands, now."

"Oh, Midge, you can't spend your life worrying about what might have been. Nobody can predict the future! Yes, perhaps if you'd come with us, Cynthia might be still alive. Or maybe, all three of us would be dead! What happened, happened. We all have to play out our lives from the point in time and space where we are right now!"

"Then I didn't do the right thing?"

"You haven't done anything wrong! But I'm alive, you're alive, and Cynthia is irretrievably dead. It's time for you to go back to your proper husband, and live your own life!" I said.

"But, I'm not under his command any more."

"Kid, everybody in the army is under my command. Just who do you think runs this show, anyway?"

About then, we were coming into the local headquarters. I dismounted, gave Silver another hug, and told her that I'd be back before too long.

The guards outside of the big tent snapped to attention, with shock on their faces, as I approached them. They'd known, intellectually, that I was coming, but it hadn't seeped in emotionally, as yet.

Sir Wladyclaw and Sir Vladimir were waiting for me, sitting at a folding camp table. They, too snapped to attention when I walked in.

"Gentlemen. Old friends. Please sit down and tell me just what in the hell is going on around here. Why do we have warships that I never authorized? Why are there at least five new weapons systems that I never authorized? And just what in the hell are you doing here in Africa, anyway? I left explicit orders that if I turned up missing, no one was to come out looking for me!"

"May I answer some of your questions, sir?" Sir Vladimir said, "First off, yes you did not authorize these weapons, but you did leave Sir Piotr in charge when you left, knowing full well that he disagreed with you on a number of things. Once he was in command, he was absolutely obligated to do as he felt best. Anything else would have been a dereliction of his duty!"

Sir Wladyclaw said, "As to ordering us not to look for you, sir, well, you didn't quite do that. You just told Sir Piotr that you didn't want it to happen. That's not exactly the same thing as an order."

"You are talking like a lawyer," I said.

"Perhaps, but did you really expect us to simply abandon you? Anyway, the name of this organization is The Christian Army. We think that gives the Pope some say in what we do, and he wanted us to attack the Moslems," Sir Wladyclaw said. "And even if we never had been able to find you, we have been doing some very good work out here. Thus far, we have freed more than eighty thousand Christian slaves, as well as a like number of people from other religions. We have sent most of the Christians back to Europe. A high percentage of the freed men have enlisted in our army, incidentally. Your basic training camp, Hell, actually has a waiting list right now. That's never happened before."

I said, "Even if they were all men, eighty thousand freed slaves wouldn't fill up Hell."

"Many freed men and most of the freed women went home, all across Europe. Hearing their stories has given Christians everywhere the incentive to join in the fight," Sir Vladimir said.

"But the cost of doing all of this must be bankrupting the army," I said.

"Not at all," Sir Wladyclaw said. "In fact, last quarter, we made our biggest profits ever. True, our expenses have gone up, but our productivity has gone up much higher! There's a new spirit in the army. We were going stale, without anything great and noble to do. Now, everyone bustles around as though he was a hero from a storybook. There is no malingering, waste and poor workmanship are not tolerated by the men themselves, and it has become common to work an extra hour or two a day, without pay, for the benefit of the war effort! I once told you that a crusade was just what we needed, and I was right! Sir."

"Okay. I'll be verifying all this myself, of course, but I don't believe that you two would lie to me. Besides the slaves that you've freed, what else have you accomplished?," I asked.

"Well, we've pretty much taken out the Almohades Empire," Sir Vladimir said. "We are occupying most of it, and we're going to keep it. The plan is to keep the enlisting freed slaves from each city together in their training, and when they've graduated, they will be sent back to their old city as garrison troops. Most of them will speak the local language, you see."

"A fair thought. But from the battle I just saw, it looked to me that there a lot of Imperial troops left around," I said.

"Not really, sir. That was pretty much their last gasp, which was why they fought so hard. They have three cities left, with a few garrison troops still in them, but we'll be taking them soon, and without much effort," Sir Wladyclaw said. "The southern half of Spain is now army property, as is the Mediterranean sea coast west of here, and the Atlantic west coast of Africa, until you get to jungle country populated by Black people. We don't see them as our proper enemy, so we have left them alone."

"The Blacks are the victims of slavery, for the most part. But why did you attack Spain?"

"That happened almost by accident, sir. We had a lot of troops in northern Spain, awaiting transportation to Africa," Sir Vladimir said. "Southern Spain was part of the same empire that we were fighting in Africa. It was reasoned that if we could take and hold a road to a seaport in the south, shipping times would be reduced, and we could get to the war faster. So we took the road that went to Cartagena, as well as the city itself. The empire didn't like what we did and naturally they hit us back. Which we didn't like, of course, so we hit them back, only harder. When the smoke cleared, we owned some very nice territory, with lots of orchards and vineyards, and quite a few beautiful castles and palaces. I've put in a bid on a lovely place just outside of Seville. Taking it all was only a matter of a few months, doing the job. And I suppose that you could say that we did it with spare troops, because they were all just sitting around awaiting transportation."

I said, "Very well. Next subject. What is your situation regarding supplies?"

"Actually, they have been sending us a lot more than we need. They have been sending out full Explorer vessels, dropping off the supplies at Depots, and returning them filled with ex-slaves. They have been filling all three cargo decks with them, as well as the passenger space, but we're getting them home," Sir Wladyclaw said.

"Good. Because I've got a total of around twenty-seven thousand people with me. I've made most of the men members of the Christian Army, even including our four companies of Jews, so they will have to be brought up to snuff, properly equipped, and trained in the new weapons. Some of the non-combatants will be returning to Europe. Some of them, Arabs and Blacks, will be going back to Timbuktu, with our pack train, and I'll want to be sending a lot of stuff to Omar, the man I left in charge there. Mostly, weapons, ammunition, and European trade goods," I said.

"Someone told us that the middle of Africa was devoid of people, and that

Timbuktu was a myth," Sir Vladimir said.

"It's sparsely populated, most of it, but it's BIG, so there are still a lot of people there. Timbuktu is bigger than Copenhagen, I'd guess, and a place that we called Shangri La was densely populated. We took both cities in the last six months or so. There are a few others along the way that we didn't have to conquer."

"That's a story that I'd love to hear," Sir Vladimir said.

"I'll tell you a short version of the story over dinner, assuming that I'm invited."

"But, of course, sir!" Sir Wladyclaw said.

"Okay. Sir Wladyclaw, I want you to get together a company of your Wolves for an extended trip. I want them to go to Timbuktu. We made army style maps on the trip here, so they won't have any problems finding the place. I can provide you with translators and guides. Almost all of my people speak Pigeon. I want them to have three radios with them, two of which they will be leaving there, along with the operators. You'd better send two large artillery pieces with them, and an assortment of ammunition. There are sometimes city gates and walls to be dealt with. I want them to have about four gross of extra rifles, with bayonets, and a few dozen revolvers, with a large supply of ammunition, powder, and a reloading machine. The craftsmen in Timbuktu can cast their own bullets, if you bring them a few bullet molds. These weapons and radios will be gifts for my friend Omar. I'll brief the Captain myself early tomorrow morning."

"Very good, sir!"

"And now, I suppose that I should contact my wives."

Sir Vladimir said, "Uh, I took the liberty of contacting your wives yesterday, when we first heard that you were alive."

"Good. That will simplify things. Now, do you have any paper and pens around, so I can write them a radiogram?"

"Well, yes, but wouldn't you rather just talk to them?"

"Talk to them? You mean that you've got voice communication radios available?"

"Yes, sir, I'm afraid so."

"Wonderful. One more unauthorized gadget around!"

"They were developed for use in aircraft to ship communications. Using a Morse code key when you're flying an airplane proved to be very difficult."

"Very well. But broadcast radio is absolutely forbidden, and put the word out that anyone found working on a television set will be shot!"

Somehow, Midge had been able to walk into the room without being challenged by the guards, or being noticed by anyone else. Not a bad feat for a pretty, naked lady.

She said, "What's a television set, my lord?"

"It's an instrument of the Devil, that degrades the quality of life, and turns people's brains into mush!" I said to her as I left for the radio shack. "Oh, yes. Take Silver, go back to my camp, and invite Sir Stephan over here for dinner. If our ladies get back before then, invite them along, too. Inform Sir Vladimir's people of how many are coming over, once you know. Arrange transportation over here with the Big People. It's time they got acquainted. Some of our ladies are pregnant, and will need a carriage of some sort. And this time, take a radio with you! Leave it, and the operators, at my headquarters."

"Yes, my lord. Can I come to dinner too?"

"I suppose so. We probably couldn't keep you out in any event. Tomorrow, I want you and another Big Person, not Silver, to go over and talk to Juma, the Black man you saw earlier. He's a friend of mine, and he wants to meet both of you. I'll be needing Silver, and Juma couldn't talk to her, anyway. He speaks Pigeon, and a few other languages, but not Polish, and certainly not English."

In the radio shack, they had already set up a link with my family at Okoitz. Francine and Celicia talked for what seemed like hours, about the most trivial of topics, without being apparently much interested in just how I had managed to survive my ordeal. Then, there were the eight children that I had had with my legal wives, and with another thirty of so that I'd had by other women, but hadn't been able to find husbands for. I talked with them all, being told about every childhood complaint and problem known to man.

When the windy conversation was finally over, I was beginning to think that I wasn't ready to go home just yet. Maybe, the Arabs had the right idea on how to run a household. They make all of their women go down on their knees when they walk into a room. It puts the girls into the proper mind set.

I was about to sign off when the last kid in line told me that Sir Piotr had been patiently waiting to talk to me the whole time.

Well, he has a wife and kids, so I guess that he understands.

"Sir Piotr," I said. "You have done a lot of unauthorized things while I have been gone. You have many new weapon systems. Several new aircraft, and armed aircraft at that. I'm told that three new types of warships have been designed and built. And built in quantity. Have you been having fun, spending the army's money this way?"

"Fun, my lord? No, it has not been fun! This is the most miserable job that I have ever had, and I am grateful that you are finally back, and can relieve me of my command here. But at the same time, I must insist that the things that I have done were NOT unauthorized. They were authorized, because I authorized them. You left me in command here, so I commanded as I saw fit."

"Do you think that I wanted you to start a war with the entire Moslem world? Especially with the Mongols liable to attack us at ant time?"

"No, but both King Henryk and the Pope demanded that we go on Crusade. The whole army, and most of Christendom wanted war as well. There are limits to the pressure that one inexperienced man can endure! Especially with you being missing and presumed dead! You can hold me responsible for the new weapons systems, if you want to, but this war was not my fault! Now, may I please be relieved of my command?"

"No. You got us into this 'Crusade', and you will have to see it through. As to the new weapons and the invasion of North Africa, well, if our armies hadn't taken out the Almohades Empire, I never could have made it alive to the Mediterranean Seacoast. I guess that I owe you one for that."

"My lord, so you are saying that I've saved your life, but that I still have to keep working at this horrible job? You have a strange way of saying 'thank you'."

"Yeah, well, war sure is hell, isn't it. I've got to get to dinner, now. Keep up the good work!"

"Oh, thank you, sir!" I could hear him scowling over the speaker.

We had a pleasant dinner, with mostly canned food served, but in the Polish style. It was especially good since Sir Wladyclaw had put in a stock of that wonderful dark beer from Tallinn. He served it, well, not cold, but cool, by exposing the barrels at night, and keeping a thick layer of blankets over them during the day. All of my twelve ladies, and Sir Stephan's four, were able to attend, having elected to simply ride their camels over to where the feast was being held.

My officers had brought their women along. Some were wives, some were not. They were still using the fashions popular in Poland when I had left, with the female guests being bare breasted, and the serving girls being nearly naked. My own girls, and Sir Stephan's, looked at each other, nodded, and stripped to the waist. I thought that it was an major improvement. A woman who is in her second trimester is particularly lovely, with lush breasts and a glowing complexion. God must have done that to make sure that we men kept them around when they needed us so much.

Most of the casual talk at dinner was perforce in Pigeon, since women tend to monopolize a conversation. Pigeon is an easy language to learn, but it's fairly awkward in social situations. It lacks the subtleties. I told the girls that as soon as they got to Poland, they would have to work very hard at learning the whole, ancient language.

I told the story of my trip, how I was washed overboard, our horrible problems on the shipping container filled with fiberglass, and our encounter with the Twaregs.

"You will be pleased to note that we have killed many thousands of those bastards," Sir Wladyclaw said.

I soon noticed that my subordinates had three attractive secretaries, all of them female, taking careful notes of everything I said. Later, a fairly accurate account of my adventures was published in the Christian Army Magazine.

Maybe my wives would learn of the story from there.

I talked about my journey to Timbuktu, how I was sold as a slave, and about my eight months in a barrel, pumping water. I told them about how my face and teeth healed, how my hand grew back again, and how Omar and I fought our way out of the barrel, started a slave rebellion, and eventually conquered the ancient City of Timbuktu. Then I talked about our new laws for the city, and how I formed up the African Corps of the Christian Army. Finally, there was the whole saga of our trip north.

Really good beer sure makes a man talkative! And the cigars that were served out after dinner helped a lot, too! The ladies smoked them as well as the men, I was surprised to note. We definitely had a profitable product, here.

Before the evening ended, Midge was prevailed upon to dance for us. The regular army people had seen her do this many times, but my African Corp folks were amazed!

Jasmine said, "Do you think that she could teach me to do that?"

I said, "I doubt it, love. Midge isn't exactly human. She is much stronger than you or I are. But I think that it might be possible for you to teach her, or her kind, something about your style of dancing. There are many of her sisters living at Okoitz. Once you have given birth to our son or daughter, you might want to look into it."

Sir Vladimir said, as we walked back to the tents that had been assigned to me and my ladies, "I've gotten strange reports this afternoon about what your Black troops are doing to the Imperials they killed in the battle. What's going on out there?"

"They were gutting and cleaning their kill, Sir Vladimir. By now, they will have roasted them and have started to eat them. It's sort of a religious thing with Juma's people. Welcome to the African Corps of the Christian Army, my old friend."

Chapter 44   Re-equipping – 'A Man Must Wear His Loincloth'

I found a few more things to send to Omar, some felt tip pens, some lighters, a few flashlights, and some lighter fluid. One of the translators had a spare copy of an Arabic-Polish dictionary, a copy of the Explorer's Corps book on Pigeon, and a children's book on learning Polish, which I sent along as well. I'd written Omar a letter, which I thought would have to be translated from Polish to Pigeon to Arabic for him, only to find that Sir Vladimir could lend me a scholar who knew both Polish and Arabic. This simplified things considerably.

The usual company in the Wolves also had six big, container sized carts, which were pulled by two Big People each, and rode on big, balloon rubber tires. They had a coil spring suspension system, similar to a McPherson Strut, and shock absorbers. I was told that for really rough roads, sand dunes, and steep inclines, more Big people could be used to help out, with riders pulling on ropes running back to the carts.

They were loaded with supplies and gifts for Omar and his army in Timbuktu. It turned out that there was room for five times as many weapons as I had first ordered, and that these guns and ammo were available, so Omar made out quite nicely. I also sent him back what was left of the city treasury, as well as my share of the booty from Shangri La. Since I was back in the old Christian Army, I could just sign for anything that I wanted.

I also picked up a new revolver for myself, replacing the one that went to the bottom of the Atlantic Ocean. It felt good on my right hip, balancing the sword on my left.

Two guides and the translator were assigned Big People whose riders had been killed in the last battle. The whole augmented company left by mid morning.

On Big People, what with the time saved by eating canned or dried rations that only had to be heated, and not cooked from scratch, and with the easily set up army dome tents, they could travel at twelve times as many miles per day as our caravans could. And the Big People provided security at night, while they were eating, so palisades, night guard duty, and other defenses weren't necessary.

Captain Fritz, the commander of the expedition, had been at last night's feast, and heard the story of how we got here. He had studied our maps, and said that he could probably get to Timbuktu in ten days. He would spend at least two weeks there, or several months, if that was necessary, training Omar's army with the new weapons.

Perhaps two months later, the full caravan would arrive, with a lot more presents and merchandise. They would be able to travel faster going south than they had going north, since they wouldn't have non-combatants walking beside them any more. Also, they would have our old camp sites along the way that they could use, some of the time. Canned army rations would help, too, although they would be taking the bread oven back with them, remounted on a rubber tired army cart.

Sir Vladimir had liked the idea, and had ordered six more bread ovens made up for his own forces.

Since the African Corps had to walk, at least most of us, it would probably take us four days to get to the nearest Depot, even though the way there was across a coastal plain, where we wouldn't have to go single file. I decided that it would be best to stay where we were, and let my people collect up. We needed a rest anyway.

I wandered around, studying the new guns, mostly. They were straight forward, simple designs, the sort of thing that I had always tried for. I still wasn't entirely happy about the resources that had been spent on them, but the engineers that I had trained had learned well.

The African Corps should be able to pick up on using them fairly easily. Actually, the use of firearms is a lot easier to learn than, say, a bow, a sword, or a spear. It was much the way a steamship was easier to master than a big sailing rig.

Looking out over yesterday's battle field, I saw that Juma's people were helping with the cleanup, in their usual fashion. Other people were giving them a wide berth, not wanting to get involved.

Sir Vladimir was standing beside me before I noticed him.

I said, "Did Midge teach you that stunt?"

"In a way. She said that the trick is to watch your man's eyes, and when he blinks, or looks away, move quickly and quietly. Of course, no ordinary human is anywhere near as fast as she is. I see that your African friends are at it again."

"True. It bothers me, too, but they are very good and loyal troops, and they never kill anyone just to eat them, so you don't have to worry about that."

Sir Vladimir said, "That's a relief to know."

"What they have been doing is a sort of Rite of Manhood, with some things in common with our own Sacrament of Confirmation, or the Jewish Bar Mitzvah. Only in Juma's tribe, to become a man, to marry, and to have a family, you must first kill an enemy in combat, or at least in a fair fight. And then you eat his body, with the help of your friends and male relatives."

"Interesting. What if he kills you?"

"Well, if they can get the body back, your friends and relatives hold another ceremony, during which they cook and eat you! It is felt that this keeps your strength, loyalty, and courage within the tribe," I said.

"Remarkable. Do we really need this in the Christian Army?"

"I think that we do. My father once told me that it takes all kinds of people to make a world, and I think that he was right. Anyway, Juma is a friend of mine. Get to know him. Perhaps you will like him, too."

He said, "Perhaps, Conrad, but somehow, I doubt it. Do they have something similar for their women?"

"Yes, actually. To be truly an adult, a girl must present her husband with a healthy male child. Only then does she get the full status and prestige due to her."

"I am amazed, and I'm glad that I am not a member of their tribe. But on other subjects, what are your plans, now?" Vladimir and I had been good friends for over thirty years, and when in private we never had been formal with each other.

I said, "I was thinking of resting here for a while, and collecting up my other caravans. Then we'll be proceeding mostly on foot to this Depot of yours."

"I expect that we'll be staying here for four or five days, as well. I have a lot of wounded who need the rest and recuperation time. That was a very rough battle, yesterday. The imperials knew that they had to beat us, or they were finished. Of course, they never had a chance, but that's war for you. But as to your people walking the whole way, I don't see any reason for it. Since we're standing down right now, you could borrow some of our Big People. They can make it to the Depot and back in a single morning, and make two trips a day if need be. This would let your combatants start getting re-equipped and trained a week earlier."

"That's not a bad thought. I'd like to see just what they have at this Depot, anyway. I'd also like to know about the availability of Big People."

He said, "I think that there might be around ten thousand spares in Africa. We'd never taken them into combat before, and we thought that the loss ratio, men to mounts, would be about the same as it would be with men and horses. However, Big People turn out to have a very high survival factor, being able to live through some very serious wounds. They are even tougher than the optimists among us thought. We actually loose a lot more men than we do Big People."

"Then I can likely mount everyone I have, even some of the non-combatants, without stretching you too thin." Vladimir thought in duodecimal terms. A thousand to him was one thousand seven hundred and twenty-eight in decimal.

"I would guess so, and the girls have been very frustrated with coming here in hopes of getting a partner, and then only doing guard duty someplace that really didn't need guarding. This will make them very happy. I'll radio the quartermaster department and make sure about the numbers available. I'll also tell him that you have a large body of men coming in that will need to be fitted out with clothes, equipment, and armor."

"Thank you. What say I collect up the two companies of cavalry that I have locally, and we'll run them over to the Depot on your Big People," I said.

"Right after lunch? Fine. And I trust that 'we' implied that I was invited, too."

"Certainly! It looks like a fine day for a ride!"

I sent a runner out to tell Sir Percy that he was about to be reequipped, and that he should have his men ready right after lunch, but not his horses and camels. The men were also required to leave their spurs and whips behind. One doesn't use such things on a Big Person.

When the time came to leave, I had three companies of cavalry. Our advanced guard had been found and had returned. I might be ticked at their Captain, but that wasn't any reason to delay reequipping his men.

When three companies of my riders were assembled, I thought it best to introduce them to the Big People.

"Listen up, People!" I shouted in Arabic, the language we all had in common. "You are about to be equipped in the fashion of the rest of the Christian Army. You will be issued a full set of new uniforms, a fine set of plate armor, some new weapons that will likely amaze you, a few odds and ends, and you will be introduced to a new partner, one of the Big People. I'm riding one right now. You will notice that she isn't wearing a bridle, and that I am not wearing spurs. These things are no longer necessary. In fact, they are forbidden. So are whips. Deliberately injuring a Big Person in any way is a very serious offence, but we rarely punish humans for it. Big people can take care of themselves, and they have my permission to do what ever is necessary to protect themselves. Be warned!

"The thing that you must remember about Big People is that while they look like horses, they are not horses! They are people! They are members of the Christian Army, just as you are! And they are paid, just as you are! Or, at least you will be paid, once we get things squared away with the Accounting Department.

"Big People are more intelligent than the average human in most matters, which means that they are way smarter than most of you! Never forget that! Trust your partner!

"Their eyesight, hearing, and sense of smell are superior to any human's. They don't get lost! They can see in the dark! If they sense danger, believe them!

"They can survive by eating almost anything, including whole trees, although they prefer fresh grass, when they can get it. But they can thrive where a camel would starve to death. If you are on a seacoast, they can drink sea water! They can even feed you! Their breasts can become functional, if you ask them to do it, and their milk is very good.

"Most of you have learned Pigeon, which is fortunate. The Big People that you will be assigned as your partner can also understand Pigeon, and Polish, besides. They can't speak, but they will understand you. You will be taught a sign language we have worked out which lets them talk to us.

"Big People are superb fighters. I have been jumped by more than a dozen thugs, and Silver here wiped most of them out, herself. I never had a chance to do more than draw my sword!

"They don't seem to need sleep, so they can stand night guard duty, and graze, while you get a good night's rest.

"We refer to them as 'the ladies', and we sometimes call the one we are talking to 'my sister'. And we mean it! Once you are assigned a partner, she will be welcome in your camp and in your home. She will become a member of your family. They have very clean habits, and your wife and children will be safe around them. Very safe!

"We will be riding over to the Depot where we will be reequipped on some borrowed Big People. Just remember that one is always very polite to a Big Person. Ah, here they come, now."

Three companies of big people were approaching us, without any humans guiding them. They were from the Mounted Infantry Brigade, judging by their equipment, and they were fully equipped, including the weapons.

Our usual saddle had a big saddle bow, to protect the rider from his waist to his mid thigh. It also held various kits and gadgets, a canteen, and some ammunition. The cantle, in back, was fairly low, about like an American 'western' saddle, to make for easy mounting. It wouldn't have made a good saddle for jousting, but for warfare, it made a lot of sense.

The Wolves used two sub-machine guns as their primary weapons, one in each hand. Spare clips of ammo were arranged against the Big Person's neck, which also armored it. A revolver was used as a side arm, along with a saber, and they usually carried a lance attached to the saddle, which was rarely used for anything but holding up their family crest. The Wolves were all members of the 'old' nobility, and sometimes they were fairly snobbish about it. In return, our regular forces told a lot of jokes about them. A rifle was also carried by the Wolves, but rarely used, except in extreme situations. These guys liked to get in there and mix it with the enemy.

The rifle was the primary weapon of the Mounted Infantry, along with the bayonet. They usually dismounted for a fight, to take advantage of the long range accuracy of their rifles. They carried two large horse pistols, for use when mounted. These were smooth bore, six shot revolvers that fired a small shotgun shell. Shooting accurately from a galloping Big Person was more than most men could accomplish. They also carried a saber attached to the saddle, since rapiers don't work very well when you are mounted. They used a standard revolver as a side arm, along with a rapier carried over their left shoulder. These people were mostly from agricultural 'snowflake' forts.

Mounted Infantry machine guns were towed behind many Big People on two wheeled carts, but these had not been sent along.

"Listen up!" I shouted, "I notice that the big people who will be taking us to the Depot are fully armed. You don't know how to use these weapons yet, so don't you dare touch them! If the gun doesn't kill you, I might!"

The Big People went among our ranks, and they picked the men that they were willing to carry. The men mounted up, awkwardly, without any reins to hold.

We were about to leave when Juma rode up. His Big person was wearing a double saddle and Midge was riding in front of him holding his shield and spears, while he clutched the saddle bow with both hands. Juma was wearing boots and a pair of pants, but had his loincloth on over the pants.

"May we join you, my brother?"

"Certainly, Juma, welcome along, Midge, and you too, my sister. I see that the three of you have become acquainted."

"Yes, and they are both marvelous people, but I feel ridiculous in this outfit!"

"Wearing a loincloth over a pair of pants is ridiculous, yes, but so what? Personally, I think that your outfit needs a cape. Maybe you'll start a new fad."

"Well, a man must wear his loincloth!"

It was a good ride, with a clear blue sky and fresh green grass growing beneath our Big People's hooves! Racing swiftly across the Mediterranean Plain on Silver's back was a pure joy!

The men of my three companies had huge grins on their faces. They had never dreamed of mounts like these, with their incredible speed and power! A big person could travel as fast as a thoroughbred race horse, but the horse could keep that speed up for only a mile or two, and with but a small jockey on his back. A Big Person could do it with a fully armed and armored man riding her, and keep it up all day long! And all night as well, in an emergency!

Sir Percy pulled along side of me wearing the biggest smile I'd ever seen on him. It was too windy to talk, but he gesticulated to me with his thumb pointed up in the air, meaning, 'This is good!"

The Quartermaster's Corps was waiting for us when we got there. The army can be very efficient, when it wants to be.

Sir Vladimir went back to the battlefield along with his Big People, but promised to get the rest of my new troops there as soon as possible. He also promised to bring enough experienced men to us to handle weapons training.

The Quartermaster's people had picked a flat stretch of grassland that was to be our bivouac and training area, and had drilled some tube wells for us. Latrines, we were told, were our own responsibility, but we should keep them far away from the wells.

Each lance of men was issued a six man octagonal dome tent, tall enough for a man to stand in. These had cloth floors, zippers on the doors and windows, and window screens. They could be set up by one man in minutes, once you knew what you were doing, which of course, my new people didn't.

Our standard layout had seven of these tents in a circle, six for Warriors, and one for the knights, with the knights toward the center of the company. All of these men reported to a single Knight Bannerette. Six of these circles were grouped into a bigger circle, surrounding a tent for Knight Bannerettes, the company commander's tent, which doubled as his office, and a headquarters tent. The company's six carts would also be parked here, once we got them.

In under an hour, we had housing up for three companies. My personal tent was in the middle, with Juma's next to mine. I made sure that there was room for all of my household, once they had arrived. There were wide streets separating everything, with plenty of room for the Big People.

Now that we had a place to put our stuff, we went back and got some. Clothing was first. This was only for our current assignment. Dress clothing and winter clothing would come later. Much later.

From the bottom up, each man received a pair of walking boots, cap toed, and laced up, similar to a modern paratrooper's boot. The Quartermaster's Corps was very careful, making sure that everything fit properly. Each man also got a pair of knee high, slip on riding boots, with a thick heels and pointed toes. Then there were three pairs of socks for each sort of boot. Two sets of long underwear. Four sets of short underwear. Two pairs of pants. Three shirts. A light jacket. A rain cape. Two sets of armor padding. The regulation garrison cap was eschewed by the Africa Corps in favor of the triangular Arab headgear we'd been wearing all along. It made much more sense in this climate.

Appropriate insignia was handed out, which was a horizontal axe for the Warriors. A second and third axe might be added later when they got enough time in grade. Knights wore a vertical sword, with two for Knight Bannerettes and three for Captains. They didn't have the triple star thing that I was entitled to, but my ladies could embroider that on once they got here.

Finally, we were each given a duffel bag to put it all in. We each carried our bags back to our tents, and returned for more.

We each got a canteen, a mess kit, a sewing kit, a first aid kit, a weapons cleaning kit, a personal hygiene kit with towels, a lighter, and a bayonet. We were each issued a down filled sleeping bag with two washable liners, and another bag to put all this stuff in. Now that rubber was available in quantity, I suppose that I ought to tell somebody about air mattresses. Someday.

Each lance was issued two metal buckets, an axe, a shovel, and a pickaxe. The shovels were put to work, digging latrines, before darkness set in.

Each company was issued a clock. This was a new design, and used a flywheel on a spring in place of the usual pendulum. It wasn't as accurate as the old ones, but it was small enough to put in a saddlebag, and the radio could always tell you the exact time. In conjunction with a bell that was rung every quarter hour, it made for a considerable improvement in unit efficiency.

Back at our camp, fire wood had been delivered, but we were told that from now on, we'd have to find our own.

Three wagons had been delivered to each company, plus an additional one for me and Juma. They were mostly filled with cans of food. The labels, in Polish, had snappy titles like 'breakfast', 'lunch', and 'dinner', but nothing else was admitted. The food itself wasn't bad. It was meaty, high protein, high calorie stuff. Something designed for a very active man.

Our personal wagon also had a case of my private stock whiskey in it, which was welcome, but it got me to wondering if someone had raided my cellar, and was shipping this rare, twenty year old stuff everywhere!

The wagon also contained a large supply of cigars.

Juma and I ate, smoked, and drank. I sat on the whiskey case, and Juma sat on the ground, as was our custom, with a small camp fire between us.

"It has been a remarkable day, Conrad."

"I suppose it has been, especially for you. What impressed you most? Midge? The Big People? Our Supply Depot?"

"What impressed me most was knowing that one of my Warriors can get along quite nicely with nothing but two spears, a shield, and a loincloth!"

Chapter 45 Retraining – Whiskey and Women, Juma Takes a Ride

After a bit, the Depot's Quartermaster came by.

"Is everything to your satisfaction, my Lord Conrad?"

"As far as I'm personally concerned, yes," I said. "But I want some changes made to the army policy on labeling food cans. I want every can to list exactly all of the ingredients used to make it. If there are animal products in the food, I want a picture of that animal on the label, too. You see, the Christian Army is expanding. We will have four companies of Jews coming in a day or two, and these people have different dietary requirements than we do. We have a company of Arabs here right now, and if they found out that they were eating pork, they would be at least as upset as you would be if you found out that you had been eating dog meat! I want you to write a letter to whoever is providing this food, which tastes very good, incidentally, and tell them that they must change their labeling practices, immediately! You will tell them that this is a direct order from me, the Hetman!"

"Yes, my lord! I'll do it tonight, before I sleep! But, we don't have any special rations for Arabs, sir!"

"We have plenty of Jews in the army. Arabian dietary laws are almost identical to theirs."

He said, "Yes sir! We have plenty of Kosher food. I'll have their food wagons exchanged before breakfast, sir!"

"Good! Next subject. When I was adrift on the Atlantic Ocean, we were happy to find a bottle of my own private stock hidden in the container of fiberglass we were floating on. Now, I find a case of the stuff delivered to me in a place where nobody could have reasonably expected me to be. Why is this happening? This was all whiskey that I made myself, for my own private enjoyment. My thought was that my great grandchildren would someday be enjoying it, and thinking good thoughts of me while they drank it. Now, I seem to be finding it everywhere!"

"My lord, I have no idea of why there was a bottle of your good whiskey in a container of fiberglass, but I do know the story of the case that you are sitting on. Your wife, Lady Francine, sent it to me, as she sent a case to each of the eleven other Quartermasters in Africa. I was told to keep it safely for you, in case you happened to arrive, and that if you were ever conclusively proven to be dead, my men and I were to drink it to your memory."

"Hmmm." I said, "That was a nice thought on her part, don't you think?"

"Yes, my lord, but I have always wondered what it tasted like."

"Well, now's the time for you to learn!" I said. I handed him the bottle, since nobody had issued me a glass yet.

He took a drink, smiled, waved his arm, palm down, to the side, and said, "Smooooth!"

"Thank you. Have a seat."

There was room for him on the case since Juma, as always, preferred to sit on the ground. He had once explained to me that the Earth was our mother, and that it was good to be close to one's mother.

The cigars turned out to be a private gift from the quartermaster. He'd read my articles on them in the Army Magazine, and had thought that I would enjoy them. Usually, they were for sale, and not a part of normal rations. Since the men hadn't been paid yet, except for the booty they had taken at Shangri La, which half of them had already gambled away to the other half of them, I asked him to distribute some cigars to my troops at my own expense. I'd sign for it later.

We were trying to speak Pigeon, so Juma wouldn't be left out of the conversation, but we kept unconsciously dropping back into Polish, a much better language for casual conversation. Juma was patient with us.

We were into the next bottle and a third cigar each when Sir Percy dropped by.

"Greetings, my lords and gentlemen. I just dropped by to find out when we might expect to become acquainted with our new partners, the Big People," he said.

The quartermaster said, "Well, sir, your people are scheduled to get your armor fitted tomorrow morning. The Big People should be looking you over and choosing their partners just after that. They'll be coming in from all of the Depots in Africa, almost eleven thousand of them."

"That is wonderful," Sir Percy said.

"Isn't it, though," I said. "But for now, let's get out another shipping case, so you can sit down and join us in a drink. It's from my private stock."

No blacksmithing work was normally needed to put together a suit of army plate armor. Every piece came in dozens of sizes, so it was a simple matter of measuring the Warrior very carefully and then assembling the pieces.

They also came in two colors. Warriors got nickel plated armor, and officers, knights and above, got theirs gold plated. It was pretty, which was good for morale, and the plating kept the spring steel inside from rusting, so time wasn't wasted in polishing your armor. In the old days, when every armored man had plenty of servants around, this wasn't important, but now it was.

It wasn't all that much more expensive, and we already had the gold, left over from fighting the Mongols.

Big People had been nosing around our troops since mid-morning, and more and more pairs of two different kinds of people were agreeing to a name for the Big Person, and eventually going over to the area where saddles were being given out.

The ladies would all be Christened next Sunday afternoon. It wasn't as though they were born with any original sin, but Big People were all very religious. If they wanted to be Christened, they would be Christened. Juma and I had pulled rank to get our armor without standing in line. Juma let them fit him out, but you could see that he was dubious about the whole thing.

He wasn't pleased to be wearing the stuff, but he promised to give it a few days before he made a final decision on wearing armor.

Swords, pistols, rifles, and sub-machine guns – but not ammunition – came next. The cavalry had opted to be fitted out in the same fashion as the Wolves. So did a few other companies that Sir Percy talked into becoming part of an increased cavalry command, which he ended up being in charge of. Our infantry companies would get Mounted Infantry equipment, when they got here.

Within minutes of being fitted out, Juma spotted a Big Person who had noticed him. It seemed to be love at first sight. He went with her to get a saddle, loaded it with his new weapons, and then they left the area at a gallop.

Our men were told that they could keep their old weapons, if they wished, or they could store them at the Depot, or they could donate them to the Christian Army

Fund, which would sell them as curiosities in Europe. The money would be used to support the army's various charities, like supporting widows and orphans. Very few men of the African Corps donated them to the fund. After you've lived with a weapon for a while, you don't like to let it go, even if you get a better one.

I donated my hand made armor from Timbuktu to the fund, along with a note to prove its authenticity, so that they would get a good price for it, but I kept Hajji's bow and quiver. And nobody is ever going to get my sword away from me again!

By noon, twelve more of my companies had arrived, along with six companies of Sir Vladimir's men, who would be acting as instructors.

Juma's men were staying back near the battlefield, since he wasn't convinced about the program, yet. I just gave him time, figuring that he would come around, eventually.

Sir Stephan had come with this group, to get fitted out and re-trained. So did my five non-pregnant serving wenches, and my lance of seven runners with their ladies. My own campsite was soon bustling, and three companies had become twenty-seven by evening.

I told each of my ladies, and the other girls of my camp, to each get a revolver, a gun belt, a rifle, and a bayonet, because you never can tell what might happen in combat. They were put on the firing range schedule, to learn how to use their new firearms.

I also told each of them to find a Big Person who liked them, and to get a saddle for her. Our days of moving as slow as a camel were over!

I sent word to my Captains that any woman who wanted to stay with our troops had better get herself armed, trained, and mounted. Those who wished to return to Europe, or to Timbuktu, shouldn't.

In Europe, during a Mongol attack, it might happen that the men were all out fighting while the women had to defend the fort. Because of this, we did have armor for women, but none of it had been sent with the African Expeditionary Forces, which had at least started out as an all male force.

The girls had designed their own outfits, and it was pretty stuff, with a mini-skirt reminiscent of something that might have been used by the Roman Legions, rather than full leg armor. This was acceptable because the ladies normally fought from behind their castle walls, and not in the field. The high crested helmets might have been ancient Greek, and their breast plates had exaggerated breasts on them.

That evening, things were very pleasant. My five ladies and my household's seven others had decided that canned army food, while good enough for an emergency, just wouldn't do for a man of my status.

They'd somehow managed to bring cooking utensils and dinnerware with them, and they scrounged up a dozen folding tables and six dozen camp chairs. I don't know where they got it from, but we were served fresh stewed lamb, rice, and fresh vegetables. Ladies are wonderful people.

And their music and dancing were very good, too. Even Midge was impressed.

I'd invited all of my household, as well as all of my leaders, Captain and higher, including our instructors and the Quartermaster's men, to the feast around our campfire.

Juma came to the campfire while food was being served. He asked for help in getting his armor off, which he left scattered on the ground, along with the rest of his western clothing. He put his loincloth back on, sat on the ground, and ate without further comment. He left early, and apparently just went to sleep in his own tent.

He seemed to be a man with a decision to make.

Midge was prevailed upon to dance as well, and when she accepted, I suggested that some musical accompaniment might be nice. My servants couldn't be expected to learn any new songs that night, but they got together with Midge, and worked out some hand signs for louder and quieter, faster and slower, and within minutes she gave one of the finest performances we'd ever seen.

We put a serious dent in my case of whiskey that night, but the quartermaster said that other drinks, although perhaps less noble, were available. That, and eleven more cases of private stock were coming in from the other Depots in Africa. Also, there was all that brandy that I'd left behind at my campsite near the battlefield, but which would soon be brought over when Mohamed showed up. We wouldn't be in need of potables for the foreseeable future.

The next morning, we held our usual Sunrise Ceremony, which our Big people always attended, silently raising their right hooves to the sun higher than a normal horse could. Right after it, Juma put a few cans of food in his saddlebag an rode off, wearing nothing but his loincloth and a pistol. He took his spears and his shield, as well. I guessed that he just had to find out for himself.

I spent an hour on the rifle range, checking myself out with the new rifle. I always had been a good shot. My new pistol was not exactly the same as my old one had been. It looked the same, but my old one had been a single action revolver, while the new ones had been upgraded to double action. You could still cock it manually, for better accuracy, but it also worked by pulling the trigger alone, if you were in a hurry. The instructors glanced at my targets, saluted me, and left me alone. They probably decided that I knew what I was doing. Maybe they recognized me, even though I wasn't wearing any insignia yet.

On the bayonet range, they did come over and show me some of the fine points, since I'd never used a bayonet before. I probably wouldn't again, either. Not when I had my sword, anyway.

I decided that a swim in the nearby Mediterranean Sea might be a nice idea, and that Silver and I could use a bath anyway. I was soon joined by my runners, the twelve girls of the household, and Midge. They were all mounted now. It was an impromptu, forty-two person skinny dipping party.

It was fun, especially since the bathing suit hadn't been invented yet.

Back at the camp, we sponged ourselves off in fresh water, rinsed down the Big People, and had a canned lunch.

Then I spent the rest of the day mostly lazing around, attended by my lovely ladies. I was getting old. I felt it in my bones.

Juma got back after dark. There were a lot of scratches on his feet and lower legs, but he did not walk like someone who had just lost most of the skin on his crotch.

"Conrad, we must talk."

"Certainly," I said, handing him the bottle. "Pull up some dirt."

"Thank you." He sat on the ground and took a drink. "First off, your Big People are magnificent beyond belief! Eagerly would I welcome them into my tribe! K'Koma Sut already is a member of my family. She is like a sister to me!"

"Yes, I feel much the same way about Silver. You haven't brought K'Koma Sut over and introduced her yet. You should, you know. What does her name mean?"

"In my people's language, it means 'Daughter of the Winds and Shadows.'"
I said, "That's beautiful, poetic, even."

"I will bring her tomorrow, for I have already sent her out to spend the night eating," he said. "I am very impressed with much of your equipment. Your tents are absolute marvels! The screens on the windows work very well to keep the insects out, and your zippers amaze me. I want my men to have them."

"I'm glad that you like them. They are yours."

He said, "Your weapons are also astounding. I would like to see my men equipped as your Mounted Infantry are, but without the rapier. We will be keeping our spears, instead."

"As you wish," I said.

"Your food is adequate, and since it is already cooked, but does not rot, somehow, it could be very useful in the field, although I wouldn't want to eat it all of the time."

"These are my feelings as well," I said. "But it will spoil, eventually, once you open a can or jar."

"But your clothing is ridiculous! It requires too much time for maintenance, and I, for one, find it very uncomfortable."

"Midge has much the same thought," I said.

"Yes. She is a very fine lady, and a Magnificent Warrior! Were she not already married to another man, I would beg her to be my wife!"

"She could never give you sons, you know. Her people, like the Big People, give birth only to women like themselves. We call it parthenogenesis."

He said, "She has told me this. But about clothing, I have found that it is not necessary to wear pants and boots while mounted. I have just ridden all day without any discomfort."

"Indeed? Your feet and lower legs are bleeding in at least a dozen places."

"Riding through thorn bushes did that," he said. "But I have a solution for the problem. I have talked to some craftsmen attached to the Depot this evening, and they are making a modification to the stirrups for me. It will have a wooden plate on the bottom, as big as a man's foot, and heavy leather covering a man's toes, and the front of his legs to above the knee. We will not be needing your boots, either."

"I suppose that this would work, but your armor will protect your lower legs, in any event."

"We will not be wearing armor! Besides being unmanly, your armor is absolute torture to wear! I believe that if I forced them to wear it, even my men would be insubordinate to me!"

I said, "But armor would save a lot of their lives!"

"You should know by now that we are not afraid of death!"

"I never said that any of your people were afraid of anything. But as their leader, it is your duty to lead them to victory, not to their deaths!"

"I know what my duties are, Conrad, and I say that my men will not wear armor!"

"You sound very adamant on that point."

"I am. If you force us to take it, we will throw it away!"

"Huh. You know, I believe you," I said. "Very well. I don't like this, but it shall be as you wish, Juma. I do not want to lose you."

I never was sure how Juma and his people managed to ride without pants on, but I have a theory about it. Black physiology is basically a hot weather adaptation. That tightly curled hair acts as a sun helmet, the black skin is impervious to Ultra-violet rays, and they have more sweat glands than a white person does. I think that the extra sweat was lubricating his butt on the saddle.

Over the next few days, the rest of my Warriors arrived, some fifty-four companies of them. Not that Juma's men were organized into our companies. I never figured out how they were organized, or even if they were organized at all! All I know was that when Juma gave orders, things got done. That was enough for me.

Their campsites weren't like ours, either, but were rather just a random placement of tents, where any European would have gotten lost in minutes. Juma said that it was more natural that way, like the trees in a forest.

Sir Vladimir's Training Instructors seemed to be doing a good job with training the rest of the army, in our usual fashion. This involved a lot of shouting and not quite obscenities, but it got the job done.

They didn't have much success with Juma's people. Shouting at one of these Blacks usually got you a calm statement about how they didn't understand what you were upset about. If you tried to explain, they gave you a polite, reasoned argument that proved to their personal satisfaction that you were wrong. These Blacks didn't care about how to roll their socks or fold their underwear, in part because they didn't have any socks or underwear. But even if they had had these things, they wouldn't have cared.

The usual TI's first reaction to this sort of indifference was to challenge the offender to a fist fight. The Blacks were always agreeable to this, once the Marquis of Queensbury rules were explained to them, but they won at least half of the time, and since students considerably outnumbered instructors, the instructors eventually desisted.

At my suggestion, they simply concentrated on explaining our weapons systems to their African students, at which time the Blacks became very obedient. When they were interested, they learned quickly.

Captain Fritz got to Shangri La without difficulty. The natives there were still sufficiently cowed to welcome him profusely, once he told them that I had sent him.

They immediately swore allegiance to the Christian Army, promising to obey all of our dictates.

The even changed the name of their valley to Shangri La, to please him, since Captain Fritz couldn't pronounce the original name, either. He stayed there for two days, enjoying their ladies and their brandy before he moved on. But he left six lances of his troops behind to help out with their defense, and to build them some simple machines, mostly wheelbarrows, wind mills, and waterwheels, to help replace all of the slaves that they had lost.

Sir Fritz also requested that Sir Vladimir send an additional company, largely composed of engineers, to Shangri La, to show the flag, and to help these people out. They were, after all, on our side now.

Sir Vladimir sent his company of engineers to Shangri La.

The rest of my caravans had collected up at the battlefield, and after a day's rest for the last one, they had headed for the Depot, under the command of Mohamed. They were being escorted by four companies of Sir Vladimir's Mounted Infantry, who were also taking their severely wounded men, slowly, back to the Depot for shipment back to the hospitals of Europe. Uncle Tom's magic cure could wipe out most infections and diseases, but it didn't help much when you had an arrow in your lung, or a broken leg!

Sir Wladyclaw took his battalion of Wolves, along with the artillery and the balance of Sir Vladimir's men, east, to see what could be done about those last three Almohades cities.

Everything seemed to be in order, the instructors seemed to be doing their jobs well, and Juma's men were keeping him busy. I just stayed around my personal campsite, enjoyed my ladies, and rested.

I slept, ate, and drank well. Damn, but I was tired!

Chapter 46   Many Departures – We Go To War!

The arrival of the non-combatants was received with great joy in my extended camp, and I decreed a special holiday to honor it. Having Jasmine, and my other expectant ladies, at my side again was a special joy.

There wasn't room in the military area for our families (except for mine), but the Mediterranean plain is very large, and no one was more than a mile from his loved ones. With the Big People, that was a short trip.

We got the dependant's and non-combatant's camp set up well before dark. The Quartermaster was generous with supplies of food and equipment, once I'd signed for everything, and the Accounting Department had finally gotten everybody paid, so they could all buy all of the drink that they could stomach.

Hundreds of camp fires were burning. The Jews in particular seemed to be having a good time, dancing around a huge fire, even if they don't drink much. Even their Big People were doing a Hoare.

I'd had Hajji's silk tent set up. If the bugs got bad, we could always retreat to my army tents, but until that time, well, the big blue silk tent with embroidered gold trim had class!

After a morning mostly spent sobering up, I called a meeting of my officers, Captains and above.

"Gentlemen. We have arrived. We now have to decide where we go from here. Mohamed will soon be taking a caravan that will include all of the horses, mules, and camels back to Timbuktu. He will be loaded with weapons for Omar's army, and various European trade goods. I imagine that most of the Arabian and Black non-combatants will want to return with him.

"I'm making arrangements for our Christian and Jewish Non-combatants to be shipped home to Europe.

"There is a war going on, so I expect that many of our trained and armed forces will be participating in it, but I want to get your reaction to this. I am sure that our Christian forces will want to go on this crusade, but how do our four Jewish companies feel about it?"

A Jewish Captain raised his hand, and I nodded to him. "Sir, that decision will have to be made by our counsel, but I can assure you that they will vote to go. To be able to return to Jerusalem, as part of a well armed group, why, this is an ancient Jewish dream! We will go with you, and earn our place in the front ranks!"

"Thank you. Now, what about our Arabian companies?"

An Arabian Captain said, "Sir, my company was originally one of the three camel cavalry units that Omar loaned to you. We have served you well, I think, but we never signed on for a long term war, especially one aimed specifically at the people of my own religion! Also, we have wives and families back in Timbuktu. With your permission, we would like to go home. However, many of the Islamic companies who were formed from slaves freed on our trip will probably prefer to stay with your army. I suggest that you let them decide as individuals whether to go on this crusade or to return to be members of the Army of Timbuktu."

I said, "That would take a lot of re-organization, but I suppose it could be done.

Omar should have a strong army. Those Twaregs are a menace, and should be wiped out. And there are still many other cities in the south where slaves are being held. What about you and your people, Juma? Where do you want to go?"

He said, "Back to Timbuktu, eventually. But we still have a few months before my wives start giving birth to my sons, and I would like to test these new weapons in combat. I have been studying some of your maps, with the help of a translator. I think that we will have time to go east with you as far as Alexandria, and then join the expedition that you will have to send south along the Nile river. From there, we can travel west to Timbuktu. I have found a guide who knows the route."

"That sounds like a reasonable program," I said.

"One other thing," Juma said. "I still have four thousand of my men in Timbuktu. You will be sending Omar sufficient weapons to arm them, but I would also like them to have Big People. When the Arabians ride south, could they be accompanied by enough Big People so that all of my men can be mounted?"

"I will have to check with the Quartermaster about the exact numbers available, but certainly we can send many Big People down there. Since we have consistently been losing more men in combat than Big People, the army doesn't need any spare mounts at all.

"Very well, gentlemen. Discuss the options with your people, and we'll meet here again in one week.

"One other thing. Tomorrow we all will be taking 'the cure'. Make sure that your people, and all of the non-combatants, understand what that means.

"Dismissed."

Juma had moved his tent so that he could be with his men, but that evening, he rode over to my camp.

He sat down in front of my stool, so I handed him the bottle.

"Conrad, did you know that twenty-eight men have not been able to bond with a Big Person?"

"No, I didn't. Do you know what's happening there?"

"I have an idea. First, many men without manna have paired up with our sisters, but all of the men who have not paired have no manna at all."

"Curious," I said.

"Yes. I asked my sister about it and all she will say is that they are bad men. We have been able to eliminate all of the truly bad men in the African Corps who have manna but we could do nothing with those who do not have manna. I think that our sisters can see something that those in my tribe cannot. I also think that we should kill these men."

"I am loathe to kill some of our own men who have done nothing provably wrong, but…" I said, and then switched over to English, "Silver, come over here, please. There are twenty-eight men who none of the Big People will accept. Do you know about this?"

Silver nodded 'yes'.

"K'Koma Sut thinks that they are 'bad' men. Do you think so, too?"

She nodded 'yes'.

"Juma thinks that we should kill these men. Do you think that we should do that?"

She stared at me for a moment, and then nodded 'yes' once more.

Switching back to Arabic, I said, "Damn. Silver agrees with you, and I've never heard of a Big Person being wrong on a question of character. On my head be it. Juma, get these men away from camp on some pretext, and then kill them. Do it discretely. We'll put it out that they are AWOL, perhaps because the Big People wouldn't have them."

"You are doing the right thing, Conrad. We will eliminate them tonight."

I drank more than usual, that night, and took none of my ladies to bed with me.

The next day, there was something that army regulations required us to do. At least once a year, every Warrior was required to 'take the cure', to use my Uncle Tom's three part cure for just about everything. I myself was remiss in this, and most of our people had never taken it at all.

Right after the Sunrise Ceremony, all twenty-seven thousand of my people, and most of Sir Vladimir's instructors, were given pats of the butter, which had to be eaten in the presence of someone in authority. Then we all walked down to the beach, shovels in hand. The Big People knew the drill, and left the camp, taking the few pets people had with them. We didn't bring any food with us, but we brought lots of water.

The men were separated from the women, and went about a mile apart, since many of our people had a nudity taboo, and 'the cure' was best taken naked. That, or you had to spend a day trying to wash the vomit and shit out of your clothes.

We dug a hole, a latrine of sorts, for every person. With the cure, when you had to go, you had to go, and waiting in line was impossible.

I'd explained the whole thing to Juma, but he was uneasy about this strange ceremony that I'd insisted that he and his men participate in, so I joined his people and sat on the ground with them, while the medics handed out the cheese, one small square to each person.

The Blacks with Juma were a mixed force, and more than half of them were not members of his tribe, but were simply freed slaves. He had mixed them in with his own men, to better train them, and it had seemed to work.

Someone trained by Sir Vladimir's medics was coming up the line, using a pair of tongs to but a piece of the cheese into each man's mouth.

As I watched, a Black man simply keeled over. He fell on his face and didn't move any more at all. Then another fell, and another!

"STOP!" I yelled at the top of my lungs. "You! Medic! Stop what you are doing!"

He looked at me, confused, but he carefully took the cheese that was in his tongs out of the next man's mouth.

"Sir?"

"Look behind you, man!" I shouted.

He turned around to see more that twenty men laying motionless on the ground! More were falling over as we watched.

"Sir? But, I did exactly what they told me to do!"

"I'm not blaming anybody, yet! But put that jar down, and back away!"

Juma said, as he walked quickly over to the fallen men, "These men are all from my tribe! Those who are not don't seem to be affected!"

"Don't touch them, Juma! We must figure out what is happening!" I said, "I've taken this cure a dozen times. Let me examine them!"

I did so. They were all dead, with not a trace of pulse or breathing.

"Juma, are you sure that all of these men are from your tribe?"

"I am absolutely certain! There can be no doubt!"

And yet the other Blacks had not been killed. My Uncle Tom's medication worked by first marking every cell in the body as human, with the butter. Then the cheese killed everything that was not marked. This could only mean that by the medication's definitions, Juma's people were not human! Certainly, there was a lot about them that was strange. They must be a mutation of some sort, which their marriage customs must have perpetuated!

"Juma, I want you to get everyone from your tribe out of here! Go and join with the Big People, and don't try to come back for a day. I'll explain as best as I can later, but for now, take all of your people and go!"

"To hear is to obey, my brother!"

Thirty-three of Juma's people were dead on the ground.

"Those of you who have not yet had the cheese, gather fire wood, a lot of it! We must cremate these fine Warriors. Juma's customs would require that their dead brothers be eaten, and if they did that, they would die, too!"

A few thousand men can get a lot of fire wood in a hurry, and soon a huge blaze was going.

Then, I took a square of the cheese and ate it in front of the troops. Then I told them that it was their turn. Most of them were nervous about it, but not one man proved to be a coward!

Of course, we all had a perfectly miserable afternoon, but nobody else died. At dusk, we all had a cleansing swim in the sea, covered up our latrines, picked up our clothes, and went back to our camps. The next morning, the oil was distributed, and we all rubbed it in.

I spent a few hours apologizing to Juma for what had happened, and explained as best as I could what caused it. I'm not sure if he understood, but he trusted me enough to forgive me. I tried to get him to take the oil with him, and use it, but he declined. I couldn't really blame him.

Chapter 47 In Uncle Tom's Control Room

Tom hit the pause button.

"That tears it! I'm getting to the bottom of this one!"

He was typing madly at his keyboard, a strange thing, actually.

We had some very well developed artificial machine intelligence. Most people here, including me, used it regularly when we needed information, or help from the computers. You just asked the machine about what you needed to know, and they told you, verbally, or in hard copy.

Only, we had to do that on the sly, without Tom finding out.

Tom was convinced that using a computer to do anything but compute was a sure route to cultural degradation. He insisted that nothing but a keyboard could be used to communicate with a computer.

I never met anyone who agreed with him, but he was the boss, so we let him think that he was having his own way. The artificial intelligences helped out, of course.

I said, "The bottom of which one?"

"Of this whole alien manna thing! Look, the human race started in Africa, and until very recent times, the last five thousand years or so, only a few small groups made it out to the rest of the world. It stands to reason then that there would be far more genetic variation among sub-Saharan Africans than in the people of the rest of the world, and that's exactly what you find. They are forty times as variable in their genetic makeup as everyone in the rest of the world combined. But there is no way that a mutation could develop that was so different that those people could be considered a different race!"

"So what are you doing about it?"

"I've put a team from the Historical Corp on tracing Juma's people back as far as they have to go to find out when they became mutants. I've put a team of physicists and physiologists to isolate some people who have who have this manna stuff, and some who don't, and to try to figure out what's happening. And I have a team of bio-engineers going at finding out why the Big People and the Servants both seem to have manna," Tom said.

"How long are these studies going to take?"

"Oh, a few hundred years, I suppose."

"Wonderful," I said, hitting the start button.

Chapter 48   Leaving my Ladies for War

I'd been calling home every other day. Marina and Celicia knew me well enough to expect me to have collected up some more women, and had become tolerant enough over the years to not be angry about it. They promised to take good care of Jasmine and her six pregnant friends. They also promised to have them speaking, reading, and writing Polish by the time I got home, in six months or so. I'd get into the subject of marrying the new girls once I got back to Poland, in six or eight months or so.

I found that our only Liner, the Duke Henryk the Bearded, was in the area on a trip from Constantinople to Gdansk, so I told the Captain to drop by to pick up Jasmine and my other girls, Sir Vladimir's wounded, and as many of our Christian and Jewish non-combatants as he had room for. He was hesitant about upsetting his schedules, and the Depot didn't have the sort of special dock that his ship normally operated out of. Also, since we had many warships in the area, they'd finally let him resume commercial operations. It had been a while since he'd been able to make a profit.

I told him that since he had left me in the middle of the Atlantic Ocean, sitting on a shipping container, he owed me some favors!

He agreed with that, so I didn't have to make more serious threats. He called in a Frigate and three Explorers to help him make the transfer from land to his ship. This gave him a total of nine lighters to speed the loading.

I also told him that my ladies would be staying in Noble Class accomodations, and that the wounded would be in at least Standard Class. Healthy freed slaves could be put down in the top four unused cargo tunnels, if necessary.

He also off loaded some cargo which I commandeered for Omar. Three containers of glass ware, four of window glass, three of various cloths, and some odds and ends. Some amber, some furs, and six cases of lighters. There were pens, paper, and a lot of books. There were eight containers of plumbing parts, tools, and clocks.

There wasn't room enough for everybody on the Henryk, so I also commandeered the three Explorers, sending one to Italy, one to Spain, and one to France. By temporarily leaving most of their cargo at the Depot, this gave us enough space to send everyone to Europe who wanted to go.

Curiously, Komander Meier, the Captain of the ship that went down off the coast of Africa five years ago, elected to leave the African Corps, and to return to sea duty. He also turned down my promotion to Komander, returning to his old rank of Captain. This cut his pay in half, but that wasn't what he cared about. He said that in the seagoing army, Komanders were desk jockeys, and he wanted a ship again. None of his former subordinates, most of whom were at least Captains in the African Corps, went with him.

The Accounting Department gave each of the non-combatants a free pass, good for three months, on any army railroad or ship, and a reasonable supply of currency to get them started somewhere.

I tried to give Hajji's money chest to Jasmine, but she would only accept half of the money. She said that the girls still with me would need the rest.

It was a tearful departure, with many promises made, but the girls left none too soon. I didn't want my ladies to have to give birth on a tossing ship!

Komander Walznik came over and inquired if anyone had heard of the two men he had sent in a Dhow from the belly of Africa to Lisbon, with the news that I was still alive. Inquiries were made on the radio, and no one had heard anything about them. Certainly, their message had never been delivered. The only thought that anyone had was that they must have been lost at sea.

Captain Fritz made it to Timbuktu without incident, barring two run-ins with bands of Twaregs, which his men totally destroyed, man, woman, and child. He even shot the camels! Then they burned the camps, and threw the swords and other weapons into the fire. This was Standard Operating Procedure in Sir Wladyclaw's forces. The sheep, though, he just let run free.

This was brutal, to be sure, but once you have killed all of a tribe's men, you would not be doing the women and children a favor by letting them live. They would just die a slow and ugly death on the desert. Camels are the life blood of these nomads, and leaving the camels to be found by other nomads would be counter-productive. The sheep would all die without someone to protect them, but they weren't worth the ammunition to finish off.

War is an ugly business.

Omar was astounded with the radio, and it was a while before he finally believed that he was actually talking to me! But he was ruling peacefully, and there had been no unrest in the city. Various civic projects had been completed. There were now beautifully carved fountains in every marketplace. Juma's people had built African villages on top of all of the palace buildings, walls, and half of the city walls as well. Plans were being made to build a bridge across the Niger River, one that could be easily defended.

I told him about the gifts we were sending him, I read him the manifests, and he made me repeat them. He said that he'd known that I was rich, but he had never imagined that I was that rich! Over four thousand square yards of window glass? Zounds!

I would have talked for hours with him, but Juma was getting antsy beside me. He wanted to talk to his half-brother, Mishaba, first, and to his senior wife, right after that!

When Mishaba arrived at the palace, Omar and I agreed to talk the next day. He wanted to go and look over the things that Captain Fritz had brought him, anyway.

Juma spent the next six hours on the radio, talking in his native language.

Mohamed left three days later, with a huge train of animals, moderately loaded with many gifts and weapons, but mostly carrying the civilians. He had three dozen of the big, rubber tired army carts with him, loaded with gifts, each towed by four horses. The carts themselves were another gift for Omar. The six thousand non-combatant Arabs and Blacks with Mohamed would spend much of their time taking care of the animals.

He had the original three companies of camel cavalry with him for security, but since they were now mounted on Big People, and were armed in the fashion of the Wolves, they shouldn't have any difficulties.

And Mohamed had a radio with him, to call for help in case he did. Army radio carts had a generator built into the rear axel, to keep the batteries charged. They also contained something that looked a bit like a bicycle, which a man could use to charge the batteries when they were stationary for a while.

His orders were to bring with him any slaves who came to him and wanted their freedom, but not to attack any slave holding societies. We'd send an army through to free those people later.

In another week, my troops' weapons training was declared complete, we had a nice graduation ceremony, and then we too departed.

We had six companies of Arabs who had elected to go on crusade with us, four of Jews, Juma's forty-five hundred men, the equivalent of eighteen companies, and twenty four companies of Christians. This made us a nearly full battalion, even without Juma's men.

Sir Stephan was promoted to Baron, and was put in command.

Since Juma had a full battalion of men if you counted the four thousand men he had left in Timbuktu, I promoted him to Baron, as well. He didn't seem to care much about it.

Most of our Arab troops were going to Timbuktu, along with four thousand extra Big People for the rest of Juma's men living there. For now, they were doing duty as pack animals, carrying supplies and more gifts for Omar.

Three companies of Arabs had elected to go to Shangri La. This was an option that I hadn't considered, but since the valley was on our side now, I didn't see anything wrong with it. For most of the men, it was their home town. But they had left as recently freed slaves, and they were going back as armed, free men.

Once the Arabs had left, I raised my arm, sword in hand, and pointed it forward, to the east.

"Brothers! Sisters! We go to war! For God and Poland!"

Chapter 49 In Uncle Tom's Control Room

As soon as I got there the next morning, Tom said, "Did you see the preliminary report on Juma's people?"

"No, I didn't. I thought that wasn't supposed to come out for hundreds of years, yet."

"Well, they do have over four hundred man years into the project so far, but when you have time machines, you don't have to wait around for the news."

I said, "Right. So what did the report say?"

"First off, something is definitely going on there. This is not your usual psychic phenomena hoax. Juma's tribe has a massive genetic mutation. The usual definition of a species is that it cannot breed with any of it's closer relatives, and Juma's tribe fits that definition."

"They don't look any different. Are they actually a separate species?"

"Yes!" Tom said, "What's more, they have carefully kept themselves apart from the rest of humanity for at least forty thousand years. That's an amazing length of time for a cultural tradition to survive, but it was backed up by the fact that after a few thousand years, they couldn't interbreed with the rest of humanity. You probably noticed that Juma wasn't interested in sex with anyone but his own tribal people, any more than you would be interested in having sex with a dog."

I said, "Well, with a dog, no. But I've certainly been attracted to those serving wenches of yours, and they are not the least bit human."

"That's a special case. They were designed to be attractive to humans, and to put out all of the proper pheromones. Juma's people have some major differences from the rest of us throughout their genome. That probably accounts for their ability to see this manna thing, although we don't have the foggiest idea how that works."

"Well, the Big People, your wenches, and Juma's people all seem to be able to do the same thing. Is there any similarity between Juma's DNA and the Big People's?"

Tom said, "None at all. Our engineered critters don't use DNA. Instead, they use a much tougher three stranded chemical, that resists mutation. A natural life form has to be able to mutate slowly, so that it can evolve into something more complicated than a slime mold. When you are designing something, you don't want it to go around changing on you."

"Then how about going about it from the other end? Do your people have any idea just what this manna stuff is? If we knew what they were looking at, we ought to be able to figure out how they were seeing it."

"A good thought, but no cigar. We have put the thing through every scientific test anybody has been able to come up with, and it comes out a goose egg. There's nothing there! Or at least it is not any sort of energy or matter that we know about."

I said, "Then how do you know that this thing is real?"

"By the results that all three types of critters come up with. Remember when Juma said that they had killed about two hundred people in Conrad's army because they had bad manna? Well, actually, the real number was five hundred and thirty-one. He rounded downward to spare Conrad's feelings. But, we have traced the history on every one of those people, and the nicest of them was a multiple felon! In any court of law, every one of them would have been given a maximum sentence, if the truth came out. To my mind, getting it one hundred percent right proves that something is happening."

"How about those twenty-eight guys without manna that Juma's people slaughtered?"

"The same thing. Sadists who liked torturing children, mother rapists, mass serial murderers, you name it! Hell, one of them raped his own father! No, Conrad and Juma did the right thing there."

"I suppose so. I wonder how many thousands of man years of research time this project will take to resolve."

"More like millions, I imagine, which is wonderful!" Tom said, "These people are academics who just don't have enough to do, you know. Without something that interests them, too many of them just drink themselves to death. But we're on to something new here, and that's just what the organization needs!"

"Yeah. Well, keep me posted, Uncle Tom."

THE END

Made in the USA